CONSPIRACY

Book Four: The Alex and Cassidy Series

Nancy Ann Healy

ISBN 10: 0692608907

ISBN 13: 978-0692608906

A Note from the Author

When I began writing the Alex and Cassidy series, I had no way of knowing where it would lead me. In many ways, I did not know where it would lead these characters. I am often asked what the books are about. Are they lesbian romances? Are they political thrillers? Are they crime novels? Novels and stories, no matter their genre are about people. Characters become people to the author and hopefully to the reader. The plot moves stories along and offers characters challenges and experiences so that the characters may grow and change. Sometimes, the plot is also meant to convey deeper messages.

As I write Conspiracy, our world and our country are facing numerous upheavals and crises. We are divided on many issues. We face struggles abroad and challenges at home here in the United States. In our effort to understand our world, we often make broad, sweeping statements and assessments about each other. We label groups. We determine that individuals are either good or evil, moral or immoral, compassionate or bigots, heroes or villains based on tidbits of information we see at a distance. People are holistic beings, within them resides the capacity to accomplish extraordinary things or to strive only for mediocrity. The characters in the Alex and Cassidy series are no exception.

What makes someone a hero or a villain? Is it their intentions or their actions? At the end of this series, that is a question for each reader to pose about each character. Who are they? What motivates them? Why do we consider one a beacon of morality and goodness, and another the epitome of selfishness and evil? As the author, I cannot tell you what to believe. That was never the purpose of these stories. It is for you to decide who Alex, Cassidy, the congressman, Claire, Krause, Eleana, Fallon, Tate, Merrow, Jane, Edmond, Viktor, Rose, Helen, Nicolaus, James, Brady, and all the others you have met are. Is any one of these characters a hero? Is any one of the people you have encountered on the page a villain? If so, why?

We create this world. In this series, all of the characters have an active role in shaping the world that they live in. They see that world through different colored lenses, just as we do. I hope that you have enjoyed getting to know this colorful cast of characters as much as I have enjoyed creating them. Their journey has allowed me to travel places that were once only in my imagination. That has reminded me that from our dreams we create our reality. Everything we create changes us and the world we live in. We may not think so, but it does.

As I close this chapter of the series, I want to thank those who have traveled with Alex and Cassidy on this journey. I have laughed with these characters, cried with them, screamed at them, cheered for them, and marveled at the love they share along the way. I hope that you have too. So, what is the series? Is it romance? Thriller? Crime? It's about relationships. It's about people. Hopefully, it is about the extraordinary power of love that connects us in unexpected ways, and in so doing demands that we strive to become our better selves.

I know that taking this journey has enriched my life. I would be remiss if I did not take a moment to say *thank you*.

Thank you to all the readers. I cannot express my gratitude enough to all of you for your enthusiastic support. The heartfelt emails and messages, the witty and amusing memes and videos, questions, comments, and rants that I have received over the last two years have amazed me. You have made me laugh and brought me to tears with your personal stories and observations as much as any of these characters have, and I thank you from the bottom of my heart.

Special thanks to my wife, Melissa and my son, Christopher for enduring my late nights, constant jokes about tacos, occasional tantrums, increased travel, and the need for quiet when they would have preferred noise.

Thank you to MC and Natalya for their willingness to act as translators. Your knowledge, time and friendship are appreciated more than you will ever know.

Thank you to Jay, Kim, Caroline, Chelsey, Tami, Angie, Robin, Robin Lynn, Charlotte, Tina, Heather, Mary and the host of other people who have been with Alex and Cassidy since day one, and have supported not only their journey, but mine. To the many friends that have encouraged me over the course of my life, I want to say this—I do believe friendship is the light of life, and that belief is subtly embedded in every word I write.

Finally, thank you to the many mentors that I have had over the years who encouraged me to reach higher. In particular, Mrs. Jamo and Mrs. Agnew, the two teachers who made the greatest impact on my young life. To my parents, and my Nana, most of all my mother for teaching me the power that unconditional love has to heal and to strengthen us through both adversity and triumph. And, to Pina and Renée for the work they shared with me, helping me to open myself in new, sometimes frightening ways, giving me new found courage to live my life with an open heart and mind. I would not be walking this path without all of you, and I am grateful every moment for the impact you have each made on my heart and my life.

This book is for all of you. I leave you with a quote from a book that captivated my imagination as a youngster. It reminds me a bit of the world that Alex and Cassidy live in as they confront Conspiracy—a world, not unlike our own.

"Yet man will never be perfect until he learns to create and destroy; he does know how to destroy, and that is half the battle."

~Alexandre Dumas, *The Count of Monte Cristo*

Chapter One

"**N**o, it isn't fine," Alex Toles blared into the phone. She continued her nervous pacing in the office as she listened to the man on the other end of the call. "Listen to me. This merger has been in the making for over six months," she said firmly. "I don't care what you have to do, just get it done!" Alex pinched the bridge of her nose and groaned in frustration. "Just get it done, Jason. MyoGen is key to Carecom's future. Yes, well, if you had wanted to give me a present you would have taken care of this—yesterday. Call me the minute you know something. I don't care what time it is," Alex instructed. "Yeah, I know. You too," she said, finally taking a seat at her desk. "Just what I need," she grumbled.

Alex had been burning the midnight oil for the last three weeks in an attempt to solidify a merger between her company Carecom, and the genetics and bioengineering company MyoGen. It was a merger that she had poured all of her energy into. MyoGen was ahead of the curve in the development and research of genetic applications in pharmaceuticals. Of course, that was an unofficial program. Officially, they developed everything from life-saving medicine to designer drugs. Most of Alex's life was officially unofficial. She had been at the helm of Carecom for well over a year. On the surface, Alex was building her father's business into a mini-empire to honor his legacy. Beneath those calm surface waters lay a tumultuous undertow—the truth.

Carecom had been distributing medical supplies globally since the end of World War II. Alex's grandparents had built the company. It had been engineered to provide a reliable cover operation for the newly organized intelligence community. Over the years, Carecom delivered far more weapons, money, and state secrets than it ever hoped to distribute IV bags, syringes, or surgical implements. Carecom was a CIA controlled business. At least, it was intended to be. When that had changed, Alex still was not certain. She did know that her father had been engaged in numerous illicit activities. Moving money to foreign governments through Carecom channels was only part of his legacy. Carecom also assisted in the delivery of technology to rogue groups, warlords, and terrorists under the guise of military medical shipments. It was all part of the landscape of international intelligence. Alex had wondered many times who came up with that term—intelligence. At one point in history, the intelligence game had been focused on gathering information to provide a tactical advantage in warfare. The end game had been to ensure the physical and financial security of a nation. That had not been the reality for many years. The intelligence community, Alex often mused, should have been called the arrogance community.

The Central Intelligence Agency was anything but a cohesive unit. It existed officially in the unofficial world of espionage. Accountability, Alex had learned, became an impossible task when there were no rules and no transparency, but rather endless veils that concealed countless secrets. Alex had become immersed in a world that was still unfathomable to her most days. Her father had been part of this world. Her grandparents had been part of this life. Her brother was in as deep as anyone she knew, and all of that meant that her family was continually at risk. That was what had led her here—her family.

Alex looked at the pictures on her desk and smiled. Just seeing the faces of her wife and children always seemed to calm her anxiety and frustration. It was ironic, Alex thought, that had she never met Cassidy O'Brien, she likely would never have ended up here in this office. It started as a simple investigation. At the time, Alex was working with the FBI. She had been sent to investigate threats against a congressman's ex-wife. Alex picked up a photo on her desk of Cassidy and chuckled. It still amazed her that one assignment had changed her entire life. She fell in love with Cassidy O'Brien in what seemed like an instant. Alex suddenly had a family. That initial investigation had uncovered the tip of an iceberg. An iceberg that many had hoped to keep hidden below surface waters forever. An iceberg in scale that Alex had never imagined possible. An investigation into what had been considered a simple stalking had turned out to be not so simple. It led Alex into a hidden world of false identities, hidden agendas, money, and greed; a world full of men and women with an insatiable lust for power.

Cassidy's ex-husband, Congressman Christopher O'Brien had been recruited and used as a pawn in an international, high-stakes chess match. He had been a well-placed pawn whose arrogance had put Cassidy and her son Dylan at risk. Dylan's paternity, while not public knowledge, further complicated Alex's mission. The man who had fathered the boy Alex now called her son was not Congressman O'Brien. Dylan's biological father had been Alex's best friend, John Merrow. He had served as her colonel during her tour in Iraq. Merrow had become a senator and finally one of the most popular U.S. Presidents in recent memory. And, he too had been in service of the agency. Alex was convinced that his efforts to derail much of the agency's unofficial work had led to his assassination. Alex's father's dealings had resulted in his death as well. Her family was at constant risk. Merrow and her father had been part of a faction known as The Collaborative. The Collaborative utilized the Central Intelligence Agency along with all the government resources that the agency gave them access to. On the record they were legitimate agents. Off the record, they functioned outside of any government oversight. The Collaborative was an international conglomerate comprised of corporations, heads of state, and military leaders. Their objective was simple from what Alex could tell—make money, lots of it. If innocent people got hurt in the process, that was just the price of war. This was a war as far as Alex was concerned. She was determined to shake the foundations of The Collaborative until it cracked. Then, she would shake it some more until it broke into pieces. That was Alex Toles' plan. MyoGen was the next hammer she would use to chip away at that foundation. Alex set down the picture of Cassidy, closed her eyes, and massaged her temples.

"Napping?" a voice called from her office door.

"If only," Alex answered without moving at all.

Jonathan Krause made his way into the office and took a seat across from his sister. "Bad day?" he asked knowingly.

"Just a day," Alex responded as she slowly opened her eyes. "What brings you down here?" Krause smiled and sighed. "Oh, that's not good," Alex surmised. "What gives, Pip?"

"You first," he said. "Let me guess? Issues with the MyoGen merger," he surmised. Alex groaned. "Alex, it will work out. Jason knows what he's doing. They're not going to bail."

Alex shook her head. "I don't know. Rand Industries is in play, making overtures at the eleventh hour. I don't like it," she said.

"Look, you know this is part of the game. You've managed to acquire seven major players in the pharmaceutical industry in less than a year. They're going to hold out until the last minute. It will be fine."

"You are awfully calm about this," Alex said with a questioning gaze. "You and I both know that Rand is in Viktor Ivanov's pocket. That doesn't concern you? ASA has made its share of acquisitions too. If Viktor and the Russians get hold of…"

"Alex, they won't. Trust me."

"I wish I had your confidence on this one. And, I'm still curious why you seem so unconcerned about this. We both know that MyoGen is crucial in undermining The Collaborative. We fail to control their access and…"

"I am concerned, but this is your department and you haven't failed yet," he reminded his sister.

Alex sighed heavily. Jonathan Krause was the most unlikely best friend she could have imagined. She'd pondered their relationship for months before discovering that he was her half-brother. It was a discovery that took them both by surprise, and yet seemed to answer a million unspoken questions that they each had been asking. Alex was grateful for her older brother. They were kindred spirits. She loved her younger brother, Nick, but they were different people. She was Nick's protector, his advocate, his cheerleader. She was the big sister. Krause was different. They were closer in age. They were alike in many ways. They had similar interests, similar ideas, similar talents, and even a similar taste in women. Krause had proved the big brother Alex had never imagined having. They were equals on every level, but he felt a fierce protectiveness of Alex and her family. Some of that Alex understood was rooted in his long-term friendship and affection for Cassidy. A good deal of it stemmed from the knowledge that his childhood best friend was Dylan's father. There was no denying those factors. Alex also realized that Jonathan Krause had come to value her not just as a partner and friend, he loved her as his sister. He valued their relationship on levels that continued to surprise Alex. She was grateful for him, far more than she had verbalized to anyone. "Pip?" Alex gently urged him. "You either give me too much credit or there is more to this than you are telling me."

Krause nodded. "The Sparrow," he said.

Alex groaned dramatically. "What's going on with Claire?" she asked. Claire Brackett continued to be a thorn in Alex's side. The DCIS agent's loyalty was constantly wavering. Claire had lost the woman she loved to her arrogance. She had lost her lover to the game they were all immersed in. That made her even more unpredictable. She had no anchor. Claire Brackett's allegiance blew with the wind, and Alex wasn't sure which way the wind was blowing now.

"This ghost she's been chasing," Krause said.

"Yeah? I thought that was just some folklore the locals had?"

"Maybe," he said.

"Or?"

"Or, maybe not," he offered.

Alex sighed. "So what?" Alex watched as Krause's eyes narrowed and his brow furrowed. "Okay. You think this person exists?" she asked. He just tipped his head to signify the possibility. "Well, okay. So what if he does? Pip, let her chase this ghost. If that keeps her out of our hair...."

"Alex, you know she is not chasing this on her own accord. Why do they keep digging? Claire's been in Russia and Ukraine more in the last six months than she has in her entire life. Why not let it drop? Who sent her? Something tells me it wasn't Viktor."

"You think her father sent her?" Alex asked. William Brackett was another entity that Alex kept close tabs on. She wasn't certain what motivated his actions. That made him a dangerous player in this game.

"Maybe. I'm more worried about who they are looking for."

"They're looking for a ghost," Alex reminded him.

"Yeah. That's what worries me," he said.

***

"You sure you are feeling up to this?" Cassidy asked her mother-in-law.

Helen Toles smiled. "Cassidy, I am fine. I already have one daughter ready to tie me to a bedpost, don't you start. You're my sanity," she chuckled good-naturedly.

Cassidy offered the older woman a sympathetic smile. Alex could be overbearing at times. Most of the time it was endearing, but Alex's protectiveness could test a person's patience from time to time. Cassidy had experienced that a bit when she was pregnant with their daughter, Mackenzie. Alex had been watching Helen like a hawk for weeks. "She means well," Cassidy said.

"I know. I have to get moving. You heard the doctor," Helen said.

Cassidy smiled as she fed a spoonful of peas to Mackenzie. Mackenzie promptly spit them out and Cassidy rolled her eyes. "You are just like your mother. Not everything in life is sweet, Kenzie, I hate to tell you," Cassidy laughed as she wiped her daughter's mouth.

Dylan came bounding over and looked at his baby sister. He wrinkled his nose at the green gush. Mackenzie started laughing and banging her tray in excitement. Dylan repeated his expression.

"Oh, you're a big help," Cassidy playfully scolded her son with a laugh.

"What's going on in here?" Alex asked, coming into the kitchen and setting down her briefcase.

Cassidy smiled. "I would call it an exercise in futility," she said.

Alex looked at her mother who was merrily going about the task of placing cookies on a cookie sheet. "Can I talk to you for a minute?" Alex asked her wife.

Cassidy scratched her brow and sighed softly. "Dylan, see if you can't entertain your sister by getting her to actually eat, will you? Please?" Cassidy asked her son.

"Sure, Mom. Come on Kenz, look…Mmmmmm," Dylan said spooning up the peas and making a face. Kenzie reached for the spoon and smeared it onto the tray. "Kenzie," Dylan laughed.

Cassidy rolled her eyes as she followed Alex into the living room. "Your daughter is as picky as you are," Cassidy began. Alex turned around to face her and Cassidy sighed again.

"What is going on?" Alex asked pointedly.

"I'll assume we are not talking about your daughter's aversion to anything green," Cassidy replied. Alex's expression was harsh and Cassidy met it with an equal stoicism.

"What the hell is Mom doing in there?" Alex asked.

"I'm pretty sure that was obvious. She's making cookies."

"Yeah, I saw that. Why is she making cookies, Cass?"

Cassidy took a moment to compose herself. She did not appreciate the tone in her wife's voice. It was one thing for Alex to be protective or concerned. It was another to speak to Cassidy as if she were Alex's child. "I would guess she's doing it because she wanted to," Cassidy answered evenly.

"Cassidy. Jesus. She just had a heart attack. She shouldn't be…"

"She had a mild heart attack a month ago, Alex."

"You know," Alex began to raise her voice.

"What I know is that if you don't lower your voice, this conversation is over," Cassidy said pointedly. Alex took a deep breath. Cassidy could see her wife simmering. "I understand that you are worried, Alex. She knows her limits. Her doctor encouraged her to get moving. You need to stop treating her like a child. She's not your child. She's your mother," Cassidy reminded her wife.

"You don't think I know that?" Alex barked.

"Actually, Alex, I'm not sure what is going on with you right now."

"She should be relaxing. That's why she is here. You know…"

"I know that I am not your child either. I have two of those already," Cassidy said. She loved Alex beyond words, but she had no intention of being interrogated like a teenager that got caught taking the car without permission.

"She's staying here so that she can rest, not cook!" Alex snapped.

That was it. Cassidy was done. She nodded and took a step closer to her wife. They rarely argued. When they did, it was almost always caused by some outside pressure that made Alex short with her wife, or made Cassidy irritable enough that she snapped at Alex. The first had started this altercation, the latter would finish it. "Keep this up Alex, and your mother will be home before you want it. This house is not the Army, Captain Toles. You're my wife and Helen's daughter. You want to have a discussion? Fine. You want to express a concern? I will listen." Alex started to interject and Cassidy warned her with a glare. "Don't you come in here and dress me down like some soldier in your command. When you are ready to talk to me like the woman I married, you let me know. Right now, I need to feed our daughter and help your mother. Contrary to what you seem to think, I worry about her too." Cassidy turned on her heels in disgust and left the room.

Alex closed her eyes. She knew Cassidy was right. "Shit," she mumbled. She hated feeling guilty. The guilt just made her frustration and anger rise closer to the surface. Alex headed up the stairs, taking them two at a time. She quickly shed her suit and slipped into her running clothes. She needed to calm down. She needed perspective. She needed to get away from everyone and everything. Alex needed to run. She hoped the cold February air might cool her off. Cassidy heard the front door close with a bang and jumped.

Helen smiled at her daughter-in-law. "No cookies for her," she joked.

Cassidy appreciated the levity. Dylan had settled at the far end of the kitchen table with his homework. Kenzie was banging on her tray, and Cassidy laughed softly. "Tell me about it," she said to her daughter. Kenzie pounded harder. "Why do I think you are going to be just like her?" Cassidy asked as her daughter began to throw a fit over her food and threw the peas forcefully onto the floor. "That was not nice," Cassidy said gently, but firmly. She picked up the jar and tried not to laugh at the quivering lip her daughter sported. Cassidy wiped Mackenzie's face and looked at her seriously. "Not nice to throw things," she repeated, placing a kiss on Mackenzie's head. Mackenzie reached out for her mother and Cassidy lifted her happily, delighting in the way the baby clung to her. "Yep, just like her," Cassidy smiled. "I am in so much trouble," she said.

Helen laughed. "That's an understatement."

***

"What is so important about this ghost of yours?" Claire Brackett asked her father.

"Let's just say that I am curious if such a person exists, and why that person would hide his identity for so many years."

Claire swung her feet up onto her father's couch and reclined casually. "Please, you obviously have some idea who this is. Maybe you should just put his picture on a milk carton and see what you get."

"You are the milk carton, Claire," Admiral William Brackett explained.

"Just who do you think this is?" she asked. "Wait! I know! Peter Pan, right? Jesus, you have me chasing a shadow."

The Admiral laughed. "Cute, Claire. I'm glad you find this task so amusing."

"I don't. I find it pathetic."

"Pathetic? I see. I would say vigilant," her father answered.

"You're afraid," Claire said. She sat upright and regarded her father carefully. "The great William Brackett afraid of a shadow."

Admiral William Brackett swirled the scotch in his glass and considered his response. He turned to his daughter slowly and nodded. "Not a shadow, Claire—a ghost. A shadow you can see. It reflects an object's existence. Ghosts are careful never to project a shadow. A ghost is present and unseen, not the same thing. Ghosts move without your knowledge. They see things. They move things. They change things without you ever knowing. You should be afraid of ghosts."

Claire snickered. She often thought her father should have written science fiction or fables. He had spent hours reading tall tales to her when she was a child. This mission her father persisted with, finding this ghost, was out of character for him. She followed his directives mainly out of curiosity. She was beginning to question her father's sanity. "Pretty soon you'll be telling me this guy pulled the sword from the stone," she said with a roll of her eyes. "Or better yet, he holds the keys to the Lost Ark of the Covenant," she said with a caustic chuckle.

William Brackett sipped his scotch. "If he exists, you have no idea how close to the truth that may be," he murmured. "No idea."

***

Cassidy stood in the doorway of the nursery and watched Alex as she stood over Mackenzie's crib. Alex had been on edge more than usual the last few weeks. Helen's heart attack had shaken Alex to her core. Alex had spent years estranged from her parents. Over the last couple of years, she had not only rekindled a relationship with her mother, but the two had also become closer than Alex could remember. Cassidy was certain that the thought of losing her mother now frightened Alex beyond what she was able to articulate. There was more driving Alex's earlier tension and outburst. Cassidy knew that as well.

"I don't think she's planning to escape—yet," Cassidy said from the doorway. She heard Alex sigh through an uncomfortable chuckle and made her way across the room. Cassidy wrapped her arms around Alex's waist and kissed her back.

Alex sighed again and closed her eyes. Cassidy's touch always soothed her anxiety. "I'm sorry," Alex said softly.

"I know you are," Cassidy replied. Alex turned and pulled Cassidy to her. "You all right?" Cassidy asked. Alex nodded. "Not very convincing Agent Toles," Cassidy said with the raise of her eyebrow. Alex nodded again and looked back at Mackenzie. "Alex, what's got you so upset?"

Alex pinched the bridge of her nose and shook her head. She bent over the crib and touched Mackenzie's hair. "It's hard to believe that this time last year we hadn't even met Kenzie," Alex smiled as she spoke. Cassidy watched silently and waited for Alex to continue. "I'm always thinking, how do I take care of you? What if something happened to me or what if I…"

"Alex," Cassidy pulled Alex gently to face her.

"I do think about all of that."

"I know you do. It's part of having a family," Cassidy said. Alex nodded, closed her eyes, and started rubbing her temples. "Honey?" Cassidy called to her wife. Alex tried unsuccessfully to smile. "Come on," Cassidy said, leading Alex across the hall to their bedroom. Cassidy shut the door and watched as Alex flopped back onto the bed in defeat. This was not Alex's typical demeanor. Cassidy had seen Alex injured, in pain, even sick. There were only a handful of times in their relationship that Cassidy witnessed Alex feeling defeated. The first was when John Merrow had been assassinated. The second occurred when Alex's father had died. And, the third happened when Helen was rushed to the hospital just after the New Year.

Cassidy crawled onto the bed beside her wife and laid her head on Alex's chest. "I know you are worried about your mother. She knows her limits. If she didn't, she wouldn't have agreed to stay with us," Cassidy reminded Alex.

"I know," Alex said.

"Um-hum. And, I know there is something else bothering you, so spill."

Alex closed her eyes and took a moment to gather her thoughts. "This merger with MyoGen," she began and then hesitated.

Cassidy was aware of the reasons for MyoGen's acquisition, perhaps not in detail, but Alex did not hide anything she deemed important from Cassidy. "Go on," Cassidy encouraged her wife. Alex just sighed. "Alex, are you worried that the merger will fall through?"

"Not really," Alex confessed softly.

"Okay? What is it?"

Alex sighed and turned on her side to face Cassidy. "Jason called on my way home tonight." Cassidy watched Alex closely as she continued. Alex had hired Jason Stratton soon after assuming her father's role at Carecom. He was a Harvard educated economic guru. Alex had learned a great deal about corporate life and managing a company, but that was not her area of expertise. She had been concerned about how to manage the business successfully while still utilizing Carecom's resources for her investigative efforts. Alex's time and attention would always be split. Jason Stratton had been her answer to that equation.

Cassidy noted the tension that was pulling at the corners of Alex's eyes. "Alex?"

Alex let out a heavy sigh. "There's going to be layoffs, Cass. No way around that." Alex always worried about the people Carecom employed and the people who would be affected by any of their acquisitions. It was Alex's nature to be a protector. While Cassidy understood that Alex loved a challenge, it was her desire to protect others that drove Alex's decisions. Cassidy smiled and her eyes twinkled slightly. "Why are you smiling?" Alex wondered.

"Just remembering why I love you so much," Cassidy said.

"Yeah? I'm glad you do because I don't like me very much right now."

Cassidy kissed Alex gently. "How many people?" she asked.

"I don't know yet. As few as possible. If I didn't think this was so important…"

"You would cancel the merger?" Cassidy guessed.

"Yeah. I would."

"I'm sorry," Cassidy said sincerely.

"Those people have families, Cass. At least, a lot of them do," Alex said sadly. "How did he do this all those years?"

"Your father?" Cassidy asked.

"Yeah. How did he do it? I mean all the things he did."

Alex's discoveries regarding her father's business dealings had been unsettling to her. He had directed funds to warlords in Northern Africa, engineered the use of Carecom for the delivery of weapons and parts to terrorists in Iraq, Afghanistan and a host of other nations. He had managed to funnel currency from illegal arms sales to foreign governments and devised secure pathways for money from campaign donations to the Central Intelligence Agency's many business fronts. He had done it all through loopholes. Nicolaus Toles was a legal genius. The discovery that surprised her most was the evidence of his concern for Carecom's employees. She had confided in Cassidy more than once that living in her father's world only served to confuse her more about the man. It was the only puzzle in Alex's life that she seemed incapable of solving.

"I don't know. How do you do it?" Cassidy asked.

Alex shook her head. "Some days, Cass….I'm not sure what I am doing. It's bizarre."

Cassidy caressed Alex gently. "Alex, you can't save everyone all of the time. You know that."

"This morning I was in meetings about salary reviews and benefits. This afternoon Pip was sitting across from me."

Cassidy took a deep breath. "Everything okay with Pip?"

Alex chuckled. "You mean professionally or personally?" she asked.

Cassidy didn't answer. Alex pulled her a little closer. Cassidy adored Jonathan Krause, but Alex knew that the mention of her brother's name when it came to business always made Cassidy uneasy. Alex suspected it conjured images of danger. That was justified. It always brought Cassidy back to the time Alex had been shot. Alex held Cassidy and attempted to lighten the mood. "I think his personal frustrations might be making him see things," she chuckled.

"What do you mean?"

"Oh, it's nothing. He's following Claire, worried about what she is doing," Alex commented.

Cassidy propped herself up. "You think it's because of Eleana?" she asked curiously.

Alex groaned. "Only partly. There's reason to be vigilant where Claire is concerned."

Cassidy lifted her eyebrow. She had little use for Agent Claire Brackett. The first time she had crossed paths with Alex's brief lover had been less than pleasant. Alex's revelations that Claire had moved onto an affair with Cassidy's ex-husband, Christopher O'Brien, deepened Cassidy's dislike and distrust in the woman. It was Claire Brackett's role with her ex-husband in Alex's injury that tipped the scales completely. Cassidy had been surprised to learn of the love affair between Eleana Baros and Claire Brackett. Eleana was intelligent, beautiful, and genuinely kind. Claire was beautiful. Cassidy could not deny that, but she was also conniving. That made her ugly in Cassidy's estimation.

"I don't trust that woman," Cassidy said.

Alex laughed. "Neither do I."

"Do you?" Cassidy asked again. "Do you think that this is about Pip's feelings for Eleana?" she clarified.

Alex took a deep breath and let it out slowly. She and Cassidy were both aware that Krause had feelings for Agent Eleana Baros. Eleana had become as much a part of their family as he had. The two were nearly inseparable, but something consistently held them back from a romantic relationship. Alex suspected that Eleana's history with Claire Brackett was the primary driver, perhaps more so for her brother than for Eleana. Alex also knew that Krause's concerns about Claire were warranted. Krause was an adept agent. He'd been immersed in the world of international espionage longer than Alex. He had learned to obey his senses as much as the information he gathered. Alex understood that. Her gut inclinations and reactions were almost always correct.

"I do—partly, only partly. Claire is up to something and that never leads to anything good." Cassidy's face grew concerned and Alex kissed her gently. "He's on his way to talk to Edmond in Paris. We'll see what develops from there. Nothing for you to worry about."

"Alex…"

"I'm sorry, Cass, about earlier."

"I know you are," Cassidy said. "I know that you are worried about your mom. I am too."

"I know that. I didn't mean to take it all out on you," Alex said. Cassidy snickered. "Cass?"

"Does that mean you are willing to make it up to me?"

Alex tried to conceal her grin. "Did you have something specific in mind?" she asked Cassidy suggestively.

"Yes, actually," Cassidy said as she nuzzled Alex's neck seductively. "I do."

"And, that would be?" Alex breathed heavily.

"Oh, well," Cassidy continued her assault between words. "You see," she stopped and kissed Alex tenderly. "It seems," she stopped again for another kiss. "That I have a little problem," she began to explain while kissing her wife's neck.

"Anything I can help with?"

"Mm...Possibly. Are you willing?" Cassidy asked as her hands lifted Alex's T-shirt.

"Anything," Alex whispered.

Cassidy smiled deviously down on her wife. "Glad to hear that. Your mother has an appointment tomorrow and your son has a birthday party at the same time. I'll let you pick," she said pulling back from Alex with a playful grin.

Alex narrowed her gaze at her wife. Cassidy was pleased with herself. Alex could tell. It was a tiny, harmless bit of revenge after Alex's earlier attitude. Cassidy was on the verge of laughter when Alex grabbed her and flipped them around. "Okay. Tomorrow we will decide who plays Mom and who plays the daughter," Alex said.

"Oh?" Cassidy asked. "And, tonight?"

Alex's answer was a passionate kiss. "Questions?" she asked her wife.

Cassidy smiled. "Only one." Alex raised her brow. "Who's on top?" Cassidy asked, flipping their positions again and straddling Alex.

"That would be you," Alex admitted defeat happily.

"For now," Cassidy replied as she happily gave over to her wife.

Chapter Two

"How is our guest today?"

Agent Steven Brady shook his head and rolled his eyes. "Disagreeable as always," he said. The older man laughed. "Why keep him at all? I mean, he's given you absolutely nothing of consequence. Do you really think that it's worth the risk of someone finding…."

"Finding out he's alive or that I am?" James McCollum inquired.

"Sir, all due respect, but there has been a great deal of interest in this ghost," Brady observed. McCollum smiled. "Sir? What if they find you? If Claire…Well, Alex and Krause will follow her."

"Oh, Agent Brady, that is only a matter of time. It always has been. Even a ghost cannot stay hidden forever, not even out here."

"I don't understand," Steven Brady admitted.

"I know you don't. What matters is who comes. There is no if in this equation. Now, what of the sparrow?"

"Same, just like him," he pointed to the man on the other side of the glass window. "A puppet."

"Yes, but whose puppet, Agent Brady? Who is pulling Claire's strings these days?" McCollum posed the question rhetorically.

"Kargen and Ivanov?" Brady guessed.

McCollum smiled. "I don't think so. You go keep our guest company for a bit."

"Today's agenda?" Brady asked.

"I want to know who sent him to The Broker," McCollum said.

"Krause recruited him. I'm sure the introduction was made before any campaign funds were deposited or diverted…"

"No," McCollum stopped the man. "No, he went to The Broker not long before he received the first threats against him. That is unusual. Contact with The Broker is limited and for good reason. As brash as O'Brien is, he would not have made that move on his own. I still don't know who sent him there. The answer to that question is the key to many things."

"You mean he had gone to The Broker before the president sent Alex to New Rochelle?"

McCollum nodded. "Yes, I do. That is why Alexis was sent to Cassidy and Dylan. Jonathan was not involved in O'Brien's meeting with Nicolaus. Trust me on that. It would surprise me if Jonathan even knows that they met. O'Brien knows something. He may not even realize what he knows. Who wanted those threats sent to him? Who orchestrated that? And, why involve Cassie?"

"Wait. What are you saying? You're telling me….Jesus, Alex's father orchestrated her being sent to Cassidy. You think O'Brien knows that?" Brady asked. McCollum's jaw became taut, but he did not answer. "You think O'Brien was in on the threats themselves? Why would anyone tell him they were going to do that? Why haven't you asked him before?"

McCollum stood silently watching the subject of their discussion. He had kept Congressman Christopher O'Brien in his custody for nearly a year. He'd made the congressman moderately comfortable during that time, utilizing more abstract fear than physical intimidation to secure information from the man. He had been patient, biding his time carefully, waiting for the right moment to press for what he needed to know. Timing was everything in James McCollum's world. Some who had known him in his past life would have claimed that McCollum had a sixth sense about things. He seemed to possess an innate ability to anticipate a change in the weather. The storm he had been awaiting was finally gathering strength. He cleared his throat. "Timing, Steven, timing is everything. Now is the time to press, before our company arrives."

"If Claire discovers…."

McCollum turned to Agent Brady and smiled. "Claire will not be ringing our doorbell," he assured the younger man. He noted the puzzled expression on Brady's face. "Someone else will, and sooner than you might think."

"You want them to come," Brady surmised in amazement.

"There is a time for everything, Agent Brady."

Steven Brady looked back at the congressman in the sound proof room and shook his head. "They'll kill you," he observed. "They will certainly kill him."

"We've both been dead a long time," the older man said. Brady looked at McCollum in disbelief. "Go spend some time with my former son-in-law. See what he has to say."

"How far should I press?"

"Don't break him. Bend him as far as he will stretch," the older man directed stoically.

Agent Steven Brady watched the older man for a moment. McCollum remained still, never changing expression. Brady had been with the man for a year in this underground hideaway. The assignment had been given with no explanation and little detail until he had arrived in Siberia. He had been told simply that he would be reporting to a senior agent, the codename given was Lynx. He recalled the brief conversation with his handler well.

"Siberia?" Brady clarified.

"Yes, Agent Brady," she repeated her directions.

"Why? Taylor is gone."

"I know. And, that is all the more reason that you are the right person for this, Agent Brady," she said. "You need distance from this. Believe me, when Alex learns that Taylor is…"

"I know what Alex will do. This is your answer? My banishment?"

She sighed. "The man you will meet—he is called Lynx."

"So? And, when you call on me I am Stallion. What of it? I don't understand this. I got you Mitchell's information. I followed, gave it to Taylor. I took care of O'Brien as you instructed."

She shook her head. "Do you know why he is called that? Lynx?" she asked. She watched as Brady's expression hardened. "A lynx has second sight. That is what they say." She noted the crease deepen in Steven Brady's forehead. "Listen to me, you will understand more when you meet him," she said thoughtfully.

"Just tell me," Brady asked. She met his gaze. "I'm not coming back, am I?" he asked. She smiled. "Jane?"

"I don't know, Steven. We have all chosen our path now—all of us. That path sometimes leads us in unexpected directions," Jane Merrow answered. Brady took a deep breath. He had just closed his eyes in resignation when he felt her hand on his. "I do believe, if he has anything to say about it, you will make it home again," she said.

"Just who is this man?" Agent Brady asked.

"Just a ghost from the past," she replied.

Steven Brady took one last look at the man beside him and headed off to his appointed task. Living in these conditions for the last year had afforded Brady the opportunity to get to know the older man. It would have been impossible for most people to believe that this man had served as the heavy hand of The Collaborative for many years. James McCollum was soft-spoken and mild-mannered, even in the presence of a man like Christopher O'Brien. Brady turned his attention to the former congressman sitting in an over-sized chair across the large room. He looked back at the mirror behind him, unable to see the expression of the man on the other side. He imagined it remained stoic, even passive. Brady gently bit the inside of his lip and steadied his breathing. Mild-mannered, passive, stoic—it was funny he realized, those were the attributes required in this line of work. Only a few men could endure these conversations, whether the interrogator or the subject. A calm exterior often concealed an inner beast that raged supreme when set free. A controlled beast, as Brady had learned, is the most dangerous. Its prey are left unsuspecting, deliberately allowed to gain false confidence. They never see the beast lurking beneath the surface until it is ready to devour them. That was the manner of things in Steven Brady's line of work. "Well, Congressman, I guess it's time we had a little talk."

***

February 21st

"You are going to see my father," Eleana said flatly.

"I am," Jonathan Krause replied.

Eleana regarded the man before her as he finished packing his suitcase. Jonathan Krause's jaw was taut and his temple was occasionally twitching on its own accord. Seldom could anyone detect stress in Jonathan Krause's demeanor or stance. His need to always conceal his emotions frustrated Eleana at times, even if she did understand its origins. Over the last year, she had learned to read the subtle signs that slipped out from underneath his control. The telltale signs of stress or concern only revealed themselves when she and Krause were alone or in the presence of Krause's family. Looking at him now, Eleana was sure that there was something he was not telling her. Visiting Edmond Callier was no cause for stress or apprehension and Jonathan Krause was obviously anxious. Krause suspected something. Either that, or he was concerned about protecting Eleana from something.

Eleana and Krause's relationship had grown well beyond professional respect and kinship. Eleana had been waiting for the aloof agent standing before her to admit his feelings for her. She sensed his reluctance and was well aware of its cause. Now, a new tide was rising in their lives. Everyone in the life they shared could sense it. Eleana noted the increased tension that permeated the room when their small group of fringe agents and operatives had met just before the New Year. Alex had been uncharacteristically impatient. Jane Merrow had been unusually quiet. Her father had been deliberately evasive. After the meeting, Krause had grown distant. Eleana was the youngest in the group. She understood that Jonathan Krause often mistook her lack of field experience for naïveté. Eleana was no more naïve to the workings of the world than she was aware of the emotions that coursed between her and Krause. She'd let him dictate the pace of their work and their personal connection. A vague shadow of fear in Krause's eyes compelled her to change that dynamic now.

"What aren't you telling me?" she asked him pointedly.

"Nothing," he said with a smile. "I just need to follow up on a few things." Eleana nodded. Her expression was a roadmap to her suspicions. Krause smiled again. "Your father hasn't told us everything," he said. "You know that as well as I do. He has held back. It's time. We need to know. Something is festering. I can feel it."

Eleana sighed deeply. "You think Claire's ghost is real, don't you?"

"I think someone thinks it's real," he corrected her.

"No," Eleana said flatly. "You wouldn't be going to France now unless you believed she was chasing something that might undermine our efforts."

"Eleana, it's just a precaution. We have to know what your father is holding back. There is something."

"Fine. Then I am going with you."

"No," Krause said emphatically as he closed his suitcase.

"Yes. I am," Eleana said.

"Eleana…"

"Don't," she warned him. Krause stepped back slightly. Seldom did Eleana Baros become cross. "Don't tell me what I am not doing. You aren't expecting a quick visit to France."

"I have no idea where this will lead."

"Don't lie to me, Jonathan," Eleana said.

"I'm not lying to you. I don't know."

"You know perfectly well that this trip will not end at my father's villa. Where exactly do you think it will end?" she asked. Krause remained silent. "That's what I thought."

"Eleana, I have no idea what I am going to confront…"

"You mean who you are going to confront," Eleana said. She shook her head. "You think you are going to cross paths with Claire."

"I don't know," he admitted.

"You think I will fall apart if I see her," she surmised.

Krause shook his head. "No," he told her. He massaged his aching temples for a moment and looked back at the woman glaring at him. Krause wasn't sure he could pinpoint when it had happened, but at some point, he had fallen in love with Edmond Callier's daughter. Alex had seen it before he had. He still had not told Eleana what he felt. Jonathan Krause had spent many years loving a woman that would never return his affection. That was not a pain that he planned to endure again. He was sure that Eleana felt something for him. He was also sure that Eleana loved Claire Brackett. He'd witnessed it in her eyes repeatedly when Claire's name would arise. Now, those same eyes penetrated him with a defiant gaze he could not recall.

Eleana stepped directly in front of Krause and placed both her hands on his chest. She looked up at him and held his stare with her own. "You are not going this alone," she said.

"It's not safe."

"For whom?" she asked him.

"For both of us," he replied honestly.

Eleana shook her head and took Krause's face in her hands. "It's not me who needs to let go of Claire," she told him.

"What the hell are you talking about?" he asked.

Eleana smiled and her expression softened. "Jonathan. Please," she shook her head slightly. "I know you. I can see it in your eyes. You're worried."

"I'm cautious. If this person exists, this ghost of Claire's…Who could be so important that the admiral wants her to follow? That your father would not tell us? We are standing at the edge of something, something that people have gone to great lengths to keep us from. Don't think they won't go even further if they need to," Krause explained.

Eleana closed her eyes for a moment. "You don't expect to come back," she surmised painfully.

"I never know what to expect."

Eleana reached out and took Jonathan Krause's face in her hands. She opened her eyes and looked into his. "I can't lose you too," she whispered.

Krause felt his heart rise into his throat. He wiped a single tear from Eleana's cheek. "Eleana…"

"No, Jonathan. I am going with you," she repeated her demand firmly. Krause started to speak and Eleana stopped him. "I need you, Jonathan."

"You don't need me," he said softly.

"You're wrong," she said.

"Eleana, if Claire…I can't promise you…"

"I know," she said. "Look, I will always love Claire," she confessed. "I loved her my whole life, but life changes. I understand that. Claire never has."

"Eleana, I know…"

"I love you, Jonathan. I can't lose you."

Krause took a deep breath and tucked an errant strand of hair behind Eleana's ear. "I will be back."

"I'm not taking that chance," she told him. She looked up at the man before her and smiled.

Krause leaned over and brushed his lips against her forehead. There was a great deal that he needed to say. It did not feel like the right time. He was positive from the look in Eleana's eyes that the words she spoke were true. And, he was sure that she was aware of his feelings. His reluctance to allow Eleana to accompany him was not simply about Claire Brackett. Edmond Callier was Eleana's father. Jonathan Krause had developed a new perspective on family over the last year. He intended to press Edmond as hard as was necessary to obtain the information he needed. It no longer mattered what Callier's reasoning or intention was in withholding information. Being an ally did not guarantee one's honesty and it definitely did not ensure transparency of any kind. Everyone had an agenda, something to protect. Krause believed that Callier's motives were pure. That simply did not matter any longer. Information was not only power, but knowledge was also security. He did not want to subject Eleana to the possibility of seeing him press her father physically. On top of that, Claire Brackett remained a wild card. Claire delighted in the adventure of an agent's life. She could be impulsive. Krause also understood that Claire loved Eleana. That concerned him. He had witnessed loss enough times. He did not want to subject Eleana to that. He sighed and held Eleana close. He surprised himself with his words.

"I wish you would walk away from this," he whispered.

Eleana listened to Krause's heartbeat in her ear as he held her. "You mean the agency or do you mean you?" she asked him softly.

Krause sighed. "It's not safe."

"I've never known anything worthwhile in life that was," she told him.

"Perhaps so," he said.

"Now," she began as she continued to lean against him. "When do we leave?"

***

Cassidy and Helen walked through the front door and Cassidy stifled a giggle at the sounds coming from the distance. She gestured to her mother-in-law to step softly so as not to alert Alex to their presence. Cassidy had a strong desire to see what was unfolding in the living room.

"Moo!" Alex's voice carried through the house.

"Bah Bah!!" a small squeaky voice babbled.

"Not bah, Kenz. Bah is a sheep, silly. MMM…OOOO… MOO! That's what the cow says. MOO!"

Cassidy and Helen looked at each other in amusement, both struggling to contain a burst of laughter.

"Try again, Kenzie. Like Momma. Moooo!! Mooo!! Mooo!" Alex repeated. Each time Alex released the sound, Mackenzie would giggle uncontrollably. "Moo!" Alex howled again to Mackenzie's delight.

Cassidy shook her head and motioned for Helen to follow her.

"Moo is an easy one, Kenzie. Moo! Then we have to learn oink. That one is harder," Alex said seriously. "Cows say moo. Pigs say oink. Ducks say quack. Sheep say bah."

Cassidy stepped into the doorway and smirked. Mackenzie was on Alex's knees lying on her back. Her eyes were wide as she watched and listened to Alex. Each time Alex made a noise and a silly face, Kenzie would erupt into a belly laugh. Cassidy looked at Helen, who was stifling a laugh and shook her head at the seriousness in Alex's plea to their daughter. "Good luck," Helen whispered. "I'm headed for my first glass of wine in over a month," she said with a wink.

Cassidy smiled. Helen was feeling better and more confident after a positive visit to her cardiologist. Cassidy understood. She was looking forward to a nice glass of wine soon as well. She watched Helen head back down the hallway and turned her attention back to the farm animal lesson in the next room.

"Hoping she'll catch on to your language skills early, huh?" Cassidy called over. Alex looked at her wife and flushed with embarrassment. That prompted more laughter from Mackenzie. Cassidy could no longer contain herself. She made her way to the pair on the couch and leaned in to place a kiss on Alex's cheek. "Dare I ask what brought about the Farmer Brown lesson?" she joked.

Mackenzie looked up at Cassidy the moment she heard Cassidy's voice and Alex chuckled. She lifted Mackenzie up and set her between them on the couch. "God, she looks so much like you, Cass," Alex remarked.

"You think so?" Cassidy asked.

Alex laughed. "Like your very own Mini-Me," Alex said. Cassidy looked at Mackenzie and shrugged. Alex watched as their daughter reached for Cassidy's hair and began to twirl it in her fingers. She'd done that from the moment Alex had placed her in Cassidy's arms. Alex never grew tired of watching Cassidy with their children. Both Mackenzie and Dylan resembled Cassidy, but Alex marveled at the likeness between mother and daughter. Mackenzie's eyes were just like Cassidy's. They changed from deep tones of blue to light green depending on her mood. Just like her mother, excitement and contentment sparkled a bluish green while frustration and upset darkened her irises like a storm on the horizon. Right now, Mackenzie's eyes twinkled sea-green. Alex looked at Cassidy and smiled when she noted the exact same color in her wife's eyes.

Cassidy felt the weight of Alex's stare. She did not need to ask her wife what she was thinking. It amused her and touched her the way Alex became entranced by the smallest things. It was true, Mackenzie did look a great deal like Cassidy. Cassidy also understood that often people saw with their hearts more than their eyes. When Cassidy looked at Mackenzie, she saw Alex staring back at her. Mackenzie was spirited and playful, and extremely willful, far more so than Dylan had been as a baby. Dylan had loved to play, loved to cuddle. He had been a good-natured baby and that had followed him into childhood. He had his occasional outbursts and mishaps, but overall Dylan was even-tempered. He enjoyed trying new things, but he often required encouragement to become adventurous. Cassidy could see the difference in her children clearly.

Mackenzie was prone to defiance already at the tender age of seven months. She also seemed to be curious about everything. Often, Cassidy would snicker at the expressions on her daughter's face when she was amused or even irritated. The mischievous glint in her bluish-green eyes was all Alex. Mackenzie was a Toles at least as much as she could ever hope to be a McCollum. Cassidy looked down at the baby and sniggered. "Now, Kenzie, tell Mommy what Momma was teaching you," she said. "What was that sound? Was it bahhh?" Cassidy asked. Mackenzie laughed. "No? Hum. Was it oink?" Cassidy asked with a quick tickle to her daughter. Mackenzie laughed again. "No, huh?" Cassidy asked. She looked at Alex whose face had turned a lovely shade of pink. "I know!" Cassidy exclaimed. "It was…Moooo!" she made the sound loudly. Mackenzie shook with laughter.

"Bah," Mackenzie babbled.

"No, Kenz," Alex corrected. "Moooooo! Like a mooooo cow."

Mackenzie laughed harder. Her tiny body quaked as she giggled uncontrollably at her parents' antics.

"Are you two buying a farm or something?" a voice called into the living room. Cassidy focused on her daughter, enjoying Mackenzie's laughter.

"I don't think so," Alex said. "She's not ready for that. She'd be feeding the cows the pigs' slop and trying to milk the ducks at this rate," Alex said. Cassidy swatted Alex playfully. "What?" Alex feigned innocence before joining Cassidy in her laughter.

"Uh-huh," Rose McCollum said.

"Not that I'm not happy to see you," Cassidy looked up at her mother as Alex took hold of Mackenzie. "But, what are you doing here?"

Rose chuckled. "I have a date with a glass of red wine to celebrate my best friend's liberation."

Alex looked at Rose and then at Cassidy to explain. Cassidy let out a small sigh and smiled. "The doctor cleared your mom for a few more things."

"Let me guess," Alex began, "at the top of that list was wine." Cassidy lifted her eyebrow. Alex groaned a bit.

"Oh, relax," Rose gently chastised her daughter-in-law. "I promise I will keep her in check," she said. Alex frowned and Cassidy bit her lip to conceal her amusement. "Are you implying something, Alex?" Rose asked cheekily.

"No offense, you promising to keep my mother in check is a bit like Cass and I agreeing to let Dylan watch Mackenzie for an entire evening."

Rose rolled her eyes. "I'm sure he would do just fine," she said. "He's very attentive to his sister," she said before winking at the two women on the couch and making her way toward the kitchen to find Helen.

Cassidy laughed at her mother. "You never did tell me," she said as she turned to Alex.

"Tell you what?" Alex asked.

"What possessed you to start teaching our daughter farm animal sounds."

"Oh, that."

Cassidy's lips turned upward into a smirk. "Yes, that. French, I would have expected. Maybe even Army lingo…"

"Army lingo?" Alex asked through a chuckle.

"Yes, Cap," Cassidy returned smartly. "Can't say I saw farm animals on the horizon."

"I like farm animals," Alex grumbled.

Cassidy raised her brow. "You certainly are full of surprises, love."

"Very funny, Cass," Alex answered. "All right. I dropped Dylan off at his party and they were playing some weird version of pin the tail on the donkey."

"Weird? How can you make pin the tail on the donkey weird?" Cassidy inquired.

"Pin the soccer ball in the goal," Alex answered disgustedly.

"Well, that certainly is creative," Cassidy commented. Mackenzie was beginning to fuss and she reached out for her mother. "I still don't follow. How did soccer lead to farm animals?"

"I told you," Alex said as she passed Mackenzie back to Cassidy. "Pin the tail on the donkey. I had a lengthy discussion with Kenzie about the correct way to play party games," Alex explained. Cassidy's brow lifted again. "What?" Alex asked. "She needs to know that some traditions should be respected."

Cassidy nodded and tried to suppress her laughter. "I see. I never knew you were such a party purist."

"Cute," Alex said. "Why is it so strange that I want to do the traditional things with our kids?"

Cassidy smiled. Mackenzie was lying against her and quickly falling asleep. She looked down at the baby and shook her head. Alex looked at the pair and was taken back by the tear falling down Cassidy's cheek.

"Cass?" she asked gently. Cassidy continued to gaze at their daughter. "Cass? Why are you upset?"

"I'm not upset, Alex."

"You're crying," Alex noted the obvious.

Cassidy sighed. "I was just thinking about my dad," she said softly. Alex placed her arm around Cassidy. Cassidy collapsed against her gratefully. "I wish he was here to see them. I missed so many things with him," she said.

"Like party games?"

Cassidy nodded. "Yeah, that too, I guess. I missed him walking me down the aisle. I missed him interrogating my boyfriends—interrogating you," Cassidy added lightly. Alex smiled. "I guess I just still miss him sometimes. I don't want us to miss any of those things with Dylan and Kenzie."

Alex pulled Cassidy closer. "We won't," she promised. "So, you don't think it's strange then?"

Cassidy looked up at Alex and strained to place a gentle kiss on her lips. "No."

"Not even the farm animal lesson?" Alex asked.

"No. Besides, you're cheaper than a See 'n Say."

Alex laughed. "You want me to take her and put her down?"

Cassidy shook her head. "No. I just want to stay here for a while."

Alex looked down at Cassidy just as Cassidy closed her eyes in contentment. She looked upward and said a silent prayer. She'd never had much of an inclination to pray. Alex had always placed her faith in herself. Believing in others was an uphill battle for her. It took time to earn Alex's confidence, and she tended to remain cautious. After many years of walking a tightrope with the people in her life, Alex had learned to rely on the woman in her arms for both strength and guidance. Life was anything but solitary for Alex now.

Cassidy amazed Alex in every moment. She was gentle, honest, and compassionate. She was also spirited, opinionated, and intelligent. What Alex admired the most in her wife was Cassidy's capacity for love and forgiveness. Cassidy saw goodness and possibility in the most difficult situation. Alex sometimes lost sight of the reality that her wife had experienced great loss and sadness in her life. Cassidy did not dwell on those moments. She spoke of her father often. She treasured her recollections of the man. She seldom mentioned the loss itself, choosing instead to slip into happy childhood memories. Occasionally, she recounted moments with her ex-husband. In spite of his repeated betrayals, Cassidy endeavored to focus on the lighter moments she and Christopher O'Brien had shared with Dylan.

Some of that was for Dylan's benefit. Alex understood that. More than that, it was simply Cassidy's nature to look at the best in everything and everyone.

Alex kissed the top of Cassidy's head and held her hand over Mackenzie. She offered another silent plea to whoever might be listening to keep them safe—all of them. One thing that Alex had grown to understand unequivocally, was how deeply Cassidy's father's death had shaped Cassidy's life. In spite of the upheavals in her own family, Alex thought of her father often. She even missed him. Alex often wondered what Nicolaus Toles would say, do, or think about a decision she needed to make or about the life she now led. She could not fathom experiencing such a profound loss as a child. "I wish I could give you that back," Alex whispered aloud without thinking.

"What did you say?" Cassidy asked without opening her eyes.

Alex took a deep breath. "Nothing. I love you, Cass."

A smile edged its way onto Cassidy's lips. These simple moments meant everything to her. The pain of the past and the confusion that often permeated life faded away in Alex's arms. "I love you too, Alex. More every day."

***

"Are we ready?" a deep voice asked.

"We've been ready for months, Sir. The only thing holding us up is your say so," a younger voice responded.

"Good. You understand what this entails, Captain?" the older man asked.

"I do."

"You agree with this action, and you are prepared for that inevitability?"

"Sir, all due respect, it is not my place to agree or to disagree with your command. My duty is to follow your orders, Sir."

The older man smiled triumphantly. "We would be living in better times, Captain if more men thought as you do."

"Is that all, Sir?"

"Yes, Captain. Keep me apprised of the timeline."

"Sir," the younger man gave his formal agreement.

"Dismissed, Captain."

""Vy ponimayete, chto eto znachit? (You understand what this means)?"

Admiral William Brackett straightened his jacket and faced the man beside him. "Da, Viktor. YA tol'ko nadeyus', chto mi ne zhdali slishkom dolgo. (Yes, Viktor. I only hope that we have not waited too long).

"Kak vy dumayete, on pridet? (Do you think he will come)?" Victor Ivanov asked.

"Yesli on zhiv, on pridet. Eto ne vopros. Vopros v tom, za kem oni stanut? (If he is alive, he will come. That is not a question. The question is who will they follow)?" the admiral answered. "I za kem oni stanut opredelit mnogiye veshchi ... dlya vsekh nas. (And, who they follow will determine many things...for us all)."

Chapter Three

February 23rd

"**H**awkins," Joshua Tate addressed the woman before him.

"Nice to see you too, Joshua," she said.

"I wish I could say the same," he replied.

"Where is your flunky?" she asked him.

Joshua Tate took a deep breath to steady his frustration. The woman now seated across from him had a unique ability to pull Joshua Tate's strings. She had been technically under his command for a year but marched to a beat laid by a different drummer. His lip twitched slightly and he conjured an insincere smile. "Agent Fallon is anything but a flunky—as you put it."

The woman shrugged. "If you say so."

"I do," Tate responded just as Fallon made his way into the coffee shop.

"Director," Brian Fallon greeted his boss.

Tate smiled. He watched as Brian Fallon's eyes tracked slowly to the unfamiliar face seated at the table. "Fallon, let me introduce Agent Charlie Hawkins."

"Hawk," the woman corrected her superior. "Nice to meet you, Agent," she mustered a polished sincerity.

Fallon looked at Tate quizzically and then back to the woman at the table. He suppressed a slight snicker. Hawk, as she called herself was a stunning beauty. Fallon wondered silently if sex appeal was somehow a prerequisite for women at the NSA. He shook off his musing and extended his hand. "Brian," he told her. "Or Fallon."

"Sit down, Fallon," Tate directed.

"I guess I can safely assume this meeting is not about coffee," Fallon joked. Tate pushed a small envelope in Fallon's direction and indicated that Fallon should open it. Fallon complied and removed a piece of paper. He studied it for a few moments before placing it back inside and sliding it across the table. "Does Alex know?" he asked Tate directly. Joshua Tate shook his head. Fallon nodded. "You have to tell her."

"I agree," Hawk said.

Tate's lip twitched again and he shook his head. "No."

"She has a right to know," Fallon said.

"I agree," Hawk concurred.

Tate glared across the table at the younger woman before meeting Fallon's steely gaze. "It's conjecture. And....There are more pressing concerns that we need to address."

"If you are talking about Agent Brackett," Fallon began, "I have no reason to think she has made any headway in this area."

Tate nodded. "I'm not talking about Claire," he said flatly. "Ambassador Daniels is in town."

"So?" Fallon questioned. "He is an ambassador. They tend to visit on occasion," he reminded the NSA Director.

"Exactly," Hawk supported Fallon's assessment as she looked at Tate.

Tate warned the woman with his eyes. Fallon watched the exchange curiously. "Yes, but not the week after he met with the Russian Prime Minister," Tate responded.

"Are you sure about that?" Fallon asked. Tate nodded. Fallon hesitated to continue.

"Agent Hawkins already knows the drill, Agent Fallon. You can speak freely," Tate assured his friend.

Fallon remained skeptical. "No offense," he said to the woman. "I don't know who the hell you are."

Hawk laughed. "Alex was always discreet. I will give her that much," she said. Fallon bristled at the comment and looked at Tate.

"Enough," Tate warned Hawkins. "Hawkins and Toles were partners briefly at the NSA," he said.

"I thought Alex worked in decryption?" Fallon said.

Tate's lopsided grin told Fallon there was more to Alex's time at the National Security Agency than she had shared. Alex was not one to divulge specifics about any investigation unless it was warranted. She was even less likely to share tidbits of her past personal entanglements. Alex had never boasted about her conquests, neither the ones she made in the field nor the ones she made in the bedroom. Fallon looked at the female agent across from him and nodded. The fact that she had been as bold as to insinuate a personal relationship with Alex only served to deepen Fallon's unease.

Hawk regarded Fallon thoughtfully, studying his expression. "Relax, Fallon. I have nothing but respect for my ex, both professionally and personally."

Fallon was taken off guard by the candid response. He nodded but remained silent.

"Jane sent Hawkins to me," Tate explained. "She's been working with General Waters for nearly four years," he said.

Hawk smiled at Fallon genuinely. She had been skeptical of the ex-cop turned FBI agent turned NSA. Law enforcement and espionage were not the same things. Fallon's caution and his obvious loyalty to Alex Toles reassured her of his commitment and comprehension of his role. She sighed. "Look, Agent Fallon, I'm not here for Alex nor am I here in spite of her, okay? I don't happen to agree with the director here on his approach," she said. She turned her attention back to Tate. "She has a right to know what we suspect."

"Yes," Tate agreed. "But, we don't yet know who planted that seed. You know that as well as I do," he said. Tate took a deep breath and exhaled it forcefully. "Daniels did not just meet with Kabinov," he said. Both Fallon and Charlie Hawkins narrowed their gaze in questioning. Tate sighed again. "Anton Petrov was there."

"Ivanov's business right hand," Fallon observed.

"I suspect it's worse than that," Hawk surmised.

"It is," Tate told them. "Petrov is in town too. Wait for it," he said. "Meeting with none other than Kyle Becker."

"Fuck," Fallon groaned.

"The head of Rand Industries?" Hawk asked for clarification. Tate nodded.

Fallon looked up. "MyoGen," he muttered.

"Yes," Tate responded. "The question is—what is it that they are planning?"

"You think they are making an aggressive play to grab MyoGen out from under Carecom?' Fallon asked.

Hawk closed her eyes for a moment and then looked at Tate knowingly. "That's our best case scenario," she said flatly.

Tate's silence served as his response.

"That doesn't change," Fallon began.

"It changes everything," Tate said. "You let Krause chase Claire and her ghost," he told Fallon.

"And me?" Fallon asked.

"You two are going to find out what Petrov, Daniels, and Becker are up to," Tate said.

"Wait a minute," Hawk held up her hand.

Tate laughed. "You think Jane sent you to me as a parrot?" he asked her. "You know better than that," Tate said.

"I'll kill her," Hawk grumbled.

Tate chuckled. "I'd like to see you try," he challenged her. "I should think you two would fall right into sync with all of your common experience." Both Fallon and Hawk looked at Tate in disgust. "Nothing to Toles yet," Tate reaffirmed his position. "Let's deal with reality before we send her reeling on some ghost chase."

"You should, at least, tell Jonathan," Fallon said.

Tate shook his head. "Krause and Baros are in France. Edmond…"

"Are you telling me Callier knows?" Fallon demanded.

"I'm not sure anyone knows anything, Agent Fallon. You have your directive. Let's make sure we know what pieces of the puzzle we have before we try and fit them together," Tate suggested.

Fallon remained unconvinced. Hawk shrugged and looked at her new partner. "Guess we'll be taking our coffee to go," she said lightly.

Fallon chuckled. "Fine by me. You are buying," he told her.

"Why me?" she asked.

Fallon shrugged. "Guessing you make the bigger bucks," he said.

Tate watched the unlikely pair of partners head toward the counter and ran his hand over his face. He pulled a folded piece of paper from his jacket pocket and scanned it slowly with his eyes. "Oh, Jane. I hope you know what you are doing."

***

"Alex?" a small voice called from the hallway outside of Alex and Cassidy's bedroom.

Alex looked up and smiled. "Hey, Speed. What's up?"

Dylan sauntered into his parents' bedroom and hopped onto their bed while Alex sat in a chair tying her sneakers. "Are you going running?" he asked.

"I was going to. Did you need something?" Alex asked. Dylan looked down and shrugged. "Dylan?"

Slowly, Dylan looked up and met Alex's eyes. "Can I go?"

"Can you go where, Speed?" Alex wondered. Dylan shrugged again. "You want to go running with me?" she asked him. Dylan nodded. Alex watched her son carefully. He rarely asked to join her on a run. "It's cold, Speed."

"Never mind," he said.

Dylan hopped off the bed and started to make his way out of the room. Alex stopped him. "Hey," she said gently. "You can come with me if you want to," she told him. Dylan looked up hopefully. "I just wanted to remind you that it's cold. That's all. Put on a pair of long underwear and a sweatshirt," she told him. Dylan nodded and took off in a sprint down the hallway toward his bedroom, nearly tripping Cassidy on his way.

"Where's the fire?" Cassidy called after him.

"Sorry, Mom!" he yelled back.

Cassidy shook her head in amusement and walked into the bedroom. "Need some air?" she joked to her wife.

Alex smiled. "Mm...Going to have to pass on the quiet time, though," Alex said.

"Huh?"

"Dylan asked to go with me," Alex explained. Cassidy nodded. "You don't seem surprised," Alex noted.

Cassidy shrugged. "I'm not."

"Did something happen this morning when I was out with Mom?" Alex asked, wondering if Dylan had been scolded while she was out.

"No. Nothing out of the ordinary." Alex was puzzled. Cassidy reached for Alex's sweatshirt and shrugged again. "I think he just misses you," she said honestly.

"Misses me?" Alex asked. "I'm home now more than I used to be."

"Umm…and you have someone else vying for your attention," Cassidy said.

Alex sighed. "You think he's jealous of Kenzie?" she asked.

"Maybe a little," Cassidy said with a grin.

"Shit." Alex frowned. "Cass, I haven't ignored Speed, have I?"

Cassidy smiled broadly and kissed Alex on the cheek. "No, not at all."

"I don't get it," Alex confessed.

"Alex, he's always had you to himself. The minute you walked through the door, he was at your feet," Cassidy said.

"But…I still…."

"I know," Cassidy said. "He knows. He just needs a little time with you to himself," Cassidy said. "You know, he has always had me. You also know that Chris was not around much."

"Shit…Cass…I don't mean to dote on Kenzie so much. I mean, it's not like I don't want to spend time with Speed. It kind of seems like he has had other things to do," Alex said honestly.

Cassidy arched her brow and snickered. She enjoyed watching Alex and Dylan from a distance. Mackenzie had added a new dimension to their family. Both Dylan and Alex were enthralled with the baby. Dylan loved his baby sister. There was no denying that. Alex lit up like a Christmas tree every time she looked at her daughter. That was a fact. Cassidy understood that despite the affection they both had for the newest addition to the family, there was a bond between Alex and Dylan that went far beyond description or explanation. Alex was Dylan's hero. Dylan held Alex's heart. Alex could not have loved Dylan more if she had given birth to him herself. They had grown used to each other's undivided attention. And, both were just a tiny bit jealous of the wrinkle Mackenzie caused in that equation. It was endearing beyond measure to Cassidy.

"I think, maybe you two should take the car, take a run in the park and then go pick out some Lego project you can immerse yourselves in this afternoon," Cassidy suggested.

"What about you?"

"Kenzie and I will find something to do. Maybe I will talk to her in French all day," Cassidy winked.

"She's struggling with cow, Cass. French might be a stretch," Alex laughed.

Cassidy shrugged. "You go do your Superhero thing. I will worry about our daughter. I will even make tacos for dinner."

"I see. You are just setting us up so Speed and I will have to do the dishes."

"Another reason I am grateful I married a butler," Cassidy cracked. She kissed Alex gently. "Go get the Dark Knight, Alfred. I'll see you back at the manor later," Cassidy said as she headed out the door.

"Yep. She's got us pegged, Speed. We get tacos and dishes," Alex said. "Maybe I can convince her to let me give her a lesson in billiards tonight," Alex laughed.

***

"Mr. President."

"Ambassador," President Strickland greeted Paul Daniels. "You've been busy."

Daniels smiled. His perfect white teeth knitted tightly together, concealing little of the contempt he held for the man across from him. "Simply doing my job, Mr. President."

"Diplomacy?" the president asked sarcastically.

"Diplomacy has many faces," Daniels replied.

"I'm not sure most people would agree with that assessment—not if they knew what you were referring to," Strickland said.

"War has always been at the heart of diplomacy, Mr. President."

"And terrorism?" Strickland asked. "Does that hold one of the many faces you refer to?"

Daniels offered the president a sardonic smile. "The goal of diplomacy is to secure a strategic advantage. That remains the same in peace and in war," Daniels said. "An adept diplomat makes alliances and uses whatever tactics necessary to secure the end goal—strategic advantage. I do not see that as terrorism."

President Strickland's forehead wrinkled in consideration. He nodded and changed the course of the conversation. "What of Petrov?"

"He and Becker will deliver," Daniels said.

"Have you determined the target?" the president inquired.

"The targets were determined long ago," Daniels said.

President Strickland endeavored to remain stoic. "Targets?"

Daniels' lips curled again. His smug smile turned the president's stomach. "Mr. President, a simple assault or strike on an embassy in a foreign country will not suffice. Look at my good friend Ambassador Matthews' death. Mourning, grieving, disbelief and anger immediately erupt in passionate displays," he said. "Then? It dissipates into nothingness. We solved the problem of one man's interference. Nothing more. People do not live there. Secretaries and dignitaries in a foreign land, even children....That is removed from people's reality. It's nothing more than a five-minute scene from an action movie," Daniels said. He noted the president's discomfort. "What? You are the leader of the free world," Daniels laughed. "Did you think that was preserved through banquets and speeches? It's sustained by an economy, not only of money—of blood."

President Strickland nodded. "American casualties?" he asked.

"Difficult to project. Substantial."

"And, the Russians?"

"Measured."

Strickland forced a smile. "When can I expect delivery?" he asked.

Daniels chuckled. "Even I am not privy to that," he said. "Over time. That is best to shift perception. Best you receive the news as it unfolds."

Strickland bristled. "That is not acceptable. I need to be…."

"You need to show the world your shock and horror, Mr. President. Surprise is your ally in that endeavor. I'm sure the admiral agrees. "

"Where?" Strickland demanded.

"Everywhere, Mr. President. One at a time. That is how you change perception. How you wage a war. Not all at once. One incident at a time that creates anxiety."

"Where?" Strickland pressed.

Daniels smiled. "Where they will least expect it."

***

"Jonathan," Eleana placed her hand on Jonathan Krause's arm. "It is possible that he knows nothing," she said.

Krause turned to the woman beside him. His faint smile portrayed his skepticism clearly. He desperately wanted it to be true, even to be possible, that Edmond Callier would prove to be as in the dark as the rest of their group. That was not only unlikely, Krause understood it was unreasonable to entertain the notion at all. Callier's close relationship with Admiral William Brackett, with Anthony Merrow, and with his own parents was all the proof he needed. Krause shook his head. Brackett was a wild card, Merrow and Nicolaus Toles were dead. They all knew something. They had built this alliance they called The Collaborative. If Callier didn't know anything concrete, at the very least he had suspicions he had not shared.

"I wish that were true, Eleana," Krause sad sincerely. "You don't know how much."

Eleana nodded. "Then let's go. Promise me one thing?" she asked. Krause looked at her expectantly. "Let me talk to him before you press him."

Krause nodded. Eleana had no illusions walking into her father's villa. Edmond Callier would be forthcoming one way or another. Krause hoped her presence, if not her tactics, would prove effective.

***

Alex slowed her pace so that Dylan could meet her stride as they ran through the park. "You okay, Speed?" she asked.

Dylan nodded. Alex smiled at the quick puffs of cold breath that hovered above him in short succession. She was tempted to stop their run and let him catch his breath for a moment. Alex saw a familiar sparkle in Dylan's eyes when he looked up at her—determination. She kept her pace even and continued forward. She suppressed a chuckle at the boy beside her as his arms pumped more furiously than was necessary to propel him forward. A few more yards and she would slow them to a walk.

"Are we stopping?" Dylan asked through his panting.

Alex leaned over and placed her hands on her knees. "Yeah. It's hard to breathe in the cold sometimes," she said. Dylan mirrored Alex's actions as she spoke. "You feeling okay?" she asked him. Dylan nodded.

Alex suspected he would never have confessed to the cramp she was certain he was feeling in his leg. His stride had become a tad wobbly and the way he bit his lower lip had not gone unnoticed. She was quite impressed with her son, not because of his speed and not because of his endurance, because of his perseverance. Part of it, Alex understood, was Dylan's desire to impress her. More than that, it was Dylan's nature to want to do his best. He pushed himself. While he was athletic, Dylan was also less adventurous than Alex. Alex had been a daredevil as a child. Dylan was a bit more reserved. That didn't surprise Alex. Both of Dylan's parents were more reserved than she was. Cassidy and John Merrow were also two of the most determined and committed people Alex had ever known. They were also two of the most intelligent and caring people Alex had ever met. Dylan was his parents' son.

Alex saw a little of both Cassidy and John Merrow in Dylan every day. Most days, it warmed her heart. At times, it made her heart just a touch heavier. She missed John Merrow. There was a great deal she wished she could ask him now. And, Alex could not deny that a part of her missed being a part of Dylan's life—missed seeing him born, seeing him walk, or hearing him talk for the first time. Sometimes, she would watch Mackenzie do something and find herself wondering when Dylan had done it for the first time. Did he throw his peas? Did he twirl Cassidy's hair? Did he laugh like Mackenzie? Did he like his first bath or did he cry? Alex simply didn't know. She could ask Cassidy, and sometimes she did. More often than not, Alex kept to her silent pondering. It felt strange to ask. She hadn't been there. She was here now. Watching Dylan straighten up slowly, Alex realized that she had been missing him too. He had friends to play with, homework to complete, and his own interests. Slowly, he was beginning to need both Alex and Cassidy less. Alex had stepped back, thinking that was what her son needed. Maybe it was. She still needed time with him, even if he sometimes needed to go his own way.

"Mom suggested we spend the day together," Alex said as she resumed a slow pace forward.

"Really?"

"Yeah. It is cold, though," Alex observed.

"Yeah, and not enough snow," Dylan griped.

Alex laughed. Dylan loved to go sledding and skiing. It was certainly cold enough, but there was barely a sporadic dusting of snow on the ground. Alex was not a skier. Dylan loved it. Cassidy's parents had a cabin in Maine that he loved to visit. The last two years had not seen much time for winter sports. "Hasn't been the best winter for sledding," Alex agreed.

"Or skiing."

Alex nodded. "You'll be doing that soon," She reminded him of their upcoming trip to the cabin. "What about if we build something together instead?" she suggested. Dylan brightened. Alex put her hand on his shoulder. "What do you say we hit the store before we head home?"

Dylan nodded. "Can we stop for hot chocolate first?" he asked hopefully. Alex pretended to consider the request for a moment, amused by the pleading look in Dylan's eyes. "Please?"

Alex smiled. She could tell that Dylan was not quite ready for their outing to end. In truth, neither was she. "Hot chocolate it is, Speed."

***

"Edmond," Jonathan Krause greeted his old friend.

Edmond Callier embraced his daughter with a smile, released her and then promptly turned to pour two glasses of scotch. He turned back toward Krause and handed the younger man one of the two glasses. "A vote santé (to your health)," Callier raised his glass as a toast.

Krause set his glass on the table beside him without as much as a sip. He regarded the older man intently, his eyes clear and his focus sharp as a razors edge.

Callier took another long sip, set down his glass and pressed his lips together tightly. He released a heavy sigh and offered his daughter a reassuring smile before turning his attention back to Krause. "Qu'est-ce que vous voulez savoir? (What is it that you want to know?)" Callier asked.

"Whatever it is that you have failed to tell me. What is it about Claire's ghost?" Krause replied.

Callier nodded and closed his eyes momentarily as if to gather his thoughts. He shook his head.

"Papa," Eleana urged her father emotionally.

Edmond Callier looked at his daughter and smiled softly. He took a deep breath and turned to Krause. "Etes-vous sûr que vous voulez cette réponse? (Are you sure you want that answer)?" he asked pointedly. Krause's only response was a stoic gaze. " Très bien. Peut-être que vous devriez vous asseoir. (Very well. Perhaps you should sit)," Callier suggested.

"I'm fine," Krause responded.

Callier smiled knowingly at Krause's deliberate response in English. It was an unspoken rule in the world that Callier and Krause called home, a measure of respect to speak in the native tongue when a guest. Krause's statement was clear. Krause was here for information. Callier's response would dictate the younger man's role—ally or adversary. "Chasing ghosts is usually a futile endeavor, Jonathan," Callier said. He noted Krause's unwavering expression of stolidity and took another deep breath. "I do not know if the ghost exists, Jonathan. It's a legend that has existed many years, long before either of you were a part of any of this," he began.

Eleana looked to Krause. His demeanor remained impassive. She noted the slight twitch in his temple and understood that he would not be deterred in his mission. "Papa," she turned to her father. "S'il vous plaît. Papa. Nous devons savoir. Vous devez dire à, Jonathan. S'il vous plaît. (Please. Papa. We have to know. You have to tell Jonathan. Please)," Eleana urged her father.

Edmond Callier moved to his daughter. He took Eleana's face in his hands. He leaned in and whispered in her ear. "Il aura besoin de vous maintenant. (He will need you now)," he told her. He kissed her cheek and turned back to Krause. "Many years ago, there were five of us who made a pact. A pact not unlike the unspoken agreement you have now with Alexis and this small group. An agreement that we would—that before all else, we would protect our children. That was our vow to one another."

"Continue," Krause said.

"We lost one of our five sooner than any of us expected. The details do not matter now. Not long after his death, stories began to surface. Stories of an American ghost. A man haunted by some past who saved a young girl."

"And, this is the man Claire is chasing?" Krause asked.

Edmond shook his head. "In a manner of speaking, I suppose so."

"You don't think he exists," Krause asked skeptically.

"That depends on what you mean," Callier answered. He saw Krause's jaw tighten. "Legends come from somewhere, Jonathan. Someone creates them whether intentionally or not."

"Edmond…"

Callier shook his head and made his way to pour himself another drink of scotch.

"Edmond," Krause urged his old mentor.

Callier swished the scotch in his glass and took a long pull from the glass, savoring the sting on his lips and the burn in his throat. "I think that the ghost was just that for many years. Until about a year ago," Callier said.

Krause suppressed a rising tide of emotion. He nodded, understanding instinctively the suggestion that Callier was making. "He's dead, Edmond."

Callier smiled sadly. "Perhaps. Perhaps not,"

"What are you two talking about?" Eleana interrupted.

"You think he is Sphinx," Krause surmised.

"Indeed," Callier replied. "Not everyone remained dedicated to that pact. There is only one man I know who was more committed than he and I, Jonathan. And, that man is long dead."

Krause's pupils narrowed to pinholes. He shook his head in disbelief.

"Jonathan, ton père (Jonathan, your father)," Edmond began.

"My father is dead. Both of them," Krause answered harshly. Eleana rose and came to Krause's side. She placed her hand firmly against his lower back to steady him.

"Perhaps," Edmond said. "There is only one way to know that for certain. Nicolaus would have moved the heavens for his…"

"Enough," Krause stopped Edmond's exposition. "Where is he?"

"I don't know that, Jonathan. Follow the legend and perhaps you will discover the ghost," he suggested. He crossed the room to the young pair before him and shook his head. "So much you have yet to understand. So much you have yet to accept. Sometimes it is better to let the ghosts lie in the past, my children. You keep looking, you will always find something.

The question is, do you truly want to find it? Let it go," Callier pleaded quietly.

"I can't," Krause confessed.

Callier nodded his understanding. " C'est faux, ce qu'ils dissent—que la vérité vous rendra libres? Parfois, elle vous tiendras en otage. (It is not true, what they say—that the truth will set you free? Sometimes, it only holds you hostage)," the older man advised. "Faites attention à ce que vous cherchez. (Be careful what you seek)," he said. Callier kissed Eleana's cheek, turned and handed Krause an envelope. "Soyez certain que vous êtes prêt à affronter le passé avant que vous ressuscitez les morts. (Be certain you are ready to face the past before you raise the dead)," Callier advised. He looked at Jonathan Krause warily. With a nod of respect, the older man slipped quietly from the room.

"Jonathan?" Eleana called for his attention. Krause managed a contrite smile and opened the envelope Callier had passed him. "Jonathan," Eleana repeated.

"Get some rest," Krause suggested to her. "We have a lot of ground to cover tomorrow."

***

Alex sat facing Dylan as he searched through model parts that were spread across the floor. He had opted for a model airplane. Dylan had been markedly quiet for quite some time. She watched him curiously as he diligently worked to put it together with minimal assistance every now and again.

"Alex?" Dylan looked up from his project to meet Alex's eyes.

"Yeah?"

"Do you miss your dad?" he asked.

Alex bit her lower lip. Dylan looked back at the half constructed model on the floor. "Sure, I do," she admitted honestly.

"Mom misses her dad too," he said a bit sadly.

"She does," Alex agreed. She regarded Dylan closely as he snapped a small piece into place. She could tell his mind was working on something more than the puzzle of a model plane. She wasn't certain what he was trying to piece together. "Speed?"

Dylan kept his focus on his hands. "Did you ever think you were adopted?"

Alex sucked in a ragged breath. She and Cassidy expected that her formal adoption of Dylan would be granted in a few weeks. She wondered if he was worried, but decided to play along with his line of questioning for the moment. She chuckled a bit. "A few times," she confessed. "Why do you ask?" she wondered. Dylan shrugged. "Speed?"

"I will be adopted," he said.

"That's true, Dylan. Does that bother you?" Alex asked. Dylan shrugged. Alex's heart sank. "Dylan, I don't have to adopt you. We can stop…" Dylan looked up at Alex with tears in his eyes. Alex immediately pulled him into her lap. Generally, he had begun to shy away from this type of affection. Now, he accepted it gratefully. "What's wrong, Speed?"

"I want you to be my dad. You can't be. You can't be."

Alex closed her eyes and held Dylan close. "No, but I can still be your parent."

"But, not really," he cried in her arms.

"What? Of course, really," she assured him. "Dylan?"

"Why couldn't you be?" he cried.

"Dylan…"

"Kenzie is yours. I'm nobody's."

Alex fought back her tears. "That's not true, Speed. That is not true. I love you every bit as much as I love Mackenzie. Don't you know that?"

"It's not the same," he whispered.

Alex let out a long breath and placed Dylan in front of her. "Dylan, I want you to listen to me, okay?" Alex said. He nodded. "I wish every day that I had been there to see you be born. I wish I had seen you throw your peas. I even wish I had been there to change your diapers," she said with a grin. Dylan smirked slightly. "The thing is, Speed…I know this is hard to understand, if I had been around then, you wouldn't be you. You'd be some other Dylan. I love this Dylan. I don't want any other Dylan to be my son," she said honestly. "That doesn't mean I don't wish I could have been there, Speed. I do."

"Alex?" Dylan asked shyly.

"Yeah, Speed?"

"Can…."

"What is it?" she asked him.

Dylan shrugged. "You're Kenzie's momma," he said.

"Yeah. But, I'll bet she won't always want to call me that," Alex chuckled.

"Then what will you be? I mean if Mom is Kenzie's mom?" he asked.

Alex pondered the question for a moment. "I don't know," she told him.

"Kenzie won't call you Alex," he murmured.

Alex sighed, suddenly understanding what was driving Dylan's insecurities. "No," she said. Not if she wants to live to adulthood. "I don't know what she will call me…Maybe Ma, maybe she'll call me Mom too."

Dylan kept his eyes on the floor. "Can you…I mean…Can I…"

"Can you what, Dylan?" Alex asked.

"Can I call you that?" he asked timidly. "I mean, just when we are alone or whatever."

Alex quickly wiped a tear from her eye. "Anytime you want," Alex said honestly. Dylan looked up and Alex wiped a tear from his cheek. She could see the blush of embarrassment and insecurity creeping up his neck. "Speed…it's okay," she said. "You can always tell me anything, okay? Anything at all," she told him as another tear cascaded over her cheek. Dylan collapsed against her as he used to when she had first met him. Alex closed her eyes and savored the moment. It was a moment she was positive would not be often repeated in the future. She couldn't help but think about her father, about Cassidy's father, about Dylan's father. She could tell that Dylan was quickly falling asleep. It had been a busy day already, and an emotional one. She kissed the top of his head and rocked him gently. "I love you, Speed—more than you will ever understand.

Chapter Four

"Unclear. Movement in Ukraine. Movement in London and Paris as well. Los Angeles and New York have been mentioned. I suspect it will begin in earnest abroad before we see it directly."

"Are you certain?" McCollum asked through the phone line.

"Unfortunately, yes," Jane Merrow answered.

"This is worse than we had anticipated," he said. "They'll be moving soon."

"Yes," she agreed.

"And Jonathan?" he inquired.

Jane sighed heavily. "I imagine he is speaking to Alex," she said.

"Mmm."

"Jim," she called to him over the line. "I need Alex here."

"I agree," he replied. "What made Strickland call?"

"This is not a legacy any president wants," she said frankly. "It may not be his conscience, it certainly is his common sense. Where do you think they will strike first?" she asked.

"Hard to say. London? Maybe even Paris," he said without hesitation. "They are not afraid. Wherever it is, it will pave the way."

"The Cesium," Jane surmised. "And then?"

"I think you can guess," McCollum said. "They will be looking for assets to deploy. We both know where that will lead them."

"MyoGen."

"Yes, and Carecom. They will try to tie Alexis's hands."

"What are you thinking?" she asked.

"Anderson," he replied.

Jane let out a low groan. "You want to bait Claire? That is a wild card."

"Fifty-fifty," McCollum said.

"What about O'Brien?" she asked.

"Time for a heart to heart—face to face," he said.

"You honestly think he knows more?" Jane asked skeptically.

"Without question."

"All right," she agreed. "I can't keep Jonathan at bay long."

"Don't keep him at bay at all," McCollum replied.

"You want me to lead him there?" Jane clarified.

"The sooner, the better."

"Jim…You think they will hit Carecom this soon?"

McCollum made no response. "Not just Carecom. And, yes, it's time," he said. "In fact, it's overdue."

"Edmond?"

"Leave him as he is," McCollum responded. "He's played his role—better than the rest of us," McCollum said. "This is not his war."

"He won't see it that way," Jane said.

McCollum chuckled. "No, I don't imagine he will," he said. "I owe him this much. One of us should be able to face our children as an honest man," he said.

Jane nodded on the other line, silence hovering for a moment. "I'll expect you."

"No. I have other business first."

"Jim...."

"I'll see you soon enough," he said as he disconnected the call.

Jane Merrow looked at the phone in her hands and sighed. "I hope we are wrong."

***

Cassidy entered the bedroom after tending to Mackenzie to find Alex sitting on the edge of the bed with her face in her hands. Alex had just returned home after receiving a call late in the afternoon. "Alex?" Alex looked up slowly with a weary smile. "What is it?" Cassidy asked.

Alex held out her hand to Cassidy. Cassidy crossed the short distance and Alex wrapped her arms around her wife's waist, collapsing her head against Cassidy's stomach. Alex held on tightly and inhaled deeply, allowing Cassidy's hold to calm her as only Cassidy could.

"Alex?" Cassidy called again with growing concern. Alex finally looked up and smiled at her wife. Cassidy returned the loving expression. "Tell me," Cassidy urged gently.

Alex merely smiled. She reached up and touched Cassidy's cheek. "I love you," she said.

"I know," Cassidy replied. She took the opportunity to sit on Alex's lap. Cassidy searched Alex's eyes for some clue as to what was traveling through her mind. "Do you want to talk about it?" Cassidy asked.

Alex closed her eyes and nodded. "Jonathan called," she said.

"That's why you stepped out earlier," Cassidy surmised.

Alex had left abruptly, explaining that there was something that needed to be addressed at Carecom. She had apologized profusely to Dylan for having to abandon their taco night. Cassidy had assumed that it had something to do with the MyoGen merger that had been plaguing Alex's time and concerns for weeks. Alex had been gone for nearly six hours before she returned. Cassidy had chalked up the lengthy absence to Alex's need to address details. A call from Jonathan Krause likely meant something else needed to be discussed—something that required security.

"You went to Natick?" Cassidy guessed. The Carecom office in Natick possessed a secure room. Cassidy had never seen it, but Alex had explained that it was one of the main reasons she would never venture to close that office. "Are you leaving?" Cassidy asked. Alex shook her head. "Alex?"

"I can't leave right now," Alex said. Cassidy was puzzled. Alex looked at her and shook her head again.

"Alex?"

Alex sighed. She pulled Cassidy down again and kissed her reverently. Cassidy pulled back slightly to regard her wife. Alex tucked Cassidy's hair behind her ear and smiled genuinely. "Right now, I just want you."

"You have me, Alex."

Alex smiled and pulled Cassidy down to her. "I know," she said as she repositioned them on the large bed, Cassidy now beneath her.

Cassidy had grown to understand Alex. Inevitably, Alex confided her concerns, her fears, and her dreams to Cassidy. They had promised each other long ago that there would be no secrets between them. Neither would ever break that promise. There were times, and Cassidy understood this, that Alex needed to cross an emotional bridge first. She needed to feel Cassidy, to connect in a way that defied words. Cassidy looked up at Alex knowingly. This was a familiar dance—a dance that Cassidy prayed they would never grow tired of.

Alex's lips met Cassidy's softly. Cassidy's lips parted and invited Alex in. Alex held herself just above Cassidy, their bodies pressing together gently. Their kiss continued, searching and speaking all at once. Alex felt Cassidy's hands moved tenderly over her back, communicating both a growing need and a deep understanding of what coursed between them. She pulled back slightly and began to lay a trail of kisses over Cassidy's throat, lingering slightly whenever Cassidy's breath would hitch in response.

Cassidy closed her eyes and held onto Alex as Alex's hands deliberately addressed the buttons of her blouse. She could feel Alex's eyes upon her as Alex opened the blouse and her fingertips brushed faintly across the swell of Cassidy's breasts. Familiar and completely new all at once, making love with Alex was always that way. It never ceased to amaze Cassidy, the way Alex could convey so much with a tender caress. Cassidy opened her eyes as Alex's kisses fell like soft raindrops over her skin, sending shivers up her spine. She reached out and touched Alex's cheek. Cassidy's eyes met Alex's in silent understanding. No words. Some declarations and promises went beyond words, needing to be felt rather than heard. Cassidy let her head fall back and submitted to Alex's touch willingly and gratefully.

Alex was lost in the woman beneath her. She marveled at Cassidy in the simplest of moments. Watching Cassidy feed Mackenzie, talking with Dylan, when Cassidy was cooking dinner, or even brushing her teeth—moments that people often took for granted, Alex considered the most breathtaking in life. She looked at Cassidy and smiled earnestly. "Tu es ma vie (You are my life)," Alex whispered before continuing her loving exploration of Cassidy's body.

Cassidy sighed deeply and tugged at her bottom lip when Alex's hands took hold of her jeans and began lowering them. Alex's hands held Cassidy's hips as she lowered her lips to taste Cassidy's skin, lightly bathing Cassidy's stomach in a flurry of kisses. Alex lifted herself higher and teased a taut nipple, soliciting a short gasp followed by a pleading moan from Cassidy. Alex glanced up and lost her breath at the expression on Cassidy's face. While she craved Cassidy's touch, nothing set Alex ablaze the way making love to Cassidy could. It had been that way from the first time they had made love, and Alex had no doubt that it would remain that way until death one day parted them.

"Alex," Cassidy called to her wife breathlessly.

Alex lifted herself higher yet again and placed a delicate kiss on Cassidy's lips. "You are everything, Cass," she whispered as tears began to bathe her cheeks.

Cassidy took Alex's face in her hands and caressed Alex's cheeks with her thumbs. She wiped away a falling tear that had begun to trail down Alex's face and smiled. "Show me."

Alex's hand quivered slightly as it slowly fell over Cassidy's skin, tracing feather light patterns along its way. She delighted in the way that Cassidy moved with her, gliding sensually against her. Needing to feel closer, Alex sat up momentarily and pulled her shirt over her head. Cassidy looked up at Alex appreciatively. Alex kissed Cassidy's fingertips as they reached out for her and then placed Cassidy's hands over her head, holding them firmly in place as she placed a seductive kiss on Cassidy's lips. She faintly brushed her lips over Cassidy's again.

Alex leaned in and whispered in Cassidy's ear, her breath caressing Cassidy's skin as her words embedded themselves in Cassidy's soul. "Permet-moi de te faire l'amour. (Let me make love to you)." Cassidy sighed, turned her head slightly and Alex took the opportunity to nip lightly at her wife's neck. "Si belle. (So beautiful)," Alex said reverently.

Steadily, Alex's body glided against Cassidy's, descending gradually in constant admiration, as if she were seeing her wife for the first time. Cassidy's breath had grown shallow and her hands had again found the expanse of Alex's muscular back, mapping out Alex's flesh and gripping gently to her in a feeble attempt to steady a rising tide of pleasure and emotion. Alex's lips dropped deliberately over Cassidy's center and Cassidy whimpered in anticipation. Alex lost herself again in a familiar dance. She held onto Cassidy as Cassidy's hips rose to meet her in a desperate plea.

Tenderly, Alex began her exploration of the woman she loved. Cassidy was the most gentle, giving person Alex had ever met. More than anything in life, Alex desired to give to Cassidy as honestly and completely as Cassidy always gave of herself.

Cassidy had always been astounded by the tenderness in Alex's touch. It was always soft and loving, no matter how playful or demanding it became. Making love with Alex was a paradox, a contrast, and complement of strength and gentleness, connection and desire, love and lust. It was intoxicating to them both no matter how many times they came together.

"Alex," Cassidy cried when she felt Alex enter her.

Alex pulled Cassidy closer. She glanced up to meet Cassidy's gaze and held Cassidy's eyes without any hesitation in her touch. Alex felt her heart skip and her skin flush with excitement when Cassidy's head fell back in response to the wave of sensation Alex was evoking from her body. Alex closed her eyes as Cassidy's hands wove themselves through her hair and then deliberately searched out Alex to ground her.

Alex took Cassidy's left hand in her right. Cassidy grasped on tightly, needing Alex to somehow tether her to the ground as she rose higher and higher. Alex caressed Cassidy's hand with her thumb and teased her with a tentative kiss that steadily grew to circle Cassidy's need. Cassidy's hold tightened on Alex's hand as her other hand grasped the sheets desperately. Watching Cassidy, feeling Cassidy's body move, and hearing the sensual sounds that slipped from her lips was beginning to make Alex dizzy with desire. Her body had begun to move of its own accord in time with Cassidy's.

Cassidy felt as if she were floating. Alex had lifted her to a precipice that left her breathless. She felt no inclination to urge Alex on. She would float happily as long as Alex wanted to keep her suspended in this place. When she finally fell, she knew that she would land in Alex's waiting arms. This journey had only one destination. Knowing that had never diminished the intensity of the climb nor the fall. Cassidy felt Alex's touch begin to grow more insistent, her teasing giving way to a palpable yearning.

"Alex," Cassidy called to her wife just as an unexpected wave crested and pulled her under. "I love you," Cassidy called desperately. "Alex…"

Alex held on to Cassidy firmly and guided Cassidy through another series of forceful waves. Gradually, the waves moved from tossing Cassidy about violently to rolling over her in gentle crashes. Finally, Cassidy's eyes opened as the waves shifted again to a series of soothing ripples, the kind that raindrops often left in a stream. Alex held onto Cassidy until she felt Cassidy release a deep breath and her hands relax in time with the rest of her body. She kissed a pathway up Cassidy's body until their eyes met.

Cassidy caressed Alex's cheek. Alex's eyes were a doorway to her soul, at least, they were for Cassidy. She searched the stormy blue eyes above her and sighed. "I love you," Cassidy said.

"I know," Alex replied. "Sometimes, Cass, I don't know why you do. I'm just grateful that you do," she confessed.

Cassidy pulled Alex into her arms, Alex's head coming to rest on her breast. She pulled the elastic from Alex's hair and prompted the soft wave of dark curls to fall into her hands. Alex closed her eyes and caressed Cassidy as Cassidy held her. "Do you want to talk about it?" Cassidy asked.

Alex sighed and nodded against Cassidy. She let Cassidy's touch calm her as she began to replay Jonathan Krause's call earlier that evening. "I'm not sure where to start…or how," Alex admitted.

Cassidy kissed Alex's head and stroked her back lovingly. "Whenever and however you need to," Cassidy said compassionately.

Alex sucked in a nervous breath and released it uneasily. Instinctively, her hold on Cassidy intensified. "I think my father might be alive."

***

Earlier that evening

"Pip," Alex answered her phone. "How are things in the land of love?" she teased him. Alex's playful nature dimmed in response to the eerie silence her comments were met with. "Jonathan?" she called to her older brother.

Krause swallowed hard. He had excused himself from the large parlor of Edmond Callier's home, leaving father and daughter to speak freely in his absence. It had taken him nearly half an hour to muster the courage to call Alex. He had thought that he had prepared himself. It was odd, he thought. Jonathan Krause had witnessed death. He had, in more than a few instances, been death's hand. He was familiar with the cruelty that life could often dispense. In the realm of his chosen career, lies, betrayals, death, even committing murder were all considered acceptable behaviors when circumstances warranted their need. Krause had been a party to all of it. He had even assisted in creating believable scenarios of death—just more lies.

He closed his eyes as he mentally berated himself. How many families had he watched mourn a loved one? How many times had he watched that loved one mourn the loss of their family at a distance? A new identity given seemed always to be met with little life and even less happiness. Perhaps his past had come now to haunt him. Krause could accept facing those demons. He had entered this life of his own will, on his own terms. Alex was different. Everything was different now for Jonathan Krause. He'd always felt alone, the outsider in his family. He had loved his mother deeply. But, in the circle of family gatherings, under the gaze of a demanding father, Krause had learned to grow cold on command. He had tried to please the man who had raised him. He had attempted with every fiber of his being to belong. His efforts had been fruitless. No words, no sentiments, and no promises had ever served to change the alienation of a young boy amid the people he was told he should trust the most. John Merrow had been his rock. His friendship with the former president had carried him through the worst of times in his childhood. As they grew, roles changed and expectations shifted. While the devotion between them remained, Jonathan Krause and John Merrow's chosen paths paved the way for distance to creep between them. Krause had mourned the only man who he truly considered a brother. He had faced the pit of loneliness in his life and accepted it on its merits. It had been his doing after all. Then came Alex, a sister—his sister.

Krause fought off a wave of nausea as Alex called to him over the phone. Everything had changed. He could face these demons, perhaps even accept them. He deserved whatever he might be handed. Alex? Alex Toles reminded Krause repeatedly what and who he once had strived to become. She did not deserve this betrayal. How could he tell her? How does a person tell someone they love that they have been lied to in the cruelest of ways?

"Jonathan?" Alex called again with deepening concern.

"Alex," he replied with a deep breath. "I don't..."

Alex felt her heart rise and her stomach fall. "What happened? Eleana?" Alex began guessing.

"No," Krause assured her. "Eleana is fine. She is with her father."

"What is it?" Alex asked.

"Edmond believes in ghosts," Krause said.

"You mean he believes in this ghost Claire has been chasing after?"

"Yes."

"Do you?" Alex wondered.

Krause swallowed hard. "I've seen ghosts," he replied. "In fact, I've created them, so, yes."

Alex groaned. "What aren't you telling me?"

"Alex...What if...What if this ghost is someone we know. Someone that we..."

"Pip!"

"Fuck," Krause mumbled. "He thinks it's your....Edmond...He thinks our father might be alive."

Alex froze. Her heart stopped for several beats and then sped erratically. "You were there," she said. "You saw the...."

"I saw the casket," Krause said. "I've seen many caskets, Alex."

"This is insane. He's dead," Alex said flatly. She heard Krause sigh heavily. "Jonathan? Don't tell me you believe this? Either Edmond is playing you or he's lost his mind. My mother found him. I saw her face. I saw the..."

"I know," Krause said.

"You know?" Alex barked. "What the fuck? You can't seriously think..."

"Alex. Stop," Krause said. "Think about it. Just think about everything you have learned this last year. Think about what you have seen...It makes sense."

Alex began kneading her temple forcefully. "How?" her words fell so softly through the phone line that Krause was not certain she meant to speak them at all.

"There are a number of ways," he answered her honestly. "Look, it's all speculation..."

"You don't think it's speculation," she observed candidly.

"Your father..."

"Forgetting something?" Alex challenged Krause. "He's your father too," she reminded him more harshly than she had intended.

"By blood," Krause replied stoically. He heard Alex sigh. "Alex," Krause stopped to gather his thoughts.

"I'm sorry," Alex said.

"No. I'm sorry." Krause rubbed his eyes in frustration. He found himself wishing he could be with Alex—with his sister. This was not the kind of news that should be delivered over a phone line.

"You're going to look for him," Alex surmised.

"I have to," he told her.

"Why?"

"Whoever it is..."

Alex chuckled caustically. "Yeah. Jonathan....I can't leave. Not now, and not...My mother...if this..."

"I know," he said. "Alex, I..."

"What?"

"I'm sorry. I hope it's not..."

"Yeah," Alex said. She collapsed her head on her hand. "Are you going to be all right? If you find him, I mean...If it is him."

"I'll be fine," Krause promised.

Alex laughed. She could detect the tremor in her brother's voice. "You really should be better at lying after all those years as a spook," she teased him.

Krause chuckled uncomfortably. Few people would have detected his uncertainty—very few. The truth was, the majority of Krause's trepidation in seeking this "ghost" surrounded his family, namely Alex. The truth escaped him without any conscious thought. "If he is alive, I might kill him for hurting you so much."

"You're past that," she reminded him. "But, thanks."

"Yeah, well…and last I checked we were both spooks."

"Don't remind me," Alex said. "Jonathan," she began seriously. "Be careful."

"Worried about me?" he asked lightly.

Alex swallowed hard. She and Krause had a unique way of expressing their affection and emotion toward one another. Generally, it entailed playful jabs. Alex was not feeling particularly humorous nor playful. She pinched the bridge of her nose and spoke evenly. "No matter what he says," she began, "and, no matter what he does. If you find him….It changes nothing between us," she said flatly.

Krause smiled at the determination in Alex's voice. "Nothing will change that, Alex. Not now."

"Be careful," she warned him again.

"It might not even be him," he pointed out the obvious. "Besides, you and I are too old to be afraid of ghosts."

Alex shook her head. "Just…"

"I'll be careful."

"Jonathan…If you find…"

"Alex, I promise you I will find out if he is alive. If he is, I will find out why," Krause said. Alex could not answer. "Alex?"

"I need to go," she confessed. "Be safe," she said again as she disconnected the call before he could respond.

"Son of a bitch!" Krause screamed and hurled his phone across the courtyard.

A gentle grasp of fingertips encompassed his wrist. "Jonathan," Eleana called to him cautiously.

"I'll kill him," he muttered.

"No, you won't," she said assuredly, taking a step in front of him. She lifted her hand to his cheek. "You won't because you love her." Krause closed his eyes tightly and shook his head. "You know, you might try telling her that. She is your sister."

"She knows," he said quietly.

"Yes. I'm sure that's true. That doesn't mean that she couldn't use to hear it," Eleana told him,

Krause looked down at the brown eyes looking up at him. "Maybe so," he confessed.

Eleana placed her head against his chest and closed her eyes. She wondered when he would learn. She inhaled his scent as Krause wrapped his arms around her. The words were so difficult for him. Eleana wondered silently if perhaps something within her was flawed. It seemed everyone she loved struggled with the mere concept of loving at all. What was it, she wondered, that frightened the strongest people she knew about love? Why did they seem to see it as weakness? Eleana held onto the man holding her more tightly. She could sense his turmoil.

"I do love you," she said.

Krause rested his head on top of Eleana's. "I know," he said. "I just will never understand why."

Eleana nodded against him. "Maybe you should stop questioning why so much all of the time."

Krause snickered. Eleana was not one to mince words. He understood she was not only referring to their relationship, whatever relationship they were attempting to build. And, she was right. He knew it. He wasn't certain he would ever be able to understand why, why anyone would love him. His father hadn't. His mother left him suddenly and without the truth. His brothers were strangers. His best friend had often questioned his methods. Krause could not look on himself with pride. There was simply too much he wished that he could change, and that gave all of his uncertainty free reign in his mind. "I wish it were that easy," he admitted.

Eleana pulled away slightly and looked up at him. "It gets easier once you start," she told him. "You have to start somewhere."

Krause smiled at her. Eleana was beautiful, and not only because of her physical appearance. Somehow, even in the midst of so much misfortune and deceit, somehow Eleana remained gentle enough to see the possibility of everything. It made his heart ache to protect her from the inevitable truths that might taint her youthful ideals. "I suppose I do," he said before leaning in and placing a tender kiss on her lips.

"We'll find him," she said as he pulled away slowly.

"That's what I am afraid of."

***

Cassidy listened silently as Alex recounted her conversation with Krause. She felt the warmth of Alex's tears bathe her skin and stroked Alex's hair.

"I can't…Why would he do that?" Alex asked hoarsely.

Cassidy placed a kiss on Alex's head and allowed her lips to linger. "I don't know," she confessed.

"I could never do that," Alex said as her tears continued to fall. "What do I tell Mom?"

Cassidy was at a loss. "Nothing," she finally replied. "Not unless you have to."

"It will kill her," Alex observed fearfully. "I can't risk losing…"

"No one is losing anyone," Cassidy promised.

"Jonathan…"

"Pip will handle it," Cassidy said.

"I don't know, Cass. You didn't hear his voice. It is his father too."

"Mmmm."

"What?" Alex asked.

Cassidy shifted lower on the bed and took Alex's face in her hands. "I don't think it is facing your father that Pip fears," she said. Alex's confusion was evident. Cassidy wiped the tears from Alex's cheeks. "Pip loves you, Alex."

"He's…"

"He is your brother," Cassidy said with a knowing smile. "Just like Nick, but different. I understand. You love them both. But, each is different. You aren't betraying Nicky to love Pip."

Alex huffed. Sometimes, Cassidy's ability to read her unsettled Alex slightly. It was true, her younger brother had struggled with Krause's entrance into their family. For a while, Alex had assumed that Nick's stand-offish manner stemmed from his anger at their father. Nick had always been close to Helen. Over time, and with a bit of hinting from her mother and Cassidy, Alex began to understand that Nick felt some pangs of jealousy over her relationship with Krause. Now, that plagued her mind. How would she explain to her younger brother that their father was still alive? If he was, how could Alex break that news to her mother? She'd witnessed the devastation in her mother's eyes the day her father had died. Fear coursed through Alex now. Too many questions that she could not answer flooded her thoughts. It mattered little that the man Krause was pursuing gave them both life. Alex wondered what any man capable of faking his own death could be capable of. If Nicolaus Toles was alive, Alex was not at all sure she could look at the man as her father ever again.

No matter how much Krause had tried, regardless of hours and years of his training, Alex had learned something important in her time with her older brother. A compassionate person could learn to mask their emotions, but they would never be able to banish them. She had seen that in her older brother, in Edmond Callier, even in Claire Brackett. Alex could not begin to fathom how Krause would react if he actually was forced to confront Nicolaus Toles, a man he had known simply as The Broker for years.

"It's not just Nicky," Alex said. "I wish he could understand. I wish he would let Jonathan...Now...I just..."

"Alex, you are his hero— still—after all these years, Nick sees you as his protector. He doesn't want to lose you. You know?"

"He could never lose me," Alex said flatly. "It's not a competition," she said and then shook her head. "But, this...Jonathan...I don't want to lose..."

"I know that too," Cassidy said. "Stop trying to cross bridges you haven't even come to yet," she said with a compassionate smile.

Alex moved and reversed their positions, pulling Cassidy into her arms. "I could never do that."

"What?" Cassidy wondered.

"These things, Cass...My father, John...If he is...If my father is really out there, I don't know that I can..."

Cassidy stretched and placed her fingers over Alex's lips. "Stop. Don't," she instructed Alex. Cassidy replaced the fingers resting on Alex's lips with her own. She kissed Alex lovingly. "Quiet," Cassidy whispered as she lightly caressed Alex's forehead with her fingertips. "Always thinking," she smiled knowingly.

Alex closed her eyes and exhaled. Cassidy was often the only thing that could silence the constant spinning of her thoughts. Sometimes, it only required a glance from across the room. Cassidy would sense Alex's growing anxiety and smile from a distance at her. The whirlwind that was Alex's mind would slow its pace. Other times, when Alex's emotions began to dance with her reasoning, Cassidy would reach out and lay a gentle hand on Alex's arm, stifling all of Alex's thought in an instant. Alex relaxed under Cassidy's caress.

"I'm here," Cassidy whispered. "No matter what. I'll always be here," she promised.

Alex pulled Cassidy to her. She sighed and let her thoughts wander. It was impossible for Alex to fathom her father's actions. He was a complete puzzle to her. For years, he had left Alex feeling cold and inadequate. Over the last two years, she had discovered sides of Nicolaus Toles that perplexed her. Her mother had attempted to fill in some of the gaps. Alex remained apprehensive where her father was concerned. At times, Alex would find herself looking at Mackenzie or listening to Dylan and wonder how any parent could deliberately pull away from their child. There was nothing and no one in the world that Alex Toles loved more than her family, her wife and her children. Sometimes, she wished for a simpler life, one that brought her home at five in the evening each day. That had never been Alex's life, but at times, she found the thought appealing. Home grounded her. Home was a refuge from the ills that often plagued her days. When Alex found herself doubting that humanity could save itself after confronting the selfishness and greed in the world, she would wander into one of her children's rooms and watch as they slept peacefully. She would listen in the distance as Cassidy sang to Mackenzie or read to Dylan. It gave her a sense of hope and possibility. Alex smiled as her thoughts turned yet again.

Cassidy felt Alex chuckle against her cheek. "What are you thinking?" she asked. Alex did not answer. "Alex?"

"Nothing. I was just thinking about football."

Cassidy shook her head and kissed Alex's chest. "Uh-huh."

"What?" Alex asked innocently.

"Maybe we could finish training before we add to the team," Cassidy suggested.

Alex laughed. "First rule in training, Cass."

"What's that?"

"Recruits learn more from each other than from you," Alex said.

Cassidy laughed and smacked Alex's stomach playfully. "We'll negotiate, coach."

"Oh, it's gonna cost me, isn't it?" Alex replied. She could not see Cassidy's smirk in the now darkened room. "Cass?"

Cassidy smiled against Alex and bit back her laughter. If Alex could, Cassidy was certain that she would assemble an entire football team with their children. In the midst of upheaval, chaos, and loss, the family they had created always served to remind them both of what mattered most—this was it. No one could ever take that away from them. Cassidy was confident of that.

"Cass?" Alex called to her wife nervously.

"Go to sleep, coach. I need my rest with all this recruiting you've got going on."

Alex snuggled closer to her wife. "I love you," she whispered.

"I love you too," Cassidy answered. "Now, go to sleep. I'm serious about the rest."

Alex laughed. She banished all thoughts of the father she had always wished to impress and failed to understand. Cassidy was right. There were things Alex needed to say. There would be bridges she would inevitably have to cross. Home always awaited her. Home meant family. That family had grown. She closed her eyes and let herself begin to drift away. "Just be safe, Jonathan. Please," she offered a silent prayer. "Just be safe."

Chapter Five

"**I** was surprised to get your call," Claire Brackett said as she stretched her legs out in front of her and reclined on the small sofa in her home.

"Nice to see you too," Agent Anderson replied with a chuckle.

"I'm sure it is," she winked at him. "So? What can I do for the NSA?" she asked.

"As usual, your arrogance is charming," Anderson noted.

Claire shrugged. "Do we need wine for this?" she asked him. "We're not on the clock, are we?"

"We don't punch clocks," he reminded her playfully.

Claire stood and stretched her long form like a cat about to go on the prowl. She moaned appreciatively at the pull in her muscles and smiled amusingly at Anderson. Anderson intrigued her. There were only a handful of people that Claire Brackett respected. Unfortunately for her, most of them had become adversaries—formidable adversaries. Anderson was an unknown quantity. Technically, his designation was NSA. Technicalities mattered little in Claire Brackett's world. Every agent technically reported to someone, and more often than not their loyalty could be found elsewhere. She padded carelessly to the kitchen with Anderson trailing casually behind.

"You know, you might want to slow down with that," Anderson cautioned as Claire began opening a bottle of wine.

Claire turned the corkscrew smoothly, freeing the plug, pulled down a glass and filled it. She swished the red liquid gently and smile lasciviously at the man in her kitchen. Slowly, she brought the glass to her lips, taking a moment to allow the soft aroma of plum and vanilla to tickle her nose. She lifted the glass to her lips, glancing over its top at Anderson, who was leaning against the wall. Anderson grinned at Claire's blatant seductiveness.

"Does that work for you?" he asked her lightheartedly.

"Normally."

Anderson nodded. He pushed himself off of the wall and walked past Claire casually. Claire watched as Anderson sniffed the cork from the bottle appreciatively. He raised a brow and smirked at Claire as he moved to pour the contents of the bottle down her sink.

Claire pouted. "Waste not, want not," she sighed.

"I'm not sure you know what you want," Anderson said.

Claire chuckled. "I wanted wine."

Anderson's expression darkened. "Is that right? That's what drives you, Claire? Wine?"

"It's dependable," she explained. Anderson pursed his lips and nodded. He snatched the glass from Claire's hand and tossed its contents into the sink. "Hey!" Claire complained.

"If you are looking for dependable, perhaps you should consider a dog."

"When did you get a sense of humor?" Claire asked.

"I didn't."

"What is it that you want, Marcus? Why do I find it hard to believe Joshua Tate sent you here?"

"Maybe because he didn't. He doesn't trust me. He certainly doesn't trust you," Anderson said.

"That's fair. I don't trust you either. Then again, I don't trust anyone," Claire said flatly.

"I'm not sure that is true." Claire dismissed his assertion with a roll of her eyes. "What is it that you are looking for?"

"Me?" Claire asked. "What do I want?"

"Yes."

Claire sighed dramatically. "I told you—waste not, want not. You want something in this world, Marcus, you take it before someone takes it from you. Lesson one? Someone is always ready to take it from you," she told him as she turned to retrieve another bottle of wine.

"Yes, they are. And what if, someone wanted to take the only thing you wanted at all?" he asked her.

"I've never been into monogamy," Claire returned.

Anderson chuckled. "The bedroom is not the only place for conquest."

Claire turned with a smirk. "I can be flexible."

"I'm sure," Anderson said. "Storm is brewing," he said.

"Storms are always brewing," Claire dismissed him as she turned back to her project and opened the bottle of wine.

"Yes, but not all of them are headed straight for the one thing you care about."

Claire spun on her heels. "She made her choice."

"And now, you will have to make yours."

***

Steven Brady walked into a small room. James McCollum sat behind a metal desk, his wire-rimmed glasses sitting precariously on the tip of his nose as he studied a paper in front of him. Brady stared at the older man silently. Brady was positive that McCollum had sensed his presence long before he stepped through the doorway. McCollum did not avert his gaze from the paper in his hand.

"And? How is Mr. O'Brien?" McCollum asked evenly,

Brady remained still. He had spent more than two hours in the company of Christopher O'Brien. He had pushed the former congressman to the limits of human tolerance mentally and physically. As ordered, Brady had bent O'Brien as far as he could without breaking him completely. The experience had left a multitude of burning questions in Steven Brady's mind. O'Brien had reacted exactly as any seasoned agent would have been taught that a weaker person without any training would react. He had pleaded. He had begged. He had offered what Brady was certain was erroneous information without any relevance—information that implicated known figures. That was the problem. The entire exchange was textbook. Brady had felt at more than one juncture as if he were back in a training exercise. Nothing unexpected happened. After years in this line of work, the one thing that Steven Brady had come to expect was the unexpected. Nothing was ever textbook.

"Who exactly is Christopher O'Brien?" Brady asked, a hint of accusation coloring his voice.

McCollum folded the piece of paper in his hands and slid it into a small envelope. He removed his glasses, folded them deliberately and set them on the desk. McCollum looked across at the younger man and extended the envelope forward. Brady looked at the man across from him curiously. He took a step toward the unflinching, expressionless man and accepted the envelope. Brady opened it and retrieved the same piece of paper that McCollum had been perusing just seconds before.

McCollum smiled at the questioning eyes before him. "I trust you know how to proceed," McCollum said.

Brady was puzzled. "Why now?" he asked the older man.

"Why not now?"

"You're not going to tell me, are you?" Brady asked.

"Tell you why you are being called in now? I suspect you can draw the right conclusions about that."

"No, tell me who O'Brien is."

McCollum nodded. "Who do you think he is?" he asked Brady.

"He's not who he's led us to believe. There is something you are not telling me. He anticipated every move I made."

"That is interesting."

"Jim…"

"You have your orders, Agent Brady."

"You are leading them here, aren't you? Why?" Brady asked.

"So concerned about the whys. Worry about the now, Steven," McCollum advised.

"What about…."

"I will deal with my former son-in-law."

"What aren't you telling me?" Brady asked.

"Quite a lot, actually. Quite a lot."

✳✳✳

February 28th

"What are we doing exactly?" Fallon asked. Hawkins held him back with her hand and kept her eyes locked on movement across the street. "Hawkins, do you really think some ambassador is going to hold a clandestine meeting in an alley?" he whispered.

Charlie Hawkins had been working in covert operations for most of her adult life. She'd seen the most unlikely scenarios play out before her. But, that was not why she had led her new partner here. Hawkins had often reasoned that espionage was a great deal like a massive game of hide and seek. To be victorious, you had to discover the whereabouts of your opponents. As you uncovered their secrets, you drafted them to become your allies, until one by one each participant was revealed. She heard Fallon groan quietly and forced herself not to laugh at his impatience. She smiled triumphantly when a figure began to grow larger in her sight.

"He's here," she said.

"Daniels?"

"Not exactly," Hawk pulled on Fallon's arm until he came even with her.

"Who the hell is that?"

Hawk's grin grew wider. "Glad you could make it," she said.

"You could have let me sleep for a few hours," the man replied.

"What the hell?" Fallon muttered in disbelief.

"Nice to see you too Agent Fallon. Last time I saw you, you had a gun pointed at your head."

"It was you?" Fallon asked in disbelief.

"You're welcome," Steven Brady replied.

"What the hell is going on?" Fallon looked at the pair before him.

Hawk shrugged. She turned to Brady with a smile. "Buy you a drink in our old haunt?" she asked Brady.

"Sounds agreeable," he said.

Hawk and Brady began walking toward a seedy bar that lay at the far end of the alley.

Fallon looked at the two agents suspiciously. They appeared to be friends. That caused him concern. He called after the pair. "Do you mind telling me what the hell is going on?"

Brady and Hawk turned abruptly to find Fallon standing firmly in place. Brady shrugged and looked at Hawk. "Better make his a double," he surmised playfully. He noted the determination in Brian Fallon's eyes. "Trust me, Fallon, you might need more than a double for this." Without another word, Brady placed his arm around Hawk's shoulders and the two continued their stroll down the alleyway.

Fallon watched from a distance for a moment, considering his options. As far as anyone he knew was concerned, Agent Steven Brady was dead. Moreover, the agent's motivation and loyalty had been in serious question. Why, Fallon wondered, would Brady reappear now? If what he claimed was true, why did he save Fallon from Michael Taylor's gun only to run away? It made no sense. Fallon shook his head slightly and began following behind. He momentarily considered calling Alex before continuing. Something was clawing at the back of his mind, warning him to listen before he made that call. Fallon doubted that Alex would be thrilled at the news of his new partner, and he was positive given both Hawkins' and Taylor's demeanor that Alex had not been apprised of that decision. Brady added another wrinkle. Alex had considered the NSA agent a trusted friend. Fallon sighed heavily as his feet dragged toward the bar's back door. Betrayal was something a person never got used to. He stopped just shy of the door and contemplated the parties awaiting him. "What the hell is going on?" Fallon took a deep breath and opened the door. He scanned the small room, taking in the tacky red leather booths and chairs, the worn pool tables, graffiti behind the bar, and noted the stale stench that years of alcohol spills, and other fluids produced. He caught sight of his compatriots sitting at a small booth in the corner and forced the roiling of his stomach to abate. "Well, one thing's for sure, we aren't finding any ambassadors here," he mumbled.

Alex stopped outside Mackenzie's room to listen to Cassidy holding a conversation with their daughter.

"You will love the cabin, Kenzie. It's Mommy's favorite place away from home. You know why?" Cassidy asked Mackenzie rhetorically. Mackenzie blew some bubbles and giggled. "Mmm. Because, Kenz, it was Grandpa's favorite place to take her. That's how Mommy learned to ski. Shhh. That's our secret, though. Momma doesn't know how well Mommy can ski," Cassidy whispered.

Alex stepped into the room. "Holding out on me, hey?" Alex asked. Cassidy spun around with Mackenzie in her arms. "I thought we agreed—no secrets," Alex said as sternly as she could manage.

Cassidy rolled her eyes. "It's not exactly a secret."

"Afraid I will beat you in a downhill challenge?" Alex asked.

Cassidy pursed her lips and shook her head. "No more than I am that I could beat you in a hurdle race, coach."

"Ouch," Alex laughed. "You're that good, huh?"

Cassidy shrugged as Alex reached out for Mackenzie. "I can hold my own."

Cassidy did not talk a great deal about her ability. In fact, she had not skied once since Alex had met her. Rose had taken Dylan to the cabin she owned in Maine a few times, and she had offered it to Nicky. Alex's younger brother had jumped at the chance to take Cat and Dylan for a weekend. Alex had jumped at the chance for alone time with Cassidy. Dylan loved to ski. He talked about it constantly—skiing, soccer, and airplanes—Dylan's passions. He had been talking for weeks about the coming trip and how his mother would finally be able to ski with him this season. All of it piqued Alex's curiosity.

"Come on, Cass, your Mom brags all the time about it. I thought she was kidding about the Olympic thing."

"She was exaggerating," Cassidy said.

"Really?" Alex asked doubtfully.

"I never wanted to compete."

"But, you could have," Alex guessed.

"I guess so. Probably. My dad was an expert," Cassidy explained. "He started teaching me as soon as I could stand."

Alex noted the melancholy in Cassidy's voice. "Cass?"

"I didn't ski for three years after he died," Cassidy explained. "And then, I don't know, I just lost the desire. I liked to ski by myself—just me. It made me feel closer to him. It was our thing. I didn't want to share that with anyone, I guess."

"You sure you are okay with going to the cabin this weekend?"

"Yeah, I am. It's been too long. It'll be good for us all. Dylan has Monday and Tuesday off. He's been begging Mom. Besides, I think your mom is looking forward to it."

"All true, but what about you?" Alex asked.

"I just miss him when I am there sometimes," Cassidy said. "I know it's stupid after all these years. I just always feel like he should be there—like he's going to walk through that door any minute. Crazy, I know."

Alex shook her head and looked at Mackenzie, who was reaching for Alex's ponytail. "Not crazy at all, Cass."

"What about you? I thought you were headed to the office today?"

Alex grimaced slightly. "I have a meeting tomorrow morning."

"Problems?" Cassidy asked. Alex's lips turned into a crooked smile. Cassidy sighed.

"I don't really know," Alex confessed. "Seems the former first lady will be in Boston late this evening on her way back to Washington. Wants to say hello tomorrow before she leaves."

"You're headed to Natick?" Cassidy surmised.

"More specifically, Boston. I'll be here tonight, Cass. I'm not leaving until morning. You leave tomorrow after school so it…"

Cassidy stepped in front of Alex and kissed her on the cheek. "It's okay, Alex."

"No, it isn't," Alex said. "I promised Speed I would be here when you all left."

"He'll understand."

"Maybe."

"He will," Cassidy said. "Just spend some time with him tonight."

Alex nodded. "I suck."

Cassidy chuckled. "No, you work. Dylan needs to understand that, Alex. He's familiar with work commitments."

Alex felt the unintended sting of Cassidy's words. Cassidy had meant the statement as reassurance. To Alex, the statement smacked of Christopher O'Brien's parenting style. That reminded her of her father. Neither were models she held in high regard by parental standards. She pinched the bridge of her nose and sighed.

Cassidy mentally slapped herself. "Alex," she reached out to her wife. Mackenzie started babbling and squirmed to leave Alex's embrace for Cassidy's. Cassidy caught her and chuckled.

"See?" Alex said.

"See what?" Cassidy asked.

"She's not even a year old and look."

Cassidy laughed. "You need to stop comparing yourself to anyone else," Cassidy said flatly. "And, you need to stop beating yourself up over work." Cassidy saw Alex about to protest and raised an eyebrow. "I mean it."

Alex flopped into the rocking chair. She hated disappointing Dylan. Cassidy had reminded Alex often that change was part of life and so was learning to deal with disappointment. Parenting meant navigating the minefields of both. In Alex's mind, Dylan had suffered enough loss and disappointment for a lifetime. He hadn't even turned ten yet. She was acutely aware that Dylan saw her as his hero, and she never wanted to let him down. Lately, she felt as if she had been walking in the footsteps her father had left. There always seemed to be some last minute pressing commitment that she had to attend to. Alex looked up at Cassidy. Cassidy was focused on Mackenzie. Mackenzie was twirling Cassidy's hair between her fingers, giggling at her mother. Alex watched for a moment and smiled.

"What was it like?" Alex asked softly.

Cassidy turned her attention to Alex. "What?"

"Having a dad who wanted to spend time with you," Alex said. "I mean, what was that like?"

Cassidy regarded Alex thoughtfully. She placed Mackenzie on the floor with one of her toys and sat on Alex's lap. "It was wonderful," she said softly. Alex nodded sadly. Cassidy put her arms around Alex's neck. "But, Alex, he was away a lot too. I guess I just don't remember that part. Maybe that's because he died when I was still so young."

"Cass…"

"No, it's okay," Cassidy said. "I just remember the times he was with me, you know? It's like I forgot about the times I missed him. I miss him every day. I've thought a lot about it lately."

"Really?"

"Yeah."

"How come?" Alex wondered.

"I'm not really sure that I know," Cassidy admitted. "Maybe it's because we are talking about when to have another baby. Maybe," Cassidy paused and took a deep breath. "Maybe it's because sometimes I really miss teaching."

Alex narrowed her gaze and pulled away slightly from Cassidy. "Do you want to go back to teaching?"

"Someday. Yes, I think so."

Alex nodded. "If you want to…"

Cassidy smiled. She could tell where Alex's thoughts had turned. "Right now, I want to be home with our kids," she said. "That really is what I want. That doesn't mean that I don't miss teaching. Sometimes….Alex, sometimes I need a little time too—to explore other things."

Alex sighed heavily. "I'm sorry, Cass."

"Sorry? No," Cassidy chuckled. "You are not listening to me, Alex. You're just hearing my words and taking them to mean what you think they should. You aren't listening to what I am really saying."

"Go on."

"I'm telling you that you need to stop thinking that your work demands somehow marginalize your parenting. It doesn't. I promise. You spend time with all of us whenever you can—quality time. That's what Dylan and Kenzie will remember…and whoever else might come along," Cassidy winked.

"You know what I wish sometimes?" Alex asked.

"That I would make tacos more often?"

Alex laughed. "That too," she said. "I wish that I knew what it was like to miss my father that much. I just question what he would think all of the time or why he did the things he did. I don't have those memories."

"That's not true, love," Cassidy said. Alex looked at Cassidy in confusion. "Every time we go to Boston you think of him. Every time you build a model with Dylan, you recall him afterward. Think about those things more," Cassidy suggested as she placed a tender kiss on Alex's lips.

"Bahhh!" Mackenzie's melodious voice carried through the room. "Moooo," she laughed. Alex and Cassidy both looked down at their daughter. Mackenzie looked up to her parents' inquisitive gazes. "Mooooo!" she repeated the sound.

Alex moved Cassidy and sprang to her feet. "Kenzie! That's the cow. What does the cow say?" she asked excitedly.

"Bahhhh!" was Mackenzie's reply.

Cassidy broke out into laughter. "She is definitely yours," she laughed. "So many languages already—doesn't get that from me."

Alex pursed her lips. "Do you pass any farms on your way to the cabin?"

"What? Probably. Why?"

Alex picked Mackenzie up and looked at Cassidy seriously. "Maybe if she sees a real cow…"

Cassidy covered her face and shook her head. Alex was relentless. It was utterly adorable to Cassidy. She rolled her eyes playfully, stepped up to Alex and kissed her. "I'll see what I can do about the farm animals. You see what you can do about teaching her how to do dishes and clean her room before she reaches her teen years, Alfred."

"Ha-ha," Alex retorted. Cassidy winked and started to leave the room. "Hey, Cass?" Cassidy turned back. "Thanks."

Cassidy looked adoringly at Alex holding Mackenzie and nodded. "I've told you before," Cassidy began, "I married a butler for a reason." She left the room smiling. *If only she realized how lucky these kids really are.*

***

Fallon swirled the beer in his bottle while he listened to Hawkins. He still was not certain what to make of the agent. Who was she, really? Why had Jane Merrow sent her to Tate? Why did Tate think she should work with him?

"Where have you been hiding?" Hawk asked Brady.

"I wasn't hiding. You don't have to hide where I was. It's that hidden," Brady joked. Fallon looked at Brady with disdain. "Skeptical, Brian?"

"Understatement," Fallon replied.

Brady nodded. "All right, just remember that I suggested a double," Brady said as he raised his glass of scotch.

Hawk took a sip from her glass of water and smirked. "So? Daniels is here in town meeting with some interesting people."

"Not that interesting," Brady said. "Not that surprising either."

"No?" Fallon asked. "I suppose where you have been is more intriguing."

"It's definitely a bit more difficult to believe. Let's save all of that for later, shall we?" Brady suggested. "Daniels is no surprise. You're following the wrong leads, kids."

"How so?" Hawk asked.

Brady swirled his scotch again and sniffed it appreciatively. He took a small swallow and savored the burn. "Daniels is here on business."

"Yes," Hawk agreed. "But whose business? And, what is on the agenda?"

"I think you already know that. They want to choke out MyoGen. They'll do it any way that they can. If they can't stop the merger with Carecom in the board room, they'll seize it another way."

"What other way?" Fallon asked. Brady's rueful smile made Fallon's stomach turn violently.

"You think they'll use a heavy hand?" Hawk asked.

Brady's expression grew dim. "What do you know about MyoGen, Hawk?"

Hawk shrugged. "Officially or unofficially?" she asked. Brady remained silent and waited for her to answer her own rhetorical question. Hawk groaned. "Officially, the cutting edge of pharmaceutical development, not just experimental drugs, the process of manufacturing those drugs."

"And, unofficially?" Brady asked.

"Experimental programs for the CIA including sleep deprivation studies, altering sleep patterns, the utilization of drugs for interrogation purposes, genetic engineering for bioweapon applications."

"Long list," Brady interjected. He set his scotch on the table and sat back in the booth. "You've heard of The MK-Ultra Project."

"Mind control?" Fallon scoffed. "What does that have to do with MyoGen and Carecom?"

"Agent Fallon, what does everyone fear the most?" Brady questioned him.

Fallon looked at Brady curiously. "Death," he answered.

"Good answer. Think about this for a minute," he said. "For years, people have feared a nuclear accident or attack. Now, we find chemical and biological warfare at the center of political debate. The media latches onto it, just like they latch onto new designer drugs, new breakthroughs in medicine. Disease, Agent Brady, potential infection, a potential disaster is what the public is fed. MyoGen, Carecom, Rand—what do they do? They provide a solution, right? It might be for profit, but they provide the public with some assurances that there is hope when these infections strike. The public might claim to hate them. They might mistrust them, but they depend on them. We need them. They provide the perfect cover for the development of the ultimate weapon."

Hawk scratched her brow. "Are you saying that MyoGen is working on mind control?"

Brady laughed. "The entire complex is working on mind control, Hawk—yours, mine, everyone's. That's what we do, right? It's always about control, who has it and how they will use it. What better way to maintain control than to control thought itself?"

"That's insane. No one can do that," Fallon said.

"Really?" Brady challenged the agent. "You don't think people can be programmed, Agent Fallon?"

"No."

Brady chuckled. "Well, whether or not you believe it, Agent Fallon is really of no consequence. The fact is that most people in our field do believe it works. They believe that enough that they have invested trillions of dollars in research over the last century. Billions in altering perception any way that they can. You want to know why MyoGen is so key. Ask yourself where the power lies, Fallon? Control perception and you have gained control."

"I don't…"

"The details aren't the important part, Fallon," Brady said. "The perception is. Ivanov sees MyoGen as The Holy Grail. MyoGen is not a new entity. It only has a new name. Perception, Agent Fallon, is everything. MyoGen's mother was Drake Industries, sister to Rand. Once upon a time, they were DR Development, Drake, and Rand, Agent Fallon. The two split in 1973. Why? Perception. Just two months later, the CIA destroyed the files on MK-Ultra, most of them anyway."

"So, Ivanov wants to merge them again?" Hawk asked.

"Ivanov wants what MyoGen has. Even I don't know what that is," Brady said. "I only know that the work continued at MyoGen."

"Mk-Ultra?" Fallon asked.

"In essence. It was called Project Lynx—second sight. Carecom has eaten away at the complex slowly," Brady explained. "Rand has still had a healthy hand in MyoGen. Don't fool yourself. If Alex succeeds, she'll be cutting off more than a funnel to monetary assets."

"You're saying that Alex and Krause don't know about this program at MyoGen," Hawk surmised.

"That's exactly what I am saying."

"How is that possible? Nothing can stay that well-hidden," Fallon argued.

Brady chuckled. "You'd be surprised what people will believe," he said. "They see what they want to see, Agent Fallon. They believe what they are told. They just have to choose who to believe. Perception equals control. Control equals power. People do not like to lose their power," he said.

"What are you thinking?" Hawk asked. "They'll discredit Alex somehow? She's smarter than that, Steven. You know that as well as anyone."

"Intellectually? Yes. They will hit her full force, implicate her by leveraging people's darkest fears," Brady said.

"Fuck," Hawk mumbled. "They're going to attack here." Brady nodded.

"Attack with what?" Fallon asked.

"What people fear, Agent Fallon. Imagine an explosion that's fallout is more explosive than all the flames it evokes. Imagine, your research is the reason for thousands of deaths. Imagine you lose everything. The people you love, the business you've built, and the identity you have created for yourself. That is how they will strike."

"When?" Hawk asked.

"When we least expect it."

"We need to see Alex," Hawk determined.

Brady shook his head. "Someone else will deliver her the message, Hawk. That isn't our role."

"Then what is?" Fallon asked. "We have to stop…"

"We have to change the perception, Fallon."

"How do you suggest we do that?" Fallon asked.

"We visit Rand and make a contribution."

"I was afraid you'd say that," Hawk said. "When do we leave?"

"Have another drink," Brady suggested. "We have more to discuss before he arrives."

"Who?" Fallon asked

Brady smiled deviously. "Ah, Agent Fallon, that is a question even I cannot truly answer."

Chapter Six

March 1st

"What is this place?" Eleana asked Jonathan Krause. "You really think there is something here?" she asked skeptically.

Krause took in their surroundings methodically. The building seemed to be whispering something to him. He had found it curious how easily he had gained information from the locals. How, he wondered, had Claire Brackett not been able to acquire the same knowledge? Claire might have been cocky, but Krause would never have denied her abilities to leverage difficult situations. Claire Brackett was an adept agent, a master manipulator with more than one formidable weapon in her arsenal. He'd been rolling a number of possibilities over in his mind.

"There is something here," he said quietly. He looked at the paint peeling ceiling, allowing his eyes to scan over it slowly. Krause listened to every subtle sound. His eyes fell to the floor which was littered with old papers, bent metal framed desks, and remnants of paint that had peeled and fallen like snowflakes. Krause thought it the perfect setting for an apocalyptic film. He momentarily entertained the notion that he might be in one and he chuckled.

"Jonathan?" Eleana's voice stirred Krause from his thoughts.

Krause turned, his hand still hovering over his sidearm. "The question isn't if there is something here. I just wonder…"

"What?"

"If what we are looking for is looking for us."

"Do you think we are bait?" she asked.

"I don't know. I think we were led here by whoever Claire has been tracking."

"Do you think she's here?" Eleana wondered.

"No. Something tells me Claire gave up the ghost."

"Because of us?"

"I don't know," Krause admitted. "It just…I feel it….Something is not right."

Eleana followed Krause closely, nearly walking in his footsteps. She could see them. His boots left a print in the dust and paper as he walked through the large room. She followed his line of sight to a narrow hallway a few paces away. It was dark. Eleana imagined that at one time this structure had been impressive. The locals had indicated that it had once served as a school. Eleana caught a glimpse of a paper lying in the debris. It commanded her attention immediately. Little existed here in any discernable form. There were a few signs that indicated exits, and there was the furniture, but otherwise nothing that pointed to what had occurred here. Had it been abandoned as a result of force or left for some benign reason to fade into oblivion? She crouched down and retrieved the paper at her feet. She studied the faded writing:

Первое главное управление

16 июня 1992

Реферировано

Проект Монарх

"Jonathan?" Krause turned and accepted the paper from her hand. Eleana watched the crease in his forehead deepen. "This is a KGB document," she said. He looked up and met her gaze.

"First Chief Directorate? Project Monarch? Jonathan, Monarch has never been proven…"

Krause nodded and tossed the paper back on the floor. Project Monarch had been billed over many years as the hysterical idea of conspiracy theorists. Several notable people had claimed to have been part of the sub-project under the CIA's infamous MK-Ultra Project. Krause let his eyes roam over the floor for any other discernable documents. He had been in the business long enough to know that almost every theory that gained traction had some roots in fact. Facts might be distorted, even created, but if a claim gained traction, it had been allowed to for some reason. Either someone wanted to create a distraction from a viable program or someone determined that some fragment of the truth in public discourse would benefit their objective. Both programs had supposedly been abandoned in the 1970s. Krause groaned inwardly. His eyes narrowed in on a paper crumpled by the last desk inside the room. He moved to retrieve it.

Первое главное управление

Справка

Рысь

Официальный статус

умерший

назначение

Проект Lynx

12 июня 1986

14 мая 1992 года в

Место нахождения

неизвестный

"What is it?" Eleana asked as she moved to peer over Krause's shoulder. "What the hell is Project Lynx?"

"I don't know," he answered truthfully. "Never heard of it."

"But?" she asked. Krause did not answer. He let out an anxious sigh. "Jonathan? What?"

"I have heard of Lynx."

"You know who it is?" she asked.

"No, but from what I do know, I'm not surprised the Russians would find him interesting," he commented. "Come on," he instructed Eleana as he let the paper in his hand fall. Halfway down the corridor, he motioned for Eleana to stop and be silent. Krause held his breath and concentrated. It was faint, but there was definite sound from below the floor. He shook his head, motioned again for Eleana to remain silent and stay where she was. Krause slowed his breathing until it was nearly imperceptible, even to him. He closed his eyes and concentrated on the sound. He could not hear voices. He could not discern one sound from another. It was a rumble almost like a motor in the distance. He reached the end of the corridor and felt the wall— solid. He listened again.

Eleana watched Krause carefully from her vantage point. His eyes moved continually, even when his body remained still. She wasn't sure what he was hoping to find. She let her eyes wander from his endeavor and turned slightly. A flicker, that's all she saw. It was out of place. Slowly, Eleana pivoted and walked toward it. Krause's focus shifted to the woman in the distance. Her attention was fixed on the floor as she moved. He followed quickly behind her.

"Eleana," he called to her. Eleana squatted and allowed her hand to brush the floor. "It's just metal," Krause said.

Eleana looked up at him and shook her head. She looked back at the floor and swiped away a large swath of paper and dust. Krause's eyes flashed with surprise. She looked up again, her hand resting on a large grate in the cement floor. "No, it's not."

***

Alex strolled casually into the quaint restaurant that Jane had chosen. She was curious about her friend's reason for this meeting. Where Jane was concerned, there were always competing motives. They were friends, close friends. Although, Alex could not deny that Jane Merrow had become far closer to Cassidy on a personal level than she and Alex had ever been. The two remained close, but there was a comradery between Cassidy and Jane that sometimes surprised Alex, a sense of mutual understanding and respect that had grown into deep affection. When Jane was with Cassidy, it was always personal. Time with Alex was divided. There was almost always something more to a suggested get together than simply catching up. Alex let out a small sigh as she approached the hostess. A persistent nagging sensation in the back of her mind told her that Jane was worried about something.

Jane caught sight of Alex approaching the table and smiled. "Glad you could make it," she said as Alex took her seat.

"Me? Turn down you buying breakfast? No way."

"How are you, Alex?" Jane inquired.

"I'll be better once you feed me."

Jane laughed. "Not enough coffee yet?" she guessed.

"There's never enough coffee," Alex replied. "So?"

"So?" Jane parroted back the word. "How's Cassidy?"

Alex scratched her brow. "Whatever is on your mind must be really bad."

"What?" Jane asked.

"Oh, come on. You don't need me to tell you how Cass is. You two are like old hens yacking on the phone all the time."

"Old hens?" Jane asked. She laughed. "I see. She did mention you were doubling as a See 'n Say these days."

"Ah-ha! See? You know more than I do half of the time. So? What gives?"

"Maybe I just wanted to see my friend," Jane offered.

"Yeah, and I'm The Pope."

Jane shook her head and sighed. She looked up as the waiter approached. "Let's order," she suggested.

Alex nodded her agreement. She chose something quickly, eager to move the meeting along. After finishing pleasantries with their waiter, she turned her attention back to Jane. "Is this about MyoGen or my father?" she asked pointedly.

Jane offered her an awkward smile. "Neither directly."

"Okay, how about indirectly?"

Jane reached into her bag and retrieved an envelope, sliding it across the table to Alex. "Before you open that," she began. Alex took the envelope in her hand and looked at Jane anxiously. "You need to know why Rand is so interested in MyoGen."

"I already know. They have the same parent. MyoGen is at the forefront of new chemical engineering…."

Jane shook her head. "True, but that's not it completely."

"Explain."

"There are many things that can be explored with chemicals, Alex," Jane said cryptically.

"Yes, I am aware. Isn't this why we discussed the importance of MyoGen as a Carecom asset?"

Jane nodded. "It is. Alex, there are programs at MyoGen that even I am not fully versed in."

"What kind of programs?" Alex asked cautiously.

Jane shrugged. "If you want that answer, you will have to make a visit to Rand."

Alex leaned over the table and lowered her voice. "Are you suggesting that I speak to someone at Rand or that I seek something within Rand?" she asked. Jane remained still. "I see. And, what do you suggest I do? Call Fallon to back me up?"

"Perhaps. He might beat you there."

Alex immediately noted the way Jane's eyes diverted from hers slightly. "Jane? Where is Fallon?"

"Relax, Alex, he's in capable hands."

"I'm sure I don't want to know."

Jane smiled. "He's with Hawk."

Alex's jaw tightened and her temple twitched. "Excuse me?"

"She's been on Rand's tail for over a year, Alex. It made sense with Paul Daniels in D.C."

"Maybe I should try and have dinner with my good friend the ambassador," Alex suggested. "That doesn't explain Charlie," she said. "You send my former partner to Fallon? Why?"

"Alex, she's an excellent agent. She knows Rand inside and out and she cares about…"

"Don't say it," Alex warned.

"Well, she does," Jane said. "Don't tell me you don't trust Hawk?"

"Outside of our group, Jane, I'm not sure who to trust, and even that is a stretch for me some days," Alex admitted.

"Look, there is something there. Something tied to MyoGen and not just money. There's a reason they do not want to lose this one, Alex. You need to know that reason."

"Why do I think you know more than you are telling me?"

"Probably because I do," Jane responded. Alex's expression darkened. "You wouldn't believe me if I told you, Alex. I know you. Besides, anything you find could be useful later. You and I both know that Ivanov is planning something. We all know."

Alex began to answer when the waiter returned with their meals. She nodded her thanks and turned her attention to the envelope Jane had given her. Alex studied it for a moment and moved to open it.

Jane reached out and stilled Alex's hand. "Later."

"Getting into Rand…"

"Trust me. It's all in there. You'll have cover."

"Why me?" Alex asked. "Don't you think I am a bit close to this to…."

"Yes, and that is exactly why it is you. I told you, you need to see it. You might believe more from someone other than me."

"Jane, might I remind you that you haven't given me the slightest idea what I am looking for?" Alex said.

Jane gestured toward the envelope on the table. "Later, Alex," she said. "Now, tell me, what is this I hear about Cassidy and skiing?"

***

Eleana followed closely behind Krause as he made his way around the dilapidated building. "There has to be a way down there," he said. He had explored the space beneath the grate in the building. Krause had little doubt given its location and size, at one time it had been used as a vehicle for communication, perhaps some type of dummy waiter that allowed correspondence between the school and whatever existed below. If he was right, there had to be another way in. Krause was determined to find it.

"Jonathan, maybe it's abandoned just like the school."

"Only one way to find out."

"What are you looking for?" she asked. Krause's eyes narrowed to almost slits and then he smiled. Deliberately he headed for some tall brush a few yards away. "Jonathan."

Krause picked up his pace slightly. It only took a few steps for Eleana to see what seemed to be commanding Krause's interest. Underneath the overgrown bushes was some type of cement structure. "What is it? Drainage?" she asked.

Krause tore away some of the brush that was lying in front of the cement pipe. "Maybe, at least, that is what we are meant to think," he replied. Eleana was curious. "This is cut," he explained. "It's not rooted in anything."

"Which means?" Eleana asked.

"It leads to something," he replied. "Come on." Krause cleared the remainder of the brush to reveal the large opening. He stepped through, Eleana following just a pace behind. Immediately, both noticed the vines that hung just inside the large pipe. "Help me cover this a bit."

"You think someone is following us?" she wondered.

"Right now, I don't know what to think," Krause confessed. "Stay right behind me."

"Worried about me?" she asked lightly.

Krause turned and Eleana was surprised to see the apprehension in his eyes. "Stay right behind me, Eleana," he directed her again firmly.

"Jonathan, are you...."

"Let's go," he said as he began his movement forward. *I really hope this is just a ghost story.*

***

"Dylan," Cassidy gently scolded her son, "stop complaining."

"Mom...Can't you make Kenzie stop?" Dylan whined. He caught sight of his YaYa's house up the street and groaned. "I thought we were going to the cabin?"

Cassidy rubbed the back of her neck and took a deep breath. Mackenzie had been fussing on and off all day. At first, Cassidy had chalked the fits up to being overtired. But, the persistent wail in the car began to concern her. She suggested that Rose stop at Helen's house and drop her off. Now, as they pulled into Helen's driveway, Cassidy was certain she was going to lose her cool. Dylan was not normally one to complain. She was certain that he was disappointed that Alex was not joining them at all for the weekend. And, she had to admit that Mackenzie's mood was nerve-racking at best. She sighed. Sensing Cassidy's discomfort, Helen chimed in.

"We are going, Dylan. We're just dropping Mom and Mackenzie at my house first," Helen explained.

"Now, you're not going either?" Dylan asked. "Who is going to ski with me?"

Cassidy felt the pressure in her head building. "Grandma will take you, Dylan."

"But, you said I could…."

"Dylan," Cassidy warned him. "That's enough." She turned in her seat to face him. "Something is bothering your sister," she said. Cassidy had noticed that Mackenzie kept rubbing at her ear in the car. "Now, you know how it is when you don't feel well," she said. Dylan groaned. "Dylan…"

Rose pulled the car to a stop and turned to her grandson. "You know, we can always stay here if you would rather," she said. "Or, YaYa and I can just take us all home instead."

Dylan shook his head. Cassidy made her way out of the car and opened the back door to get access to Mackenzie. Helen smiled at her as Cassidy unclipped the car seat and took hold of her daughter. "Come on, Dylan," Helen said. "Let's help your mom get settled and then your old grandmas will take you skiing."

"You ski, YaYa?" he asked.

"I've made a run or two in my day," she told him.

"No way!" Dylan exclaimed with excitement. "I'll bet Alex is an awesome skier."

Helen tried not to laugh. "Actually," she said, "Alex never did much skiing." She could tell that Cassidy's interest had been piqued immediately. "Not so fond of the lifts," Helen whispered. Cassidy smiled. "Don't ever tell her that I told you that," Helen pleaded.

"And, how did she think she was going to challenge me?" Cassidy asked.

"You know her," Helen said.

"Yes, I do," Cassidy said. She looked down at Dylan as Rose retrieved her bag and Mackenzie's from the back of the SUV.

"Are you sure that you don't want me to stay with you?" Helen asked.

Cassidy shook her head. "No," she said as she jostled Mackenzie. "I'm going to take her to the walk-in clinic. The way she is digging in that ear, I have a feeling we have a date with some penicillin. Don't worry about us. I will call you when I get back."

Helen nodded and accepted her fussing granddaughter from Cassidy so that Cassidy could address Dylan. "I'll get her into my car for you," Helen offered.

"Thanks," Cassidy said with a gentle rub to her mother-in-law's arm. She watched Helen walk away and turned her attention back to Dylan. Not for the first time in recent weeks, she noticed how tall he had gotten. He was standing even with her chin. Cassidy took a deep breath and smiled at her son. Before she could address him, Dylan spoke.

"I'm sorry, Mom," Dylan said.

"I know. Listen, I'm sorry that I have to miss this trip," Cassidy said. Dylan nodded. "I really am, Dylan."

"I know. Is Kenzie okay?" he asked.

Cassidy smiled. She could see both guilt and concern in Dylan's eyes. "She'll be fine," she said.

"I wish you were coming."

"You wish Alex were going," Cassidy joked. She was surprised when Dylan looked up at her sadly. "Dylan?"

"I really wanted to ski with you," he said honestly. Cassidy sighed. "We didn't get to go last year."

"I know, but that's because we were all waiting for Mackenzie."

"Yeah, but we didn't go this year either, not yet."

"Dylan, I promise that we will have plenty of times to ski again, okay?" Cassidy promised. He nodded.

Cassidy watched her son closely. Growing a family always had its challenges. Cassidy understood that Dylan loved his little sister, but he had been an only child for eight years. Sharing Cassidy, sharing Alex, it was not always easy for Dylan. It had helped that Dylan was beginning to become more independent, wanting to spend more time with friends, and engaged in sports. It also had helped that he had his cousin Cat. Cassidy and Barb remained extremely close friends. They often discussed Cat and Dylan's challenges with their big brother roles. Some days the boys embraced that role with excitement. Other times, the boys became jealous and frustrated by the attention their younger siblings demanded. It was normal. Cassidy wished that Dylan and Cat had more time to spend together. However, the introduction of Jonathan Krause into the Toles' family had caused a slight strain between Nick and Alex. That strain had been felt by everyone, including the two boys.

"You know, maybe we should talk about the three of us taking a weekend away together," Cassidy suggested.

"You, me, and Kenzie?" he asked.

"No. I mean you, me, and Alex," Cassidy explained.

Dylan's eyes widened. "Really?" he asked. Cassidy nodded. "But, what about Kenzie?" he asked. Dylan shook his head. "We can't leave Kenzie out, Mom."

Cassidy smiled proudly. "Well, you are going without Kenzie this weekend."

"Yeah, but that's with Grandma and YaYa."

"Yes, and Kenzie gets stuck with me. So, don't you think Kenzie should get a chance to spend a weekend with YaYa and Grandma too?" Cassidy suggested.

"I guess," Dylan said." I didn't think about it like that."

"You be careful," Cassidy told Dylan. "Listen to Grandma."

"I will."

"I mean it," Cassidy said. "Take it easy."

"Hey!" Rose chimed from behind Cassidy. "What are you saying? I think I can manage more than a little bunny slope, thank you. What do you think? You pass sixty and you become invalid?"

Cassidy rolled her eyes. "Just drink the wine at the bottom of the hill," she told her mother.

Rose whacked Cassidy gently. "Let's go, Dylan. Your mother has lost her mind."

"Me? What about you?" Cassidy asked.

"Me? Oh no, you get it all in the will, what's left of it anyway," Rose winked.

Cassidy accepted a hug from Dylan before he ran back to the car. "Just be careful," Cassidy said to her mother seriously.

"Cassie, I know my limits," Rose assured her daughter.

"Mom..."

"Since when do you worry this much?" she asked. "Cassie, I have been skiing since before you were a thought."

"I know that. That was over..."

Rose covered Cassidy's mouth. "Watch it," she warned Cassidy as the garage door rolled open.

Cassidy laughed. "Okay, I get it. Stop mothering my mother."

Helen came even with the pair and handed Cassidy her keys. "Taking lessons from my daughter?" she asked Cassidy.

Cassidy held up her hands in surrender and laughed. "No fair double-teaming," she told the two older women.

Cassidy adored both her mother and her mother-in-law. She often found herself musing about how lucky she was to have them both in her life. They had become nearly inseparable, and Cassidy truly thought of Helen as a second mother. She knew that Alex felt the same way about Rose. Rose and Helen together were a formidable pair. They were both intelligent, witty, compassionate, and full of life. And, they shared a pain that Cassidy hoped she would never know. Both women had lost the love of her life. Somehow, watching Helen suffer through the loss of Alex's father made Cassidy realize that loss could not be mitigated by time spent together. She had watched her mother attempt to disguise her grief after Cassidy's father had died. She had witnessed the same challenge in Helen. Neither wanted to burden their children, no matter their children's age. Cassidy understood that the kinship between the two women was rooted in two major things: a deep love of their daughters and a shared sense of grief that few could understand.

"You two are impossible," Cassidy laughed.

"You're sure that you don't," Helen began.

"You go," Cassidy told Helen. "Kenzie and I will be fine. Besides, I sort of promised Dylan that Kenzie would get her turn with you two soon."

"Uh-huh," Rose chimed. "Stock that wine rack," she said.

"Will you go already?" Cassidy said.

Rose leaned in and kissed Cassidy's cheek. "Call us when you know about Kenzie?"

"Promise," Cassidy told the pair. She waved to Dylan and received a wink from Helen. With a deep breath and a forceful exhale, Cassidy made her way to Helen's car. "Well, Kenz, it's you and me, and I'll just bet some penicillin."

"Bahhh," Mackenzie groaned.

"I agree," Cassidy said as she turned the key in the ignition.

***

"What is this place?" Eleana whispered from behind Krause.

Krause had been in his fair share of dark places. This place, whatever it was, gave even the seasoned agent chills. The air itself was cold. It seemed to crackle with foreboding energy. The drainage pipe served as exactly what Krause had expected. It provided access to a series of tunnels that he suspected led to something housed beneath the structure they had just been exploring. Navigating them was proving difficult. While they were largely clear of any debris, they remained dark and damp. A putrid smell, one that Krause had come to associate with death hung heavily in the air. It sickened him to his core. The absence of sound that accompanied the presence of death was ironically deafening. Krause sensed the shuddering of his companion. He stopped and turned to her.

"Eleana, you don't have to do this."

"Yes, I do. I'm okay," she told him. Krause's skepticism was both evident and well placed. "I promise," she said with a gentle grip on his forearm. "I just, I can't place it."

"What's that?" Krause asked.

"This place. It's a feeling, like…"

"Death," Krause said. "It's death." Eleana shuddered again, this time visibly. "Are you sure…."

"Let's go," Eleana said.

Krause nodded and began moving cautiously forward again. He noticed a break several yards ahead in the tunnel and stopped.

"This place is a maze," Eleana observed.

"Deliberately so," he agreed. Krause gestured for Eleana to be quiet. He detected something faint in the distance. It sounded like a soft rumbling. He tuned his senses toward the sound.

"Jonathan?"

Krause grabbed Eleana's arm forcefully. "Run!" he directed her, pulling her toward the tunnel on the left. The faint sound grew quickly from a soft rumble to a deafening roar. Eleana struggled to keep pace with Krause's long strides. "Keep moving!" he implored her. "Come on, Eleana!"

A stale stench grew as the source of the sound became apparent—water. More accurately, some type of sewage. Eleana had no desire to know what it was composed of. She was taken off guard when Krause lifted her from the ground and she felt slammed against something hard. Krause had discovered a small opening in the wall of the left-hand tunnel and made the decision to shelter in place. Eleana coughed into his chest, struggling to catch her breath. His body pressed firmly against hers and he whispered in her ear. "Breathe."

Eleana continued to choke. Feeling herself beginning to wretch violently, she attempted to pull away from his grasp. Krause tightened his hold. "Shallow breaths, Eleana. Don't try to breathe in deeply. Easy and shallow," he instructed her.

Krause felt Eleana collapse into him as support. He had been inclined at several junctures to insist that she stay behind. It wasn't that Eleana was incapable. She was as capable as any agent he knew. What she lacked was exposure. The only way to achieve the level of experience that Krause had was to immerse an agent in the worst of scenarios imaginable. The truth was, he did not want Eleana tainted by those. A person could not remain softhearted in this business, not in the world that Jonathan Krause had traveled in for many years. Death was something a person never got used to. It was something a person in Krause's line of work had to become hardened to. Eleana was not meant for hardness. He silently battled with himself for allowing her to accompany him at all.

The thundering sound was gradually being replaced by a swishing that sounded like a distant echo. Krause felt Eleana's breathing even out as the smell and sound abated. Instinctively, he kissed her on the forehead. "I wish you would not have come," he admitted.

"You can't protect me from everything."

"No, but you don't need to see this. Not this."

"We don't even know what this is yet," she reminded him.

Krause stepped back and nodded. He did not know what was lying in wait at the end of the tunnel, but he was certain it would not be a fairy tale ending. He envisioned something more along the lines of unearthing Dr. Frankenstein's lair. He gently tugged on her hand and led her back down the way they had come.

"Where are we going?"

He smiled at Eleana. "You don't want to know. We need to move fast." Realization dawned on Eleana. Krause was leading her directly down the path that had almost washed them away. She looked at him. "Keep up, and don't let go of my hand."

Chapter Seven

Fallon reluctantly followed his new partner and Steven Brady on their trip to the Rand Industries Headquarters complex. Brady served as the navigator. Fallon had stayed in the back of the large delivery van while Hawkins and Brady passed through the security gates. Now he watched buildings pass by out of the tinted back window. He was still unsure as to what Steven Brady hoped to accomplish with this trip. Fallon sat on a large crate and stroked his chin in contemplation. No matter how he tried, no matter how long he had been immersed in the NSA, he still felt a constant sense of disconnect. Police work was different. The FBI had been focused on investigation. At least, that had been his role—find the bad guys. Fallon wondered how anyone could tell who the "bad guys" were in the NSA. If he was not mistaken, Brady and Hawkins planned to plant some type of false information at Rand, something that would implicate Rand in illegal activities.

This was a world that Fallon puzzled over. How, he wondered, was this supposed to protect Alex or Alex's work? Wasn't Alex's goal, wasn't the mission of this small group to which he had been admitted to thwart this type of activity? Fallon shook his head ruefully. He had seen some strange things in his career. Fallon startled when the small window that separated him from his comrades slid open.

"You ready?" Hawk asked.

"Not sure how to answer that, since I'm not sure what I am supposed to be ready for," Fallon answered abruptly.

Hawkins smiled at her new partner. "Fallon, look…The hope is that if we can compromise Rand—if we can put them on the defensive, we might buy a little time."

"I get that," Fallon said. "But, buy time? Is that enough?"

Brady's voice carried through to the back of the van. "If it helps, what we are exposing is something that Rand is completely guilty of. It's just that we are placing it prominently."

"And that accomplishes what?" Fallon wondered.

"On its own, nothing," Brady admitted. "When it lands in the hands of the press—time, Agent Fallon. Right now, time is not a luxury we have. We're stalling. That is all," Brady said as the van finally came to a stop. Brady unclipped his seat belt and made his way to the back of the van. He opened the doors to find Fallon sitting, waiting for a better explanation. "They're not above using anything at their disposal, Brian," Brady told him.

"What would that accomplish? What?" Fallon challenged Brady.

"It would set us back. Give them more time to regroup. It might get Alex off the trail altogether depending on where they hit and who is implicated or…"

"Or what?" Fallon asked.

"Executed," Hawk answered.

Fallon swallowed hard. "Cassidy?"

"They already made that play, Agent Fallon," Brady said.

"What?" Fallon asked

Brady ignored Fallon's question. "Coming or not?" he asked.

Fallon took a deep breath and hopped out of the back of the truck. Brady nodded and gestured for Fallon and Hawkins to follow him. "I don't like this," Fallon thought silently as he watched Brady lead them away. "I have a very bad feeling."

***

Alex turned the paper in her hands over for what she imagined had to be the millionth time in less than a few hours. She glanced out of the airplane window and watched the stars as they flew by. A late night meeting at Rand Industries with Robert Gray had been arranged for her. Gray was Director of Research at Rand. The meeting would be billed as a precursor to a joint project with Carecom that Rand was proposing. "More games," Alex sighed.

She looked back at the paper in her hands and shook her head. Jane's cryptic nature was not unusual, but Alex would have expected a more detailed explanation before sending her off on what Alex surmised might be a wild goose chase. She had suggested that to her friend. Jane had laughed at Alex's doubtful inclination. It wasn't until Jane divulged the source of the information in her hand, and the driving force behind the meeting that Alex's interest was piqued.

"Why on earth would President Strickland suddenly reach out to you?" Alex asked. *"Why you? Why now? Doesn't that concern you?"*

"Of course, it concerns me, Alex. I have known Larry for years. There isn't much that he values more than his image. His legacy is the biggest part of that."

"Okay? And, how exactly does any of this impact his legacy?"

"Look, Alex, the attack on the embassy in Russia last year has already tainted public perception of his administration. What do you think would happen if someone utilized that Cesium Claire liberated? What do you think would happen if someone struck here at home? It will be seen as his weakness."

Alex sat back in her chair and pursed her lips. "Is there a credible threat that I should be aware of?"

"Specifically, no. Alex, there is always a credible threat. You know that. The question is never if, it is always who, where, and when," Jane reminded Alex.

"Okay. Who, when, and where?" Alex asked.

"You. I don't know and any day now."

"Me? You think someone wants to kill me? Why?" Alex asked.

"Killing you might be a bonus for some people. Eliminating your ability to function would suffice. You do the math."

"This is nothing new, Jane. Unless, there is something else that I should know about this merger."

Jane gestured to the envelope again. "You read that on your way. Your itinerary is attached. Matt will arrange your flight out of Hanscom this afternoon."

"You think it's wise that General Waters get this close?" Alex asked.

"I told you, Matt is making the arrangements."

Alex groaned softly as she recalled the conversation with Jane. The distinction between Matthew Waters, brother to Jane Merrow, and General Waters was not as clear cut as Jane was attempting to claim. General Waters had been engaged in investigating The Collaborative from a Department of Defense standpoint for several years. He had uncovered a host of disturbing trails that led to DOD personnel, The CIA, FBI, NSA, ATF, The Department of State, Homeland Security, and The Department of Treasury. Those connections led to an array of corporations, foundations, even universities implicated in The Collaborative's dealings. Determining which entities and individuals were aware of their involvement versus those who were used unwittingly remained a daunting task. She glanced at the paper in her hands again:

Central Intelligence Agency Directive

Subject: Project Lynx

12 June 1986

1.   Project Lynx is a continuum of the project formerly established as MK-Ultra, which originally sought methods by which to alter

human perception, cognitive recognition, and the fundamental aspects of stimulus-response systems within the human biological system. Investigations will be conducted for the purpose of manipulation that may lead to possible integration and/or submission.

"What the hell is this all about?" Alex wondered aloud.

"Captain Toles," a young Air Force Lieutenant called for Alex's attention.

"Yes, Lieutenant?"

"Major Allen wanted you to be aware that we are ten minutes out of Andrews."

Alex nodded her understanding. The last time she had stepped foot on Andrew's Air Force Base, she had been in a race against the clock to reach Cassidy. Alex looked out the window again and grabbed the bridge of her nose. She recalled that flight vividly. Cassidy had been in New York, held captive by a rogue agent named Carl Fisher. Alex thought it eerily ironic that she was headed back to Andrews now. The destination conjured memories of John Merrow and unsettling images of emergency vehicles surrounding Cassidy's home.

Alex closed her eyes momentarily in an attempt to banish the past from her thoughts. She wasn't certain what anything she had read meant. Somehow, she understood it was a thread to the past. Whatever was beginning to unravel was exactly what she had been digging for these last two years. As she felt the plane dip into its final descent, Alex couldn't help but wonder if she wanted those answers at all. The past had a way of shadowing the present. Alex massaged her temples and folded the paper in her hand. "Oh, John…What is this all about?" she wondered.

***

"How's Mackenzie?" Helen asked Rose.

"From what Cassie said—grumpy," Rose replied with a chuckle. "Dylan give you any grief?"

"No," Helen said, accepting a glass of white wine from her friend. She took a seat on the sofa, leaned back and sighed in contentment when the wine brushed against her lips.

"I'll tell you a secret," Rose began.

"Should I drink more of this first?" Helen inquired.

Rose laughed. "No, but there is plenty if you need more later. I wish Cassie could have been here…"

"But?"

"But, it's kind of nice getting away with Dylan."

Helen smiled at her friend. "It is, isn't it?"

"He adores you, you know?" Rose pointed out the obvious.

"Well, I adore him," Helen said. "I swear I will never forget the first time Alex brought those two to the house."

"I just remember Alex begging me to tag along. I'll bet it was strange, all of us converging on you," Rose guessed.

"Oh, I don't know. I do know that I'd never seen Alexis like that before. Never saw Nicolaus act the way he did after you all left, either."

"What do you mean?" Rose wondered.

"He was quiet. Don't get me wrong, Nicolaus was a man of few words often. I think it affected him deeply seeing Alexis with a family. I'm not sure either of us ever envisioned that," Helen admitted.

"I think I understand."

"We've never really talked much about it," Helen said.

"About what?" Rose asked.

"Alexis and Cassidy. I mean, it must have surprised you at first," Helen guessed.

Rose shrugged. "I suppose, if I were to be honest, it did—just for a minute. I'm not sure I can explain it, but from the moment I walked into that kitchen and saw the two of them together—I don't know, they just fit. I've never been one for sappy romance novels," Rose admitted. "It wasn't like that. It was just as if that one thing, that one part of both their lives that had been missing suddenly clicked into place. It strangely made sense."

Helen nodded. "I understand."

"Me too. When I think about it, that's how it was with Jim. I certainly didn't know that I was in love with him the first time I saw him, but when I think about it now, I felt something immediately."

Helen looked into her wine glass sadly. "I knew the moment I met Nicolaus. I'll never forget that night."

"Made that much of an impression, huh?" Rose prodded lightly.

"Well, it was an unforgettable day. We were at a wedding. Kind of a miracle it happened. It came very close to being postponed."

"Cold feet?"

Helen shook her head and sighed. "No, it was a cold November day, though," she recalled. "November 22, 1963."

Rose closed her eyes. "Good Lord. What a day to have your wedding anniversary."

"I know," Helen agreed. "It was the most bizarre day. Surreal, you know? Here, I had been with my best friend—the bride, passing the time listening to the radio while her sister fussed with our hair. Then all hell broke loose. I remember the crackle of the radio and the news that President Kennedy had been shot. That entire day seemed to pulse with emotion," Helen recalled. "At first, I thought that was it—when I saw Nicolaus, that is. All that raw emotion, and here was this dashing man ready to sweep me off my feet. Camelot had ended and yet here was the dashing prince I had dreamed about. I'd seen him before at a distance. Our parents were friendly. He was older, and so he never paid me much mind. I just went about life as it was. Until that night when he walked up and asked me to dance."

Rose smiled at her friend. The blush that colored Helen's cheeks made her look twenty years younger. Rose felt a strong pang of affection and compassion for her best friend. It was far from the first time that Rose realized how much they shared in common. "I'll bet he was charming."

Helen laughed. "And then some," she said with a wink. "And, he knew it too! Like father, like daughter," she joked.

Rose chuckled at Helen's observation. There was no denying the fact that Alex Toles possessed a unique charm. Rose had noted that same palpable energy radiating from Jonathan Krause. Even Alex's younger brother Nick possessed it, albeit in a more unassuming manner. She had also witnessed similar qualities in the woman before her. Helen was more reserved than either of her children, or her husband. Loving someone with such an immense personality often meant taking a softer approach, learning to linger a bit in the background. Few would have believed that about either woman now, Rose was sure of that. But, Rose had played that role for many years with Cassidy's father. She easily related to what Helen was saying.

"Jim was the same way," Rose fell into a memory.

Helen watched as Rose began to lose herself in her private thoughts. They had discussed their marriages and their children many times. Neither woman had a tendency to replay the most emotional moments, and neither had spent much time recounting the early years of her marriage. Conversation naturally wound itself to their children and grandchildren, and the pair would muse over what their husbands would have thought of all of it. Helen reached across and took Rose's hand. "I'll bet he was quite handsome."

"He was," Rose said. "Everyone says Cassie looks like me, but the eyes, those are all Jim's, so is her disposition."

"Oh, I don't know, I see an awful lot of you in her," Helen said.

"Her sense of humor," Rose agreed with a smile. "Somewhere along the way Cassie became more than just my daughter. She became my best friend," Rose said. "But, believe me, she is very much like her father. Calm. Cassie possesses an eerie calm about her even when she is furious. Jim was the same. I could see the storm brewing in his eyes, but he seldom raised his voice. He would grit his teeth and bite his bottom lip," she recalled. "That's what he always did when Cassie tested his patience," Rose laughed. "And, she did, although she doesn't remember that," she said.

Rose got up from her seat and made her way to a desk that sat at the far side of the room. She opened up the bottom and retrieved an old scrapbook. "It's funny, I'm not sure I've even shown this to Cassie," she said. Rose sat down beside Helen and opened the book.

Helen looked at the picture on the first page. She'd seen a wedding photo of Rose and Jim McCollum, and a handful of the family that Cassidy kept in frames, but that was the extent of her familiarity with the man. "My God, Rose, I thought Mackenzie looked like Cassidy."

Rose smiled. "She does. The eyes, I told you," she said. Rose turned another page and Helen smiled a bit more broadly, noting the mistiness of Rose's eyes. "He thought she hung the moon," Rose said. "No matter what else happened, the moment Cassie walked into the room, he lit up."

Helen sensed a change in Rose's mood and looked at her to continue. Rose turned another page and looked at the pictures while Helen kept watch on her. "I don't really know what happened," Rose said. "Jim was never a drinker, never smoked. He was a health nut before they invented health nuts," Rose joked. "He just was so tight lipped. When the drinking started…"

Helen sighed. She looked down at the page in the album that Rose had turned to and felt her heart plummet in her chest. She could hear Rose speaking, but suddenly none of the words were registering. Helen's hand lifted to cover her mouth and she closed her eyes.

"Helen?" Rose reached over and took hold of Helen's hand. "Are you all right?"

Helen opened her eyes and looked at Rose fearfully. She shook her head in disbelief and looked back at the album. "Rose," she began cautiously.

"What is it?" Rose's concern began to swell.

Helen's hand dropped and traced a picture in the book. "What did Jim do?" she asked.

Rose was puzzled. "For work?" she asked. Helen nodded. "He was a biological and chemical engineer, why?"

Helen nodded again. She took a breath and exhaled it steadily. "Do you know the men in this photo?" she asked.

Rose shook her head again. She was beginning to feel a sickening sense of foreboding. "Helen? What is it?"

Helen tried to find the right words. "Who did he work for?" she asked quietly.

Seeing the pallid color of Helen's cheeks startled Rose. She began to worry about her best friend's heart. "Helen? Do you…"

"Rose," Helen said with the shake of her head. She pointed to the picture. "That man next to Jim? That's Edmond."

"Edmond?"

"Callier, Rose. That's Edmond Callier."

"Eleana's father?" Rose asked. "That's strange. I mean…"

"Rose," Helen tried to steady her nerves. "Edmond is not just Eleana's father. He's Alexis's godfather."

Rose looked up from the album and met Helen's startled eyes. "I don't understand," Rose said nervously

"Neither do I," Helen said. "That symbol on his jacket," Helen pointed to the photo. The photo was of Cassidy's father, Edmond Callier and another man that Helen did not recognize. Both Jim McCollum and the unidentified man were wearing jackets with an insignia of some kind on the right breast. "Right there," Helen pointed.

"Yes? I don't really recall that," Rose said. "Strange, I don't even remember that jacket."

"I do," Helen said. Rose looked at Helen again curiously. "Nicolaus had one. I'd never seen it before. I found it in an old trunk in the attic a few months back."

"I don't...."

"Rose," Helen said with a deep breath. "How much do you know about Alexis's work?" Helen asked. Rose shook her head. Helen nodded. "I think it's time we had a talk," she said. She saw Rose's expression darken and painted on a comforting smile.

"What is going on?" Rose asked.

"I don't know," Helen said honestly. "I'm beginning to wonder that myself."

***

Cassidy yawned and stretched. It had been an incredibly long day. Finally, Mackenzie was asleep. Cassidy reached over for her phone to call Alex and noticed the missed call. She sighed.

Hi. It's just me.

Cassidy smiled at the sound of Alex's voice.

You're probably sitting sipping wine with the grandmas.

"No, I'm sipping ginger ale while our daughter sips Tylenol and pink goo."

Jane asked for you, not like you don't talk to her all the time, but I promised I would let you know.

"Mm-hm. What is going on with you, Alex?" Cassidy wondered. Alex's voice sounded strained, almost sad.

I had to make a quick trip. Anyway, it just kind of got me remembering some things.

"What things?" Cassidy asked aloud as she continued to listen to Alex's message.

I guess, I just miss you. I wish I were with you guys. If all goes well here, I'll be back in Natick tomorrow. I miss you, Cass. Kiss Kenzie for me, and tell Dylan I will make this up to him. I promise. I'll call you as soon as I can. Love you.

Cassidy disconnected the message and looked at her phone. For the first time since watching her mother and Helen pull away with Dylan in her car, she saw a bright spot in her changed plans. She hated that Mackenzie was so miserable, and she was disappointed about missing the ski trip with Dylan. Cassidy realized there might have been a bigger hand at work. She could detect the despondent tone of Alex's voice. Perhaps if Alex knew that Cassidy and Mackenzie would be waiting for her in her childhood home, she might feel a sense of relief and happiness. Cassidy placed the phone back to her ear.

"I just heard your message. Sorry, that I missed your call. Sounds like you are on the run again. I wish you were with us too. I have some bad news and some good news. Ready? The bad news is that our daughter has a nasty ear infection. The good news is that I am at the house in Natick right now with her. No skiing for Kenzie and me. So, we will be waiting here for you when you get in. If you are really nice and stop and pick up some white wine, I might even make you tacos. I'll see you tomorrow. I miss you too, Alex. Be safe. I love you."

Cassidy finished her message and placed the phone beside the bed. She pulled the covers over her and let out a contented, albeit exhausted sigh. "Well, maybe we will get a few hours alone if Kenzie starts feeling better," Cassidy mused. She closed her eyes and began conjuring images and possibilities for ways to welcome Alex home. "Might turn out to be just what the doctor ordered after all."

***

Krause pounded his fist against the metal door in frustration. He was certain that this was the final access point. The access point to what, he did not know. He did know that he needed to get the door open before he and Eleana were caught in a flood of toxic soup. He studied the door again and shook his head. There was no obvious place for a passcode. "Fuck," he groaned.

Eleana's eyes scanned the door methodically. She stopped and zeroed in on a small silver panel at the bottom of the door. "Interesting."

"What is it?" Krause asked.

Eleana squatted down and looked at the silver rectangle closely. "It's worn off," Eleana said. She stood and let her eyes track across the door again. She allowed them to roam past the blue steel and down the wall. Her feet carried her along.

"Eleana, stop."

Eleana offered Krause a triumphant smile. "Any ideas what the passcode might be?" she asked. Krause thought for a moment. Eleana shrugged and reached for the panel.

"Eleana, it could have a trigger," Krause warned as he grabbed her hand.

"Maybe. Do you have any ideas?" she challenged him. Krause remained silent. "Okay, then we will try mine. If I am wrong and we end up the victims of some booby trap, so be it. I'm not waiting around for that decaying sludge to drown us. So, either you have a crowbar in that jacket somewhere, or we are trying it my way."

Krause smiled in spite of the situation. He had no argument to mount. Eleana reached out and typed several letters in. She held her breath—nothing. "Damnit!" she yelled.

"It's all right, Eleana," Krause began just as a loud pop filled the air.

"We're dead," she commented, believing the roll of toxic waste was headed their way

Krause shook his head and pointed to the door. "Not today," he told her. Eleana looked past Krause and breathed an audible sigh of relief at the sight of the door ajar. "Just out of curiosity," he asked her as they began to make their way through the narrow passageway. "What did you type?"

Eleana shrugged. "Lynx. Just a shot in the dark," she admitted.

"That's what they call sharpshooting," he complimented her. "Come on."

***

"Bob," Alex said as she extended her hand.

"Alex, thanks for making the trip on such short notice," Robert Gray replied.

Alex slowed her stride to walk beside him as he led her into a small building toward the back of the Rand Industries complex. "I have to admit, I am curious," she told him.

"I'm sure. Lots of curious things happening these days, I would say," he offered cryptically.

"So, I've heard."

Gray slid his identification card into a door panel and invited Alex through. "This way," he said.

"I can't imagine your boss would be very pleased to learn who you are entertaining," Alex said.

"Depends on which boss you are referring to," Gray countered.

"Touché."

Gray led Alex down a winding corridor. She watched him cautiously, noting the confidence in his gait.

"Not concerned who might see us?" Alex asked.

"Let's just say that I have bigger concerns right now. Better that we are out in the open. There are a million reasons I could justify this meeting. I'm not sure that I could find a way to justify avoiding it," Gray told her. He pressed his thumb to a panel on the wall and waited for a door to slide open. "Follow me," he instructed Alex.

Alex followed him through the door into what appeared to be an observation room of some kind. She was familiar with the layout intimately, the window that undoubtedly appeared as a mirror on the other side, the long table that sat in front of it, and the intercom at its center. At one time, Alex would have found the reality curious—an observation room within the halls of a pharmaceutical company. The last year, while much of what she encountered had piqued her curiosity, had also banished any element of surprise. Industrial espionage was at the center of the entire spy game. Corporations were the soft arm of the intelligence complex. At times, Alex had learned, corporations also employed the complex's strong arm. She groaned inwardly. No matter how she attempted to see the bigger picture, it seemed to Alex that the reasoning behind everything in her world was money. Money equaled power. There was no denying it for Alex. She watched as Gray dimmed the lights in the room and the world beyond the two-way mirror revealed itself.

Alex's gaze narrowed. She was not certain what she was attempting to bring into focus. Drug trials were not uncommon. Her trained eyes scanned the room beyond. Three hospital beds sat approximately five feet from one another. IV racks stood beside each bed. Monitors adorned the walls behind each bed. She looked upward and noted the lights suspended from the ceiling. What was this, an operating theater? Why on earth would there be more than one bed present? Why, Alex wondered would Rand Industries be performing any type of surgery?

"Ask," Gray suggested.

"I'm not sure what the question should be," Alex replied. She turned her attention to the man standing beside her. "So? What is this about?"

"Alex, what do you know about psychotropic research?"

"Enough," Alex said. "It's a primary research endeavor at MyoGen. Antidepressants are a big industry, Bob. I don't have to tell you that."

"No, you don't."

"So? That's what this is? What about it? MyoGen has similar facilities for testing and observation. Why don't you clarify things for me?" Alex challenged the man. Her patience was already wearing thin.

"It's a disguise, Alex."

"Come again?"

"This," Gray waved his hand. "It's a disguise. The trials we are engaged in. When we test new chemical compounds on patients, they have only a cursory understanding of what we are administering."

Alex's temple began to twitch. In the past year, Alex had presided over the merger of Carecom with several large pharmaceutical companies. She had command of the way in which business was conducted. She had challenged several of the executives that had been brought into Carecom on the ethical nature of their practices. Patients were not lied to, they were also not given a clear and full picture of what they agreed to. Preying on the weak made Alex nauseous and angry. She had shut down several projects at the last company Carecom took control of after reviewing the standard practices, and speaking with patients herself.

One program sought to inhibit anxiety responses in children with varying Pervasive Development Disorders including autism, and children suffering from acute anxiety and depression disorders. Alex had taken a particular interest in the program, making a trip to the company's research facility in North Carolina. She was astounded at the lack of transparency given to the parents of subjects who had submitted for trials. For weeks, Alex had reviewed forms, documents, and reports that concerned the program. It had consumed so much of her time that Krause had taken it upon himself to intervene. Alex had thrown a folder of her findings at her brother in anger. She had called an emergency staff meeting and moved to end the program completely. Money. She had been met with strong resistance. It always came down to money.

Alex took a deep breath and released it slowly. "All right, Bob, you have my attention. What does this have to do with Rand and MyoGen?"

"At one time the two were..."

"I know the history," Alex interrupted his thought. "Tell me what I don't know. That's why we're here."

Gray nodded and leaned against the long table. "For the last fifteen years, Alex, MyoGen and Rand have been competing for the front spot in psychotropic drug research."

"And?"

"Where do you think that funding is coming from?" he asked her. "Do you know who the main investor in Rand Industries is? Where the money comes from for our research projects?"

Alex folded her arms across her chest. "Aside from the obvious government grants?" she interjected.

"Right. Aside from that."

"Enlighten me," Alex said.

"Advanced Strategic Applications," he told her.

"ASA is funding your research?"

Gray nodded. "Not just ours, Alex—MyoGen's too, at least, that was the case until recently."

Alex pressed on her temple with her thumb. She was beginning to see the pieces of an equation more clearly. She still wasn't certain what it all added up to. For years, her father had funneled money through Carecom to ASA. That had abruptly ended shortly before his death. Alex had still failed to determine his reasons. Now, she wondered how the pieces fit together. Jane had been adamant that bringing MyoGen under Carecom's control was essential to undermining The Collaborative and rooting out its core elements. Alex had suspected for a long time that neither Jane nor Edmond had been completely forthright with her. This visit solidified that belief. She found her thoughts drifted to Krause, wondering what he might find on his trip to Russia. More accurately, she wondered who he might find.

"Why? What interest does ASA have in pharmaceuticals? Other than the obvious financial gains, what does a weapons company want with Rand or MyoGen? You trying to tell me that this has something to do with chemical or biological warfare?" she asked.

Gray laughed. "That would be the simple explanation, wouldn't it?" he asked. Alex did not share his humor. "Of course, they are interested in those applications, Alex. That's an easy one. They don't need us for that. The work we provide is more nuanced."

Alex felt a chill pass over her skin. The veiled meaning was becoming apparent. She hoped that she was wrong. She regarded Gray silently for a moment. "You provide guinea pigs."

"So to speak."

"You're telling me that ASA is interested in the effects of neuro-inhibitors? Is that what you are saying?"

"ASA develops more technologies than missile delivery systems, Agent Toles. You know that as well as anyone."

Alex smirked. She did know that. ASA and Technologie Applique had both been at the forefront of subliminal testing all the way back to the nineteen-fifties. That research and testing had continued well into the twenty-first century. It was no secret, at least not in Alex's circle. She had encountered multiple programs at the NSA that sought to embed messages in what appeared to be benign communication. For her part, Alex found the entire notion absurd. She didn't doubt that there was interest, or perhaps even a marker of merit in the programs, but she doubted seriously that they had any real impact. To Alex, it was simply another means of generating capital and spending that capital. People would believe anything, even some of the most intelligent and educated people Alex knew fell into that category. The truth was, people did not like to challenge their already strongly held assumptions on any topic. Programs like these simply fed those assumptions. Alex suspected what Gray was alluding to crossed a different line.

"If you are suggesting that somehow MyoGen is tied to research that goes beyond the basic applications for psychotropic drugs...."

"We are all involved in that. You are not that blind," Gray interjected. "The issue, Alex is that you have a reputation for putting an end to those programs—programs that lay at the core of both MyoGen and Rand."

"I should think that would make your bosses happy, Bob," Alex observed.

"As I said, that depends on which bosses you are referring to."

Alex pursed her lips and pinched the bridge of her nose. She looked directly at Gray and made her assumption known. "And, should I be familiar with those entities, Agent Gray?"

Gray smiled. "I would think they are known to you," he answered her evenly. "You pose a threat to years of work," he told her.

Alex chuckled. "I certainly hope so."

"I understand, Alex. I'm not sure you grasp what I mean. They are not going to let go that easily on this one."

Alex's patience had reached its end. She was a master at solving puzzles, but she had no desire to stay on this merry-go-round that Gray had her spinning on. So far, he had told her nothing that she considered enlightening. She moved to end the conversation. Alex took a step forward. "Is there anything else I can do for you?" she asked Gray pointedly.

Sensing her shift, Gray sighed. "Alex, you do not understand me. We are on the same team here. Rand and MyoGen hold answers to…"

Alex held up her hand. "I will assume that I can thank my good friend, Mrs. Merrow for this circular talk of yours. I will take that up with her later," Alex said assuredly. "If there is nothing else…"

"They won't let you interfere, this time, Alex—not with this. They will employ whatever means necessary to secure what MyoGen has. You have ties to Wade, Speritus, and Solomon now."

Alex's temple began to twitch noticeably. Speritus and Solomon had been close partners with Carecom for decades. One of Speritus' major projects was innovating methods for the disposal of nuclear waste and the storage of nuclear material. The Cesium that Brackett had liberated over a year ago from a warehouse that Carecom utilized was a Speritus sample. Solomon was a new acquisition for Carecom. On its face, it was a pharmaceutical company that developed immunosuppressant drugs. The application for control of the human immune system was being explored both as a potential biological weapon as well as a means to counteract any number of biological weapons that might be employed. Alex and Krause had spent many hours reviewing the programs at Solomon. There was promising research regarding the ability to both suppress and stimulate the immune system. She also understood that if Solomon possessed that technology, it stood to reason that so did others, perhaps others with a much different agenda than Carecom's. Gray's statement was clear. The Collaborative would use Alex's acquisitions against her. That did not come as a surprise. If Jane had thought this visit necessary, Alex surmised the threat was growing.

"Is that a threat?" she asked Gray directly.

"Not from me. It is a reality. You acquire MyoGen and the gloves are off," he told her. "If that means some type of nuclear compromise or misstep in your chemical and biological divisions....I can't..."

Alex had just begun to address Gray when a loud beep sounded in the room. Gray turned on a monitor and shook his head. "Friend of yours?" he asked.

Alex looked at the screen. "Fuck. What the hell is she doing here?" Alex watched as Charlie Hawkins crossed the screen. She inched closer and brought the two men following her into view. "Brady? What the hell?"

"I don't know what they are doing here," Gray commented. "But, I do know they are headed straight for a section they will never get out of."

"How far?" she asked.

Gray was already on the move. "Follow me," he instructed her.

"Goddammit," Alex mumbled as she ran. "What the hell are you doing, Hawk?"

Chapter Eight

"Jesus, what is this place?" Eleana asked.

Krause shook his head and kept moving forward. To his trained eye, this appeared to have been some type of hospital or research facility at one time. Krause had to admit it had the air of an asylum. They had passed several rooms with equipment that he recognized immediately. Krause had seen electroconvulsive therapy at work. He'd been subjected to it as part of his training. This place, whatever it had been, had clearly utilized methods Krause was well accustomed with. He kept moving forward cautiously, looking in each room that they passed for any clue as to what the purpose of this place had been or continued to be.

"Jonathan, there is no one here," Eleana observed.

Krause ignored the comment. Something was pushing him forward. If he had taken even a moment to analyze it, he would have found his inclination to press on peculiar. By all indications, Eleana's assessment was correct. A persistent nagging in the pit of Krause's stomach told him there was more. He rounded a corner and stopped abruptly at the lights hanging at the far end of the corridor ahead. Until now, he had required the aid of his flashlight. Krause took a deep breath and turned to Eleana.

"Just stay close," he told her.

Eleana nodded her understanding and followed Krause's direction. He looked left and then right again before proceeding down the narrow corridor. He passed several doors and tried the handles—locked. He peered in the small windows that were fixed in the doors—empty. Each room was completely empty. Strange, he thought to himself, that these rooms would be locked. He continued on toward the beckoning lights. He stopped just shy of the next door and reached out for the handle. He pulled gently but again the door was secured. Krause looked down the hallway and then stepped in front of the door. This room differed. There was no window in the door. Instead, a narrow slot sat midway in the center of the steel. Krause knelt down and pried it open gently. He peered through and strained to see into the darkened room.

"What the...."

"What is it?" Eleana asked. Krause stood and reached into his jacket. "Jonathan?"

Krause retrieved a small pick and set about working on the lock in the door. Expertly, he manipulated the mechanism until he felt the signature pop. He turned to Eleana with his unspoken question. She nodded her assent and Krause opened the door. A chair sat at the far side of the small, darkened room. Krause noted the hands tied behind it. He approached slowly and methodically, controlling his heart rate and breathing as he had been taught over many years. He stepped up behind the chair. It was heavy, almost immovable. Krause took a deep breath and stepped around it to face its occupant. A bloody cough greeted him.

"Huh, look like you've seen a ghost, Jonathan," a raspy voice crackled.

"What the fuck? What the hell is this?"

"I see you've met my guest," another voice sounded from the doorway.

Krause looked across the room as Eleana turned to the direction of the voice. "I should ask why you are entertaining a dead man. Who the hell are you?" Krause asked.

"Another ghost," O'Brien coughed. He caught the surprised expression on Krause's face and laughed through another coughing fit.

"Not who you expected, I take it," McCollum guessed.

"What the hell is this?" Krause asked.

"Vy Khotite skazat' yemu, ili ya dolzhen? (Do you want to tell him or should I?)" McCollum directed his question to O'Brien as he made his way past Eleana. "Eleana," he greeted her with a smile. "Vy pohoza na svyu mamu (You favor your mother)," he told her.

Eleana looked to Krause in bewilderment. Krause returned his gaze to the older man who was approaching. Instinctively, he reached for his sidearm.

"You don't need that," McCollum assured Krause. "Does he, Christopher?" McCollum asked. O'Brien laughed hoarsely. "Vy khotite skazat' yemu? Kristofer? (You want to tell him? Christopher)?" McCollum asked again as he rounded the chair to stand beside Krause. McCollum leaned over and whispered in O'Brien's ear. "Come now, Christopher. We are all family, after all. I'm sure Jonathan will understand."

The closeness of Jim McCollum made O'Brien seethe. McCollum had interrogated him for hours. He had the marks to prove it. He had not broken to the older man's will. Now, all eyes were upon him. O'Brien was less a fool than he knew many supposed. His time was limited and he knew it. He felt McCollum's hot breath on his face and lifted his eyes directly to the older man.

"Vam povezlo shto ya s nej perespal. Eto spaslo yey zhizn' (You are lucky I bedded her. It saved her life)," O'Brien spat.

Krause's surprise was evident. He caught Eleana's shocked glance and looked at O'Brien. The words were clear. Russian? Why was O'Brien speaking Russian? The meaning was obvious to all in the room. Krause's shock morphed into unbridled anger. O'Brien's crass assessment of his marriage to Cassidy infuriated Krause. He cocked his fist, aiming it directly for O'Brien's bloody face. "You son of a bitch!"

McCollum caught Krause's hand midair. He spoke softly. "Easy, Jonathan. Easy."

"Who the fuck are you?" Krause blared.

O'Brien cackled. His laughing caused another round of coughing accompanied by small sprays of blood. "Legche bit ubitim, chem umeret.'

Kessidi skorbit za mnogimi muzhchinami v yeye zhizni. Mozet bit eto i khorosho, ona i Aleksis. (Easier to be killed than to die. Cassidy mourns many men in her life. Good thing maybe, her and Alexis)," O'Brien laughed.

Krause's eyes lifted back to McCollum. "Where is my father?" he asked the older man expectantly.

Sadness painted the older man's eyes. "Not everyone becomes a ghost, Jonathan. Some of us just die. I'm sorry."

Eleana studied the older man in the distance. She had been thrown by O'Brien's use of Russian. It was perfect, the accent, the phrasing, it had been flawless. She was widely considered one of the most fluent and polished Russian translators in the world. It was the skill that had ensured her placement within the Central Intelligence Agency. It was evident to Eleana that Russian was, at the very least, frequently used by the former congressman. O'Brien's command of the language rivaled hers. She suspected it was native to him. That realization caused her to look at the older man with fresh eyes. Who would have suspicions about O'Brien? Who would have an interest in O'Brien at all? The pieces fit. She looked at the older man. The eyes, she had seen those eyes before. Recognition came to her—Cassidy. "It's not possible," she said softly.

"Observant," McCollum said to her. "Edmond must be proud."

O'Brien snickered. "All this reminiscing," he said dryly. "What will you tell your daughter?" he asked McCollum in amusement.

"Jesus Christ," Krause said.

"Not really," O'Brien laughed.

"Shut up, you son-of-a-bitch!" Krause yelled. Before McCollum could intervene, Krause had backhanded O'Brien forcefully.

O'Brien spit out a tooth, a red pool landing at his feet and trickling down his cheek. "Feel better?" he spit out again. Krause cocked his fist for another blow.

"Enough!" McCollum bellowed. Krause froze and stared at him. "We don't have time for this," he said. He lowered himself to O'Brien again.

"Last chance, Congressman. Kto poslal vas k Nikolayu? (Who sent you to Nicolaus)?" McCollum asked.

"Come on now, Dad," O'Brien answered smugly. "I thought we were all family?" he chuckled. "I've been dead a long time," O'Brien observed. "What are you going to promise me? Resurrection? Fuck you, McCollum."

"Peace," McCollum said. "I'll offer you peace."

"I had a piece," O'Brien retorted. "A piece of yours, a piece of The Admiral's," he gloated. "Missed that piece behind me," he said. "Chto by vash papa skazal, Eleana? (What would your daddy say, Eleana)?"

Krause lunged at O'Brien and McCollum pushed him back. McCollum withdrew a pistol from his pants and placed it to O'Brien's head.

"Your time is up," McCollum whispered in O'Brien's ear.

" Eto nichego ne menyayet. Vy ne mozhete ' nas videt. My prjiachemsa priamo na vidu. (It changes nothing. You cannot see us. We are hidden in plain sight)," O'Brien declared. His words were silenced by a deafening pop that echoed through the room. Eleana jumped and then closed her eyes.

"Jesus Christ!" Krause yelled. He looked at the slumped figure in the chair, blood pouring from the side of Christopher O'Brien's head. "What the fuck did you do that for?" he asked.

"He wasn't going to tell us anything," McCollum asserted. "That's all we were going to get. It's enough. It's confirmation."

"Confirmation of what?" Krause demanded.

McCollum placed the pistol back in its home and straightened to his full height. "Not now," he said. "We need to get to your sister."

"We can't just leave him here," Eleana said awkwardly.

McCollum smiled at the innocence of the young woman. He looked at his former son-in-law lying cold in the chair. "Like he said, he's been dead a long time. I promised him peace. He has it. Let's go," he said in a commanding tone.

Krause remained still. "We're not going anywhere until you tell me what the hell is going on and just who the hell you really are," Krause demanded.

McCollum turned. "The first will take some time—time we do not have. As for your other question, if you want to keep your sister safe as much as I do my daughter, you will follow me—right now, and stop asking so many goddamned questions," McCollum said. "You are worse than your father," McCollum chuckled to himself. "Let's go."

***

"Are they there?"

"On route," the Colonel replied.

"Good," Admiral Brackett answered. He leaned back in his leather chair.

"Strickland went for aid," Paul Daniels told the pair.

Brackett smiled smugly. "I'm not surprised. He has no convictions and little courage. Let him fly. It is inconsequential now."

"How do you figure?" Daniels asked.

"I think we can guess who he called. Who will intervene?" the Admiral asked rhetorically. "Krause is on a wild goose chase."

"The same wild goose chase you had The Sparrow on for months," Daniels observed.

Admiral Brackett shrugged off the observation. "The point is that he is on the other side of the world. Alexis is around the corner. This is Dmitri's window. The play is now."

"I hope you are not underestimating them," Daniels said.

"Colonel Marks, explain to the good ambassador here why his concerns are unwarranted."

Colonel Marks turned his attention to Paul Daniels. Marks was reserved, a soldier who knew how to lead but prided himself on understanding when to follow orders. That was the nature of his life and his career. Admiral William Brackett had been calling the shots for decades. It was not Marks' place to agree or disagree. Some might have considered that following blindly. Marks considered it duty. Admiral William Brackett had earned the right to make demands. Marks did not ask questions unless he required the answers to complete a mission. He had learned over the last twenty years that there was a reason for everything Admiral Brackett said and did. If he had to describe The Admiral in one word, he would have chosen the word deliberate. Marks had not once witnessed William Brackett act impulsively. If Brackett had any concerns now, they were secondary to his objectives. And, he had confidence in his players.

"Dmitri can handle this situation, Ambassador," Marks said. "It's a simple mechanism. Once it is in place, we will have full control. Eyes, Ambassador, and ears, if need be—teeth."

Daniels regarded the men before him thoughtfully. There were two things that Paul Daniels considered sins—apathy and arrogance. Most people regarded Daniels as the epitome of arrogance. He was confident, even cocky, but he was not careless. Carelessness was the fine line in Daniels' experience that separated confidence and arrogance. Daniels had known Alex Toles for many years. He was well-acquainted with Jonathan Krause's work and reputation. In his estimation, the current situation teetered on the edge of carelessness.

"You know, there are other ways to address…."

Admiral Brackett let out a raucous laugh. "Ambassador, are you gaining a conscience? I know you are partial to Mrs. Toles," he continued in amusement. "Who knows? Perhaps she will play the role of grieving widow in need of comfort."

Daniels did not share his superior's amusement. "Your end game is Alex's death? What about Baros? What about Claire?" he asked.

Admiral Brackett nodded. "The end game is never about death, Paul. It is always about perception. You know that as well as anyone. I've done what I could. I made a promise long ago and I have done my best to fulfill it. I cannot protect them from themselves. If they choose to follow this path, they will collide with our direction. That is inevitable."

Daniels chose silence as his ally at the moment. Admiral William Brackett had set his course. He was the navigator on this ship, a ship he had deemed unsinkable. Daniels had accepted an appointment to his command. As he watched the Admiral sip his scotch and shift the conversation to small talk with the Colonel beside him, Daniels found himself secretly hoping that they were not headed straight for an iceberg.

***

Alex emerged from Gray's car in a fury. "Just what the hell are you doing?" she called across the small parking lot.

Fallon and Brady turned immediately to the sound of Alex's frustrated voice. Hawk blew out a heavy breath and stilled herself for battle. The last person she expected to see this evening was Alex. Alex was approaching the threesome rapidly with Gray in tow. Hawk pivoted to face her former partner.

"Alex," Hawk held up a hand in mock surrender.

"Don't you Alex me," Alex chastised her. "What the hell are you doing here, Hawk?"

"Well, Agent Fallon and I...."

Alex let out an exasperated groan and shifted her attention to Brady. "You look pretty good for someone who is dead," she said flatly.

Brady chuckled. "Long story."

"Always is," Alex observed.

"One we do not have time for. You are on the radar," Gray said. "We need to get you out of here fast."

"Nice to see you, Robert," Hawk greeted the man.

"Hawk," he replied.

Observing the familiarity between her former partner and the Director of Research for Rand, Alex rolled her eyes. "I am sure I do not want to know," Alex commented.

"One of us needs to stay put," Hawk told the group.

"Now, I'm sure that I am the one who doesn't want to know," Gray said. Hawk shrugged. Gray shook his head. "Your credentials are still good," he told Hawk.

"Then it's settled. You get this motley crew out of here," she said to Gray. "I'll deliver the package."

"Hawk," Brady cautioned.

"What package?" Alex asked pointedly.

"Later," Hawk told Alex. Alex groaned.

"Come on, Alex. Let Hawk finish what they came for," Gray suggested.

"Pretty amicable to that scenario," Alex said.

"Like I said, it depends on which boss I am answering to. Come on," he instructed her. He looked at the service van and turned to Brady. "You came in here with that?" he laughed.

"Yeah?" Brady responded indignantly.

"Brave," Gray laughed again. "You have papers, I assume?" he asked. Brady nodded. "Good. You drive. Alex, you and Fallon get in the back. I'll get us through security. My car won't rouse any suspicion out here. Hawk will have time."

Alex reluctantly climbed in the back with Fallon. Fallon smiled sheepishly and started to speak. "Don't," Alex held up her hand. A persistent buzzing in her pocket caused her to shift her position. She retrieved a small, black phone. "Oh shit, now what?" Alex looked at the message display. 4-1-1. ECHBOR TTU - 3-5-2. "Fabulous," she mumbled. Alex slid open the window and peered into the front seat. "Don't suppose you have a plane you'd like to lend us?" Alex inquired jokingly of Gray.

"Can't say that I do," he replied.

"That's what I thought."

"What is it?" Brady asked.

Alex pressed down her frustration, anger, and her inclination to question her old friend. "Compromise at home base. That means the Natick facility. Timetable unknown."

"Threat?" Brady asked.

"To be determined."

Brady nodded. "Faster if we drive."

"We are over four hundred miles from Natick," Fallon piped up.

"Alex?" Brady asked.

Alex massaged her temples forcefully. "How about a car?" she asked Gray.

"Funny you should ask. I think I might have just what you are looking for," he replied.

"Great," Alex said as she slid the gate closed again. Fallon looked at Alex expectantly. She shook her head. "Don't even tell me right now. We'll have six hours to catch up."

"Six? Alex, it's over an eight-hour drive to Natick," Fallon reminded her.

Alex just smiled. She needed silence now. She'd felt the storm brewing for months. They all had. A dark, cold night seemed appropriate to her. She needed to get her bearings. Something told her that the skies were about to open. "Here we go," she thought silently. "I just wonder where the hell we are being led."

***

March 2nd

"You're sure about this?" Claire asked Anderson.

"As sure as I can be. The source is reliable," he answered her.

"What makes you think Eleana is in any danger?" Claire challenged him.

Anderson glanced over at Claire, who was sitting in the passenger's seat of his car. "Claire…"

Claire shook her head. She turned to look out of her window. Anderson did not need to complete his statement. Eleana had made a choice. Although Claire had not seen her old friend in many months, she was well aware of the changes in Eleana's life. Eleana had aligned herself with Alex Toles and Jonathan Krause. It was not surprising. Claire let her thoughts wander to her former lover. Eleana had always possessed a moral compass that pointed directly north. Claire chuckled softly. It was the reason Claire loved Eleana. For many years, Claire regarded Eleana's conscience and compassion as naiveté. Claire closed her eyes in resignation of the truth. Eleana was not naïve, nor was she weak in any way. Eleana was simply put, an honest woman with a genuine heart. Where Claire's moral compass spun wildly, Eleana's had remained steady. The only thing that surprised Claire in the least was the knowledge that at some point, Eleana had fallen for Jonathan Krause.

All indications were that Krause's compass mirrored Claire's more closely than it ever could Eleana's. The senior agent had been involved in numerous activities that Claire was certain would send shivers up Eleana's spine. While, she may not have been naïve, Claire understood that Eleana would always remain somewhat idealistic. She wondered how Krause had captured Eleana's heart. She was certain from what she had observed at a distance, and what she had been told that he had. Perhaps, she mused, Eleana was not so concerned about the past. Krause seemed to have taken a different track in the last year. Claire suspected, however, that no matter his motivations, he still gravitated more toward Claire's inclinations than Eleana's. Perhaps it was as much those similarities, as the different paths they had taken that drew Eleana toward the man.

Claire derived a sense of pleasure, albeit temporary, from power and violence. She enjoyed the rush of physical exertion, the thrill of a chase, and the exhilaration that accompanied danger. Eleana, Claire had no doubt, could navigate any scenario that presented itself expertly. Eleana was intelligent, thoughtful, and discerning. Claire also knew that Eleana was a skilled fighter. She had proven that to Claire many times. Most people would never expect the beautiful Eleana Baros to possess expertise in several martial arts forms. Eleana was slight in appearance. Claire imagined that appearance itself would give Eleana an advantage against an unsuspecting foe. Her unassuming demeanor would likely evoke false confidence in an adversary. While Claire knew that Eleana detested guns, Eleana was also an expert marksman. Eleana had bested Claire many times in a sparring ring and at a shooting range. Claire smiled as she recalled one of their sparring matches. Eleana's cool demeanor gave her the upper hand in confrontations. She could easily sense the frustration in Claire, and used it to her advantage.

"Something amusing?" Anderson inquired, hearing a snicker slip from Claire's lips.

Claire shook her head. "Just remembering something," she told him.

Claire continued to gaze out of the window, watching the scenery as it passed by. She had been feeling unsettled for months, not that the sensation was foreign to her. Claire had felt deeply discontented for most of her life. She had never gained a real sense of self, only of self-defense. Eleana had always been the one person, the one place that Claire had been able to calm herself, to be still, and to be content in the stillness. In every person's life, one thing held purpose above all others. Claire had been raised by a man whose purpose was a sense of duty that she could scarcely comprehend. For as long as Claire could remember, only one thing held any meaning in her life at all—Eleana.

"You ready for this?" Anderson parked the car on a side street.

"You really think someone wants to harm her?"

Anderson observed fear and concern play over Claire's features. In her eyes, he noted something he was certain few took the time to see—sadness. He nodded. "She means something to…."

"To him," Claire said softly.

"Yes, and to you," Anderson commented.

Claire looked up in astonishment. "That gives her power," he explained. "Because she gives you both power," he continued. "And, that makes her a target as much as it makes you one."

"Me?"

Anderson watched Claire closely. She was a unique individual—charming, brilliant, and cunning, even witty. Claire was often so consumed in her own game that she failed to see what was unfolding around her. He smiled at her, realizing that his assessment of the cocky agent had been correct. Claire's bravado masked something that ran far deeper—fear.

Anderson had been chosen for his role carefully. He understood that. His skills differed from Claire's or even Alex's. Jane had brought him in two years earlier, preparing him slowly for his entrance to this world. Marcus Anderson was one of the most intuitive agents Jane had ever met. He possessed what few people in the field did, an innate ability to understand people, not in a cursory way. Anderson had a rare capacity for sensing a person's emotions, a person's inner turmoil. It was an attribute that could not be taught nor learned. It could be honed. Anderson was a master.

Claire had been a wildcard in the game that Jane found herself immersed in. It was a game that was affecting everyone central to her life. It demanded her full attention, and she made the decision to accept her role as an orchestrator. It was the only way she could seek to protect what she held most dear. Early on, she had taken the time to assess the people entrenched in the same circles. Claire presented a challenge. At some point, Claire would either need to be cut loose entirely or reeled in. Jane had left that assessment to Agent Anderson. He had made it. Now, was his moment of truth.

"Claire, she still loves you."

Claire could not meet Anderson's gaze. Eleana would always love her. She knew that. She also understood that Eleana would never hold the place in her life that she once had. She had never considered what it all meant, at least not what it might mean for Eleana.

"She might not be...."

"When they strike, they will be certain it makes the impact they desire. The right people will be present," Anderson said. "It will not be enough to destroy a building full of distant acquaintances and strangers."

Claire looked up and directly into his eyes. "How do you know they will be here, now?"

"I don't. Not for certain. This is their opportunity."

"What do you mean?" Claire asked.

Anderson debated with himself for less than an instant. Few people trusted Claire Brackett. Anderson surmised that if he were to ever hope to earn Claire's trust, he would have to show her his first. "Toles is in Virginia. Krause and Baros are across the globe."

"Where?"

"Chasing ghosts," he replied.

Claire shook her head. "More of my father's dead ends. Right where he wanted them."

Anderson opened his door. "Maybe," he said.

Claire rolled her eyes. "He always gets his way," she muttered.

"Maybe not," Anderson offered. "Ready?"

Claire chuckled. "You make it sound like a date," she told Anderson.

"I've had worse," he joked

Claire smiled at him. "You might just be crazier than me, Marcus."

"Maybe."

***

"What are you doing?" McCollum asked Krause.

"Calling Alex."

"Bad idea, Agent," McCollum gave his unsolicited assessment.

"You want me to show up on her doorstep with her dead father-in-law in tow? Think that is a better idea?" Krause spat vehemently.

"We'll have time, Jonathan, time for you to do as you see fit. She's in Virginia."

"How do you know that?" Eleana asked.

McCollum winked at the young woman. "She has a meeting at Rand."

"And?" Krause asked.

"We are not showing up on her doorstep, Jonathan."

"I thought you said we had to move quickly," Krause replied.

"Good to know your hearing is intact."

Krause's patience was waning. "The least you can do is give us some answers."

McCollum sighed and nodded. "There are people who deserve those answers first," he said honestly.

Krause's posture stiffened. Eleana put a hand on his knee to calm him. "Jonathan," she whispered. "He is right."

"Look," McCollum began. "There's a lot you need to know, all of you. I promise you that when we reach Boston, I will explain things as best I can. What I can tell you is that Dmitri had been sent to Carecom in your absence."

"For what purpose?"

"My assumption is that they intend to place a mechanism."

"A bomb?" Eleana asked.

"Perhaps or perhaps something more subtle, something that can be triggered at a great distance, something with eyes as well as teeth," McCollum said.

"To what end?" Krause asked. Before McCollum could respond, Krause continued. "And, just what the hell did we walk into back there?"

McCollum shifted in his seat as the plane began to take off. He had expected questions. He had anticipated anger and confusion. He had promised himself that the answers to these questions were owed to Cassidy and Alex before he dove into them with anyone else. He realized now that his hope had not been realistic. Krause needed some perspective. Moreover, the pair before him deserved it.

"For a long time, we suspected that O'Brien had been placed. It was a suspicion, Jonathan. One for which no one had gained any confirmation."

"Placed? Placed by whom?"

"That remains the question," McCollum said.

"I don't understand," Eleana admitted. "You mean that someone placed him in Congress? That's how it's done, isn't it?"

"No," McCollum said. "I mean that he was placed in Cassidy's life."

Krause felt a wave of nausea roll through him. "To what end?" he asked.

McCollum's lips tightened. "To try and flush me out."

"Jesus Christ," Krause mumbled. "What about Alex's father?"

"Your father is gone," McCollum said honestly. "I wish for all my life that were not the truth, Jonathan. While, I am sure nothing I say will hold any truth for you yet, I swear to you that is the truth."

Krause's gaze was impassive. Eleana smiled sadly at the older man accompanying them. The tension in the plane was thick, heavy like the air in the tunnel she had traversed earlier.

"He was Russian," Eleana observed.

McCollum shook his head. "He was American, Eleana. Who placed him—that remains the question."

"His Russian was impeccable," she said flatly.

"As is yours," McCollum reminded her.

"Yes, but I was raised with the language," she said.

She recalled her mother in that instant. Maria Baros had been an amazing woman and mother. She had raised Eleana as best she could with a sense of who both her parents were. Maria's father was a Spanish businessman who had fallen in love with a Russian dancer. Maria had been raised in Spain, but with the languages of both her parents. At seventeen, her father had purchased a vacation home for the family in France. It was there that a young Maria met a much older Edmond Callier and fell in love. Eleana had lived a charmed life, one much different than her older brother had in London. She spent winters with her mother and grandparents in Spain and the rest of the year with her parents in France, until her mother's illness compelled then to send her away to school. She adored both of her parents. She considered her exposure to language a priceless gift that her family had given her. Spanish, French, English, and Russian were all as familiar to her as her own skin.

"To be able to speak with that confidence," Eleana began, "that was not so much taught as given."

"Mmm," McCollum hummed his agreement. "Given is an excellent word," he told her. He turned back to Krause. "I will tell you what I know about where we are headed and why. The rest, you agree to wait for," he said. "I cannot give you what you seek before I give it to her."

"You mean Cassidy."

"If it comes to that, yes. At the very least, I owe it to Alexis," he said. Krause reluctantly nodded. "This new merger you two are hell-bent on," McCollum began. "It's the proverbial straw on the camel's back," he said

"Why?" Krause asked pointedly. "Carecom has taken control of at least four major competitors to MyoGen and Rand over the last year. Alex has…"

"Alexis has no idea what she is taking over," McCollum said.

"And you do?" Krause asked skeptically.

"I should. It was my project," McCollum replied.

"Lynx," Eleana whispered, more to herself than to the two men with her.

McCollum looked at Eleana proudly. "You are your father's daughter, Eleana. Where did you hear that name?"

"It was on some documents we found," she told him.

"Well, you are further ahead than I expected then."

"Somehow, I doubt that," Krause interjected. "So? Why the rush now? Why come out of hiding now, after all of these years?"

"I wish I had an answer for that," McCollum replied. "I don't have a choice now. Not now. Your father is gone," he told Krause. "And, your father," he turned to Eleana, "does not know that I am alive."

"How is that?" Krause asked. He was seething. All Krause wanted to do was reach across the seat and throttle the older man into oblivion.

"You won't believe me," McCollum asserted.

"Good bet," Krause agreed.

McCollum chuckled and then sighed deeply. "We did not want to compromise him as well," he said. "Edmond was always the barometer for us. He would never have agreed to this knowingly. Not to my exit. It was necessary to protect all of you. Part of that was closing the loops. Only your father knew for a very long time."

"And now?" Krause challenged.

"That's a discussion for later. When he became compromised, arrangements were made. We had hoped to avoid this scenario, all of us. That's not possible now. The Admiral suspects one of us is alive and that has no good place to lead. You and Alexis are on a bridge, and there is more than one person who is ready to blow it out from underneath you. That will mean compromising your work and your lives, and if you or anyone else should become casualties…Well, that is the price of war. For these people, this is a war. It's a war they make every day. You might not believe me right now if I told you the truth. Some people will not relinquish what MyoGen has. It is too valuable."

"You still haven't told me what that is," Krause reminded him.

"No, I haven't. I have my reasons, Jonathan. Look, Cassidy has lost enough. I will not allow her to lose Alexis too."

"What could be that important?" Krause asked doubtfully. "That you would come back from the dead? That you would kidnap O'Brien? I've seen some crazy things," Krause said. "What is there to gain? What are you so afraid of that you would fake your own death?"

"Let's leave it at this, the ultimate spy is the person who does not even know he is spying at all."

"What does that have to do with MyoGen?" Eleana asked.

"Everything," McCollum said.

Chapter Nine

"**M**om! It was so cool!" Dylan practically screamed through the phone.

Cassidy held the phone away from her ear slightly and winced at the volume. She chuckled at the thought that if Dylan continued at this decibel, she might receive some hearing loss. "I'll bet it was," Cassidy replied, a smile lighting her face.

"Grandma said to tell you that she and YaYa only have wine at the bottom of the hill like she promised."

Cassidy laughed. "Tell Grandma I am glad to know I won't have to ground her when you get home," she joked. "I'm glad that you are having a good time."

"Oh! We saw a moose too!" he told his mother. "Man, I wish you could have seen him, Mom. He was outside the cabin this morning."

"I wish I could have seen him too," Cassidy said honestly. She was thrilled to hear the excitement in Dylan's voice. Sometimes things that seemed like tragedies turned out to be blessings in disguise. She would have loved to have spent the weekend with Dylan at the cabin skiing. But, she understood that there was something magical in time away with your grandparents. Cassidy recalled those times in her childhood often. She had little doubt that what started as an outing tainted by disappointment would become a memory Dylan would cherish for the rest of his life. And, while Mackenzie was still not feeling up to par, Cassidy was enjoying her one on one time with her daughter. She did not get much of that for extended periods. Another unexpected bonus was the fact that Alex would arrive sometime today. Cassidy seemed to find silver linings everywhere.

"Is Kenzie still sick?" Dylan asked.

"She's okay," Cassidy promised.

"I wish she could have seen that moose!" Dylan exclaimed.

Cassidy chuckled. She envisioned Alex trying to ascertain what sound a moose made so she could teach it to Mackenzie. "Well, you will have to tell her all about it when you get home," Cassidy said.

"Is Alex there?" Dylan asked.

"No, sweetheart. She had a trip to make. I won't tell her about the moose. You can tell her tomorrow when you call. She should be back by then."

"Nah, it's okay, you can tell her," he said. "YaYa wants to talk to you."

"Okay. You have fun. I love you."

"I will. I love you too, Mom. Say hi to Kenzie for me," he said as he passed the phone to Helen.

"Hi there," Helen greeted Cassidy.

Cassidy was still chuckling. "I hear you've had some visitors."

"Oh yes, we love to entertain," Helen laughed.

"I wonder if your visitor was related to Marvin?" Cassidy mused aloud.

"Who?" Helen asked.

"Oh, sorry....Marvin the moose. When I was a kid, there was a family of moose that used to wander nearby the cabin. My dad named them all—Marvin, Mabel, Marian, and Martin," she explained. "He said they were spies sent by the forest faeries to see what we were doing. He had some crazy stories when I think about it," Cassidy giggled.

Helen sighed deeply. She had spent hours talking with Rose the previous evening about their husbands, divulging more than she would have ever thought about her own life. The truth was, Nicolaus had done his best to shelter her and their children from his activities. Helen's mother had different ideas as did Nicolaus' mother. They were both well aware of Carecom's dealings, and while neither divulged specifics regarding Nicolaus' role beyond Carecom, Helen had surmised a good deal just by observation.

She had seen her husband's turmoil when their daughter had chosen and insisted upon a career in the military. He had maintained it was not a proper place for a woman. Helen had been and remained certain that his concerns ran along a different line, and much deeper. For those reasons, she had chosen to share with Alex what she did know about the family and about Alex's father. It had taken Alex by surprise, the fact that her family had a legacy in intelligence. Helen knew it stunned Alex to realize that her mother had any inclination at all about any of it. There was no doubt in Helen's mind that Alex had apprised Cassidy of all or nearly all of it. Alex did not subscribe to her father's theory that keeping her wife in the dark was necessary. Alex took the approach that Helen's parents and in-laws had, she maintained transparency between herself and her wife as much as possible.

It had been an unsettling realization for Helen at first, but she understood that she and Nicolaus Toles had not found each other by accident. Nicolaus had not found his best friends through happenstance either. Everything had been orchestrated. It did not make their relationships any less authentic, but it did make them less organic. They had been led to one another deliberately, put in situations that would foster connection. It had never once occurred to Helen that Cassidy and Alex might have been pawns in a similar game, not until she had seen the photo of Jim McCollum and Edmond Callier. It was too much of a coincidence. In Helen's experience, few coincidences happened of their own accord, at least, that was not the case in her world.

Silence hovered longer than Cassidy was used to. "Helen?"

"Sorry."

"Are you okay? I lost you there for a minute," Cassidy said.

"I'm all right," Helen assured her daughter-in-law. She momentarily debated sharing what she had discovered with Cassidy, but dismissed the notion just as quickly. She would have to tell Alex. That was not a question.

Helen would leave the decision of how to proceed with the information to Alex and Rose. It was not her place. "How is my granddaughter doing?" Helen changed the subject.

"You know how Alex gets when she doesn't have coffee?" Cassidy asked. Helen sniggered. "Imagine that times five," Cassidy said.

"Oh dear."

"She'll be okay in a day or two," Cassidy said. "I just hope this doesn't end up being a common malady."

"Mmm. Alexis got them quite frequently. Almost had to put tubes in her ears, poor kid. Of all the things she could take after Alexis for—that would not be the one I would choose."

"Oh, well, she takes after her momma in a lot of ways," Cassidy said affectionately.

"That she does," Helen agreed. "Speaking of my daughter, have you heard from her?"

"She left a message yesterday. Said she would be back to your house sometime today, but I haven't heard from her since. Kind of strange. I thought she would call when I left the message that we were here."

"Well, who knows? She probably got caught up with something," Helen observed.

Cassidy groaned softly. "That's what I'm afraid of."

"I'm sure she's fine."

"I'm sure she is too. This merger has really taken a toll on her," Cassidy explained.

"I know it has," Helen agreed. "She's a lot like her father in that way. He had many a sleepless night when it came to decisions that cost people their jobs."

Cassidy listened to the hint of melancholy in Helen's voice. Alex had told Cassidy many times that she was perplexed by her father. On the one hand, he had been involved in activities that made Alex's skin crawl. At the same time, she'd found everything from documents and memos to personal notes that expressed his grave concerns about the people Carecom employed. Cassidy rarely commented. She listened attentively and let Alex express her confusion and frustration. On some level, Cassidy remained angry with her father-in-law. She had witnessed the pain that his words and actions had caused Alex. That did not bode well with Cassidy. On the other hand, when she listened to Helen, or even her wife at times, she could capture glimpses of a man whom she was certain revered his daughter. Cassidy understood Alex's confusion. Alex, much like her father, constantly worried about the people under Carecom's umbrella. She felt responsible for them.

"I imagine she is quite a bit like him," Cassidy conceded.

"He always found a way to make things work. She will too," Helen said assuredly. "You know where everything you need is there?"

"I do," Cassidy said gratefully. "I hear there is snow headed your way."

"That's what they are saying," Helen said. "Do you think we should cut it short? I mean, I know Dylan has school on Wednesday."

"No," Cassidy answered. "He's so happy right now. What's the worst thing that happens? He gets an extra day with you two? He'll be in heaven."

"You sure? That could be a possibility."

"I'm sure," Cassidy said. "Tell my mother to behave herself."

"Oh no," Helen said. "I know better than to tell your mother anything."

Cassidy laughed. "Smart woman."

"You call us if you change your mind," Helen said.

"I will, but I won't," Cassidy told her. "Say high to Marvin for me."

Helen heard the wistful lilt in Cassidy's voice. The memory she shared clearly held affectionate meaning for her. "I'll leave some snacks for him from you," Helen promised.

"You do that. I'll talk to you," Cassidy said.

"You will," Helen agreed as she disconnected their call. She set the phone down and closed her eyes.

"How were things on the home front?" Rose asked.

"They are fine," Helen said

"You didn't tell her, did you?" Rose guessed.

"Not my place," Helen said. "I'm not sure she needs to know something that we don't even know matters," Helen smiled at her best friend. "She was interested in Marvin."

"Marvin?"

"The moose," Helen explained.

A knowing smile crept onto Rose's lips. "He certainly was creative," she said. "He had Cassie searching for wood nymphs. I think she believed they were real until she was in high school," Rose mused.

"She probably did," Helen guessed.

Rose nodded. "He was her hero," she said.

"I understand. Believe it or not…While Alexis would never admit it, there was a time when she followed her father everywhere."

"I believe it," Rose said. "I just hope Cassidy can keep that image of him."

Helen nodded. "I know, so do I."

∗∗∗

"Alex?"

"I don't know what you want me to say, Steven," she told her old friend. "You haven't told me much at all."

Brady nodded. "Not because I don't want to," he said honestly.

"You see, in my experience, that's what is called bullshit," she replied. "You disappear to God knows where, and you don't think I should be skeptical about you watching my back? Or, Fallon's?"

"I would expect nothing less from you than reservations," Brady replied. "I've never lied to you, Alex. Not in all the years we've known one another."

"There's not a very fine line between deception and omission," Alex observed.

"Fair enough. For the record, I have as much to lose in all of this as any of you," he said as he brought the car to a stop.

Alex stepped out and stretched her back until it popped. Fallon watched his friend closely, noting the familiar wince and slight twitch of Alex's temple.

"Alex," Fallon began quietly as he made his way to her side. "Are you okay?"

Alex nodded in spite of another involuntary wince. Traveling as much as she had in the last twenty-four hours had stiffened her back to the point that it was difficult to move. She needed to stretch. Whenever possible, Alex avoided long car rides. Unlike most people she knew, she deliberately scheduled layovers when she flew. Her back did not cooperate with long periods of idleness, a result of the injuries she had received while serving in Iraq. She had been fortunate that to date, her injury had never seriously impacted or compromised her work. She smiled unconvincingly at Fallon.

"Just stiff, Fallon," she promised. Inwardly, Alex was hoping she could trust Steven Brady. She doubted that if they had the need to move quickly, that her body would currently comply with any agility. That only served to heighten her anxiety about her old friend.

Gray had held true to his word, outfitting the threesome with a Maryland State Police car for travel. Alex was certain she did not want to know the connections he had used to accomplish that. She'd been making mental notes about every oddity and every detail she had observed in the last day. And, she had every intention of calling Jane and demanding some concrete answers. The ride back to Massachusetts had moved between unsettling silence and heated accusation. Alex was not pleased with the turn of events. Brady was not forthcoming with information about where he had been over the last year. She pressed him. He remained unwavering. The only thing that Alex had surmised was that in some way her good friend Jane Merrow was involved—again.

Alex looked ahead at the building that held the company her grandparents had established and that her father had cared for. She pinched the bridge of her nose, stretched her back again and sighed. If she was following Gray's insinuations correctly, her determination to take over MyoGen had served to compromise Carecom completely. Something Gray had said kept repeating in her brain. "The work we provide is more nuanced." If Alex was reading the innuendo correctly, Rand and MyoGen were engaged in developing pharmaceuticals for the purpose of altering consciousness. That was territory that Alex was explicitly opposed to. She had suspected that one of the programs she had ended earlier in the year was seeking to do more than to simply create an effective drug to reduce anxiety. The world of psychotropic drugs presented a slippery slope. In the end, the aim was always to change behavior. It was not a stretch to imagine how those applications might benefit people in Alex's line of work. She was curious as to what MyoGen might have undertaken that would cause such a knee jerk reaction by the intelligence complex. Alex had seen no evidence of any programs that had given her grave concern at MyoGen, and Alex was always thorough in her assessments. That meant one of two things: either Gray was lying to her to cover up some other agenda or whatever MyoGen was involved in had been buried deeply and deliberately. Neither scenario was desirable. Alex wasn't certain which possibility gave her more concern.

"Alex, if you are not up to this," Fallon said gently.

Alex forced a smile. "I'll be fine, Fallon."

Alex looked across to Brady. He nodded his silent acknowledgment. There was no way that Alex was going to allow Steven Brady into the halls of Carecom with her to accompany him. "Ready?" Brady asked. Alex nodded. "Lead on then," Brady said.

***

"What are we looking for?" Claire asked as she rounded a corner.

"Not sure," Anderson confessed.

"That's helpful," Claire mumbled.

"What?" Anderson chimed. "You expect me to have all the answers?"

Claire spun around and glared at him. She watched as his playful expression gave way to a look of apprehension. Claire followed Anderson's line of sight and groaned. "Aw, fuck."

***

"Looks like someone beat us here," Krause observed.

McCollum nodded. He felt tired in his bones, and it was not simply as the result of sitting on a plane for nine and a half hours. Ahead of him lie both the past and the future. The present would force him to confront what had passed, and he knew that whatever came to pass now would forever change the future for the people he loved. He looked at the State Police car parked a few spaces away. It seemed too overt for Dmitri Kargen and his cohorts. That left McCollum wondering who else had been tipped off, and who had informed those parties. "The question is who."

Krause moved toward the police car and assessed it for a moment. "Not Kargen's MO," he surmised.

"I agree," McCollum responded.

Krause stroked his chin and looked at Eleana. "Any ideas?" he asked her.

Eleana shook her head. "From what I know, Kargen and Ivanov are a bit more old school, if you know what I mean."

McCollum could not help the chuckle that escaped his lips. Eleana's assessment amused him, not because it wasn't accurate, but because of Eleana's choice of words and inflection. It was a sincere observation laden with just a touch of humor. For a split second, it conjured images of old James Bond films for McCollum. Ironically, he imagined that Dmitri Kargen saw himself much in that light—a modern day Bond of some kind.

Wrong allegiances and Kargen hardly possessed Bond's magnetism. Nonetheless, McCollum could imagine Kargen making such a proclamation to his reflection.

"Something funny?" Krause asked.

"Not really," McCollum said.

"Well? What do you think?" Krause wanted to know. "Who do you think beat us here?"

"Only one way to find out," McCollum said.

***

"I wish I knew what we were looking for," Fallon said more to himself than to his compatriots.

"Nothing good," Alex commented absently. "This is like looking for a needle in a haystack. If they want to take out Carecom, there are millions of ways and a million places they could do that." Alex stopped at looked at Brady. "Why here? If it's me that they want, why Natick? This isn't my home base anymore," she told Brady.

"But, it is. How often are you still here, Alex?" Brady asked. "Where does Krause spend most of his time? Eleana? Where do you converge? They will want to see and hear before they make any move. You know that. It's the first rule of operations—listen first."

Alex heard his comment and understood his meaning. "In that case, follow me," she said.

"Alex? Do you think we should be…" Fallon began to address his friend.

Alex kept moving confidently. "This is my home. I'm not sneaking around in it," she said flatly.

Fallon looked at Brady to convey his concern. Brady shrugged. He agreed with Alex's tactic. This was indeed her turf. Anyone here, whether physically present or electronically listening was an uninvited guest. Alex needed to be confident and deliberate. She would not bend to anyone's will nor their threats. That had never been Alex's nature. The best defense was often a stellar offense. That was clearly the path Alex had chosen.

"Your call, Alex," Brady said.

"Yes, it is."

***

"Shhh," Claire warned Anderson.

"Is it Dmitri?"

"Yeah."

"Who is he with?"

"Don't recognize them," Claire whispered. She ducked behind a cubicle.

"Why here?" Anderson asked. "Seems like the warehouse would…"

Claire shook her head. "No, this is not just about taking out Carecom," she noted. "It's about taking from Carecom…Taking from Toles, if I had to guess."

"You think there is something personal here? That isn't…"

"It's always personal, Marcus," Claire said dryly.

Anderson stood behind Claire, staring at her curiously. She was completely focused on the scene unfolding ahead. Until now, Claire Brackett had always remained aloof, maintaining that there was nothing personal in her line of work. He wondered what had shifted and when the shift in her thinking had occurred.

Claire kept a close eye on Dmitri Kargen as one of his men deftly picked a lock to what seemed to be the executive offices. Claire's trained eye scanned upward and caught sight of the mirror she was certain she would find. Just to the side of it lay a camera. "We need to get closer. I need you to keep an eye out for me," she said, gesturing to the mirror. "Watch my back." Claire adjusted the piece in her ear. "This thing had better work, Marcus," she said.

"It works."

"Well, we will find out soon enough, won't we? You see anyone approaching, you..."

"I got it. What are you going to do?" he asked.

"Depends on what I see," Claire said. With that, she was on the move toward the offices a few yards away.

Anderson watched in rapt fascination. The doors and windows of what had been the executive offices of Carecom were all made of frosted glass. He had little doubt that more could be seen from the inside than from Claire's vantage point. She would need to gain access to the area if she hoped to gauge Kargen's actions.

Anderson had worked with Claire on numerous occasions. He had always admired her abilities as much as he often questioned her judgment. She was far more intelligent than many gave her credit for. Impulsive? At times, Claire's impulsivity was a danger to herself and those around her. He hated to admit it, but at times, Claire's willingness to act on sheer curiosity and instinct proved to be what was needed. Recklessness and fearlessness were sometimes necessary to achieve results. It was a reality that Anderson loathed. That did not make it any less true.

Claire navigated her way to the door and opened it slightly. She took a deep breath and held up a hand to Anderson. With a quick thumbs up, she disappeared. "Don't lose sight in that mirror," Anderson heard Claire's voice whisper.

Anderson kept focused, watching the empty hallway, wondering why Claire did not want him to follow. He was tempted to abandon the task he had been assigned and trace her footsteps. He jumped when he saw a figure growing larger in the reflection. "Shit!"

"What?" Claire asked as she moved toward another door that was left slightly ajar.

"Toles," he breathed.

"What?"

"Toles is headed your way," he repeated. "With company."

"She armed?" Claire asked.

"I would imagine so. Shit…."

"Marcus, what? Talk to me."

"Brady is with her."

"Fuck," Claire hissed.

"She's circling the opposite way. I can't see them now," he said.

"Go, Marcus."

"Go?"

"You heard me. Get the hell out of here now!"

"I'm not leaving you in the lion's den alone," he answered.

"I'm hardly alone," Claire chuckled uncomfortably. "Listen to me. You get down to security. Do whatever you have to. You get the footage from these offices."

"Claire…"

"Marcus, do it. You know I'm right. Just go. That might be our only chance to see what they are doing. If Alex gets caught…Just go. I'll be fine."

"And, if you aren't?"

Claire laughed in Anderson's ear. "Starting to like me?" she asked. She heard Anderson's soft laugh. "Go. I got this. Just trust me."

Anderson swallowed hard. Trust and Claire rarely went together in the same sentence. Her decision was selfless, something he knew few would believe. "Just be careful," he told her.

"Just get the footage," she snapped. Claire straightened to her full height and opened the door deliberately. "Boys," she greeted the men in the room.

***

"Alex, where are you going?" Fallon asked.

"We're not alone, Fallon," Alex responded.

"You sure?"

"Positive."

"What's your plan?" Brady asked.

"Well, Fallon and I will enter the offices from the back corridor. There's a door to my father's old office that is adjacent to mine."

"You still have an office here?" Fallon asked.

Alex nodded as she kept moving. "It's a necessity," she explained.

"Anything they can find?" Brady wondered.

"Not what they are hoping for, no. If they are looking for information on the MyoGen merger or any financial records, they're going to have a difficult time here. I had the system here taken off the mainframe a few months back."

"So why…." Fallon began.

"No one knows that, Fallon," Alex said. "No one but Pip and me, that is. There are records. They just are not the right records. They can hack and download for days, all they will get is old data."

"Smart," Brady observed. Alex cocked her head and grinned. "So?" Brady continued. "You and Fallon hit the offices. What about me?"

"Get down to security on the second level," Alex said. "Get whatever they have for the last few hours before anyone else can."

"Alex, are you sure you…" Brady began.

"This is my fight, Brady. You know where to find me."

"What do you want me to do with the discs from security?" Brady asked.

Alex faced her old friend. "Well, assuming it matters, I would like them to come to me and only me. I'm not that naïve, however."

"You still don't trust me, do you?" Brady asked.

"I'll trust you a little more when you put those discs in my hand," Alex returned. "Go before someone beats you to it. Second floor, room 283 is where the surveillance room is. Take the stairwell over there," Alex gestured over her shoulder. "It will drop you directly across from that room. You won't need to go through the security office."

Brady nodded. "Watch your back," he advised Alex.

"I've got it covered," Fallon replied.

Brady smiled in acknowledgment. "See you on the other side," he said to Alex.

"I hope so," Alex deadpanned. She watched Brady jog away toward the stairwell and turned to Fallon. "Ready?"

"Just wish I knew what I was ready for," he confessed.

"Be ready for anything," she said.

***

"Sparrow," Dmitri Kargen acknowledged Brackett as she entered the room.

Claire smiled at Kargen and kept her gaze impassive as if she were bored by the entire scene. She was certain her sigh and the slight roll of her eyes convinced him of her general disinterest. In truth, she was expertly noting every detail about the space. She memorized where Kargen's men stood, any doors, windows, and each piece of furniture. The office was shaped in a typical rectangle, nothing extraordinary about it. Should she need to move quickly, it would be imperative to know her surroundings.

Directly across from Claire's position was a desk that both of Kargen's men stood behind. She could see lights from the street below shining through the blinds that covered the window behind it in slivers. Off to the right, the walls were lined with bookcases. Claire noticed that more pictures seemed to line the shelves than books. She let her eyes roam left and made note of two doors. She imagined that at least one served as some type of exit, though she could not be certain which.

Claire batted her eyelashes. "Want to tell the goon squad to point those things somewhere else?" she suggested.

Kargen waved his hand as a signal for his men to lower their weapons. They both complied hesitantly. "Might I guess who sent you?" Kargen asked Claire.

"You have time for twenty questions?" Claire cooed.

"Clever," Kargen replied.

"Usually," Claire agreed. "What about you? Still doing Viktor's dirty laundry, I see."

Kargen motioned to one of his men to continue working at Alex's computer. "What are you doing here, Sparrow?" he asked Claire as he moved away from the desk.

Claire shrugged, cautiously feeling for the gun at her side. "Maybe I just missed you," she said flirtatiously.

Kargen gave a low, throaty laugh. "I'm sure." He moved toward the far said of the office and opened a closet door.

Claire chuckled. "Closets, Dmitri? You think Toles is in there? She's been out of the closet a long time," she laughed. Dmitri ignored Claire and opened the door and looked inside.

"Vy khotite vse fayly? (You want all the files)?" Kargen's man at the computer asked him.

"No, he just wants whatever girls' phone numbers you can find," Claire scoffed. "I can understand you," she rolled her eyes.

Kargen seemed interested in whatever contents the closet held and made no response. Claire had never considered Dmitri Kargen an adept operative of any kind. She'd often mused that whoever invented the word 'goon' must have been picturing Dmitri Kargen. Kargen was Viktor Ivanov's nephew. That was his ticket to infamy. He was attractive—rugged and relatively handsome. He was attached to powerful people. That is where Dmitri Kargen's allure ended for Claire Brackett. He was rough around the edges. Claire herself was often placed in that category by observers and she knew it. The differences between Claire Brackett and Dmitri Kargen, however, were substantial. Claire was not only attractive and physically agile. She was bright, intuitive, and clever. Dmitri was roguish at his best. He did not possess a stunning intellect nor any unique skills that Claire had ever discovered. It did not surprise her that he did not sense the approaching presence that she did.

Claire's hearing was not as acute as she would have liked. She had learned to tune her senses even amid noise and chaos. She was positive that someone was close, and she suspected that someone was the owner of this office. Claire understood several things: if Alex Toles were to enter this room, Alex would immediately consider Claire a threat. Dmitri Kargen would not hesitate to kill either Alex or Claire. And, if Claire in any way compromised Alex, Eleana would never forgive her. Claire kept her sight directly on Kargen as her hand reached deliberately for her gun in preparation.

Kargen's men were both behind the desk. One was underneath, presumably attempting to place some type of device. Claire made a mental note of his exact position. The other one of Kargen's men, a short, somewhat stocky man was hovering over the computer on the desk. Claire listened carefully as the second door on the wall began to open. The next few moments passed as though time had sped up and then abruptly came to a screeching halt.

"Alex!"

***

Alex took a deep breath and released it slowly. She had divided her father's sizeable office when she first came to Carecom. After years of bullpens and cubicles that were complimented by long hours of field work, the large space and its decadent furnishings had distracted Alex. She'd left this space largely untouched. Alex looked across the room at the portraits that hung over what had once been her father's and grandfather's desk. She smiled at the picture of her grandparents. Her eyes moved slowly until they focused squarely on a framed photo that sat on the bookshelf behind the desk. Alex sighed audibly and closed her eyes for a split second. Who was he?

After all this time, Alex still struggled to understand the man she knew as her father. The photo had been taken when Alex was nine. She shook her head ruefully and drew her sidearm. With one more step, Alex had reached the door to the space that still served as her office when she traveled here. "Be ready," she told Fallon.

Fallon gave Alex a quick nod and a small smile. He placed his gun firmly at his side, ready to follow her into whatever might lie behind the door. "Ready," he promised.

Alex placed her hand on the door handle. She turned her body slightly, hoping to gain a better view of the expanse of her office and maintain some semblance of protection. One more breath and a short exhale and Alex had stepped through the door. Her sight immediately fell on Brackett, more accurately on the gun that Brackett was holding that had swiftly lifted in her direction. Three voices screamed out at once.

"Drop it!" Alex screamed as she moved forward.

"Alex!" Brackett yelled.

"Don't move!" Fallon called out in warning as his gun trained on the men behind Alex's desk.

Pop. Pop. Pop.

Claire felt herself lifted slightly from the ground and thrown backward. Alex started to move forward when a voice stopped her.

"Priyatno videt' vas, Aleksis. (Nice to see you, Alexis)," Dmitri hissed. He held his bleeding right hand with his left to steady it.

Claire looked up at Alex, attempting to convey her warning.

"So? Who should I kill first?" Dmitri asked as he placed the barrel of his Glock to the back of Fallon's head. "I think it is you who should drop it, Agent Fallon. What do you say, Alexis?" Alex started to pivot.

Pop.

"I don't think so, Dmitri," an unfamiliar voice said.

Fallon felt the ringing in his ears and a familiar, unsettling warmth on his neck. "Aww, shit," he groaned.

Claire started to move and Alex aimed her gun again. "Jesus! You fucking shot me!" Claire yelled.

"You were about to shoot me!" Alex reminded Claire.

"I was aiming for Kargen, you idiot!" Claire declared.

Eleana flew into the room past Krause and McCollum. "Claire?"

Alex groaned in recognition of the truth. She turned back and saw Kargen in a heap on the floor, Fallon wiping Kargen's blood from his neck, and Krause standing with a familiar looking stranger just inside the door. Alex froze for a moment.

"Are you okay?" Krause asked as he moved to subdue the other two men in the room.

"I'm fine," Alex answered.

"You're welcome!" Claire called out.

Eleana looked down at Claire and shook her head. "Stay still," she ordered Claire as she tried to assess Claire's injuries.

"Jesus Christ!" Steven Brady's voice called into the office from the front door. "What the hell happened?"

"Nice to see you, Steven," McCollum greeted him from the back of the office.

Brady's eyes found Alex. "Discs were gone in security." He looked at Fallon. "You okay?"

"Better than him," Fallon gestured to Kargen.

Eleana looked over at Krause and shook her head. She looked back at Claire. "We need to get her some help."

"That's a newsflash," Fallon mumbled.

Alex grabbed the bridge of her nose. "Everyone shut the hell up!" she ordered. Alex looked across the office at her older brother. "What the hell are you doing here? I thought you two were looking for our father in Russia?"

"We were," he said. "There were unexpected developments."

Alex's gaze narrowed at the older man who was watching the scene unfold silently. She studied him for a moment, feeling that she should be able to place him. "Who the hell are you?" she asked pointedly.

Krause and Eleana exchanged a fearful glance. "Alex," Krause began to speak.

Jim McCollum made his way into the center of the room and stepped directly in front of Alex. He looked her in the eye and nodded slightly. "Hello, Alexis," he greeted her. "I'm sorry we have to meet under these circumstances. But, I want to thank you for taking such good care of my family."

"Excuse me?" Alex asked.

"I'm sorry about your father," he said. McCollum outstretched his hand. "McCollum...James," he said. Alex stared at him blankly. "Not the father you expected, I know. I'm afraid you will have to settle for your father-in-law."

"No fucking way," Claire's voice carried through the room.

Alex stood frozen in place. She held the older man's gaze and studied his eyes for a moment. She looked down at his waiting hand and promptly turned her gaze back to Krause. "Call Jane and make arrangements for our uninvited guests," she instructed him. She moved to face Brady. "I trust you and Fallon can handle things here until reinforcements arrive?"

"Not a problem," Brady promised. "I'm sorry about the...."

Alex held up her hand. "Not your fault. Clearly there were more invitations to this party than we were made aware of," she said.

"Damn," Claire groaned in pain. Eleana tried to keep pressure on Claire's shoulder. "Nice shot," Claire hissed at Alex. Alex grinned.

"What about Claire?" Eleana asked.

Alex considered the question for a minute. She looked at Krause. "I think I have just the place."

"Hey!" Claire called out. "What are you gonna do? Dump me with Dmitri?"

Alex shrugged. "No," she smiled. "I'm taking you home," she said casually. Alex walked past McCollum without any acknowledgment and headed for the office door.

Brady moved to Krause's side along with Fallon. "You look like shit," he said to Fallon. "This is becoming a thing with you."

"Funny," Fallon replied.

"You coming?" Alex called back as she kept moving forward.

Krause sighed and looked at McCollum. "That went well," he said before moving to help Eleana get Claire to her feet. "Can you walk?" he asked Claire as cordially as he could manage.

"I sure as hell am not having you carry my ass over Toles' threshold."

Eleana shook her head. "This is not happening."

Claire was starting to feel lightheaded from the loss of blood and shock to her system, and her knees gave way. Krause flung her over his shoulder. "Hey!" Claire yelled. She looked at the older man walking beside them and chuckled. "Bet they hate you more than they do me," she said honestly.

McCollum suppressed an earnest laugh. "Not even a question," he told Claire. "Not even a question."

Chapter Ten

Alex had remained silent on the drive to her mother's home. The only exchange in twenty minutes consisted of Eleana expressing concern over Claire's injuries. Alex had insisted on driving, commandeering a Carecom van. She needed to be in motion to still her mind. McCollum and Eleana found themselves in the back with a bleeding, irritable, and slightly silly Claire Brackett. Eleana had piped up amid Claire's babbling and groaning to urge Alex to take them to a hospital. Alex had promised that she would see that Claire got medical attention.

Alex pulled into her mother's garage and turned off the car. She was grateful for the late hour, the fact that her mother's house was set back from the road a bit and the knowledge that no one in the family was close by. "Follow me," she instructed the group.

"Where are we going?" Krause asked. He followed Alex as she made her way to the back of the house and the hatchway. "I thought you said no one was here?"

Alex ignored Krause. She led the group into the basement of her parent's home. The first room was a laundry room. The next was a large family room. Alex moved to the far wall. It was adorned with a large mural of Santorini. Alex moved a few paces left of the bar. She reached underneath and in less than a second, a panel in the middle of the mural opened.

"Holy shit! Does your dad have this too?" Claire asked Eleana sluggishly.

"She really does need something," Eleana said. "She's lost a lot of blood."

"She'll be okay," McCollum said assuredly. "She's lucid enough. If I know Nicolaus, there will be something here to at least help with the pain."

Alex shot McCollum a disgusted glare and led the group down a short hallway to another door. She typed in the passcode and directed them through. She looked at Krause and gestured to a large couch in the corner.

"Alex, are you sure this is a good idea?" Krause asked as he laid Claire on the couch.

"Fuck!" she yelped. "You could be a little more gentle!" she scolded him.

Krause glared down at Claire and Eleana stepped in. She put her hand on Krause's chest to calm him and made her way to Claire's side. Eleana shook her head at her former lover, the hint of a smile touching her lips. "Will you ever learn?" she said as she moved a pillow behind Claire's back.

"Alex," Krause began again.

"It's fine. Cassidy took the kids with my mother and Rose to Maine for the weekend. Besides, Mom has been staying with us. I told you twice, no one is here," Alex assured him. Alex turned to Eleana. She pointed to a chest in the corner of the room. "You'll find some supplies in there. I'll make a call. Just keep an eye on her," Alex instructed the younger agent with a nod toward Brackett.

"Hey!" Claire barked. "I tried to save your ass and this is my thanks? You shoot me and lock me up in some basement on a couch?" Claire complained. Eleana put her face in her hands.

Alex grinned evilly. "I can think of less comfortable accommodations if you prefer."

Claire huffed. "Jesus, I couldn't have been that bad," she muttered.

Alex chuckled in spite of the situation. Claire remained a wildcard, but Alex would have been lying to herself if she had claimed to hate the younger woman. She didn't trust Claire. She did recognize Claire's weakness and it was kneeling beside the wounded Brackett right now. "Save that bravado," Alex said. "You might need it later," she said honestly.

Alex began making her way from the room with Krause and McCollum trailing behind. She deliberately kept her back to both men as she made her way back down the small hallway. This time, she made a turn and headed up a small flight of stairs. Her thoughts had turned from the altercation at Carecom and its implications to the implications her current company held for Cassidy. Alex had scarcely had a second to ponder the reality that followed a few paces behind her. Alex pinched the bridge of her nose as she climbed the stairs and tried to comprehend who was following her lead. She opened the door that led to her father's office.

"Alex," Krause began.

Alex continued to ignore her older brother. She turned and secured the panel in the wall that led to the safe room her father had constructed years ago. Without so much as a glance, she turned and continued to make her way into the hallway. She was not ready to discuss anything, believing that a few more soundless moments would serve them all best. Alex began massaging her temples with her thumbs as she finally reached the hallway and made her way toward the large living room.

"Alexis," McCollum called in a demanding tone. "We need to…"

Alex reached the center of the room and spun on her heels to face him. "Don't," she warned him sternly.

"You can't…"

Alex's voice lowered and her expression darkened. "Don't," she repeated her warning. "I have no idea what I am even going to tell Cassidy about this."

"You have no idea what you are going to tell me about what?" a voice asked from a short distance.

Alex turned as Cassidy entered the doorway that separated the dining room from the living area. She immediately felt the blood drain from her face and her heart plummet in her chest. "I thought you were in Maine?"

Cassidy folded her arms across her chest. "I was on my way. Kenzie has an ear infection. I left you a message," she said.

For a split second all of Alex's thoughts turned to her daughter. "Is she all right?"

"Grumpy," Cassidy said. "She'll be fine. Now, what is it that you need to tell me?" Cassidy asked pointedly. She regarded Alex thoughtfully as Alex stared blankly at her. "Alex?"

"Is Dylan here?" Alex asked, partly hoping to stall for time and needing to know the answer.

"No. He stayed with YaYa and Grandma," Cassidy explained. She pinned Alex with her gaze.

"Cass," Alex drew her wife's name out and shook her head. "This is…"

"Alex. We promised each other—no secrets. None. What on earth are you so afraid to tell me?"

Before Alex could respond, a figure stepped into Cassidy's view. James McCollum offered his daughter a sad smile. It was weak, tinged by both deep regret and boundless love. Cassidy's eyes lifted from Alex's and studied the older man standing just behind her wife. She narrowed her gaze, attempting to process what her heart already knew. He had aged. His once thick blonde hair had thinned and grayed. But, his eyes—his eyes were the same. Green with flecks of gold stared at Cassidy. The brilliance and liveliness had dulled noticeably, but intelligence still sparkled clearly in the changing irises. Cassidy's lips parted slightly then closed tightly in recognition. She stood paralyzed. Time stopped. Thought ceased. Emotion evaporated. This was not possible. She was dreaming. Cassidy tried to close her eyes, hoping that when she opened them again, the figure would vanish, but her eyes would not obey her command. She could not process a thought nor any concrete feeling. Blankly, she stared at the vision before her as if the man facing her were transparent.

Alex moved quickly to Cassidy's side to steady her. She looked into Cassidy's eyes and called to her softly. "Cass? Cassidy, look at me."

"You," was the only word that Cassidy could manage, her eyes penetrating the man a few feet away.

"Cassie," James McCollum took a slight step forward.

Cassidy's eyes finally closed. She licked her lips and shook her head. "I can't," she said.

"Cass?" Alex tried to reach her wife.

Cassidy pried her eyes open and looked into Alex's. "I can't," she said. "I need to look in on Kenzie."

"Cassidy," Alex whispered.

Cassidy touched Alex's cheek to give her some sense of reassurance. "I can't," she repeated so that only Alex could hear her.

Alex watched as Cassidy shook her head again and left the room silently. She desperately wanted to follow. She wanted to fold Cassidy into her arms and take away the pain she saw flickering in the typically playful green eyes she adored. Alex fought back the urge to scream and cry out in anger at the unfairness of the world. Why Cassidy? Cassidy was the kindest person Alex had ever met. Cassidy was compassionate and giving. No one was deserving of this type of deceit—no one, Cassidy least of all. Alex's eyes tracked Cassidy until she disappeared and then turned to bore a hole into the older man facing her.

"Maybe you should," Krause chimed in.

"No," Alex responded, leaving her sight squarely on McCollum. "She needs to be alone right now," Alex said.

"Alexis," McCollum began. "This is not an ideal…"

"Not an ideal what? Situation? No, I would say not," Alex cut him off.

"Cassie will need…"

"I don't need you to tell me what my wife needs," Alex sniped.

"She is my daughter."

"You certainly have an unusual method of parenting," Alex shot.

"Maybe we should take a second here and talk about why we are here," Krause interjected with his suggestion.

Alex moved to face her older brother. "A call would have been nice," she said heatedly.

"Alex, there was no time. You were on the move. It wasn't safe," Krause said.

"It wasn't safe?" Alex asked. "Safe for whom? This is what you call safe? Brackett is bleeding in the basement, Brady and Fallon are cleaning up the mess that was Kargen, and I am standing in front of a man who has been dead for over twenty years—who happens to be my wife's father. What exactly do you find safe in this scenario?"

"Don't play semantics, Alex. You know exactly what I meant," Krause replied evenly.

"Semantics?" Alex raised her voice. "I could give a shit about what words you use, Jonathan. I thought you were looking for our father."

"I thought so too," Krause told her honestly.

"Edmond led you," she began.

"Edmond led you both to what he believes is the truth," McCollum interrupted the dialogue.

"Just how much does your being here endanger my family?" Alex asked pointedly.

"They are my family as well," McCollum replied calmly. Alex remained unflinching. McCollum sighed heavily. "The truth is, Alexis, we are safer in the open now. Hopefully, stopping Kargen will stall their plans."

"Stall?" Alex asked. "What exactly do you think they are planning?" she looked at him curiously.

"Extermination," McCollum answered evenly.

"Of?" Alex asked. She caught the tension in Krause's eyes.

McCollum took a deep breath and answered her honestly. "You."

***

Alex paced the hallway, glancing up the stairs every few seconds. She looked back toward the kitchen and shook her head. She needed to put some space between herself and everyone in the house—everyone except the person who needed space from her. "Oh, Cass," Alex looked up to where Cassidy had disappeared nearly a full hour ago. Alex was not surprised when Cassidy had sent her a text message. It was simple and to the point: Just give me some time.

"What the hell is this all about? Why didn't you warn me, Pip?" Alex mumbled to herself. She had just begun to forcefully rub her temples when she heard a car pull into the driveway. Without waiting, she opened the door and smiled at the woman approaching. "I owe you," she said.

"Again, it would seem," Major Jennifer Garrison replied with a smirk.

"It would seem," Alex agreed as she led her old friend through the door.

"At least, you're not bleeding this time," Jennifer Garrison observed.

"For once," Alex chuckled. She led the surgeon through her mother's house and into her father's study.

"God, Alex....What is this? A fortress?" the surgeon asked when Alex revealed the hidden door in her father's study.

Alex shrugged. "Not a very secure one these days it seems." She led her friend the short distance to her father's safe room and opened the door. "Good luck," Alex mumbled.

Major Garrison poked Alex lightly and made her way to the couch where Claire Brackett was lying. "What is it with your friends?" she asked Alex.

"I'm not her friend," Claire groaned in pain.

"Well, good to see you have a sense of humor," the surgeon commented.

"I'm not kidding," Claire replied.

Eleana looked at Alex helplessly and Alex sighed. "Major Garrison will take care of Claire, I promise." She noted the doubtful expression on Eleana's face. No matter what had passed between any of them, it was obvious that Eleana would always care deeply for Claire. Alex nodded. "Eleana, I promise, she is in the best hands. I promise you," Alex said. "What's the verdict?" she turned her attention to her old friend.

Jennifer Garrison looked at Alex sternly. "It passed through," she explained. "Pretty clean, but Alex, I would prefer to do this in a hospital."

"Not an option."

"Why?" Jennifer Garrison challenged.

"Yeah," Claire chimed. "You hate me that much?"

Alex shook her head. "It's not safe. And not just because I don't trust you," she told Claire. "It's not safe for you."

Jennifer Garrison patted Claire's knee and made her way to Alex. Alex shook her head again. "Alex…"

"Can you treat her here?" Alex asked directly.

"Yes, I can," Jennifer answered. Alex began to turn away and Jennifer grabbed her arm. "I would prefer not to," she said firmly. "You need to give me something here, Alex. She's lost a significant amount of blood. Enough to kill her? No, but enough that I would opt for a transfusion. We're not even beginning to cover possible infection," she explained.

Alex nodded and sighed deeply. She looked over at Claire and grabbed the bridge of her nose. "Look, I am not deliberately keeping you in the dark," Alex promised. "I can't tell you what I don't know."

"Then tell me what you do know."

"The issue is what I don't know, Jen," Alex explained.

"Alex, Kargen is dead and his men," Eleana began to protest.

"Yes, but we don't have the surveillance from the building. Not any of it. The discs are gone for a three hour period. Maybe, maybe we can recover the hard drive, but that will take time. Normally, I would opt to call in a favor at Quantico. Given certain developments, I don't think that is our best option," she said. "We have no idea who else was in that building," Alex said. "We have to assume that they all know that we were. That compromises Claire as much as it does me, you, or anyone else," Alex told Eleana.

"Hanscom is a secure facility," Jennifer started to argue.

"No," Alex said. She smiled sadly at her old friend. "You need to trust me on this one, Jen. No place is secure, least of all Hanscom. Like it or not, and believe me when I tell you, I do not like it—this is our best option right now." Alex pointed to her father's chest. "There are supplies in there," she said. "If you need something else, we'll secure it."

"Jesus, Alex. What the hell are you into?" Jennifer asked.

"Even if I knew, I wouldn't tell you," Alex said honestly. "You're safer that way. I'm not even sure I want to know," she admitted.

"Me neither," Claire mumbled. Alex smiled slightly.

"She'll need to be in a more…"

"I have a place for her," Alex said. "Just not yet, Jen. Please? You let Eleana know what you need. I promise you, I will make sure Claire gets whatever you deem necessary. You have my word."

Jennifer Garrison nodded reluctantly and returned to her patient.

"Alex?" Eleana caught hold of Alex's arm as she was leaving.

"Trust me, Eleana. This is for the best right now, for Claire too."

"I know," Eleana admitted sadly. "What about Cassidy?" Krause had brought some clean towels and some food down for Eleana and apprised her of the situation upstairs.

Alex shook her head. "I don't know," she said. "Seems I don't know much right now. I promise you I am going to find out."

"I don't know what to believe about him," Eleana referenced Cassidy's father. "But, I do believe her," Eleana admitted. Alex tipped her head in confusion. "Claire," Eleana said with a nod toward the sofa. "That she was trying to shoot Kargen."

Alex looked over at Claire and nodded. "I know. So do I."

***

"So? What's the verdict on the patient?" Krause asked Alex as she entered the kitchen.

"She'll live."

"You believe her?" Krause asked.

"That she was trying to shoot Kargen to keep him from killing me?" Alex asked. Krause lifted a brow. "Yeah. I believe her. That doesn't explain why she was there, and I can't help but wonder who she was with."

"Did you ask her?" Krause wondered.

Alex ignored the question. "Did you talk to Brady?"

"Change the subject much?" Krause challenged.

"No, I didn't ask her. In case you hadn't noticed, she's loopier than usual," Alex said. "So? Brady?"

"They're secure. Still not sure how anyone wiped the server in security," he said.

"There are plenty of people with that ability," McCollum commented absently.

Alex let out a disgusted chuckle. "That begs the question who was with Claire."

"What makes you think anyone was with Claire? This is Brackett we are talking about," Krause reminded her.

"I know. Brackett is impulsive, Pip, not stupid."

A small smile tugged at Krause's lips when Alex used his nickname. Her anger had not escaped him. He could hardly blame her. Krause was confronting a host of emotions himself. He still had no idea what to believe about the man sitting across from him. He understood that this was Cassidy's father, but a part of him still wanted to doubt that fact. He had expected to

180

find Nicolaus Toles, or perhaps no one. James McCollum had not even been a thought. He looked at the older man. "You owe us all some explanations."

McCollum nodded and looked at Alex. "There was no other way. I had to…"

"Not now," Alex stopped him.

"Alex," Krause urged her.

"Not now, Pip," Alex repeated herself. She looked directly into the older man's eyes. "I have someone else that needs me right now," she said. "It has held for over twenty years. It will hold a while longer," she said. "Find out all you can from Brady," she told Krause. "Have him get whatever Jen needs for Claire," she instructed.

"You're going to keep her here?" he asked.

"You have a better idea?"

"No," he confessed. Alex nodded and turned away. "Where are you going?"

"Where I'm needed," Alex replied.

***

Alex left Krause with Cassidy's father in the kitchen. She was frustrated and sickened by the appearance of James McCollum. There were more than a few reasons to act with caution where her long-dead father-in-law was concerned. Right now, the most important of those was upstairs. Enough time had passed. Alex needed to search out Cassidy. She climbed the stairs and made her way into the bedroom her parents had once shared. Cassidy was looking out of the window. Alex stopped just inside the door and struggled to take in a full breath. Before she could muster a thought, Cassidy spoke.

"Tell me it's not real," Cassidy said without turning to face her wife.

Alex exhaled slowly. "Cass…" Cassidy shook her head and looked at the ceiling, never turning to look at the woman who shared her life. "Cassidy…"

Cassidy turned slowly and looked at Alex helplessly. "What kind of person does that?" she asked sharply.

"I don't know," Alex confessed.

Cassidy closed her eyes and ran her tongue over her bottom lip. As her eyes opened, she looked upward reflectively. "I remember my mother, so many nights, Alex….So many nights she called for him. Her voice was always hollow when she would call his name… 'Jim…Why?' Over and over."

"Cass," Alex started. Cassidy shook her head. She felt as if her heart had been wrenched in a vice grip. "Cassidy," Alex called gently. "I don't know why. Maybe, he loved you and just saw no other way out—for any of you," Alex said honestly. "I don't know what that means or who that means he is. He is, after it is all said and done—he is your father."

"And, what kind of person does that make me?" Cassidy asked desperately.

Alex's heart broke at the sight before her. The betrayal, the fear, the disbelief she saw in Cassidy's eyes was an unfamiliar sight. Cassidy was lost. "You? You are the best person I know, Cass."

Cassidy shook her head in self-loathing. "No."

"Yes, Cass."

Cassidy looked at Alex. "Do you know how many nights I have laid awake, some small part of me wishing for this day? Do you have any idea? Any idea how many times I wished that he would walk through that door? That he would tell me it was all a mistake, pick me up and kiss my cheek like he always did?"

"Cassidy…."

"Alex….Now…Now here he is, the man I have worshiped my entire life. The man I mourned in some small way at the happiest moments in my life. Now, here he is and I can't even look at him—my own father. That look, I see it in his eyes, Alex, like it was yesterday that he said goodbye for the last time… 'See you at the castle, my Cassie,' that's what he said. That's what he always said. I can't even look at him. My own father. What kind of person does that make me?"

Alex stepped forward and closed the distance between them. She brushed her hand across Cassidy's cheek and then tilted Cassidy's chin upward. "You," Alex said. "You are the most compassionate, forgiving woman I have ever known, Cass," Alex told her wife.

Cassidy's eyes finally welled with tears. "Why?" Cassidy asked as she collapsed into Alex's arms, sobs racking her body.

Alex held Cassidy close. She felt utterly helpless as she supported Cassidy's weight and caressed her back tenderly. What could she say? There were no words for this. Alex had tried to prepare herself to come face to face with her own father. This was beyond any possibility in her imagination. She kissed the top of Cassidy's head as Cassidy clung to her and spoke the only words she could summon. "Vous êtes ma vie, Cassidy. Je t'aime ... Toujours, Cass. Toujours. (You are my life, Cassidy. I love you...always, Cass. Always)."

***

"You're sure it's done?" Daniels asked.

"It's done. The distraction worked perfectly," a young Army Lieutenant assured the ambassador.

"I hope you are right," Daniels commented.

"Relax," Admiral Brackett piped up. "It went better than we had hoped," he said as he pocketed his phone.

"Come again?" Daniels asked.

The Admiral smiled at the young lieutenant in front of him. "You are dismissed Lieutenant," he said. Admiral Brackett waited for the young man to disappear from his sight and turned back to the ambassador. "Dmitri, I understand, will be out of our hair."

"And that is a good thing?" Daniels was beginning to question Admiral Brackett's sanity.

"He was an annoying fly."

"Yes, who happens to be Viktor's nephew," Daniels observed.

Admiral Brackett scoffed at Daniels' concern. "Kargen was stupid and irresponsible," he said flatly. "He knew too much that could compromise us, and our hands are clean."

"Really?" Daniels challenged the older man. "Just how did Kargen meet his maker?"

"Unclear at this point. It appears Alexis may have taken care of that particular problem for us," Admiral Brackett gloated.

"You seem pretty sure of that. Something you would like to share?" Daniels wondered.

"Not particularly, no. It isn't important one way or the other. I don't answer to Viktor Ivanov and neither do you."

"No," Daniels agreed. "I know that and you know that, but Viktor does not share that opinion. You and I both know that. He needs to be controlled. We don't need him as our adversary, Bill. And, I for one do not want him in possession of Lynx," Daniels said. Admiral Brackett smiled broadly. "What aren't you telling me?" Daniels asked the Admiral.

"All in good time, Ambassador."

***

"What did Steven have to say?" McCollum asked Krause.

Krause sat down and leaned back in his chair. "Casual," he observed. "Your familiarity with Agent Brady is curious."

"Not so curious," McCollum replied. "Spend a year with someone in the confines of the hell hole you found me in—you get 'familiar,' as you put it."

"Enlighten me, Mr. McCollum."

"I think we've covered that," McCollum responded. Eleana chose that moment to enter the kitchen with Jennifer Garrison. "How is Claire?" McCollum asked with genuine concern.

Eleana looked at him in disgust. "You almost sound like you care."

"I do care, Eleana," McCollum said genuinely. "A great deal more than you realize."

"She's sleeping right now," Jennifer Garrison replied. She turned her attention to Krause. "Where is Alex?" she asked.

"With Cassidy," he said. "Trust me, you don't want to know."

Jennifer nodded. A corpse could feel the emotional tension in the house. "She'll need an actual bed," Jennifer told him. "She needs rest—a lot of it."

"That could be a challenge," Eleana said honestly

Jennifer grinned. She had no doubt that her patient could be a handful. Even in severe pain, with a fair amount of disorientation, Claire Brackett was a handful. She reminded the surgeon a bit of a young Army Lieutenant she had treated years ago. "I've no doubt," she said. "You need to watch her for infection. Make sure her fever does not spike suddenly, look for redness—you know the drill," she said. Eleana and Krause both nodded their understanding. "I took the liberty," she said as she handed Eleana a prescription. "It's made out for Alex. No one would question the script with her back injury. It will help with Claire's pain, and help to keep her quiet. Although, that sprained ankle will likely be the thing that forces her off her feet for a few days. If she does move, it will be slowly."

"Anything else?" Krause asked.

Jennifer considered her response for a moment. "I want to check on her in a couple days. Tell Alex that is non-negotiable. I'll stop by Tuesday sometime. Alex knows how to reach me if anything changes."

"I'll walk you out," Eleana offered. She started from the room with Jennifer keeping pace. "Major?" Eleana began as they reached the door. "Is Claire honestly all right?"

Jennifer Garrison released a slow breath. "She means a great deal to you," she observed.

"Yes," Eleana replied.

Jennifer nodded. "Physically she will recover fully. I expect she'll be wanting to move by the time I come back."

"But?"

"Eleana, what do you know about Claire's background?"

"Probably more than anyone," Eleana said.

"I had a feeling. Your presence calms her."

"Did she say something when I left the room?" Eleana wondered.

"No," Jennifer said. "Nothing discernable anyway. There are some signs…When she was fading out, she grabbed onto me as if I were a lifeline, as if something had terrified her. In another situation, I might chalk that up to trauma over today's incident—whatever led to her being shot. This," Jennifer looked over Eleana's shoulder. "Well, I think I can safely guess that the majority of that trauma will be felt in that shoulder."

"I don't understand," Eleana said. "Was she dreaming?"

"Maybe. Eleana?"

"It's nothing. It's just that was common when we were kids."

Jennifer nodded. "It's a symptom of PTSD," she said. "Sometimes, latent memory can cause it—the dreaming, I mean."

"I don't know…."

"It's okay," Jennifer said. "Just watch her, Eleana. The shock, the medication, whatever stress is occurring here…Those things might conspire to surface her emotions or if it is something she has repressed…"

"I think I understand."

"Call me if you need me or if anything changes," Jennifer said as she opened the door. "And, tell Alex she owes me—big time."

Eleana chuckled. "I'll remind her." She closed the door and leaned against it for a moment. *Oh, Claire, what haven't you told me?*

***

Alex had been gone for well over an hour. Cassidy had cried in Alex's arms for much of that time. Alex could not remember a time when she had felt so helpless. Finally, Cassidy had calmed and slept for a short time, overwhelmed by emotional exhaustion. When Cassidy awoke, she had encouraged Alex to go and let her take a shower.

Alex suspected that on some level, Cassidy hoped to wash away the anger, questions, and sadness that were encompassing her. Alex also understood that it would take a great deal more than a hot shower to accomplish that endeavor. She wasn't even certain time could heal this. Alex took a deep breath and steadied her nerves as she made her way down the stairs.

"How is she?" McCollum asked as Alex entered the kitchen.

Alex looked directly at the older man as she addressed Krause and Eleana. "I need to speak with Mr. McCollum privately," she said.

Eleana took Krause's hand. She sensed his reluctance and pulled on him slightly to lead him from the room. "Alex," Krause began to protest her request.

"It's fine," she assured her brother. "I promise, I won't kill him," she said. She waited for the pair to make their exit, her eyes burrowing into the man a few paces away.

"How is Cassie?" he repeated his question.

"Confused. Angry. Hurt. How do you think she is?" Alex replied. She desperately wanted to tear the older man limb from limb.

"You don't understand, Alexis. There was no other way to protect them."

Alex shrugged. "Could have offed yourself for real," she said honestly.

McCollum nodded. "There were things that needed to be addressed. Your father…."

"My father is not the issue."

"Your father is the only reason any of us have made it this far," he said pointedly. "He did exactly as you suggest."

"Brave," Alex commented sarcastically. "Check out when the shitstorm you created blows home."

"None of us wanted this," McCollum said. "By the time we realized how deep things had gotten, there was no other answer. They would have killed Rose and Cassie to get to me—maybe worse. They would have killed you if they had any idea Nicolaus knew I was alive. If they knew who he really was…What he had become privy to, what he was doing from the inside—they would have killed all of you, Alex. That doesn't begin to cover what they would have made of you all back then. Sometimes, you have to make sacrifices…"

Alex chuckled bitterly. "Sacrifice? What is it with you? How fucking selfish are you? If you wanted to protect her, you should have stayed dead."

"If it were Dylan and Mackenzie? If it were you, Alexis? If it were you that put Cassidy at risk? You would have done whatever you had to do, even what I did."

Alex shook her head in disgust. "No. I would never leave them, not by choice," she said assuredly. "Not ever. I promised Cass that a long time ago. I committed that to her when I married her. I promised Dylan," she said. "I promised myself." McCollum listened silently. "Don't compare me to you. And, don't compare me to my father. You both took the coward's way out. You left your children. You left them to wonder and to mourn. And, for what? To protect us? Protect us from who? You?"

"It's not that simple, Alexis. You know that much," McCollum said. "Sometimes, there is no good choice to make. Family is…"

"Everything," Alex finished his sentence. "I know. Cass taught me that," she said. Alex sighed. She looked at the older man and rubbed her temples. "You don't owe me any explanation," she said. "Don't expect me to trust you," she said honestly. "Not with my children, and not with Cass."

McCollum nodded. "Fair enough."

"None of this is fair," Alex said honestly. "None of it."

Cassidy walked into the kitchen to find her wife facing off with her father. James McCollum stood with his back to his daughter. Cassidy looked at Alex. "Alex, could I have a moment—please?"

McCollum turned deliberately to face his daughter. Alex remained still. She regarded Cassidy silently and frowned. Nothing within Alex compelled her to want to leave her wife alone with the man in the kitchen. Lineage, parentage, history aside, he was a stranger. He might have been Cassidy's father, but that did little to bolster Alex's trust in the man. She exhaled a ragged breath and remained in place.

"Alex," Cassidy called gently. "Please," she implored her wife. Alex closed her eyes, shook her head and made her way to Cassidy. Cassidy looked at her lovingly. "I'll be all right," Cassidy promised.

Alex remained unconvinced. She glanced back at the older man with a gaze that communicated her silent warning. He met her challenge without expression. Alex kissed her wife on the forehead. "I'm going to go check on Kenzie. If you need me…"

Cassidy smiled warmly at Alex. "I know," she said honestly. Alex looked back at James McCollum one last time, bent down, kissed Cassidy on the lips and hesitantly took her leave.

Cassidy stood in place and looked at the man a few paces away. She had played her questions and her words over and over again like a broken record. Now, she seemed to lose all conscious thought in a violent undertow of emotion.

"Cassie," he addressed his daughter. "She loves you a great deal," he observed.

Cassidy smiled earnestly in spite of the situation. "Yes, she does," Cassidy agreed. "Not half as much as I love her—believe me," she told him.

McCollum nodded. He was struck by the devotion to Cassidy he had seen in Alex's eyes as she addressed him. He saw the exact same expression in his daughter's now. "Cassie, I know that you…"

Cassidy held up her hand. "No," she stopped him. "You don't get to do that. You don't get to walk in here after all these years and assume you know anything about me," she said firmly.

McCollum nodded again. "You must have questions," he said.

"Right now? Right now, I am not interested in your answers," Cassidy said honestly. "Nothing you could say to me would change anything. I want you to hear what I have to say."

"I'm listening," he said.

Cassidy took a deep breath and let it out slowly. She licked her lips and pressed them together tightly for a moment. "You broke my heart," she said pointedly. "You broke Mom's heart. You left us. Worse, you left us by choice in a lie that I cannot even fathom," she said. She closed her eyes and tried to steady the wave of emotion descending upon her. "I said goodbye to my father as a child."

"I'm sorry, Cassie. I don't expect you to forgive me. If I could have changed anything…"

"What? If you could have changed anything?" Cassidy asked, her voice dripping with venom. "What would you have changed?"

"All of it," he said. "But, if I had…"

"Don't you dare," Cassidy warned him. "Don't." Cassidy looked upward, sighed heavily, and then returned her focus to her father. She closed her eyes in a futile attempt to stave off her mounting tears. "Do you know how many nights I prayed that you would walk through that door?" she asked him. Her voice dropped to a faint whisper. "Do you know how much I want to hate you right now?" McCollum took a step closer just as Cassidy opened her eyes. She shook her head and held up her hand again. "I should hate you," she said softly as her tears began to flow over forcefully.

McCollum stepped up to his daughter and wrapped his arms around her as she started to sob. Cassidy struck him with her fists forcefully. "How could you?" she pounded his flesh. McCollum only held on tighter. "How could you leave me?" she demanded. "How could you?" Cassidy collapsed into his arms.

"My Cassie," he said lovingly as he began to rock her. "I missed you."

"I should hate you," she cried, helpless to do anything but allow the man she once considered her knight in shining armor to hold her.

"I know," he said.

"Why can't I hate you?" she asked in frustration.

James McCollum kissed the top of his daughter's head. "Because you are a better person than I am, Cassie. A better person than anyone I know," he said proudly. "You don't have the ability to hate, Princess. It's not who you are."

Cassidy cried into her father's chest. "You're not real," she said repeatedly. "This is not real."

McCollum sighed. He stroked Cassidy's back and silently cursed himself for the pain he had caused the person he loved more than anyone. He could list his reasons. He could mount his defense. All of those reasons he once believed justified his actions had been suddenly reduced to nothing beyond pathetic excuses. Alex was right. He was a coward. "I love you, Cassie," he told her as she continued to sob in his arms.

Chapter Eleven

"Agent Brady, I need you to be clear," Jane Merrow said.

"I'm being as clear as I possibly can be."

"What do you mean there was nothing on the security server at Carecom?" she asked.

"What part of that was unclear, Jane?" he asked in frustration. "Who else was there?" he asked her.

"How should I know that?"

"Don't jerk my chain," Brady said abrasively. "In case you missed some part of what I just told you, Fallon nearly was killed, Alex nearly got shot, Brackett did, and McCollum offed Kargen, so I would like to know what you haven't told me."

"Steven..."

"Not good enough, Jane. I've followed your lead for the last two years. A good part of which I spent locked away in something akin to a fucking dungeon with a dead man, so do me a favor? Why don't you give me a clear picture for a change?"

"Sometimes, Steven, it is safer not to know everything. Have you forgotten that? What happens when you end up in the chair that Dmitri's cohorts are in now?" Jane challenged him.

"Protect the assets...."

"You are the asset, Steven," Jane reminded him. "You think this is fun for me? It isn't. I might remind you how I ended up in this position."

Steven Brady huffed and then relented. "I do remember," he said. "But, Jane, someone else was there. You're telling me that you have no idea who that was?" he asked her. Silence hung in the air. "Brackett did not go there alone. How would she even know to look there? Why would she bother?" he asked. Silence. "Where is Marcus?" Brady asked.

Jane sighed. "Steven, you need to trust me on this one. Please."

"It's not an issue of trust. It's an issue of transparency."

"He's on his way to Joshua now."

"Tate? Why Tate?" Brady wondered.

"Steven, Joshua can utilize things that even I cannot right now."

"Marcus took that footage," Brady surmised.

"Only part of it, and he did not wipe the server," Jane said.

"Then who did?"

"I don't know and that is a concern. If it wasn't you and it wasn't Marcus, assuming Dmitri's men are telling you the truth…"

"Who else would have interest?" he asked.

"Use your imagination," she said. "Just trust me. Let Joshua take this one."

"What about Hawk?"

"Successful."

"Do I want to know what was in the package she delivered?" he asked.

"Probably best you don't," Jane replied.

"What do you want me to do now?" Brady asked.

"Stick with Agent Fallon for now. Let Alex call the shots," Jane said.

"You know, she's not going to let you off so easily."

"No, I don't expect she will."

"What are you going to tell her?" Brady asked.

"The truth," Jane said. "It's all I have left."

***

March 3rd

The late evening had stretched into early morning quickly. Alex wanted answers, concrete ones. She needed them to plan her next move. Something more important needed to take precedence—Cassidy. The emotional tension in the house was palpable. Everyone was raw. Alex worried that the answers they each sought might serve as a tipping point to disaster if she persisted now. A few hours would not make any difference in her efforts.

Claire needed to be attended to. Cassidy needed Alex, and Alex needed to step away and be with Cassidy. She needed to center herself, and Cassidy remained the place that Alex could do that. Telling Cassidy the details of what had transpired would not be easy. Informing Cassidy that Claire Brackett would be their guest was not something Alex was looking forward to.

"Cass?" Alex asked gently as Cassidy stepped into the bedroom. She could tell from the redness surrounding Cassidy's eyes that Cassidy had been crying. "Are you okay?"

"I will be," Cassidy promised. She smiled at Alex who was stretched out on the bed with Mackenzie cuddled beside her.

"What did he say?" Alex asked.

"Nothing really," Cassidy said as she flopped down on the other side of Mackenzie. She kissed their daughter's head and looked at Alex. "I didn't give him a chance to say much," she admitted. Cassidy looked at Alex. "I love you," she said.

Alex smiled. "Where did that come from?"

"He did tell me a few things," Cassidy said.

"Oh?" Alex asked curiously.

"He told me how he ended up here," Cassidy raised a brow. Alex sighed. "Where is Claire?" Cassidy asked.

"What?" Alex startled slightly.

"He told me, Alex…What happened at Carecom tonight."

"Jesus…"

"You would have told me and I forced the issue of how he got here."

Alex nodded. "Right now, she's in the safe room."

"You can't leave her there," Cassidy said.

"I know. You're not mad?" Alex asked.

Cassidy looked down at Mackenzie and then back at Alex. "Mad? I don't know what I am, Alex. I haven't had time to examine that. From what he told me, Claire Brackett tried to save your life. Is that true?" Cassidy asked. Alex nodded. "Why?"

"I don't know. My best guess is that it has something to do with Eleana," Alex explained. "Cass, what about…"

"I don't know where to begin," Cassidy said. "I mean, I don't even know why he is back. I don't even know why he left. What do you think?" Cassidy asked Alex. "That man, he looks like my father. I know it is him, but I don't know who he is," Cassidy observed painfully.

"I know. I'm not sure right now is the time. You've been through enough today."

"What about you?" Cassidy asked.

"I'm fine," Alex said. "Just worried about you."

"Ummm. Nice try, Agent Toles. I haven't lost my sight nor my hearing. You were groaning before I came in here, and you are not exactly walking straight."

Alex chuckled. "My back is hardly anything for you to worry about."

"I always worry about you, Alex. I almost lost you tonight."

"But, you didn't," Alex reminded Cassidy.

"What now?" Cassidy asked.

"Now? Now, I get Pip and we move Claire into Nicky's old room. Your father can stay in the safe room."

"You don't think he would…"

Alex sighed heavily. "No, I don't think he's a threat to us, but I'm not going out of my way to make him comfortable." Cassidy bit back a smile at the protective tone in Alex's voice. Alex rose slowly from the bed. "Do you want me to put Kenzie down?"

Cassidy looked at their daughter and shook her head. "No," she answered. "Would you mind if she slept with us tonight?"

Alex smiled. "Not at all," she said. "I'll be back once everyone is settled. Try and rest." Alex leaned over and kissed Cassidy gently. "I love you, Cass."

"I know. Alex, I don't know how to…."

"You don't need to figure anything out now. Just snuggle Kenzie and relax. I'll be back soon, I promise."

"Alex?"

"Yeah?"

"Do you think he means it?" Cassidy asked softly. Alex was perplexed. "My father," Cassidy said.

"Do I think he means what?"

"That he loves me?" Cassidy asked tearfully.

Alex thought the sadness that rose within her would choke her. "I'm sure of it," Alex said.

"How can you be?"

Alex smiled. She hardly trusted James McCollum, and she had her own set of emotions to sort out regarding his return. She could not stand seeing Cassidy in so much pain. It infuriated her and it broke her heart at the same time. No matter what her concerns, she had seen the way James McCollum looked at his daughter. Alex had never met anyone that disliked

Cassidy. She doubted that very many people would have that capacity. She moved back to the bed and kissed Cassidy's head.

"He loves you, Cass. I can't promise you anything else, but I believe that. He does love you." Cassidy nodded weakly and pulled Mackenzie closer to her. "Rest," Alex said again. "I'll be back soon. I love you."

***

Claire moaned slightly and Eleana flinched at the sound. "Claire?" Eleana called to her. Krause set Claire on the bed as gently as he could manage and stepped away. "Claire?" Eleana called again.

"Hey," Claire opened her eyes slightly. "What are you doing here?"

Eleana smiled gently and brushed the hair out of Claire's eyes. "You don't remember," she said. "It's the medicine," she told Claire.

"So tired," Claire said.

"I know you are," Eleana replied. She looked at Claire and struggled not to cry. Claire looked fragile, lost. It reminded Eleana of a young girl she knew many years ago. "Just sleep," she said.

Krause made his way from the room, not wanting to disrupt the private moment inside. He smiled at Alex as her foot hit the top of the stairs.

"How is she?" Alex asked.

Krause shrugged. "How's your other guest?" he asked.

"I don't know, Pip. Did he say anything to you?"

"Not much."

"What do you think?" Alex asked.

"About him?" Krause asked for clarification. Alex nodded. "I don't know, Alex. I have a feeling this has something to do with some project called Lynx. That place where he was?"

"Yeah?"

"Alex, there's a lot more we need to talk about," he said.

Alex nodded. "Not tonight," she said wearily letting her gaze fall to the end of the hallway where Cassidy awaited her.

"How is she?" Krause wondered.

"How would you be?"

"I don't know," he confessed. "Honestly, I didn't know what I was going to do if...."

"If you had found our father instead. I know. I thought about that too—constantly, in fact. I just can't imagine what would make someone do that," Alex told her brother.

"You know, Claire was aiming for Kargen. We were just coming in when you knocked her back with that shot."

Alex looked toward the room that Claire was in. "Yeah, I know she did."

"You think it's about Eleana, don't you?" he asked.

Alex sensed Krause's worry. "Jonathan...."

"She still loves her."

"Maybe. She's in love with you, though. If you weren't so dense you'd do something about that," Alex said.

"I don't think my love life is really a hot issue right now," Krause replied.

"No?" Alex challenged him. "If you hadn't gotten there when you did, it might be me that Brady and Fallon were cleaning up after and not Kargen."

"Don't even go there," Krause warned. "There's no point."

"Wrong. It's the only point. Any one of us could be Dmitri. You're just wasting time," Alex said.

"Easy for you to say."

"Not really," Alex replied. "Stop fighting it."

"What about Claire?" Krause tried to change the subject.

"Time will tell. For now, we keep her close."

"You trust her?" Krause asked.

"No. I am curious. And, that is enough right now," she explained just as Eleana emerged. "How's she doing?"

"I managed to get another pill into her. I think she'll sleep for a while," Eleana said.

Alex nodded. "You have my old room," Alex said to Eleana. "Unless you prefer the guest room," she winked. "Goodnight."

Eleana smiled. "You tired?" she asked Krause.

"Not really," he said.

"Up for some company?"

Krause smiled. "Yeah, I think I am."

***

"And?" Tate asked

"They are all together."

"It worked," he said.

"It appears so. I just hope we're right about this," Jane said.

"It was inevitable. You didn't have a choice. Now, you know where The Sparrow sits," Tate said.

"Perhaps," Jane replied.

"You suspect something, don't you?" Tate inquired.

"I suspect many things."

"You think McCollum is still hiding something?" he asked.

"From me? Definitely. But, he won't hide it from Alex, at least, I don't believe he will."

"Jane, you think this is really what led to John's assassination?"

"Partly. Partly, I think it was the fact that he was onto O'Brien," Jane said.

"Any idea yet who placed O'Brien?" Tate asked.

"There are the usual trails to Congress—The Admiral, General Compton, that upper echelon. That's not what concerns me. The bigger question is whether or not someone placed him with Cassidy, and if they did, who made that call? Congress came later. The question is what O'Brien's real objective was."

"You think someone set him up at Stanford to meet Cassidy?"

"I think that is a distinct possibility—yes," Jane admitted.

"I need to ask you something," Tate said cautiously.

"Go ahead."

"It's bothered me for a long time. It's been eclipsed by more pressing matters. O'Brien's car accident that weekend in D.C.? Why? That didn't fit with the letters. Why would they implement something like that when they already had the letters?"

Jane's answer came in the form of one name. "Nicolaus."

"Alex's father arranged that?" he asked. Jane nodded. "Why?"

Jane opened her eyes and looked squarely at Joshua Tate. "At that point, he'd hoped O'Brien's demise would signal the same for Carl Fisher."

"Jesus Christ. Are you saying that O'Brien put Fisher on Cassidy?" Jane's sorrowful gaze answered the question. "Why?"

"To flush out Lynx, I would imagine," Jane said.

"Jesus Christ. The letters? He orchestrated that so Fisher could have free reign with Cassidy? Just to try and flush out someone that no one was even sure was alive?"

"It's not as crazy as it sounds," Jane told him. "Sphinx holds a lot of cards, Joshua. No one knew who that was. Everyone wanted what he had."

"And so...What? It just went awry?" Tate was confused.

"Even O'Brien couldn't have guessed what a nut job Fisher was. I doubt he expected Fisher would become honestly infatuated with Cassidy."

Jane was hoping that was the truth. She recalled that time vividly. Her husband, John Merrow had spent hours pacing the halls of The White House, worrying about Cassidy O'Brien and her son Dylan. It was a story that only a handful of people understood with any clarity, and the majority of those people still only held glimpses of the truth. And, it was the story that had led Alex Toles to meet Cassidy O'Brien.

Then Congressman Christopher O'Brien had begun to receive a stream of threatening letters. At first, President John Merrow had stayed out of the fray. When he was apprised that the letters had targeted Cassidy, his involvement had changed. John Merrow shared something with Cassidy O'Brien that only three people in the world knew about at that time. He was her son's biological father. It had never been discussed between Cassidy and President Merrow. He was certain of that truth. In her own way, Cassidy had acknowledged it silently many times, and John Merrow had no intention of allowing harm to come to his family. For the president, that family included Cassidy and Dylan. When he had begun to suspect Congressman O'Brien's connection to the letters, John Merrow had reached out to the one person he believed would help in any way that he could— Nicolaus Toles.

"Joshua, John went to Nicolaus immediately when he began to suspect that O'Brien might be complicit. He felt he owed it to Nicolaus to tell him that he was going to involve Alex," Jane explained. "And, he knew that as angry as Nicolaus would be, he would help."

"Why?" Tate asked.

Jane sighed. This was a story she had yet to share with anyone outside the innermost circle of her life. "Nicolaus, Jim, and Edmond were best friends," she said. "From what my father told John, they were more like brothers. I don't know all the details, Joshua. I know more now than I did then. There are things that they kept close to the vest, so close that even I have yet to uncover it all. I do know that O'Brien put Fisher on Cassidy— intimately speaking. At whose behest remains a question that none of us have been able to answer. And, that answer would tell us many things. That is what Jim was hoping he could get O'Brien to divulge."

Tate tried to take in all the information. "I thought Claire had been pulling Fisher's strings."

"Claire? She might like to think so, but no. She thought O'Brien was a pawn then. Really, she was his. They used her long history with Fisher. She and Fisher had known each other since childhood."

"That seems to be a theme," Tate observed.

"It is, and not an accidental one," Jane told him.

"Well, now you have them all under one roof, or close to it. You really think that's the answer?"

"I don't know if there is an answer, Joshua. At least, this might be a solution to the immediate problem. Ivanov is the least of our worries now."

"The Admiral?" he guessed. Jane nodded. "What is his agenda?"

"Duty."

"To what end?" Tate asked.

"That really is the question, isn't it?" Jane said. "The other is who is playing on his team besides Daniels. We both know there are more assets there."

"You know, I can listen in almost anywhere," he told his friend. "That doesn't mean I will hear anything that can help you."

"I know, but we have to try. Keep digging. Hawk will meet up with you before she heads to Alex."

"You're sure this is necessary?" he asked. "This plan to compromise Rand?"

"I'm not sure of much anymore," Jane said. "This has been in motion a long time. It was a contingency plan long ago. Before Viktor or The Admiral make a move, we need to put them on the defensive."

"Strickland?"

"Not my problem. He put himself in this when he…"

"You think he knew about John's assassination beforehand, don't you?"

"He knew. He doesn't know who made that final call. I intend to find that out," she said assuredly. "His ambition has always been greater than his conscience. Now, his legacy is threatened," she said harshly. "He cared more about sitting in the Oval Office than he did about John's life, maybe even than his own. But, no one wants to go down in history as the losing president in a war."

"Is that where this is headed? War?" Tate asked nervously.

"There is more than one kind of war," Jane reminded him. "There are always people who gain at the expense of those who lose. You know that. John understood that intimately. Strickland only cares about his own neck."

"That's why you want to compromise Rand?" he looked for clarification.

"Rand cannot get what MyoGen has. If Ivanov and the Russian contingent get MyoGen's research and blend it with what they already have developed—if they get MyoGen's records somehow…Joshua, that cannot happen."

"Why not just take what MyoGen has now?" he asked.

"That's what Alex is trying to do. She doesn't have any idea what it is she is taking possession of. At least, she didn't a few days ago. MyoGen is the offspring of Lynx. Trust me, we need what they have intact—for now."

"Jane, if Alex finds out that we had anything to do with Rand…."

"She won't."

"What if McCollum tells them?" he asked.

"He can't. He doesn't know."

"When?" Tate asked.

"Soon," Jane replied. "Deal with Hawk. I'll deal with Alex."

"Good luck with that," Tate said.

Jane chuckled. "Luck might be exactly what we all need right now."

***

"Jonathan?" Eleana said softly.

"Hum?"

"What is it?"

Krause offered Eleana a reassuring smile. "Just thinking."

"I see. Thinking about Cassidy?" she guessed.

"Thinking about all of us," he corrected her, "but, yes. I can't imagine how she must feel."

"I know. What do you think this Lynx program is all about? You do think that is why he left, don't you?"

"I'm sure that's the reason he will give."

Eleana studied Krause's expression. "What?"

"I have some ideas what it was or is," he confessed. "None of them are good."

"There's something else bothering you," she observed. He just smiled uncomfortably. Eleana sighed. "I see. Is it me and Claire that is bothering you or is it you and me?"

"Eleana…"

"Talk to me, Jonathan—please."

"I don't know what to think," Krause admitted.

"About what?" Eleana questioned him.

"Eleana, I'm not who you think I am."

"And, who is it that I think you are? Enlighten me. Apparently, you know my thoughts better than I do."

Krause covered his eyes. "You don't understand…The things I did…Things I have done…"

"I understand more than you give me credit for," she replied.

Krause removed his hands from his eyes and looked at her. "How can you even…"

"Can you change any of those things, Jonathan? Even one of them?"

"If I could…"

"That's not what I asked you. Now. Right now, can you change any of those moments?" she challenged him.

"No. That doesn't change who that makes me."

"It doesn't make you anyone," Eleana told him. "What makes me who I am?" she asked.

Krause smiled. "You would never…"

"You don't know that. I never confronted those choices."

"You would never have put yourself in that position," he argued.

Eleana sighed in frustration. "Jonathan, sometimes," Eleana's thoughts trailed momentarily and she closed her eyes before continuing. "Sometimes people change."

"We're not talking about me now, are we?" he guessed. "Eleana, Claire is not likely to change. People don't…"

Eleana opened her eyes and shook her head. "Claire was not always the person you know," she said honestly. "There is another Claire. Another side to her…Lost long ago," she said sadly.

"You still love her," he surmised.

Eleana smiled. "I will always love Claire," she said honestly. "I am not in love with Claire. She is not as hard as you think."

"Maybe that's what you need to believe," Krause said.

"No," she sighed heavily. "You are sitting here mulling over a past that you can't change. Thinking about your father, both of them. Thinking about John. Wondering…Am I right? How you ended up here, right now?"

"What does that have to do with anything?"

"It has everything to do with everything," she said. Eleana took a seat on the bed next to the man she loved. "Claire's father loved to tell her stories, every night, in fact," she said. Krause looked at her curiously. "When we were small and I would stay there, he would sit at the end of the bed. Sometimes he read from a book, sometimes he just made them up."

"I can't even imagine that," Krause admitted.

Eleana shrugged. "We were small. I loved going there. Claire was different then."

"As a kid, you mean?"

"Umm…until we turned thirteen. That's when it started," Eleana said. Krause wrinkled his brow as Eleana's pleasant memory gave way to something that made her eyelids grow heavy with worry. She smiled at him sadly and continued her story. "It was February," she recalled. "Claire had gone home for her birthday for a long weekend. I remember that because I was so disappointed that she didn't invite me," Eleana chuckled at the memory. "I hated being at school without her," she admitted. "I was excited for her to come back. And then…."

"What?"

Eleana closed her eyes as images began to race through her mind. "She didn't come back right away," Eleana said. She pried her eyes open and looked at Krause. "Her mother…"

"That's when she died," Krause guessed. Eleana acknowledged the statement with a solemn smile. "I knew Claire was young when she died…"

"Yes. When she came back, she was different."

"Eleana, you're not suggesting that her mother's death is a reason for all she has caused? Cassidy lost her father when she was ten…"

"Claire is not Cassidy," Eleana said flatly. "And no, I'm not," she said assuredly. "You don't understand, Jonathan. I tried for a long time to get her to talk to me. She wouldn't. Every night—nightmares."

"That's not uncommon," Krause said gently.

"No. But this? She would wake up in the night screaming, sweating, thrashing in the bed," Eleana recalled painfully. "I tried. I tried to get her to tell me. She would just say she couldn't remember. That was it. Finally, I just gave up on talking and started holding her—every night. Every night for the next five years I held her. It's the only way she seemed to be able to sleep at all. Even then sometimes I would wake to a fist balled, striking me in desperation."

Krause listened attentively. "She never told you?"

"No, but I put the pieces together. Some of them anyway. There were times she would talk in the middle of a dream."

"What do you think caused them?" he asked. Eleana shut her eyes again. "Eleana?"

"I hope that I am wrong. If I am right? I'm not sure that is my place to tell—even to you," she said.

***

Claire woke up with a pounding headache. She blinked rapidly in an attempt to process her surroundings. "Where the hell am I?" she wondered. She heard voices in the hallway and closed her eyes again to concentrate.

"You look like you are on a mission," Krause said to Alex.

"You look like you didn't sleep at all," Alex observed. "Is that a good thing or a bad thing?" she asked lightly.

"Nothing happened," he told her. "We just talked."

"You are such a girl sometimes," Alex teased him.

"Why are you in such a good mood?" he asked.

"I'm not," Alex replied. "But, I don't need Cassidy to see that."

"How is she doing this morning?" he wondered.

"Hard to say. She's quiet. She was up before me. That never happens unless Kenzie is fussing."

"What about you?" he asked.

"Me? I am headed for coffee and answers, necessarily in that order," Alex said. "I'll see you downstairs," she said just as Eleana emerged from Krause's room. Alex raised a playful eyebrow at Krause.

"Shut up," Krause grumbled.

Alex waved to Eleana and walked away laughing. She expected her older brother might provide the only levity in her day. She had meant what she had said to him. Alex expected answers, and not just from James McCollum. She would be making some demands of her good friend Jane Merrow before the day was over as well.

"Morning," Eleana greeted Krause softly.

"Hey."

Eleana stretched up and placed a light kiss on his lips. "You okay?" she asked. "You didn't sleep very much."

"That's not unusual for me."

"I'll keep that on file," Eleana said.

"What the hell?" Claire mumbled to herself in bed. "Eleana?" she strained to hear the conversation just outside the door. Claire moved abruptly to get out of the bed and promptly fell backward. "Fuck!" she groaned.

Eleana gave Krause a sheepish smile and opened Claire's door. "What are you trying to do?" she scolded Claire.

"Where the hell did you bring me?" Claire demanded. Eleana slowly made her way to Claire's bedside.

Krause peeked in the room. "Need me for anything?" he asked. Eleana shook her head and Krause took his leave.

"Am I dead?" Claire asked seriously. "I am, huh? This is my penance."

Eleana giggled. "You're not dead," she promised. "You still don't remember last night?"

Claire closed her eyes and tried to put the pieces together. She shook her head in frustration.

"It's the painkillers and the loss of blood. Plus, you haven't eaten yet. Give yourself a bit to come out of the fog," Eleana told her.

"Where are we?" Claire asked again.

Eleana smirked. "We're at Alex's parents' house."

Claire's immediate reaction was to sit up, which sent her backward again with a thump. "Damn, that hurts!"

"I'll bet it does."

"Wait," Claire started to regain her bearings slowly. "Wait…Alex shot me! Why did Alex shoot me?"

"She thought you were about to shoot her," Eleana said.

Claire closed her eyes again. "Dmitri. That son of a…."

"You certainly are sunny this morning," Eleana teased.

Claire opened her eyes and glared at her old friend. "So, what? They gave you nursemaid duty?"

"Claire…That's not fair."

"Sorry."

Eleana looked at Claire compassionately. "Come on, you know me better than that. I'm here because I want to be here."

"What does that mean?" Claire asked.

Eleana sighed. "It means that you are still someone I care about," she said honestly.

"It doesn't matter," Claire whispered.

"Everything is always all or nothing with you," Eleana observed. She rubbed her eyes, feeling her emotions beginning to surface. She did love Claire. No force on earth would change that. She just didn't love Claire the way she once had. And, Claire, Eleana suspected, did not love Eleana the same way either. But, Eleana had always been the only person Claire Brackett trusted at all. On some level, Eleana's decision to walk away from their love affair undermined that for Claire. "Claire…"

"I'm sorry," Claire said again.

Eleana smiled. Claire's apology was sincere. "Come on, what do you remember?" she urged Claire.

Claire shut her eyes tightly. Images started to roll through her mind. Eleana watched as Claire's brow twitched and her forehead creased. "Was following a lead…Anderson said they would make a play…A play for you," Claire said.

"For me?" Eleana was puzzled.

Claire nodded but held her eyes closed. "All of you, any of you…Dmitri," Claire rolled through the events of the prior evening in her mind. "Then Toles with Brady…Where the fuck did he come from? She was walking into the bee's nest…I had to go…Sent Anderson to security….Had to know who was there."

"Agent Anderson took the security files?" Eleana asked.

"Supposed to. I don't know," Claire said. "Then…Dmitri…Strange….Why is he in the closet? Why here? Doesn't add up. Toles is outside….Sure it is her….Dmitri…Shit, if she walks in, she'll never see him…."

Eleana exhaled slowly. "Dmitri tried to shoot Alex."

Claire opened her eyes and nodded. "She couldn't see him, only me."

Eleana smiled. "Why did you try to save Alex?" she asked.

Claire stared at Eleana for a long moment. "You would never forgive me."

"Claire….Maybe so, there's more, though…."

"He can't win this time," Claire said.

"Who?" Eleana asked.

"My father."

***

Alex had taken a few minutes to savor her coffee in the kitchen. She had watched at a distance as Krause led McCollum into her father's study. It was time for a long overdue conversation. Alex was determined to try and keep an open mind. That would prove to be difficult, and she knew it. This entire situation, her entrance into the CIA, her takeover of Carecom—all of it was personal. She was lost in her silent contemplation when Eleana entered the kitchen.

"Morning," Eleana greeted Alex.

Alex looked up from her study of her coffee cup and smiled. "Morning. How's the patient?"

"Her usual sunny self," Eleana replied. Alex nodded and looked back at the contents of her cup. "Not sure that holds the answers you're looking for," Eleana offered.

Alex laughed. "Would be nice."

"Yeah, I guess it would. Look, Alex....I think I know where the security footage might be."

"What?"

"Claire was with Marcus Anderson. She sent him to get it."

"Jesus! What is her...."

"Alex, listen," Eleana held up a hand to calm her friend. "I know that you don't trust her. I don't think she was there to compromise you."

"I'm listening," Alex said. Eleana gauged Alex's demeanor for a moment. "I swear, I'm listening," Alex promised.

"She's worried."

"About losing you," Alex guessed.

"Probably. She knows that part of our life is over, Alex. She might not like it, but she does know it. She also knows that she will always be part of my life. I need you to understand that too. Wherever we are going, I need you to know that I don't regret my past with Claire."

"Eleana..."

"No. You need to hear this. I don't approve of what she's done— most of it, in fact. And, if she chose to compromise us, I would do whatever was necessary," Eleana said flatly. "That means you, Cassidy, Jonathan—any of us."

"I believe you, Eleana. What I think isn't important."

"Yes, it is," Eleana disagreed. "Like it or not, you are the one everyone looks to."

"I don't think...."

"It's true, Alex. Even Jonathan. I don't know what is happening with Claire. That's the truth. I do know this is about more than me."

"Eleana, Claire is not someone to fight for the greater good. She likes the game too much."

"Maybe so," Eleana agreed. "She does have a heart, Alex." Eleana heard Alex's doubtful sigh. "I know you don't believe me, but she does."

"It's not about whether I believe it," Alex said. "It's about her track record."

"I get that."

"You really think this is some new leaf she wants to turn over? To what end? To win you back?" Alex asked.

"No. I told you that ship has sailed. She knows that."

"What then?"

"I think it has to do with her father," Eleana said.

Alex took in the information and nodded. She took a sip from her coffee cup and pinched the bridge of her nose. Fathers seemed to be able to provoke strange reactions from their daughters. Alex had dealt with Admiral William Brackett more often than she was comfortable with. Edmond had maintained that The Admiral, as he was called, might not act as Alex would, but that William Brackett was committed to the same cause. Alex had her doubts.

Alex could see a great deal of Edmond in Eleana. Knowing her own father, dealing with James McCollum for less than twenty-four hours, and observing William Brackett, it was easy to see that Edmond Callier was the idealist among the men. She'd witnessed genuine tenderness in the man, something she could scarcely recall in her father. It left Alex to wonder just what kind of impression William Brackett had left on Claire.

"Did she say why?" Alex asked.

"No, but, Alex? The look in her eyes? She acts as if she hates him."

"Maybe she does," Alex commented.

"Yeah, maybe. She's afraid of him."

Alex nodded. She filed away the information for later. "Well, we will have to see why that might be. Right now, I have to deal with my father-in-law. Interested?"

Eleana nodded. "I'll be in after I get some coffee and something for Claire."

"We'll be in the study," Alex told Eleana as she left.

Eleana poured herself a cup of coffee and took a seat at the table. "I just need a minute," she mused aloud. "What is it about The Admiral, Claire?" she wondered. "What aren't you telling me?"

Chapter Twelve

"You can't expect any of us to trust you," Krause told McCollum. The older man nodded. "To tell you the truth, I'm not sure there is anything you can say that will redeem you in Alex's eyes."

"I don't expect that anything I say will," McCollum said. "If anything, it will probably do the opposite."

Alex walked into the study and nodded. "Good bet," she said. "All right. Let's hear it," Alex demanded.

"What do you want to know?" McCollum asked.

"We could start with why you decided to play dead for twenty-five years, but since I think there is someone else you owe that explanation to, I will settle for what the hell you are doing here now."

"If you want to understand that, then I will need to answer that first question," he told her.

Alex grimaced. "Fine. I think you could give Cass the courtesy of hearing this story," she said.

McCollum's temple twitched, but he nodded his assent. Alex took a deep breath and made her way from the room. She could feel the tension pulling at her muscles. Her body's rigidness reminded her of her days in recovery after being injured in Iraq. It was painful to breathe. Physically, emotionally and mentally, Alex felt as if she had been stretched on a rack for hours. She leaned against the wall, closed her eyes, and took a deep breath.

"Alex?" Cassidy walked into the hallway and saw Alex leaning against the wall. She picked up her pace and grabbed hold of Alex's arm.

Alex opened her eyes and painted on a wan smile. "I was just coming to find you."

"Why do I not like the sound of that?" Cassidy asked.

"Your father is about to explain some things. I wanted you to know that…"

Cassidy smiled. "I don't need to know."

"Cass…"

"I'm serious, Alex," Cassidy said. "I know you don't understand. You need to know the whys. Short of him telling me that he had amnesia for twenty-five years, I really have no interest."

"Maybe it would…"

Cassidy leaned in and kissed Alex's cheek. "Maybe someday. Not today," she said. "You go." Cassidy chuckled and shook her head ruefully.

"What is it?" Alex wondered.

"Oh, I was just thinking how things change. I always wondered what it would be like if my father had been around to interrogate you. Here you are interrogating him." Alex reached for the bridge of her nose and Cassidy captured her hand. "You go," Cassidy repeated. "Do what you need to do."

"I'm more worried about what you need right now," Alex said.

"Time."

Alex nodded her understanding. "Are you sure?"

"I am. Go on. You can fill me in later on what you think I need to know."

Alex kissed Cassidy on the forehead. "I promise, I will try not to make it a long day," she said.

Cassidy watched Alex head back toward the study. Alex's gait was slower than normal, almost as if she wanted to postpone the inevitable. Cassidy waited until she heard Alex close the door to the study before heading for the kitchen. She was surprised to find Eleana sitting at the table.

"Hi," Eleana greeted Cassidy quietly.

"Morning," Cassidy offered the younger woman a smile.

Eleana thought it best to tread lightly. "How's Mackenzie?" she asked.

"Sleeping," Cassidy replied. "She was up quite a bit in the night. Finally passed out."

"Ear infections suck," Eleana said.

Cassidy laughed. "They do. Today should be better. How are you?"

"Me? I'm fine. I think I should be asking you that question."

"I'm all right," Cassidy said assuredly. Eleana looked down at the table. Cassidy shook her head. "Oh, don't you dare start," Cassidy warned playfully.

"Start what?"

"Walking on eggshells around me," Cassidy said as she poured herself a glass of juice.

"We're just worried about you."

Cassidy sat down across from Eleana. She reached over and took Eleana's hand. "I know, and I love you all for it, I do. This is something I have to deal with in my own time," Cassidy said. "And, that might take an exceptionally long time," she admitted. "I honestly can't even think about him right now. And yet, that seems to be all I can think about."

"Do you want to talk about it?"

"Not really," Cassidy replied. "What am I supposed to tell my mom?" Cassidy asked helplessly.

Eleana hung her head. In all of the emotional upheaval and chaos of the last few days, she had yet to consider that inevitable dilemma. "Maybe you shouldn't," Eleana said softly.

"I've considered that. I've considered a lot of things in the last fourteen hours. Some of them might surprise you," Cassidy told her friend.

Eleana chuckled. She had to give Cassidy credit. No matter how conflicted Cassidy was feeling, she was endeavoring to put Eleana at ease.

"Oh, I don't know. I can imagine some pretty wild things," Eleana said. "I was involved with Claire for over ten years, remember?"

Cassidy laughed. "Puts my life in perspective," she said with a wink. She heard Eleana's sad sigh. "I'm kidding," Cassidy said. "Look who I was married to before Alex," she pointed out. "Talk about self-centered." Cassidy watched Eleana turn a light shade of green. "Eleana?"

"It's nothing."

"Right," Cassidy answered sarcastically. "What is it?"

"Cassidy, I really don't think…."

"Do you consider us friends?" Cassidy asked.

"Of course."

"Good, because so do I. So, let's have it. What aren't you telling me?" Cassidy wondered.

"I don't think Jonathan has even told Alex yet."

"I see."

Eleana sighed. "I don't even know…"

"I understand."

"Cassidy, I don't want to hurt you."

Cassidy nodded. "I know. Something tells me whatever it is, it's not your fault. So?"

Eleana was positive that both Jonathan Krause and Alex would disagree with her decision. At the moment, she did not care. Cassidy was her friend. In many ways, Cassidy had assumed the role of an older sister in Eleana's life, and Eleana welcomed it. "I don't know how to tell you this."

"Just tell me," Cassidy suggested.

Eleana struggled to inhale a full breath. She exhaled it slowly with her words. "When we found your father, he wasn't alone."

"Who was he with?"

Eleana looked at Cassidy as if to beg forgiveness. "Congressman O'Brien."

***

Cassidy burst into Alex's father's study and all eyes immediately turned in her direction.

"Cass?" Alex looked over at her wife. She could see the light trembling of Cassidy's hands.

Cassidy looked at her father and shook her head, then she looked at Krause and repeated the same action. Finally, she looked at Alex. "Sorry, to interrupt your—what exactly is this?" Cassidy asked pointedly.

"Cass?" Alex called gently. Her worry was increasing by the second. "What is…"

"Alex, have either Pip or my father told you about the company my father was keeping?"

Alex shook her head and looked at the two men across from her. "Jonathan?"

"I can't believe she told you," Krause muttered.

"No? I'm glad she did. Seems mourning is a waste in my life. Who else should I expect to see rise from the dead?" Cassidy asked.

"Jonathan?" Alex asked again.

"I was getting to it, Alex. Last night was not the best time," he said honestly.

"Getting to what?" Alex asked suspiciously.

McCollum answered. "It's not Jonathan's fault," he said.

"No, it isn't," Cassidy agreed. "So? What were my dead father and my dead ex-husband chatting about?"

"What?" Alex bellowed. She looked at Cassidy and Cassidy nodded. "You're telling me O'Brien is alive?"

"Not anymore," McCollum said.

Cassidy let out a disgusted sigh. "This is a bad dream."

"Look," McCollum said. "I had to know what he knew," he explained. "Cassie, he's not who you thought he was."

"I've known that a long time, Dad," Cassidy replied.

"I mean that…"

Cassidy put her hands up. "Maybe I should, but I really don't want to know. So? Is he really dead now or should I expect him at the door soon?"

"He's dead," Krause said. "Trust me, Cassie. He's dead."

Cassidy shook her head and walked out of the room.

"What the hell?" Alex looked at Krause.

"I didn't think she'd find out before we talked," Krause said.

Alex nodded. She was certain that was true. "I'll be back," she said. "Watch him," Alex pointed to McCollum.

"Shit," Krause groaned.

"She was going to find out sooner or later, better sooner," McCollum offered.

"Maybe. It's just us," Krause said. "Who the hell was Christopher O'Brien?"

"Good question, Jonathan, an asset—just like you, just like me."

"What does that mean?"

"I told you, I don't know who placed him. I do know who created him."

"Created him? What the hell are you talking about?" Krause asked.

"Lynx, Jonathan. I'm talking about Project Lynx."

"Why do I have a feeling I am not going to like this at all?" Krause asked.

"Intuition is an excellent attribute," McCollum said. "Because you won't."

***

"Cassidy," Alex called up the stairs as she took two at a time.

Eleana was sitting beside Claire's bed. She heard Alex's voice booming up the stairs and looked away from Claire toward the upstairs hallway. "Oh shit."

"What?" Claire asked.

"Nothing good," Eleana said. "Eat that toast."

***

"Cass!" Alex practically jumped in front of her wife.

"Not now, Alex."

"Cassidy…"

"What do you want me to say?" Cassidy asked angrily.

"I didn't know. And, to be honest, I don't blame Pip for not telling me about O'Brien last night."

"I don't blame Pip for any of it," Cassidy said.

"I will find out what is going on, I swear."

"I don't know if I want to know what is going on, Alex."

"Cass, this is it, whatever your father has been doing, it's the reason John was assassinated. It might explain Carl…"

"I don't care," Cassidy said bluntly, leaving Alex stunned. "Those answers won't change any of the facts."

"No, but…"

"There is no but," Cassidy replied. "This is what you do. I get it. Get your answers."

"Don't you think that if you knew what…"

Cassidy took a breath and calmed herself. "I love you, Alex. Maybe, maybe I do need the answers. I told you, not now. The reality is enough for me to try and swallow. What do I tell Mom? I can't even begin to imagine how to cover this with Dylan."

"Maybe you won't have to."

Cassidy shook her head. "You know better than that. The truth always comes out. Look at us. Just look."

"What do you want me to do?" Alex asked. "Just tell me and I swear I will do it."

"Quit."

"Is that really what you want?" Alex asked.

"Yes, and no," Cassidy answered honestly. She reached up and cupped Alex's face in her hands. "You can't quit now. I would never ask you to. I need to step away from this for now."

"Are you leaving?" Alex asked fearfully.

"What?"

"Me? Are you leaving me?" Alex asked.

Cassidy smiled. "Never," she promised. "You're right, I will need answers. I do want to know who he was."

"Your father?"

"Both of them," Cassidy said. "He was my husband, Alex. He's the father Dylan knew. I need to know. I just can't…"

"I think I understand. I'll figure something out, okay?" Alex asked. Cassidy nodded. "I'm sorry, Cass. If I could make it go away…"

"I know. Time, Alex. Just give me some time."

Alex kissed Cassidy tenderly. "I'll figure it out."

"I know," Cassidy said.

***

"What the hell was that?" Claire asked Eleana.

"My fault," Eleana said sadly.

"Your fault? How is that?" Claire wondered. Eleana would not meet Claire's gaze. "El? Come on, it's me."

"Okay, look…"

"El, I have never once betrayed your confidence," Claire said assuredly. "Never."

"I know you haven't. When we found Cassidy's father, well….O'Brien was there." Claire was dumbfounded. "Claire?"

"No, that's impossible. I was on the phone with him when the car," Claire's thought trailed to silence.

"Claire?"

Claire closed her eyes as if someone had struck her. She pressed the heels of her hands to her forehead and sighed. "Jesus, Cassidy must be—I can't even…"

Eleana smiled. "See? It is in there?"

"What?" Claire wondered.

"Your heart," Eleana said.

Claire chuckled. "Where is he now? O'Brien, I mean?"

"Dead."

"You sure about that? Doesn't seem to stick to the men in Cassidy's life—no offense."

Eleana rolled her eyes. As quickly as Claire showed compassion, she masked it again behind her bravado. "I'm positive. I watched McCollum shoot him."

"Well, good riddens."

"Claire!"

"I mean it, El. O'Brien was a son of a bitch, trust me. There's a reason I kept him close."

It was not a secret that Claire and O'Brien had been lovers. That was part of Claire's game. She controlled people with her charm and when needed, with herself. It was another reason that Eleana could not consider a life with Claire Brackett. Eleana had accepted the terms of their relationship for years. That did not change the fact that it had always hurt her deeply.

"Really?" Eleana asked suggestively.

"Oh, please. He should have been the poster child for Viagra," Claire declared.

"What?" Eleana couldn't help but laugh. Claire shrugged and took a bite of her toast. "I think we'll cut back on that medicine," Eleana commented.

"Why? I'm not stoned, El. I was just being honest."

Eleana laughed. "You certainly are one of a kind," she said as she placed a kiss on Claire's head. "Time for me to face the music," Eleana said.

"Why? Because you told Cassidy?"

"Yeah."

Claire shrugged again. "She had a right to know."

"Yes, she did," Eleana agreed.

"Don't worry," Claire said. "He's not going anywhere."

"Who?"

"Krause," Claire clarified. "He's not a fool like I was."

"Claire…."

Claire handed Eleana her plate and pulled the covers up to her neck. "I'm tired."

Eleana nodded. She kissed Claire on the head again and felt Claire flinch slightly. "I'll check on you later."

"You don't have to," Claire said.

"Do you need," Eleana stopped when she realized that Claire had closed her eyes. Eleana looked up at the ceiling and cursed the world for the mess it seemed to have made of all their lives. *If Alex doesn't get to the bottom of this, I swear I will.*

***

"I know, Kenz. I know," Cassidy comforted her daughter. "Bananas? How about that?" she tickled Mackenzie as she walked down the hallway. She was startled when she nearly collided with her father.

"Sorry," McCollum said. "Just...Well, I was," he pointed to Claire's room.

"Going to see Claire?" she asked.

"Well, yes. Jonathan is right behind me. Just some questions about...It doesn't matter. Is that?"

Cassidy nodded. Instinctively, she turned to show off Mackenzie. "Bah...bah....Bah!" Mackenzie babbled. Cassidy chuckled.

"She's beautiful, Cassie," McCollum said adoringly.

Cassidy caught the mistiness in his eyes. She smiled. "Yes, she is."

"She looks just like you when you were a baby," he said softly.

"So Mom says," Cassidy replied.

McCollum looked at Cassidy. "How is your mother?"

"She's well," Cassidy replied evenly.

"Bah!" Mackenzie grabbed for her mother's face.

"Mackenzie," Cassidy scolded lightly. "Don't hit. Not nice."

"Not surprised you chose that name."

"Actually, I didn't. Dylan did."

McCollum nodded. "You must be very proud," he observed.

"I am," Cassidy told him. "I need to feed..."

"Of course," he said.

Krause reached the top of the stairs and stopped abruptly. McCollum and Cassidy were locked in a stare, one that Krause could tell was filled with confusion, awkwardness, and fear. He was surprised slightly by a familiar flicker he saw in Cassidy's eyes—affection. He stepped forward and broke their tension.

"Sorry, I was talking to Eleana," he explained. Cassidy shot Krause a warning glance. "I didn't give her a hard time," he told Cassidy.

"Good. See that you don't," Cassidy said.

"Protective much?" Krause asked.

"Only when I need to be," Cassidy said as she headed for the stairs.

Krause let out a sigh of relief. "Sometimes, she is the scariest person I know," he said.

McCollum let out a small laugh. "Yeah, she gets that from her mother."

***

"Well, well—look who is here," Claire said as Krause entered her room.

"Sparrow," Krause said politely.

"Claire," McCollum greeted the young woman.

Claire's eyes gave away a hint of both mirth and intrigue. "So? Your Cassidy's father, huh?"

"I am."

"Jesus," Claire commented. "Do you know my father?"

"I did—a long time ago," McCollum told her.

"Hum. I'm sure. He was certainly curious about you, or well, your ghost. Why is that?" she asked him curiously.

McCollum tried not to laugh. It was obvious that Claire's medication had reduced whatever filters she normally possessed. "You don't find ghosts interesting?" McCollum asked Claire.

"Oh, Jesus, not you too!"

"I'm sorry?" McCollum was confused.

"My father and his stories. He has a god damned story for everything. Ghosts, animals, faeries, pirates—always some crazy shit to explain his crazy theories," Claire reminisced.

Krause watched the exchange closely. McCollum seemed to take in Claire's words thoughtfully.

"Actually, when Cassie was small I used to tell her lots of stories—some had faeries and pirates," he told Claire. "She never cared much for the ones with ghosts," he said.

"Me neither," Claire said. "So? You look pretty spry for a ghost," Claire observed.

"She's loopy," Krause whispered.

"Shut up, Krause. I'm perfectly coherent. You've caused enough trouble," Claire wagged a finger at him.

"Me?"

"Yeah—you! Just be quiet and let Cassidy's father talk. It's not every day I meet a ghost."

Krause rolled his eyes. "Maybe this should wait for a bit," he whispered in McCollum's ear.

McCollum shook off the suggestion. "How is The Admiral these days?" he asked Claire.

"Son of a bitch just like every other day," Claire deadpanned.

McCollum chuckled earnestly. "Did he tell you why he was so interested in finding me?"

"Nah, he doesn't tell me anything. All about his duty, you know?" she said. McCollum nodded. "Duty for what, I don't know," she said. "Hangs around Viktor too much and that arrogant ambassador."

"Daniels?" Krause asked.

Claire shot him a furious glance and then rolled her eyes. "Was I talking to you?" She turned her attention back to McCollum. "Yeah, Daniels. Guy thinks he's fucking James Bond."

McCollum smirked. "So I have heard."

"You know who else played with Dmitri all the time?" Claire asked.

"No," McCollum said.

"Congressman Viagra," she gloated.

Krause coughed slightly. "You mean O'Brien?"

Claire rolled her eyes again. "Does he ever shut up?" she asked McCollum. She looked at Krause. "I don't like you."

"I'm heartbroken," Krause feigned offense.

"You kind of look like her, you know?" she said to Krause.

"Who?" Krause asked.

"Alex," Claire said. "She's better looking," Claire offered her assessment.

McCollum snickered. "Claire," he began to redirect the conversation.

"Hum? Sorry, El gave me those pills a little while ago."

"It's okay," McCollum said. "Do they help?"

"I guess. My shoulder feels like a hot poker got stuck in it. Alex fucking shot me, you know?"

"She didn't know you were aiming for Dmitri," Krause said. Claire groaned.

"Claire? Your father..."

"Yeah. I don't know what he is doing half the time. You know what though?"

"What?" McCollum asked.

"He had John killed. He did it. I liked him, you know? John, I mean." Krause felt his stomach lurch violently. "Then he got Fisher FBI credentials. Son of a bitch set me up!" Krause thought he was going to be sick. "And, you know what else?" she asked. McCollum shook his head.

Claire grinned. "He doesn't think I know. I know. I heard him and Viagra talking in Russian. Heard them. After that? I didn't let him far from me."

"You mean O'Brien?" McCollum asked.

"Yep, Viagra. You know," she said to McCollum. "She's better off with Toles."

McCollum smiled. "I agree."

Claire sighed heavily. "You don't like my father, do you?" she asked McCollum. He forced a halfhearted smile. "It's okay. I don't like him either, really."

"Claire? About the ghost…"

"Oh yeah. Well, I told him once he was acting like this ghost had the keys to The Lost Ark or The Holy Grail or something. You know what he said?" she asked. McCollum shook his head. "He said that if he existed, this ghost, that was not far from the truth. He's nuts! Duty has done him in."

"One more thing," McCollum said.

"Yeah?"

"The stories he told you…"

"Oh yeah! Every night. And, when I went to school he would send me tapes. Tapes of stories. Eleana and I used to listen to them. She liked them more than I did, so I listened."

McCollum nodded. "Thanks," he said.

"I didn't do anything."

"You tried to save Alex—that's something in my book," McCollum told her as he stood to leave.

"Hey?" Claire called to him.

"Yes?"

"Why did you tell Cassidy stories?" she wondered.

"I just liked to see her smile," he said. "And hear her laugh."

Claire seemed to consider his answer. "Did you quiz her?"

"Quiz her?"

"Yeah, on what they meant. The stories, I mean," Claire said.

"No," he said. "After a time, I enjoyed listening to hers more."

Claire nodded. "I'm tired."

"We'll let you rest," McCollum patted Claire's hand.

"Krause?" she called as they reached the door.

"Yeah?"

"She deserves better than either of us," Claire told him.

"Yeah, I know."

***

"Hi, Mom!"

Cassidy could've sworn that she could see Dylan beaming through the phone. She felt a wave of happiness wash over her. "Hi, sweetie. How's the skiing?"

"Good! Marvin was back," he said.

"Was he?" Cassidy asked as she headed toward Alex's location.

"Yeah," Dylan replied. "He's cool."

"Hold on a minute," Cassidy said. She took a deep breath and opened the door to the study. "Sorry."

"What's up?" Alex asked.

"Dylan," Cassidy whispered. Alex sprang to her feet. "Someone wants to talk to you," Cassidy told her son.

Alex took the phone. "Hey, Speed."

"Alex!"

"Are you having a good time?" she asked him.

"Yeah. Did Mom tell you about Marvin?"

Alex mouthed the word Marvin to Cassidy. Cassidy smirked. "No, she didn't," Alex spoke into the phone.

"He's a moose," Dylan explained.

"Really?"

"Yep. He's huge, Alex! YaYa put some vegetables outside for him," he said.

"Oh yeah, I'll bet. YaYa is good like that."

"She said she doesn't think it's Mom's moose, though."

"Mom had a moose?" Alex asked him as she looked at Cassidy in amusement. Cassidy shrugged.

James McCollum sat on the sofa in the room, listening intently. He kept his eyes on the paper in his hand, but his ears tuned to the conversation a few paces away.

"Yeah, it might be Marvin's grandson, though," Dylan explained. "They can live to be like twenty."

"YaYa told you that?" Alex asked.

"No, Grandma did."

"Ahh, I see. Grandma knows a lot of things, that's for sure," Alex chuckled.

"Yep."

"So? What are you doing now?" Alex wondered.

"We just came inside for a while."

"Hold on, Speed. I'm going to put you on speaker phone so Mom can hear. Go ahead."

"We're just taking a rest. YaYa went down Moose Run with me this morning," he said proudly.

"YaYa went skiing?" Alex asked in amazement.

"I heard that, Alexis!" Helen's voice barked.

"Dylan? Do you have us on speaker phone too?"

"Yeah," he giggled.

Alex huffed slightly. "Mom, should you be…"

"Quit your mothering, Alexis," Helen warned. "I did just fine. Didn't I, Dylan?"

"Yep! YaYa didn't fall once!"

"Thank God, all we need is a broken hip," Alex groaned. Cassidy smacked her lightly.

"Grandma says we can do a night run tonight, but only on the green circle runs. Maybe tomorrow we will do Black Bear. That's a blue square," he explained.

"Blue square?" Alex whispered to Cassidy.

"Intermediate," Cassidy whispered back.

Cassidy could tell that Dylan was having a good time. She did feel a pang of guilt. The truth was, had she been there, Dylan would have been on the intermediate runs the majority of the time. Still, she was grateful for her mother's prudence.

"I'm jealous. I love to night ski," Cassidy told Dylan.

"I know," Dylan replied. "I wish you were here, Mom."

Cassidy heard the sincerity in Dylan's voice and smiled. "I wish I was too, Dylan."

"Mom can ski Bear Claw, Alex," Dylan said proudly.

"What's Bear Claw?" Alex asked.

"Double Diamond," Dylan said. "Someday I will be able to."

"Yes, you will," Cassidy agreed. She had no doubt that Dylan would become an expert skier. He was athletically inclined and he loved skiing almost as much as his mother did.

"Yes, someday," Rose's voice sounded over the phone.

Cassidy caught sight of her father as he looked up. He bit his lower lip and looked back down immediately. Cassidy sighed.

"You two owe me," Rose said. "I expect wine and sushi, Alex."

"Yes ma'am," Alex laughed.

"Don't you ma'am me."

"Yes, Mom," Alex teased.

"Better," Rose said. "I'll let you talk to my grandson again."

"Thanks," Alex said.

"Mom?" Dylan asked.

"What, sweetie?"

"Is Kenzie still sick?"

"She's okay, Dylan. She's sleeping right now."

"Okay. YaYa took a picture of Marvin with her camera so we can show Kenzie."

"What sound does a moose make?" Alex asked. Cassidy rolled her eyes.

"I don't know," Dylan answered. "Grandma?!" he yelled.

Cassidy squinted and shook her head. Alex held the phone away from them to shield them from the volume. "Who does he get that from?" Alex asked. Cassidy shrugged. She wasn't certain who Dylan got his propensity for excited yelling from. It certainly was not her. She doubted it was from John Merrow.

"What, Dylan?" Rose's voice was soft in the distance.

"Alex wants to know what sound a moose makes."

"Give me the phone," Rose instructed her grandson. "Alex?" she asked.

"Yes?"

"Are you and Cassie planning on having moose on this farm of yours?"

Eleana gave Jonathan a perplexed look. "They're buying a farm?" she whispered. He shrugged.

"Well?" Rose prodded.

"Very funny," Alex said.

"My granddaughter does not need to know moose calls before she can say grandma," Rose proclaimed.

"Or YaYa!" Alex and Cassidy heard Helen yell. Cassidy started laughing.

"Whose idea was it to put them together?" Alex whispered to Cassidy. Cassidy kept laughing. "Put my son back on the phone," Alex told Rose sternly.

"Dylan, your mothers want to speak with you. Remind them that we have very high babysitting fees."

Dylan giggled. "Hi Mom," he said.

"I'm glad you are having fun," Cassidy said. "You just be careful out there, okay?"

"I will, Mom."

"Wish we were there, Speed," Alex said. "Next time."

"It's okay," Dylan said honestly. "YaYa and Grandma are fun."

"That they are," Alex agreed. "We'll see you Tuesday."

"Unless there's snow!" he declared happily.

Alex looked at Cassidy in confusion. "Unless there is snow," Cassidy agreed. "Don't get your hopes up for an extra day," she warned him.

"I know. I gotta go. YaYa made brownies."

"Okay," Cassidy chuckled.

"Hey! Tell them no wine with those brownies," Alex warned.

Dylan laughed. "I will. Bye, Alex. Bye, Mom."

"Bye, Speed." Alex looked at Cassidy. "Is that safe?"

"What?" Cassidy asked.

"Skiing at night?" Alex asked seriously.

Cassidy suppressed her laughter. This from the woman who gallivants across the globe and carries a gun. "They have lights," Cassidy deadpanned.

"Ha-ha. And, what is this intermediate thing?" Alex asked. "He's not even ten."

"Cassie could ski intermediate runs by the time she was six," McCollum said. All eyes turned to him, and suddenly realized he was speaking to himself.

Alex looked at Cassidy. "How did I not know this was your thing?"

"It might have something to do with the fact that I was pregnant all last season," Cassidy reminded Alex. "And," she said as her voice dropped. "I only started skiing frequently again when Dylan expressed an interest," she said. McCollum looked up and met Cassidy's sorrowful gaze. "I told you," she continued. "It was never the same after my father died."

"Cass," Alex took hold of her wife's hands. McCollum closed his eyes.

"I'm sorry I interrupted you," Cassidy apologized.

"You are never an interruption," Alex said. "And, anyway, I miss Speed."

"I know, me too. I'll leave you to it."

"Cassidy?" Eleana called to her friend. "Has Claire been behaving?"

"It's been quiet upstairs for a few hours," Cassidy told Eleana.

"I should go and check on her," Eleana said.

"No, I'll check on her," Cassidy offered.

"You don't have to…"

"It's not a problem," Cassidy promised. "You know where to find me," she said as she placed a kiss on Alex's cheek.

Alex waited for Cassidy to exit. She took a deep breath and looked at McCollum. "Sorry about that. I didn't think when I put Speed on speaker phone," she said. She remained both skeptical of the man's motives and furious at the pain he had caused Cassidy. But, Alex could not deny the pain she saw in the older man's eyes. It mirrored her wife's so closely that it made Alex's heartache in response.

"I didn't know she quit skiing," he said softly.

Alex nodded. "There's probably a lot of things you don't know about her," she said honestly. There was no malice in the statement, just fact. McCollum nodded. "So? Let's get Jane on the horn and find out where my security tapes are and why she thought it was a good idea to send Claire into Carecom."

Chapter Thirteen

assidy walked into the small bedroom carrying a tray with some soup and a soda. She walked over to the bed and placed it in front of the tall occupant.

"Jesus, what are you? The good fucking fairy?" Claire Brackett quipped.

"No, not really."

"More like Carol Brady, huh?" Claire poked.

Cassidy laughed. "If Alex gets her way that might not be too far from the truth," she mumbled.

"What?" Claire asked Cassidy.

"Nothing. And no, most days I feel more like Marge Simpson, to be honest," Cassidy shrugged.

Claire choked a bit on her soda. She studied Cassidy thoughtfully. There was no real reason for Cassidy to be here. Claire had observed Cassidy at a distance over the last day. Cassidy intrigued her. Claire had listened as Cassidy maneuvered the emotional minefield of her father's presence and had found herself feeling oddly sympathetic toward the woman. It was an emotion that Claire typically banished quickly. Somehow, that seemed impossible in Cassidy Toles' presence. In truth, it seemed the two most unlikely people in the house had the most in common—they both felt like outsiders. Claire was accustomed to that feeling. She suspected it was something quite foreign to the woman standing next to the bed.

"How are you feeling?" Cassidy asked with genuine concern.

237

"You don't have to be nice to me, you know," Claire said, teetering between going on the defensive and taking an offensive posture.

Cassidy shrugged. She had spent a fair amount of time surveying the dynamics between everyone in her mother-in-law's home. She still had not processed her reality. Everything she once believed seemed upside down. Normally, she would find refuge in Alex's arms. And, she would when evening fell again. Cassidy wished that somehow the days could be shorter. She had considered leaving and taking Mackenzie home to Connecticut, but her mother and Helen would be headed there with Dylan in another couple of days. Cassidy could not imagine how she could face her mother. What would she say? She couldn't lie. There had been so many lies, some of them of her own making. Who was she to judge anyone, she wondered?

"You okay?" Claire asked, noting that Cassidy had momentarily grown distant and a bit pale. Cassidy came back to herself and nodded unconvincingly. "You don't, you know?" Claire repeated.

"Don't what?" Cassidy asked.

"Have to be nice," Claire answered. "To him, or to me," she said honestly.

Cassidy's lips parted to speak but no sound came out and she closed them again.

Claire smiled genuinely at Cassidy. "It's just the way they are," Claire said before returning to her soup. Cassidy looked at her curiously. Claire felt the weight of Cassidy's stare and looked at her directly. "Our fathers," she clarified her meaning. "All of them. Some stupid idea that some greater purpose gives them the right to fuck with our lives."

Cassidy sighed. "I just don't understand," she said softly.

"My advice? Don't try," Claire said honestly. "It isn't worth it."

Cassidy heard Mackenzie let out a wail and offered Claire an apologetic grin.

"Better get that," Claire said.

Cassidy nodded and silently left the room. She reached back and tried unsuccessfully to rub the tension out of her neck as she made her way to the room she and Alex were sharing. The intensity of Mackenzie's cry was steadily increasing. "Oh, Kenz," Cassidy called to her daughter when she reached the small crib. "What's wrong, pumpkin?"

Mackenzie reached out for her mother and Cassidy let out a contented breath. She obliged her daughter's request and felt Mackenzie snuggle against her. Cassidy nuzzled Mackenzie and breathed in her scent. "Guess I know what woke you up," she laughed. Cassidy laid her daughter on the bed and set about the task of removing an offensive diaper, giggling at the gurgles and babble Mackenzie offered.

"All done," Cassidy said, lifting Mackenzie playfully. She made her way into the bathroom, juggling Mackenzie as she washed her hands. "I think we should go check on that other patient again, huh? What do you think?" Cassidy playfully asked her daughter.

"Bah!" Mackenzie seemed to give an answer.

"Bah to you too," Cassidy laughed as they strolled down the hallway. "You know, Kenzie," Cassidy whispered conspiratorially. "We might need to remind Momma that the whole football thing did not work out so great for the Bradys."

Mackenzie laughed as Cassidy's breath tickled her ear. "Bah!" she yelled.

Cassidy rolled her eyes as she re-entered the room Claire was in. "Are you taking her side?" Cassidy asked her daughter.

"Bah!" Mackenzie chimed.

"Is that baby for yes?" Claire asked from the bed.

"It's Kenzie for everything," Cassidy explained.

Claire nodded. Mackenzie pointed to the agent in the bed and giggled. "Bah. Bah. Bah...Brrrr."

"I think she likes you," Cassidy said.

"I don't know, that sounded like some sort of code to me," Claire said suspiciously.

Cassidy chuckled. "I just wanted to see if you needed anything else," she explained. Claire smirked. Cassidy raised an eyebrow. "Does that run in your profession?" she wondered.

"What?" Claire asked.

"That," Cassidy said. "That smug look you all get—like you can have anyone you want."

Claire gloated. "That's because we can."

Cassidy pursed her lips doubtfully. "You sure you don't need anything?"

"Take it easy, Mrs. Brady," Claire laughed. "Trust me, I've been in much worse positions. You know…"

"I don't want to know," Cassidy held up a hand. "You can come downstairs, you know—if you need something. Just let me know, Eleana or I can help you."

Claire groaned. "You might want to check that out with Mr. Brady," she suggested. Cassidy sighed. "Don't sweat it," Claire told her.

"I'll check in later," Cassidy said before turning to make her way out of the room.

"Hey, Cassidy," Claire called. Cassidy turned around in the doorway. "Thanks."

***

"Alex," Jane's voice greeted her friend. "And company I presume. So? What can I do for you?"

"You can start by having Marcus Anderson bring me the security footage from Carecom," Alex said.

"Well, I could—yes. I hate to disappoint you, Agent Anderson only managed to retrieve the three hours from part of the executive offices, a storage area on the first floor, and one back parking lot. The rest had already been wiped," Jane said.

"Shit."

"But, Joshua might have some more for you by tomorrow," Jane said.

"Really?" Alex asked doubtfully.

"We are on the same side here," Jane reminded Alex.

"Why Claire?" Alex asked.

"I am assuming that Jim has not shared all his information with you," she said.

"No, only about O'Brien," Alex said. "But, let's get this bit about Claire settled. What makes you think involving Claire is a good idea?"

"She's part of you, Alex—part of this group more than you think," Jane said. "If I am right, and I suspect that I am, she has as much to lose in this as you do, as any of us do."

"Because of her father," Alex surmised.

"Yes, but not just that."

"Quit talking in circles!" Alex lost her temper. "I want to know what the hell is going on. Do you have any idea what this has done to Cass? Jesus, Jane. You are supposed to be her best friend."

"What makes you think I'm not?" Jane responded swiftly. "Look, there is more than one thing at work here, Alex. I've had some interesting developments. Things that led to these decisions."

"Such as?" Alex demanded.

"Strickland reached out to me," Jane explained.

"You have our attention."

"Ivanov and The Admiral have an idea."

"What kind of idea?" Alex asked.

"To put lines back on the map," McCollum interjected.

"Yes," Jane confirmed.

"What does that mean?" Eleana asked.

"It means that they want to create enemies," Krause said. Eleana was still confused.

McCollum took the ball. "You're too young to remember the Cold War," he said. "Most people saw its demise as something to cheer for," he said. "Others…Well, others lost a great deal when the wall fell, Eleana. Wars are profitable for many people. Two world wars taught us that, but they came at a very high cost as well. Cold Wars keep conflicts contained."

"How do you do that?" Eleana asked.

"You create an enemy," Krause said.

"Create an enemy?" Eleana was confused.

"Every enemy we have faced since World War II, we created," McCollum said. "Some directly, some indirectly. More often than not, they were created with a purpose."

"What about Korea? Vietnam? What about now with foreign terrorists?" Eleana challenged.

"Korea? Vietnam? Contained conflicts," McCollum said. "There was no threat to our security and we knew it."

"Then why?"

"Eleana," McCollum spoke quietly. "Here, both were sold as a necessity to stem communism. In The Soviet Union? They were billed as aiding the people's united cause. The fact is, an argument could be made both ways. You want a reason? Perception. Contained wars that posed no real threat to any superpower. Russia has never had an intention of invading The United States, not any more than we have ever sought to take control of Russia."

"I understand that," Eleana said.

"Yes, but you don't understand the why. Money."

Alex shook her head. "Always about that, isn't it?"

"Of course, it is Alex. At least, it is on the international stage. Of course, it is. You think that's new? It's not. Wealth equals power. At one time, that meant land acquisition. One nation sought another's resources, be it human power, coal, oil, gold, water…Now, we live in a global economy and trade paper bills," McCollum laughed caustically. "We trade money. In fact, we don't even need the bills anymore. We buy and sell money that is nothing more than numbers on a screen. And, what value does it have?" he asked. He waited a moment. "None, in truth. Only what we perceive it to be. Why a Cold War? Why any war? Why terrorism? Perception is the greatest resource in the modern world," McCollum said. "If people believe it, they buy it. If people buy it, someone makes money. The people who make the most money? They hold the most power. But, you raise a point that has caused issues, Eleana. We had lines on a map, deep ones—namely The Soviet Union and The United States. We divided the map," he said. "Deliberately after World War II. No one got too far out of line. They'd seen Nagasaki and Hiroshima," he said. "We employed those tactics on smaller levels and still do—chemical attacks, terrorism—fear can be a tremendous motivator," he explained. "When it is used correctly. But, lines are blurred now. People like Ivanov and Bill, they see potential in what they consider the Golden Age. Go to what you know. Create a bigger enemy than the ones you both face. Become one another's enemy. That is their intention in the end."

"So, what? What does that have to do with Carecom? With Cassidy or me? With Claire?" Alex asked heatedly. She had an idea already what the answer was.

"Perception, Alex. Change perception—change anything—control anything. That's what The Collaborative has been about for almost sixty years now. You need assets to wage war. You have to know when and where to deploy them."

"Thanks for the history lesson," Alex said. "While we are discussing history, what does this have to do with Sphinx?" Alex challenged the older man. "Is that you? That mysterious person who holds the names and places—the keys to The Collaborative's kingdom?"

"I'm not Sphinx, Alex," McCollum said.

"My father?"

McCollum scratched his brow. "Sphinx was his project."

"What kind of project?" Eleana asked.

Alex bristled. "The kind that nearly killed me in Iraq."

"No," McCollum said. "That was unfortunate and not at your father's direction." Alex's posture remained rigid. McCollum continued. "Sphinx deployed assets. That was its primary mission, take the assets and place them—someone else would activate them as necessary."

"You mean weapons?" Krause asked for clarification.

"Those are vehicles, Jonathan. Weapons, schematics, drugs, those are all vehicles. And, they are all necessary for war as well, whether it is a physical war or a perceived one. Your father dealt with assets. Assets are always people. You cannot deploy a vehicle without an asset," he said. McCollum looked at Alex. "And that, Alex is where I come in. That is how you and Claire, Cassidy and Eleana, Jane and Jonathan, O'Brien and Kargen—that is why you find yourselves here. You are the assets and you don't even know it."

***

Alex needed to call a break in the study. She had the sense that what James McCollum had to tell them would change everything for all of them. It was imperative that they proceed with clear heads. They needed to know who had been in Carecom. Fallon and Brady had found no evidence of any device, short of the bugs Alex would have expected. That only served to unsettle Alex more. What exactly had been Kargen's objective the previous night? Something did not fit.

Jane had promised that the footage Alex requested would be waiting for her at Carecom later that evening. She had even promised that Agent Anderson would deliver it himself. That way, Alex could assess Anderson's allegiance for herself. Alex understood it was a longshot. She hoped whatever

Anderson had managed to download might give her some clue as to Kargen's plan, or to the other parties that might have held some interest in Carecom.

Alex climbed the stairs slowly. She was looking forward to spending a couple of hours with Cassidy before she would need to leave. Krause would spend some time with James McCollum and Jane in an attempt to determine who Christopher O'Brien had actually been reporting to and what his objectives had been. Lynx would wait until Edmond arrived the next day. That was fine with Alex. She had already reached some conclusions about Lynx. Another few hours would not make any difference on that front. And, Alex remained curious about Jane's decision to involve Charlie Hawkins as well. At least, Alex trusted her former partner. Whatever Hawkins was tasked to do at Rand, Alex was confident she would succeed. That was the least of Alex's concerns now. As always, Cassidy remained the center of Alex's thoughts.

She reached the top of the stairs and nearly collided with Cassidy as Cassidy exited Claire's room. "What are you doing?" Alex asked abruptly.

"What?" Cassidy asked in confusion. "I said I would look in on Claire."

"Cass," Alex pulled Cassidy down the hallway gently. "Claire is…"

"She tried to save your life, Alex."

Alex sighed dramatically. "You can't trust Claire."

"I don't trust Claire. Right now, Alex….I don't trust anyone except you."

Alex hung her head and her shoulders slumped slightly. Cassidy was by nature a trusting person. "Cass…"

"Alex, I just can't."

"I know," Alex said. She moved to Cassidy and kissed her on the forehead. "Claire is…"

"Alone," Cassidy muttered.

"Cassidy…"

"Alex, she is a person, you know? No matter what."

"I…"

"Do you trust me?" Cassidy asked.

"Of course," Alex said.

Cassidy looked at Alex lovingly. "Then trust that I can make a sound judgment."

Alex sighed and nodded. "I do. I just know Claire."

"You know a part of her."

"Cassidy," Alex warned. "Claire Brackett is a master of…"

Cassidy smiled. "There is more to her, Alex. Maybe something you should know."

"Did she tell you something?" Alex asked.

Cassidy shook her head. "No." Cassidy had learned a great deal about people over the years. As a teacher and a parent, she had come to understand that often what a person failed to say told a much larger story than the space they filled up with words. "Sometimes, Alex—sometimes it's what a person doesn't say that tells you everything."

Alex's lips curled into a smile. Cassidy's observation was, as usual, spot on. Of all the people surrounding her currently, Alex was reminded that Cassidy remained the one person who truly could understand people. Alex, Krause, Claire, even Cassidy's father, they dissected facts, even psychology, but it was always in an effort to predict behavior. Cassidy sought to understand a person, what a person felt, and who a person was. She endeavored to connect to people, not study them. Cassidy had suffered a massive blow to her confidence in that ability, and in her inclination to trust. If something was leading Cassidy to Claire, there was a reason. "Just be cautious around her," Alex cautioned.

"Afraid she'll give up some of your secrets?" Cassidy teased.

Alex laughed. "No. She has a lot to learn," she said, taking Mackenzie from Cassidy's arms.

"Oh?"

Alex laughed again. "Agents are dull. I married a teacher for a reason."

Cassidy joined in Alex's laughter, grateful for the solace found in a simple moment. "By the way," Cassidy began.

"Yeah?"

"I think there might be a flaw in this football theory of yours."

***

"Did you find something?" Jane asked.

Tate considered how to respond. "I'm not sure," he said.

"Joshua? What is it? Was there anything that you could recover or not?" she asked.

"Some chatter. I don't know who, Jane. And, I have to tell you it is vague at best."

"Go on."

"Something about a distraction," Tate told Jane.

"A distraction from what? What kind of distraction?" she urged him.

"I don't know. You asked. It is not the security officer speaking, although I am curious about him."

"What was the exact exchange?" Jane asked urgently.

"Just that," he said. "The rest is still indiscernible—gibberish. *Need a distraction*. Those are the words. That's it."

Jane sighed. "That could mean anything."

"I know. It could mean nothing," Tate admitted. "You want to tell Alex?"

"No," Jane said. "We don't need her chasing any more ghosts. It could be completely benign. Who knows?"

Tate chuckled. "Could be about the guy's marriage," he joked.

"Anything is possible," Jane said lightly. "Pass it to Hawk when she gets there. Let her work her sources a bit first. If you get anything else, Hawk is the go to."

"You think it could be something?" he wondered.

"Do you?" Jane returned the question.

"Right now, I wouldn't take anything for granted."

Jane agreed. "Keep me in the loop," she said before disconnecting the call. She reached over onto the end table and picked up a framed photo. "Oh, John. Things are such a mess," she said. "I don't know how he did this all those years. What was I thinking?" she mused.

"Mom?" a concerned voiced called into the room.

Jane looked up and smiled at her daughter. "Hi, Steph."

"Are you all right?" Stephanie asked.

"Yes," Jane promised. She patted the sofa beside her.

Stephanie sat down and looked at the photo now in her mother's lap. It was a picture of Jane with Alex, Cassidy, Dylan, and Mackenzie. Stephanie sighed. "Mom?"

"Hum?"

"Never mind."

"Steph? What is it?" Jane asked.

Stephanie smiled timidly. "You're close to Cassidy."

Jane nodded as a warm smile touched her lips. "She's my best friend," she told her daughter. "In fact, I'm not sure I ever had a best friend before her—other than your father."

Stephanie nodded. "Isn't that strange for you?"

"Why would that be strange?" Jane wondered.

"Mom…Come on," Stephanie looked at her mother knowingly.

"Steph, I thought you liked Cassidy?"

"I do," Stephanie replied. "It's just…I just…"

"Stephanie? What is it?"

"Dylan," Stephanie said.

"What about him?" Jane asked nervously.

"Mom. Seriously?"

"Stephanie, if you have a point to make, I really wish you would get to it."

Stephanie sighed. "Is he? Dylan? Is he our brother?" she asked. Jane was completely caught off guard. She closed her eyes and covered her face. "Mom?"

Jane let out a long, disconcerted breath. "Yes." Stephanie nodded. "How did you know?" Jane asked.

"I didn't, really. I just suspected. You'll think it's crazy," Stephanie said.

"I doubt that," Jane chuckled uncomfortably. Strange seemed to rule her life.

"I felt it," Stephanie whispered. "See? Sounds crazy."

Jane shook her head. "No, honey, it doesn't."

"And that's not weird for you?" Stephanie asked.

"What?"

"Cassidy. Being so close. Playing auntie."

Jane smiled sympathetically. She understood her daughter's question and the emotional confusion that she was sure learning the truth produced. "Oh, Steph, how do I explain this to you?"

"You don't have to."

"Yes, I do. It's time."

"Why didn't you tell us?" Stephanie wondered.

"There's a lot of reasons, Stephanie."

"Cassidy didn't want you to," Stephanie guessed.

Jane chuckled. "Actually, she is the person who has wanted to tell you the most," she said. Jane smiled at the thunderstruck expression on her daughter's face. "Why is that so surprising?"

"I don't know. I just figured she wanted to keep it a secret. You know, I'm sure it's kind of embarrassing and all. Plus, if people knew it would be everywhere."

"You think Cassidy wants to protect herself?" Jane asked. Stephanie shrugged.

"You don't know her as well as I thought," Jane commented.

Stephanie sensed that her mother had taken offense. "I didn't mean…I like Cassidy, Mom. I'm sure she is worried about Dylan. I mean, I know he's still young. But, don't you think we all have the right to know who we are?"

Jane sighed deeply. "That's an excellent question," she admitted. "The truth is, Steph—I don't know how to answer that question. I do know how Cassidy would answer it," she said.

"And?"

"She would say, yes," Jane offered without hesitation.

"Why…"

"I do know that she has every intention of telling Dylan one day."

Stephanie nodded. "Doesn't it bother you?"

"You mean the fact that your father slept with her?" Jane asked pointedly. Stephanie flushed with embarrassment and a hint of anger. "No, not really," Jane admitted.

"I'd be furious."

Jane laughed. "Your father and I were not perfect," Jane said. "I loved him. He loved me in his own way."

"In his own way?" Stephanie asked.

Jane nodded and shrugged. "Steph, you are a grown woman, so I am going to tell you the truth."

Stephanie shifted uncomfortably. Her mother had a reputation for directness. She was not certain what her mother was about to say. She braced herself for a dose of Jane Merrow's truth.

"Your father and I, our parents were insistent about our relationship. It wasn't really our decision to become involved."

"But, you loved him?"

"Very much," Jane said tenderly. "But, that grew out of our friendship for me. I accepted what was expected of us and I made the best of it."

"He didn't love you?"

"No, he did. Just not the way he wanted to. And, he did want to. Stephanie, your father and I, we came from a different time and a different world. We swore that we would give our children something different—choice."

"I don't understand. Are you saying you had an arranged marriage?"

Jane wrung her hands in her lap. "I would say that is an accurate way to describe it—yes."

"You didn't want to get married?"

"Not at the time. But, Stephanie, I don't regret it and neither did your father. You want to believe in true love, the perfect love affair. True love exists. The perfect love affair does not. What your father and I had was something I know neither of us would trade. It just isn't what either of us would have chosen for ourselves. So, you ask me if we have a right to know who we are—I'm not sure I am qualified to answer that," Jane said.

"Did you?"

"Did I what?" Jane asked. She saw the nervous twitch of her daughter's eyebrow and noted how Stephanie kept twirling one of the rings she wore. Jane reached out and stilled her daughter's hand. "Did I have any affairs?" she guessed. She took a deep breath and answered truthfully. "Yes, I did, but not until much later in our marriage," she said.

"And Cassidy?"

Jane shrugged. "That was not an affair," she told her daughter. "Your father felt horrible about it, so did Cassidy. But, they were both unhappy, both hurting, both lonely in their marriages. Sadness and alcohol can make people do things they ordinarily would not."

"Did he know? Dad? Did he know about Dylan?"

Jane nodded. "For a while, they both tried to deny it. Yes, he knew. It was an impossible situation."

"Because of his office?"

"In a way," Jane replied. "But, what you wanted to know was how Cassidy can be my best friend. That's easy. I love her."

"What?"

"Not like that," Jane laughed heartily. "I've met a lot of people in my life," Jane said. "I've seen things that I hope you never will," she told her daughter.

Stephanie watched as her mother's eyes closed. Jane seemed to be combing through memories. Stephanie wondered what her mother was seeing. Jane remained silent for a few moments before opening her eyes again. She took her daughter's hand and held it tenderly.

"I've met so many people," she said again. "People are like rocks," she smiled. "Some of them are harder than others. Some shine when the light hits them. There are some that you have to peel layers away to find their beauty. Some are rough, and some are smooth. Every once in a while, and, believe me, it is rare, you find that diamond in the rough. That's the stone that shines no matter whether dark or light surrounds it. It's nearly unbreakable, yet its strength does not dull its brilliance. It's the envy of the other stones, the thing they all wish they could be. That, Stephanie? That is Cassidy Toles."

"You make her sound perfect."

Jane laughed. "Hardly, just special and rare. Mostly because she does not see herself that way," she explained. "That's the diamond in the rough, Steph. It's what makes it unique. It lies among all the other rocks, unassuming and unaware of how beautiful it is. That's what separates a gem from a stone."

"She means a lot to you."

"Yes, she does. She is the one person who has never asked anything of me," Jane said truthfully. "Never once has she asked me to conceal the truth. Never once has she asked me to compromise my truth. Never once has she expected anything from me but the truth. And, even when I have not been able to give her that, she has still loved me. She lets me choose and she accepts my choices. That is a best friend. So? No, it's not weird for me. If anything, I am grateful."

"Grateful?"

"Yes. Things in life get messy sometimes, Stephanie. We're affected by what other people do and what we do affects everyone around us. But, in my experience, we usually end up where we were meant to."

"And Dad?"

Jane pulled Stephanie to her. "I know that this will be hard for you to believe, but he knew what he was accepting, Steph. And, when he died, he died believing he was doing the right thing—for all of us. Most of all for you and your sister...And, for Dylan."

"What about you?" Stephanie asked. "I mean, Cassidy has Alex. Jonathan seems like he and Eleana might be headed somewhere. Alexandra and I both have someone. Don't you want that?"

"You think I am missing out?" Jane chuckled. "I have all those people you mentioned. I don't need a lover, believe me," she said.

"I just want you to be happy. Lately, you seem so sad."

Jane held her daughter close. "I'm not sad, I promise. What will make me happy is to see you happy."

"I promise, I won't say anything to Cassidy."

"You can," Jane told her. "She will understand. Just don't say anything to Dylan. That is for Alex and Cassidy to decide."

"I won't. I would like to see him."

"He adores you. So do Cassidy and Alex. You would be welcome there anytime. All you have to do is show up," Jane laughed.

Stephanie snuggled into her mother. "I love you, Mom. I miss Dad."

"I know you do. I miss him too. He loved you more than you will ever know, and so do I," Jane promised.

***

Cassidy kissed Alex tenderly. "Do you really have to leave?"

"Yeah. We'll only be gone a few hours."

Cassidy put her head back on Alex's chest. She traced patterns over the skin of Alex's arm with her fingertips. "He did tell you, didn't he? Why he left?"

"Not really," Alex said. "Edmond will be here tomorrow. Jane thought, and I agree, that we should wait until then. Cass, I know it's not my place…"

"Of course, it's your place, Alex. You're my wife. Say what you need to say."

"I think they were messing with people's minds."

"What do you mean? Like, mind control? Alex," Cassidy tried not to laugh. "You have got to lay off The X-Files."

Alex chuckled and kissed Cassidy's head. "It's not as crazy as it sounds."

"I don't think it's crazy," Cassidy said.

"You don't?" Alex was surprised.

"Not really. I don't think it would surprise me if I found out he was a pod person," Cassidy joked.

Cassidy's attempt at humor did little to mask her underlying distress. Alex pulled her closer. "At least, we didn't find him in Area 51."

254

Cassidy laughed, appreciative of Alex's levity. She knew that Alex was serious. She also was sure that Alex could sense her lingering doubt and sadness. She was still not ready to know the truth. Part of her wanted to, a larger part feared she would never believe it anyway. She was thankful for some time to just lie in Alex's arms.

"Whatever it is or was, I hope it was worth it to him."

Alex responded from her heart. "I don't think anything is worth what I have seen today," Alex said.

"Neither do I," Cassidy confessed.

"I would never leave you willingly," Alex said.

"I know. Promise me you will be careful."

"I'm only going to Carecom."

"That doesn't make me feel any better," Cassidy said. "Just promise me, Alex—even if you can't, I need to hear it right now. Promise me you will be back."

"I promise."

Chapter Fourteen

"**N**o! Stop! Daddy, no!"

Cassidy startled at the screams from down the hall. She flipped on the light next to the bed. Alex had still not returned. She suspected that meant she was alone in the house with Claire and Mackenzie.

"No! Mom!"

The desperation in Claire's voice cut Cassidy through to her core. She'd heard that same terrified cadence in Alex's voice more often than she cared to recall. Nightmares, she had discovered, could be all too real. She grabbed her robe and threw it on haphazardly as she rushed to Claire's room. Claire was gripping the blanket that covered her as if it were a lifeline.

"No! He can't...Mom...Mom...."

Cassidy carefully made her way to Claire's side. She had learned long ago that waking a person from a night terror was a dangerous business. Alex once caught her with the side of a fist, leaving Cassidy with an elegant shiner for nearly four days. With a deep breath, Cassidy began to try to reach the woman just inches away.

"Claire? Claire, wake up."

"No. No. Stop him. Somebody stop him!"

"Claire," Cassidy tried one more time gently.

"Stop him, please!" Claire's ranting morphed into a sickening wail. "Please!"

Cassidy grasped Claire's wrists and shook her slightly. "Wake up! It's a dream, Claire. Wake up!"

Claire sat up abruptly, her eyes still closed. "Eleana?"

"No," Cassidy said softly, careful not to startle the young agent.

Claire's eyes opened slowly. She appeared despondent, lost. Cassidy was just about to try and speak when Claire erupted into violent sobs. "It was real. He did it. He really did it. It was real."

Claire kept repeating the words over and over. Cassidy reached out and pulled the young woman to her. "It's okay," Cassidy tried to reassure her. "Claire, what happened? Tell me what you remember."

Cassidy could scarcely believe that the woman crying in her embrace was Claire Brackett. Claire seemed so small at the moment. It felt to Cassidy as if years had been stripped away and Claire had been returned, at least momentarily, to some earlier form of herself. She was childlike, vulnerable—afraid.

"Why?" Claire pleaded. "Why her? Not her. He did it. He killed her," Claire's voice moved between desperate and broken.

Cassidy's heart lurched into her throat. "Claire," she whispered. "Who is he?"

"My father," Claire choked. She pulled back slightly and looked at Cassidy. "He killed her, Cassidy. He really did it. It's not just a dream, is it? It never was just a dream."

"Who, Claire? Who did your father kill?"

"My mother."

Cassidy fought the urge to be sick. The intensity in Claire's eyes, forlorn, yet certain—Cassidy had no doubt that Claire's claim was true.

"Why?" Claire asked Cassidy. "Why?"

Cassidy shook her head. She reached out and pulled Claire back to her. "I don't know," Cassidy said. She closed her eyes as a tear slipped over her cheek. *How many more lives have to be altered by this madness,* Cassidy wondered silently. "It's all right," Cassidy said. She understood the vividness of nightmares. Occasionally, visions of Carl Fisher hovering over her still wound their way into her slumber. When he appeared, Cassidy always woke to feel panicked and out of control. It was almost as if she could feel his breath. Alex would pull her close and hold her. It sometimes took hours before Cassidy felt safe again. "You're safe here, Claire. You're safe now."

Claire shook her head." No one is safe, Cassidy. No one."

***

Alex sat in front of a computer screen flanked by Krause, Anderson, Eleana, and McCollum. "There is nothing here," Alex huffed in frustration. Her thumbs worked to relieve the throbbing in her temples. "What did you see, Anderson?" she asked.

"Nothing more than what you see here," he said. "Probably less. I was a bit unfocused," he confessed reluctantly.

Alex pulled her gaze from the screen and looked at him to explain. "Agent?"

"I was worried about Claire—Agent Brackett," he told her. Alex listened attentively as he continued. "She was worried someone else might get the security files. She was right," he said, clearly disgusted with himself.

"I'll bet she was," Krause mumbled.

"No," Anderson jumped to Claire's defense. "It wasn't like that."

"What was it like?" Alex asked, careful to keep any accusation out of her voice.

Anderson looked back at Alex. She went ahead, had me watch the hallway. I saw you approaching. When you turned the corner," he took a deep breath. "I think she knew you were coming their way. Kargen was already in there."

"We know that," Krause said.

"Jonathan," Eleana chastised him. "Let Marcus talk."

"She told me to go. You were circling from the back. If you had gotten caught...."

"We might not have gotten anything," Alex finished his thought. Anderson nodded.

It was another jagged piece in the puzzle that was Claire Brackett. Alex still could not figure out what Claire stood to gain in any of this—other than Eleana. That didn't add up either. She looked back at the rolling footage on the screen.

"Why did she go with you?" Alex asked.

"I don't know," Anderson answered her honestly. "She would never let anything happen to Eleana knowingly. That much I know. She'd die first." Eleana closed her eyes and sighed. "I'm sorry," he apologized to her. "It's the truth."

"But?" Alex guessed he had more to say.

"I can't be sure," he said. "She's been, well, different. Reckless."

"How is that different?" Krause asked.

"Not reckless on the job," Anderson said.

"What do you mean?" Eleana wanted to know.

"Reckless. I don't think she sleeps," he said. "She drinks until she can. I've worked with her for over a year on an off," he told the group. "She lives large on and off the job. I've never seen her swim in the drink like she has the last few months."

"Any idea what triggered it?" McCollum asked. All eyes turned to him.

"She came back from looking for you," he said. "Had all these stories. Then, he called her in."

"Who?" Alex asked Anderson.

"Her father."

McCollum's sigh did not go unnoticed by Alex. She looked back at him just as he was focusing his attention on the screen.

"Where is this?" McCollum asked.

"Where is what?" Alex asked him.

"This parking lot," he pointed to the screen.

Alex moved closer. She studied it for a moment. "It's the lot adjacent to security. Why?"

McCollum backed up the footage.

"What the hell was that?" Anderson asked.

"You mean who the hell was that?" McCollum corrected him.

"Looks like a shadow of something to me," Eleana observed.

"It is," Alex agreed. She replayed the brief second. "Of a person. We were tied up at that moment. Marcus," Alex looked at Anderson and calmly continued. "I need you to think. Where did you exit the building?"

"Same lot," Anderson said.

"Think. Did you see anything at all when you were heading out? This is at the tail end of what you recovered. It had to be seconds before you were down there."

"Nothing, I'm sorry."

McCollum spoke. "Maybe you just can't remember," he looked at Alex. "I might be able to help with that."

Alex held McCollum's gaze unflinchingly. "Not without me present," she told him.

"What are you talking about?" Anderson asked. "I told you, I didn't see anything."

McCollum smiled at Alex and then looked back at Anderson. "And, I told you I might be able to help you remember what you don't know you saw."

"I didn't see anything."

"Let me be the judge of that," McCollum said. "Alexis?"

Alex nodded her agreement. "My father's old office," she suggested. "Go with Mr. McCollum," Alex told Anderson. "I'll be right there." Anderson nodded and followed the older man.

"Alex," Krause caught her arm. "You can't seriously be considering letting McCollum question him? I've seen his handy work. Anderson might be…"

"Relax, Pip," Alex said. "I think I know what he has in mind. I'm sure if it would have worked on O'Brien, he would have used it."

"You think he's going to take him under?" Krause asked.

"That's exactly what I think," Alex said.

"What's going on?" Eleana asked.

Krause watched as Alex entered her father's old office and closed the door behind her. "If I am not mistaken, I think we are getting a preview of Lynx."

"The project?" Eleana asked.

"Mmm. And, the man," Krause said. "I just hope he finds something." Eleana looked at Krause quizzically. "If he saw or heard anything, McCollum will find it."

"Is that a good thing?" Eleana asked.

"I really don't know."

✳✳✳

Alex was surprised to find Cassidy sitting at the kitchen table when she returned home. "Hey. Everything okay?" Alex asked cautiously. Cassidy looked up at Alex. She let her sight drift to the threesome trailing behind and settle on her father. Her gaze was hard, harder than Alex could ever recall. "Cass?"

Cassidy inhaled a deep breath and exhaled it slowly. She looked back at Alex, her expression unchanged. "No. Everything is definitely not all right, Alex."

"What..."

Cassidy looked directly at her father. "What do you know about Claire?" she asked him.

Eleana immediately flinched and looked at the older man beside her.

"What are you talking about?" James McCollum asked his daughter.

"You tell me," Cassidy challenged her father.

"I'm not sure I am following you, Cassie."

Cassidy nodded. She'd replayed Claire's story over and over in her head. It had taken her more than two hours to get the young woman to calm down and sleep. She pushed her chair back slightly and folded her arms across her chest. Were it not for the unusual circumstances, Alex would have started laughing. She'd watched Cassidy assume the same posture with Dylan on several occasions.

"What happened to Claire's mother?" Cassidy asked.

Alex's brow wrinkled in confusion. "Cass? What does that..." Cassidy held up her hand to stall Alex.

"Marjorie was struck by a drunk driver," McCollum said. "At least, that is what I was given to believe. I was not here..."

"Yes, I know," Cassidy said. "You were dead. Lots of death in our families."

"Cassie," McCollum began. "What is this about?"

Eleana looked at Cassidy to implore an answer. Cassidy smiled at the younger woman. "Car accidents seem to be a convenient thing for you all," Cassidy said flatly.

"Cass?" Alex looked at her wife with growing concern.

"You had a car accident. Washed away by the river. Right?" Cassidy asked her father. "Christopher, he certainly was accident prone. Why do I think you might know something about that?" Cassidy asked.

Krause felt a wave of heat flood to his face. Alex noticed immediately. "Jonathan?" she looked at him. Krause sighed.

Cassidy shook her head in disgust. "I may not be one of the chosen few for this insanity you all have going. I am certainly not stupid. You would think you people could come up with something more original to cover your tracks," she shot.

"Cassidy," Alex finally decided to be direct. "What is this about?"

"Dad? Want to enlighten the room or should I?"

McCollum closed his eyes in reservation. "I wasn't here, Cassie."

"No, but you know the truth, don't you?"

"She was a liability, a risk," he said. "She departed from the course we had set. Threatened to go public with certain operations. He had no choice," McCollum tried to explain.

Eleana went pale. "Who had no choice?" Eleana asked.

Cassidy kept her gaze locked on her father. All eyes turned to the older man. "Bill," McCollum said.

"Are you saying, Claire's father killed her mother?" Eleana asked in disbelief. "How could…"

"I wasn't here," McCollum repeated his defense. "I don't know the details, just that the accident was arranged…"

"Oh my, God," Eleana leaned into Krause.

Cassidy's caustic chuckle turned Alex's stomach. "Well, it seems Claire and I are not so different after all," Cassidy said. "I mourned my father for years, thinking he died in an accident. That's what everyone told me. Funny, I always had this dream of him standing over my bed that night. Everyone told me it was a dream. It wasn't a dream, though, was it?" Cassidy asked. McCollum sighed softly. Cassidy shook her head. "And, Claire? Everyone told Claire her nightmares were from trauma. They weren't though. She didn't imagine her father either. At least for me, my father was telling me he loved me. Claire? Her memory? Do you know what that is?" Cassidy asked her father. "No? You weren't here. She watched him choke the life from the woman who gave her life."

Alex covered her face with her hands. Cassidy finally stood. She walked directly to her father. "I don't know when it is enough for you. I do know this. There isn't one mission, not one thing more important on this earth than the children you give life to—not one. I clearly learned that from my mother," she said. She turned to Alex and kissed her gently on the cheek. "I'll see you upstairs." Lastly, she turned to Eleana. "I'm sorry to tell you this way," Cassidy said as she made her way from the room.

"Tell me that Claire is playing with Cassidy. Tell me that she is feeding her compassion. Tell me that."

McCollum shook his head. "I didn't know how it happened, Alex. I don't think anyone knew."

"Anyone?" Eleana asked. "Did he know? My father? Did he know that The Admiral killed her?" she asked pointedly. McCollum's silence served as her answer. Eleana let out a disgusted breath. She turned to Krause.

"Go," Krause told her. Eleana nodded her thanks and headed back toward the stairs. "Jesus Christ," Krause groaned.

Alex pinched the bridge of her nose. "When will it be enough?" she asked, not sure who she expected to answer, or who she was asking. Alex turned without another word and followed the direction Cassidy had taken moments earlier. She passed Claire's room and saw Eleana leaning over Claire. She wondered for a moment what they both had been like as children. Her pace slowed as she approached the room she shared with Cassidy. Cassidy was cradling Mackenzie, humming to her softly.

"Come here," Cassidy told Alex.

Alex shut the bedroom door and made her way to sit beside Cassidy on the bed. "I'm sorry."

Cassidy nodded. "I know you are. That doesn't help Claire."

"I'm more worried about you."

Cassidy chuckled and turned to Alex. She smiled earnestly. "Me? No, love. I'm okay. I have my family."

"That doesn't take away…"

"No, it doesn't take anything away," Cassidy immediately agreed. "But, Alex, I had my mother to raise me. I have you. I have our children. I've never been left to feel unprotected. Vulnerable? Of course. But, afraid? Truly afraid? Alex, I've only felt that once. That was enough. Imagine feeling that your whole life? Imagine not even knowing why you fear the one person you are supposed to be able to trust more than everyone else?" Cassidy's emotions began to surface.

Alex reached across and caressed Cassidy's cheek. "Cass, not that I am not sympathetic, but why did Claire..."

Cassidy smiled sadly. "She had a nightmare. One like you used to. One like...like the one I..."

"I understand."

"I went to wake her. When she did, she...Alex, I've seen that expression. I've felt it on my own face."

"It doesn't make the things she's done," Alex began.

"It doesn't make anything all right, Alex. I know that. Don't you think it explains some things? Don't you wonder? Even just a tiny bit who she would have been?" Cassidy asked. She looked down at Mackenzie and shook her head. Cassidy kissed her daughter and crossed the room to place her back in her portable crib. She turned back to Alex slowly. "I'm not saying that I trust her, Alex. I feel for her."

Alex smiled. Cassidy was angry, angrier than Alex could ever recall. She could feel Cassidy's resentment lying underneath her calm exterior. Most people would have been overcome by the wave of pain and insecurity betrayal produced. As always, something more powerful seemed to override those emotions for Cassidy—compassion. Alex suspected that Cassidy had yet to allow herself the luxury of feeling the array of emotions her father's return could have produced. Claire served as a distraction. Alex understood that. But, Claire was also a soul who needed nurturing. If anyone could succeed in that endeavor, it was the woman standing before her.

"Cass, you can't save everyone."

Cassidy chuckled. "Look who's talking."

"You know what I mean."

"I do. I don't want to save her, Alex. I just want to help her," Cassidy said sincerely. Alex sighed heavily. Whatever had transpired between Cassidy and Claire Brackett had affected Cassidy deeply. Alex reached for her temples and Cassidy caught her hands. "Stop worrying about me,' Cassidy said.

"Cassidy, I don't want to see you get hurt."

Cassidy's melancholic smile tore at Alex's heart. "It's too late for that, Alex. We've all been hurt. You can't save me or anyone else from getting hurt—not even our children," Cassidy said. Alex recoiled slightly at the statement. Cassidy took Alex's hand and kissed her palm. "I know you will try. I will try. You can't protect us from the world, love. You just can't."

"I know," Alex admitted.

"Alex, look at me," Cassidy implored her wife. "Maybe Claire needs a purpose."

"Claire's purpose has always been Claire."

"Maybe. Maybe that's all she knows, Alex."

"She had Eleana. She had a chance…"

Cassidy shook her head. "No, Alex. She never had a chance. Not after that day. Not with that secret to carry. A secret she couldn't even remember if I'm right."

"That might be true, Cass. Loss does things to people."

"That's not just loss, Alex. Even if it was, you're right. Loss changes you."

"You lost your father, and you never…"

"I told you, I had my mother. I always had my mother. Eventually, I found you. I've always had someone stronger than me to protect me," Cassidy said.

Alex kissed Cassidy on the forehead. Cassidy leaned into Alex's embrace. "You really do have that all backward, Cass," she said. "Okay, I hear you. Just know that Claire has a…"

"I already know what she has been. I wonder what she can be," Cassidy said.

Alex led Cassidy back to the bed. She shed her clothing and crawled in beside her wife. Cassidy's head came to rest on Alex's chest, her fingers dancing lightly over Alex's skin.

"Are you going to tell me?" Cassidy asked.

"What?"

"Why he is really back? It can't be…"

Alex held Cassidy tightly. "I don't want you to worry about that."

"We promised—no secrets," Cassidy reminded Alex.

"I know. Not tonight," Alex said. "I don't want to think about the past or tomorrow. Just let me hold you tonight."

Cassidy silently agreed. She closed her eyes and lost herself in Alex's gentle caress. She couldn't help but wonder if the past was destined to somehow repeat itself. As if Alex could read her mind, Alex put her fears to rest.

"We aren't our fathers, Cass. I promise. We will never be them."

✳✳✳

Eleana entered the bedroom Claire was in and closed the door.

"Claire?" Eleana gently shook Claire. Claire opened her eyes and offered Eleana a sad smile. Eleana said nothing. She pulled the covers back and climbed in beside the woman who had been her best friend nearly since birth. She wrapped Claire in her arms and held her. "I'm so sorry," she whispered. Eleana's tenderness opened the floodgates again for Claire, and she began to cry. Eleana rocked her softly.

"You shouldn't be here," Claire whispered.

"I'm exactly where I should be."

"Jonathan?"

"Not now, Claire. This is not about Jonathan and me. It's not about you and me. It's about you. Why didn't you tell me?" Eleana wondered.

Claire let Eleana hold her. "I could never remember," Claire confessed. "The dream," she explained. "I would wake up to flashes, but I could never put them together."

"And, tonight you remembered?" Eleana sought to understand. Claire just nodded. "Are you sure?" Eleana asked. Claire nodded again. "Do you want to talk about it?"

"No," Claire answered. She pulled away from Eleana. "You should go," Claire said.

"You don't want me to stay?" Eleana's voice was laced with hurt.

Claire smiled. "I do want you to stay. I don't think you should."

"Because of Jonathan?"

Claire took Eleana's hand. "Because I love you," she said.

Eleana was confused. "I love you too, you know?"

"I know you do, but it's not the same."

"Claire, you've been my best friend forever. I want to be here."

"I know," Claire said. "But, I need you to go."

Eleana nodded and pulled herself from the bed. "I don't want you to be alone," she said.

"El, please…Please, don't make this any harder for me," Claire begged. "You don't know how much I want you to stay."

"Then why are you sending me away?" Eleana asked.

Tears fell over Eleana's cheek and Claire felt her heart sink. Claire smiled at Eleana.

"Because, it's the right thing for you," Claire said.

"What about you?"

"It's the right thing for me too," Claire told her. Eleana nodded sadly and started to leave. "I want you to be happy," Claire whispered.

Eleana looked back at her friend. "That's all I ever wanted for you too," she said. Claire nodded. "Claire, if you need me…"

Claire nodded again. Eleana sighed and left the room. "I'll always need you, El," Claire whispered once Eleana was gone. She laid back down and closed her eyes, hoping a dreamless sleep would claim her.

***

March 4th

Alex woke early with Cassidy still in her arms. She closed her eyes in contentment and sighed.

"Not going for your run?" Cassidy asked.

"You're awake?"

"Unfortunately," Cassidy replied.

"Go back to sleep."

Cassidy snuggled closer to Alex. "Thanks for letting me sleep," she said.

"It wasn't really that hard. Kenzie didn't wake up at all—must be feeling better."

"Ummm," Cassidy sighed. Alex chuckled. "Why aren't you going for your run?" Cassidy wondered, already guessing the reasons.

"Maybe I just want to be with you," Alex said.

"Um-hum, or maybe your back is still bothering you."

"I'm okay, Cass."

"Alex…"

"The truth is, I'm not overly anxious to start this day," Alex admitted.

Cassidy propped herself up on her elbow to regard Alex. "I'm sorry."

Alex smiled at her wife. Cassidy never ceased to amaze her. "Sorry? What are you sorry for?"

"A lot of things."

"You have nothing to be sorry for," Alex said flatly.

"Yes, I do, and I have been thinking about that a lot the last couple of days," Cassidy said. Alex brushed an errant strand of hair from Cassidy's eyes and listened as Cassidy continued. "I've been thinking about why he did it, why he left." Cassidy took a deep breath and let it out slowly. "I say I can't understand. I can't. But, Alex…Part of me? Part of me does."

"How so?"

"Fear makes people do things they never thought they would do," Cassidy told Alex.

"I suppose that's true," Alex agreed. "You are thinking about Dylan, aren't you?"

Cassidy sighed. "Funny thing about lies—you can always find a way to justify them."

Alex looked at Cassidy sympathetically. "It's not even in the same realm, Cass."

"Isn't it?"

"No," Alex answered.

"But it is, Alex. It is in the same realm. Your love for me makes that harder for you to see," Cassidy said. Alex opened her mouth to speak. Cassidy placed two fingers gently on Alex's lips to silence her. "Please, hear me out," Cassidy requested. "One day, we are going to have to tell Dylan the truth, we both know that. And, no matter how much he loves me, he is going to be disappointed in me and angry."

"You don't know that," Alex said.

"Yes, love, I do. He had a right to know his father, Alex. John had that right too."

"John understood, Cassidy and John agreed with the distance. You don't have to take my word for that. Jane has told you that again and again."

"Yes, but John and I are not Dylan."

"Cassidy...."

"Alex, maybe Dylan won't be as angry as he will be hurt. He will be hurt. That doesn't mean he won't love me, I know that too."

"Cass, you are not your father."

"No, I'm not. I can't fathom what he's done, and I am sure I don't know even a fraction of it," Cassidy said. She watched as Alex's eyes cast downward. "I know he's done things that will be hard for me to believe. He's still my father."

"Do you really think you can forgive him?" Alex asked.

"I don't know," Cassidy replied honestly. "But, I do know that I still love him. That's something I can't change no matter how angry I am."

Alex reached out and traced the outline of Cassidy's face with her fingertips. She looked into Cassidy's eyes, awestruck by the woman beside her. "You don't give yourself enough credit," she told Cassidy.

Cassidy smiled. Her eyes reflected the same admiration and love for Alex that Alex held for her. "Maybe you give me too much credit," she said.

"No," Alex answered definitively. She stretched to place a kiss on Cassidy's lips. "I hear what you are saying," Alex said. "Believe it or not, I do understand. Don't underestimate Dylan. You're right—he will be hurt," Alex admitted. "But, I have a feeling it will likely be more because he will wish he could have known John more."

"And whose fault is that?"

"No one's fault, Cass. Sometimes, you do the best you can. Hindsight is always 20/20. You and John both chose the same path—for Dylan's sake."

"Yes, but also for our own," Cassidy said. "We don't get a free pass because you love us, Alex. John would tell you the same thing and we both know that."

"I did love him. I do love you—more than anything. You can only go forward," Alex said.

"I know."

"Dylan will forgive you—if that's what you are worried about. When he's ready, we'll tell him," Alex said.

"No one is ever ready for that," Cassidy replied.

Alex smiled. "I think Speed might surprise you."

"How so?"

"He's your son," Alex observed.

"He's our son," Cassidy corrected Alex.

"Yes. He has your heart," Alex said.

"See? I was right."

"About what?" Alex asked.

"You. You give me too much credit," Cassidy said. "I've told you before, Dylan got me. He chose you. Smart kid."

"Takes after his Mom," Alex replied.

"Mmm. In some ways, I guess he does."

"We'll get through this," Alex promised.

"I know we will," Cassidy said. "Not everyone is as fortunate as we are."

"What do you mean?" Alex asked.

"We have each other. We have our mothers, our children. It doesn't make it easier, Alex, but it does give us a place to land."

"You're thinking about Claire."

"I can't even imagine…"

"Cass, I'm not saying that I am unsympathetic, but…"

"I know, but you had to have seen something in her once," Cassidy commented.

"That wasn't anything. I was different then."

Cassidy smiled and kissed Alex. "A player?" Cassidy teased. Alex groaned. "I'm teasing you," Cassidy said as she placed another kiss on Alex's lips. "Alex, you might not have been into commitment, I know you. You would never have been with someone unless you saw some spark in them."

"Oh, there were lots of sparks in Brackett," Alex quipped.

Cassidy covered her mouth. "I don't want to know." Cassidy felt Alex laughing and removed her hand. "You know what I meant."

"Yeah, I do. But, you might be giving me a little more credit there than you should. You have no idea how much changed when I met you."

"You didn't change, Alex. You just learned to let go," Cassidy said. "I have to ask you something."

"What?" Alex started to grow concerned.

"Do you think it was an accident?"

"What?" Alex asked.

"Us?"

"You and me?" Alex was confused.

"No. All of us—finding each other," Cassidy clarified her meaning. Alex sighed and pulled Cassidy back into her arms. Alex was silent for a few moments, contemplating Cassidy's question. Suddenly, Cassidy felt Alex chuckle. "What's funny?"

"Nothing. I was just thinking that you would have made a hell of an agent."

"No, thank you," Cassidy replied flatly.

Alex took a moment. It was true. Cassidy was Alex's equal in every way. She was intelligent, discerning, intuitive, and even athletic. Alex had come to understand that what made her fall so deeply in love with Cassidy had been the parts of her wife that Alex still found herself in awe of. Cassidy would never have chosen Alex's career. Where Alex needed to fix things, Cassidy needed to understand them. Alex often felt inclined to punish people for their actions. Cassidy sought to forgive them. Alex marveled at all of it. She was positive she always would. It didn't surprise her to know that Cassidy had been considering all of the possibilities Alex had. Alex suspected that Cassidy had surmised more in the last few days than either Eleana or Jonathan had yet to. It was true. Cassidy would have made an incredible agent. Alex was thankful that her wife had never chosen that path. She kissed Cassidy's head and savored the feel of Cassidy in her arms.

"Do you?" Cassidy asked again. "Think it was all coincidence?"

"No, I don't," Alex replied honestly. "I don't know that it was planned either, at least, not all of it," Alex said. "I'm sure no one thought you would fall in love with me," she laughed.

"They aren't as smart as they think," Cassidy joked.

"No, they aren't," Alex agreed.

"Alex….What did they do to Claire?" Cassidy asked.

Alex sucked in a ragged breath. She didn't have that answer, but she did have some ideas. "I don't know."

"But, you have some suspicions, don't you?"

"Yes," Alex admitted.

"You weren't kidding yesterday, were you?"

"About?"

"About them messing with people's minds," Cassidy said.

"No, I wasn't."

"Alex…"

"I'll figure it out, Cass."

"Will any of that help any of us now? Will it help Claire?"

Alex shifted lower on the bed and looked at Cassidy. "I don't know. I do know Claire has to want to…"

"Change?" Cassidy interjected.

"Help herself," Alex said.

"Mmm. Maybe so, but maybe we should help her along the way."

"Don't get your hopes up," Alex cautioned.

"Hope is about the only thing I have right now, Alex."

Alex nodded. "Edmond will be here in a few hours."

"I know."

"Do you want to be there? When your father tells us? I know you said you needed time…"

"I do. But, that isn't always a luxury we have. I need to know. I can't handle any more secrets." Alex nodded and pulled Cassidy closer. "You okay?" Cassidy asked.

"I will be when you are."

"I'm okay. I just want it over—all of it."

"You're going to tell your mom, aren't you?" Alex guessed.

"No," Cassidy answered. "He is."

Chapter Fifteen

Edmond had arrived just before noon. The tension in Alex's mother's home was so thick, Cassidy thought it would suffocate them all.

"You ready?" Alex asked.

"I'll be right there," Cassidy said. She kissed Alex's cheek.

Alex watched Cassidy walk away carrying Mackenzie and telling some story along the way. Mackenzie was giggling at Cassidy, smiling brightly, and twirling Cassidy's hair between her fingers. Alex kept watching, smiling broadly.

"How is Cassidy?" Edmond asked as he came up beside Alex.

"She's all right," Alex told him.

"I can't believe it myself. I swear, I thought if this ghost existed it would be your father," Edmond said.

"I know. It's not your fault, Edmond."

"Perhaps not, but I have many things to atone for."

"We all do," Alex said.

"Will Cassidy be joining us?" he wondered.

"Yes, she will. She has a right to…"

"She has every right," he agreed.

"She's…"

Alex smiled at the man beside her. She liked Edmond Callier. He stood in contrast to her father and Cassidy's. She guessed that he had been a part of many things that she would disagree with, but she saw Edmond as a man of conscience. Her mother liked him. Cassidy liked him. That elevated the man in Alex's eyes.

"She's checking on the patient," Alex said.

"Claire?" Edmond asked in surprise. "I would have thought Claire Brackett would be someone Cassidy would want to avoid."

Alex nodded. "You don't know Cass," she told him. "Come on," she gently prodded Edmond. "I need some more coffee before we do this."

***

Cassidy stepped into the doorway of Claire's room just as Claire was trying to get out of the bed. "Should you be doing that?" Cassidy lifted an eyebrow.

"Unless she wants to share her diapers," Claire pointed to Mackenzie, "yes."

Cassidy chuckled. Claire could barely stand on her ankle and Cassidy moved quickly to help her. "Let me help you," Cassidy said. Claire huffed. "God!" Cassidy commented in exasperation. "You are as stubborn as Alex. Sit down for a second and let me put Kenzie down. I'll help you."

Claire hung her head in defeat. Cassidy disappeared from the room. Claire started mumbling to herself, frustrated by her physical limitations, the need for anyone's help, her current surroundings, and life in general. "Fuck. This fucking sucks. Asshole. Just...."

"Feel better?" Cassidy asked as she entered the room again.

"No," Claire said.

Cassidy laughed. "Come on, I will help you hobble to the bathroom."

"You're enjoying this, aren't you?" Claire asked suspiciously.

"A little," Cassidy admitted.

Claire chuckled as Cassidy led her to the bathroom door. "I can do the rest myself," Claire said.

"I'm happy for you," Cassidy quipped.

Claire chuckled again and shut the door. Cassidy waited for the younger woman to emerge again. She heard a small crash followed by a loud, "Ow!" Cassidy opened the door. She shook her head. Claire's sweat pants were around her ankles. Claire was on the floor in a position that Cassidy thought slightly resembled a pretzel.

"Don't say it," Claire warned.

Cassidy bit her lip to keep from laughing. "Are you okay?"

"Yeah, I just wanted to examine the tile. You can tell a lot about a person by their tile."

Cassidy laughed and helped Claire to her feet. She guided Claire back to the bed silently. "Claire?"

"Yeah?"

"Do you want to come downstairs with us?"

"What?"

"Edmond is here. My father, well, Alex is expecting some answers," Cassidy explained.

"Did you clear this idea with Mr. Brady?" Claire asked.

"You have as much right to be there as anyone," Cassidy said.

"Why are you doing this?"

"Doing what?"

"This. Me. This," Claire said. "Why?"

Cassidy pursed her lips and nodded. "I don't like a lot of things you have done," Cassidy said bluntly. "I don't like that you had a hand in hurting Alex. And, frankly? Your relationship with Chris perplexes me."

Claire chuckled. "Congressman Viagra was a tool," she said.

Cassidy's eyes flew open. "What did you call him?" she couldn't help but smirk at Claire's colorful description of her ex-husband.

Claire shrugged. "I don't lie as much as people think. I tend to tell it like I see it, and they prefer to see that as a lie." Cassidy considered the statement. "You have no reason to trust me," Claire said. "You have less reason to like me."

"Do you care what I think?" Cassidy asked.

Claire started to reply with a resounding 'no' and stopped. She looked at Cassidy and shook her head. Claire closed her eyes. For some reason, she did care what Cassidy thought and that infuriated her.

Cassidy watched Claire, wondering what she might be thinking. Earlier, Cassidy had found Eleana in the kitchen looking more than a bit sullen. Cassidy adored Eleana. She had from the moment she met the young agent. Often, Cassidy mused that Eleana needed to consider a change in profession. Cassidy had seen the toll that Alex's work took on her. She'd witnessed it in Jonathan Krause. Neither Alex nor Jonathan was as hard as most people thought. Eleana was soft, not weak—soft. Cassidy felt for the young woman. It had been difficult for Cassidy to imagine Eleana with Claire Brackett. But, she had seen firsthand the affection that lingered between them, even if she was sure that Eleana had fallen in love with Jonathan.

Cassidy had approached the younger woman that morning and placed a comforting hand on Eleana's shoulder. Eleana had met Cassidy's eyes with sadness. She confided in Cassidy that she was heartbroken about Claire and that she could not understand why Claire had pushed her away the previous evening. Claire had been alone, and Eleana felt an incredible sense of pain and guilt that she could not help.

Cassidy looked at Claire and sighed. She decided to answer with a question of her own. "Why did you send Eleana away last night?" she asked Claire. She had an idea what the reason was, but she wanted to hear Claire voice it.

Claire opened her eyes and looked at Cassidy. "It was the right thing to do."

"It hurt her," Cassidy said.

"Not as much as staying could have," Claire replied.

"I see."

"You think I wanted to hurt her?"

"Did you?" Cassidy challenged.

"No," Claire's voice dropped. "I want her to be happy." Cassidy nodded. "People don't change," Claire whispered sadly.

"Would you have done the same thing a year ago?" Cassidy replied with another question.

"Huh?

"Would you have sent Eleana away a year ago if she had come to you that way?"

"Probably not," Claire answered.

"There's your answer."

"To?"

"To whether or not people can change, and to why I am standing here," Cassidy said.

***

Cassidy entered the study with Mackenzie in her arms. Alex took their daughter and placed her in a small play area that she had set up.

"I thought I'd see Claire with you," Alex commented.

Cassidy shrugged. It did not surprise her that Alex had expected she would invite Claire. "She passed. I don't think she's up to this just yet."

Alex's eyes narrowed in questioning. "Do I need to call Jen?"

"No."

"What did she say?" Alex asked.

"Later," Cassidy said.

Alex sat beside Cassidy on the sofa and looked at James McCollum. "So? Lynx? Sphinx? Whoever you are, tell us…We're all ears."

***

"YaYa will be waiting to see you at the bottom," Rose told Dylan as they neared the lift to go up the mountain.

"Grandma?"

"Yes?"

"How come Mom stopped skiing for so long?" he asked.

"Oh, well, I think that was probably because it reminded her so much of your grandfather," she answered him. "Your mom never really told me why, and I never pushed her to keep going with it. She would go, but only when I made a point for us to come here."

Dylan looked at his grandmother, his forehead crinkling as if he were in deep thought. "I wish I knew him."

Rose smiled. She didn't often talk about her husband with anyone, save Helen—not even Cassidy. It wasn't because she didn't think about him. She still missed him, but the end of their time together had been immensely painful and confusing for Rose. Jim McCollum had grown distant, at times even to Cassidy, although Rose was sure Cassidy did not remember that. He bordered on the line between what she considered to be depression and anger. Rose had struggled to understand what had happened to shift his personality so drastically. He had always been an even-tempered, fun loving man. When he began coming home smelling of alcohol, Rose had deliberately put some distance between them.

He went to the cabin often that last year before his death without his family. Cassidy never mentioned it, but Rose had come to believe that Cassidy did recall that fact. She suspected that was another reason that skiing and trips to Maine had become a point of sadness for her daughter for a long time. When Dylan came along, that slowly started to shift. And, when things in Cassidy's marriage to Christopher O'Brien began to tumble into disarray, Cassidy began making trips to the cabin with Dylan for long weekends and school vacations. It was a place that held memories, both of solace and of sadness. It provided an escape for Cassidy when she needed it most, just as it had for her father.

Rose smiled at her grandson as they slid onto the seats of the lift. "Your granddad was an interesting guy," she said.

"Am I like him?" Dylan wondered.

"A bit," Rose answered.

She could not deny that she saw her husband reflected in both of her grandchildren, although Mackenzie favored him physically more than Dylan did. Cassidy had favored him when she was a baby as well. As Cassidy grew, she seemed to begin to look more and more like Rose. Rose often wondered if Dylan would come to resemble his father even more than he did currently later in life.

"He loved to build things like you do," Rose said. "Loved puzzles too, and skiing. He would lose himself up on this mountain for hours on end skiing these slopes. To tell you the truth, I think that is the reason your mom loved it so much. She just loved being with him. You, on the other hand, love to ski."

"I wish Mom was here," Dylan said honestly.

Rose nodded. Cassidy had called early that morning. Rose knew that Cassidy had it in her head that Dylan was disappointed by Alex's absence. She was certain that Dylan would have loved to have Alex with them, but on this trip, in this place, it was his mother he truly missed. She knew he was enjoying the weekend with his grandmothers, but it was not the same as it would have been had Cassidy been with them.

"Someday," Dylan said as he looked out over the mountain, "I am going to ski Bear Claw with her."

"I have no doubt of that," Rose said. Dylan was already proficient on skis. It was one reason Rose had hesitated to take him on the more difficult trails. She was still an excellent skier, but she couldn't deny that Dylan was close to surpassing her already.

"Ready?" she asked him. Dylan nodded excitedly as they approached the top of the mountain. "You know, your grandfather would have been very proud to see you on those skis ready to tackle this mountain."

Dylan smiled proudly. "I wish he could see me."

Rose felt her eyes begin to water. She wished he could too. "I'm sure he can, Dylan. Wherever he is, I'm sure he is watching over you."

***

"What are you thinking?" Fallon asked Steven Brady. "There is something you aren't telling me," he surmised pointedly.

Brady looked back at the reports Jane had sent him on Rand Industries. Most of them consisted of lists of questionable meetings. Some contained company documents. A handful were transcripts of conversations that Tate had been able to acquire. It never ceased to amaze Steven Brady who and what the NSA could find a reason to listen in on. Things just were not sitting right with him. He'd learned a great deal in the last year about the program called Lynx—more than he wanted to know. Brady had never been one to need answers. He had chosen his profession to find the "bad guys" and put them away. Some people chased street thugs and drug dealers. Brady wanted to chase the people who fed the drug dealers and employed the street thugs. He wanted to find terrorists and wipe them out. He had always believed that his job was a noble one. In the last two years, he continued to accept orders and directives while he privately began to question the ethics and purpose of the cause he found himself supporting. He wasn't sure he even knew what that cause was anymore.

"Brady?"

"Sorry," Brady apologized for slipping away. "I just don't get this. It doesn't add up. The thing is, Fallon, one plus one can only ever equal two."

"Uh-huh."

"How is it that people always think they can somehow make it equal four?" Brady asked. Fallon shook his head. "Why are we looking at this shit? Who cares who met with Bob Gray? Hell, we met with Bob Gray. Who is he? Who does he answer to?"

"Isn't that why we are looking at these?" Fallon suggested.

"No, I don't think so," Brady said. He noted the smirk on Fallon's face. "Were you going to say anything?" he asked Fallon.

"Would it have done me any good?" Fallon returned. Brady sighed. "Someone wants to keep us from something," Fallon said.

"Yeah, but what?" Brady said. "Jane had to know I would put it together eventually. She sent Alex to Gray, which means Gray is in some way taking directives from her."

"Maybe she just wanted to buy a little time," Fallon surmised. "I agree with you, but why? What was Cassidy's father in to?"

"I'm not sure you'd believe me if I told you."

"Try me."

"Programming," Brady said.

"Computers?"

"People," Brady replied.

Fallon's mouth open and closed several times. "You're not joking," he said. "MyoGen is part of that?" Brady nodded. "Rand?"

"Presumably," Brady said.

"So? You think this has something to do with what Hawkins left there, don't you?" Fallon asked. Brady tipped his head in acknowledgment. "What do you think it was?"

"Only one way to find out," Brady said.

"I hate paperwork," Fallon told him.

"See? We do have something in common. Feel like a little field investigating?"

"Who's driving?" Fallon asked.

***

"I still don't understand the relationship between Lynx and Sphinx," Eleana said.

Edmond spoke. "You are confusing the men with the programs. Sphinx is both a program and a person. Lynx," he looked across the room to McCollum. "Lynx is a program named after the man who founded it."

"You," Alex said to McCollum.

"Yes," McCollum replied. He looked at Cassidy briefly and then back to Alex. "But," he continued, "Lynx was only a continuation of existing programs."

"You're referring to MK-Ultra," Krause surmised. "So, you decided to pick up where it left off?"

"There was no picking up, Jonathan. It never ended, only on paper. You know better than that," McCollum said.

"MK-Ultra?" Cassidy asked.

Alex turned to her. "It was a project the CIA began in the fifties."

"Dare I ask?" Cassidy went on.

"It was the name of a project that served as the umbrella for hundreds of programs," Alex said.

"What kind of programs?" Cassidy urged.

"The kind that messed with people's minds," Alex told her.

"It started as a way to address issues in the field. If an agent was captured or a soldier, how could we protect information? And, if we captured a soldier or an agent how could we extract information?" McCollum explained.

"Started? What did it end up as?" Cassidy asked bluntly. McCollum hesitated. He looked at Alex.

"Go on," Alex said. "You have a captive audience."

McCollum took a moment to center his thoughts. "If you can figure out how to get people to tell you anything or to tell you nothing, it stands to reason you could tell them what to do as well."

"Don't you already do that? Issue orders and whatnot," Cassidy asked.

McCollum nodded. "Yes. But, people can say no. People can choose not to comply with orders, Cassie." He took a deep breath and looked at Alex. "What would make the perfect spy? The perfect asset in the field?" he asked. Silence loomed as everyone waited for him to answer his own question. "The person who doesn't know he is spying at all. The person who has information and doesn't know the information she has," he said. "You can't divulge what you don't recall."

Alex shook her head. "You were trying to program people."

"We weren't trying," he said.

Cassidy put her face in her hands. "This is…How is that even possible?"

"It's possible," Krause muttered. Eleana and Cassidy both looked at him. Krause sighed. "I've seen it. It's possible."

"Hypnosis?" Eleana asked. "What? Drugs?"

"Yes," McCollum said. "And other things."

Cassidy looked at her father in disbelief. He looked back at her regretfully. "What other things?" Cassidy asked.

"Cass," Alex cautioned her wife. "You might not…"

"No, Alex. I want to know—right now."

McCollum answered stoically. "Sensory deprivation, electric shock therapy, sensory overload, sleep deprivation…Do you want me to go on?" he asked. Cassidy shook her head in disgust.

"Who?" Alex asked.

"I can't answer that," McCollum said.

"You mean, you won't," Alex accused.

"No, I mean that I don't know, Alex. At least, not as much as you think."

"It was your program," Krause said.

Edmond interceded. "No program belongs to any one person, Jonathan. Jim implemented the program at Major Waters' request."

"Jane's father?" Cassidy asked.

"Yes," Edmond answered.

McCollum continued. "My work was with agents and soldiers already assigned to duty in the field," he said. "That is how it started."

"Well, we all know nothing ends the way it starts, so what happened?" Alex asked.

"It showed promise. Essentially, we were able to program someone for a particular behavior, a specific assignment and embed a keyword to activate it."

"This is ridiculous," Cassidy interrupted. "This is why you left? What's next? You are going to tell me that there is a space ship with aliens hidden in New Mexico?"

"No, there is nothing like that in New Mexico," he replied evenly. "There are other programs housed there I am certain you would not approve of."

Alex leaned into Cassidy. "Are you okay?" Cassidy shook her head. She was livid and having a difficult time believing most of what she was hearing. "If you…"

"No, go on," Cassidy said.

"What happened to the program?" Alex repeated her question.

"The research was not mine, Alex. It belonged to the CIA. They began to expand it. They wanted to see if they could grow a crop. That's what they called it—growing a crop, also known as SEED."

"Of what?" Eleana asked.

"Assets," McCollum replied.

"Agents," Eleana said.

"No, not necessarily. I mean assets," McCollum repeated.

"What's the difference?" Eleana asked.

Krause looked at McCollum closely. "Not all for the field," Krause guessed.

"No. Not at all. Some would be placed in policy making. Some would be put in business, banking, education, wherever the agency saw a need."

"Why would you need to program people for education?" Eleana asked.

"Perception, Eleana," McCollum reminded her. "Perception is everything. People will believe anything if they hear it enough, even a lie. If the person telling it has conviction? If he believes it is the truth? All the more people will believe it."

"This is their pathway to war," Eleana said quietly.

"It is the pathway to everything," Edmond told his daughter. "War is part of it at times. To maintain control of a lie, you need a support network. Media, education, business, banking, and policy all play a role. What is in your textbooks? The truth or a version of that truth that leads you to a certain conclusion?" he asked. "Does the media beg you to ask questions or does it seek to give you the answers to the questions before you can even ask them? Would you invest in a lie if you knew that it was a lie?

"Jesus," Krause muttered.

"What did you mean growing?" Alex turned the conversation. McCollum sighed.

Cassidy looked directly at her father. "They wanted to start on children," she guessed. "Am I right? The earlier, the better."

"Yes."

Alex looked at Cassidy and then at McCollum. "What happened with The Collaborative?"

"For years, The Collaborative worked outside CIA boundaries. You have to understand that oversight was far stricter for many years. The CIA and the KGB, MI6, French and German Intelligence services all had their hands tied tighter than was required."

"Required for what exactly?" Alex asked.

Edmond answered. "The biggest lie, Alexis."

"Which was?"

"The Cold War. Don't get me wrong, Communism is not something that we or most of our sister nations supported. It did provide what we needed. There has always been tension between Russia and the other nations in The Collaborative, but then, there has been tension amid all parties at different times. People get greedy," Edmond observed. "They see ways to make a personal profit. That was initially one of The Collaborative's objectives—keep the assets in line, both the human ones and the financial ones. If you want to sell a war, even a cold one, you have to pay for it. There needed to be a council if you will, that operated outside of oversight. It began small. Like all things, the more it acquired, the larger it grew, the greedier some people became."

"And? The fracture?" Alex asked.

"Greed does funny things to people, Alexis. Some people in The Collaborative agreed with the CIA's plans. Some even thought to take them further. We had an agreement, the five of us. Swore and oath, in fact, that we would do whatever was necessary to protect our families."

"It was us, wasn't it?" Alex guessed. "The children they wanted to use. It was us." McCollum's silence served as his acknowledgment.

"So you left?" Cassidy interjected hotly.

"Not immediately," he told her. "And, not for the reasons you are thinking."

"You have no idea what I am thinking," Cassidy shot.

Alex took Cassidy's hand and held it firmly to calm her. "Why leave?" Alex asked.

"The program started to spiral. It became so far reaching that Nicolaus could not even trace all of it. Everyone wanted a piece—everyone. Imagine a cadre of unassuming, loyal subjects to do your bidding, no matter what that might be," McCollum said.

Alex pinched the bridge of her nose forcefully. "So? You ran away."

"You were right Alex, they wanted you. All of you. And, they were close. They had parts of my research, but I had the core. They had bits. I took the pieces with me when I went. It set them back far enough that Nicolaus was able to keep them at bay."

"From us?" Alex asked. McCollum nodded. "But, it wasn't perfect, was it? This SEED...."

"No, it wasn't."

"You're leaving didn't stop it, did it?" Alex challenged McCollum.

"It slowed it."

"Who? Me? Cass? Jonathan? Eleana? Who? Claire?" Alex's voice rose with each name she spoke.

"You and Cassidy were not subjected to anything. My death ensured that for her. Your father assured that for you and your younger brother."

"Me?" Krause asked. McCollum offered him an apologetic grin.

"Jim?" Edmond called to his friend. "Claire and…"

McCollum looked at his old friend and shook his head. He turned his attention to Eleana. "I'm sorry," he said. "I suspected about Claire. Until I spoke with her the other day, I never considered that you might have been dramatically affected. There are schools that subtly use program techniques. But, after hearing about Bill's stories. Well, it seems, perhaps, that it is possible you did not choose this path entirely of your own will," he told Eleana.

"What?!" Edmond's voice blared through the room. "What the hell are you talking about? Nicolaus never told me…."

"Nicolaus didn't know," McCollum said. "He wasn't even certain about Claire. By the time he learned about Jonathan it was too late. I can't say how effective it was." He turned to Eleana. "You were not with The Admiral constantly, and not under his care, but you were almost certainly exposed," McCollum said to Eleana.

"Bill?" Edmond asked forcefully. "I'll kill him!"

" Il ya eu assez de tueries! (There has been enough killing)!" Eleana yelled at her father.

Edmond sat back, red-faced. Krause and Alex were both sure they had never seen Edmond Callier so furious. Alex took a deep breath. "And, Claire?"

"Most certainly," McCollum said. "I fear it only got worse after her mother's death. He sought to wipe that, replace it."

"How would he do that?" Cassidy asked.

"Please don't ask me that," he said.

"Who else?" Alex asked. McCollum shook his head and looked downward. "Who else?" she demanded.

"There are so many, Alex. That's why I went to Russia underground. Assets were passed to your father for placement."

"Assets?" Cassidy looked at Alex.

"People they were brainwashing—for lack of a better term," Alex said. "My father, it would seem, placed them in the positions they were meant for," she said disgustedly.

"As much as possible, we brought them in. I looked to uncover what their objectives had been, with moderate success. If I could not determine that, we often sought to change it. There are risks involved with it. You can never completely wash away a person's memory, neither what is organic nor what is planted. That is one of SEED's greatest failures. One mission wasn't enough. Some people went through a number of processes, multiple times. The more that is repressed, the more triggers it creates. Breaks occur."

"What kind of breaks?" Krause asked.

"Emotional, psychological....behavior changes, and ironically enough, an asset can lose control altogether, depart into a unique reality—disconnected, violent, even what you might deem evil. They become capable of things..."

"Who?" Alex demanded again. "Who? Tell me one of those names was not Carl Fisher?"

Cassidy went cold. She looked at her father as he shut his eyes tightly. "Oh, my God," she whispered.

"O'Brien?" Alex guessed.

"Likely, yes. Kargen, Elliot," he looked at Edmond, who shook his head in disbelief. "Claire...Alex, that's why MyoGen is so important. They continued, widespread, steadily growing like The Collaborative itself. Their research? Their programs? There will likely be names that we do not have."

Alex nodded and took a deep breath. She wanted this over with for both Cassidy and Eleana soon, but she needed to know as much as possible. "And, the split with Ivanov?"

"Ivanov has always been rogue. He's not his father, just like none of us were our parents. But, he shares a vision with many others that to preserve what they have, they have to stem the growth. Intelligence is business now, Alex. The big pie is being cut into smaller pieces. Ivanov, Bill—they see an opportunity. Draw those deeper lines on the map again. Give the world a reason to fear a World War. Terrorism is effective in spurts. Nuclear annihilation, invasion? Those possibilities create a different kind of fear, one that breeds order instead of chaos."

"You think someone will use a nuke?" Krause asked.

"On a large scale? No. What? You think they had Claire liberate Cesium to make Carecom look bad? Come now, Jonathan. You think they bombed the embassy in Russia to shut Russ Matthews up? John? You think his assassination was about what? Passenger planes shot down, crashing mysteriously. You've heard the conspiracy theories about Russia, the CIA—all of it. Those are only fringe benefits, the little bonuses that make it all the more enticing for them. The same types of things are happening in Russia."

"You think John's death is part of that plan? No one is talking war," Krause pointed out. "There is no massive public outcry or fear over Russia becoming a threat to our security. The conversation is about terrorism, domestic woes…There is no uprising in Russia of nationalism either."

"Yet, Jonathan. They're whispers now. In time, they will become shouts. All of that? All of those things I mentioned are seeds too. They are the seeds of perception—changing perception takes time. And, Jonathan? It would not be the first time an asset was installed in The White House only to be removed to make way for war because he acted more on his conscience than his directives."

Cassidy let go of Alex's hand and walked silently over to Mackenzie, who was playing with a toy in the play yard that Alex had set up for her. She picked Mackenzie up, whispered in her ear and kissed her when Mackenzie giggled. Cassidy turned and headed for the door. She stopped abruptly and looked at her father. She regarded him silently for a moment before shaking her head and then nodding as if she had suddenly had an epiphany.

"I do not understand you," she said. "I'm not as naïve as you might think—any of you, in fact. I've lived in this world long enough, seen enough things—lost enough people for whom I cared to understand that what you say is true. People can be greedy. They can be selfish, hurtful, vindictive— violent. You're right about all of that. You sit here and you talk about assets," she said. She looked at Mackenzie. "People are not assets. They are people. Children are people. You bring life into this world and that life knows nothing but to love you," she told her father. "You choose to create life— you assume the responsibility to care for it. You talk about protecting me— protecting any of us." Cassidy looked at Edmond and shook her head again. She looked back at her father. "I wonder what it is you think you have protected us from," she said.

"Cassie," McCollum tried to reach his daughter.

"No. You've had the floor for a while. I listened. I heard every word you said. We all did. I've watched this madness unfold for too long silently. Protect us? Here we are—all of us. Well, not all of us. John is dead.

Christopher? Claire? What about her? Do you know how many nights I still wake up and see Carl Fisher's face?"

"Cass," Alex called gently to her wife.

Cassidy ignored Alex and continued. "Do you know that Alex struggles to stand some mornings because of that IED attack in Iraq? That I almost lost her once to this insanity?" Cassidy asked. Her voice remained even. "What about Mom? Dylan? What about Jane? Or Stephanie and Alexandra? How many children have to mourn their parents?"

"No one wanted this," he said softly. "We wanted to protect you," he told her. McCollum looked up and met Cassidy's eyes. "You have every right to hate me. I need you to know that I love you. I always will love you, Cassie."

Cassidy nodded. "I know that," she said. McCollum's surprise was evident. "I don't hate you," Cassidy said. "But, I don't know if I can forgive you either. And, that is not about me. I have Alex, I have Dylan, and Mackenzie. One day there will be someone else to add to that list," she turned briefly to Alex and smiled. "I have Pip and Jane….All of it, ironically, because of this madness. But, what you caused for them? The pain you caused Mom? I don't know if I can forgive that," she said. "I love you," Cassidy said.

Eleana closed her eyes as she listened to Cassidy calmly address her father. She was certain everyone in the room could feel Cassidy's anguish in spite of Cassidy's composure. Eleana felt her anger simmering as Cassidy spoke. Krause took hold of her hand. He watched Cassidy in awe. He had not been surprised by anything McCollum offered. Little surprised him anymore and he was sure that Alex had anticipated at least some of what Cassidy's father had divulged. He was not prepared for what he was now witnessing. It was difficult to watch, as if they were all intruding on a private moment. Yet, somehow he understood Cassidy's words were meant for everyone in the room in some way.

Cassidy sighed at the shocked expression on her father's face. "You can't come in here and fix what you chose to break years ago. If you want me in your life, if you honestly feel remorse for what you created at all—you will have to build something entirely new. We all have choices to make," Cassidy said. "That is yours." She turned to Alex. Alex smiled at her. "I've heard enough," Cassidy said.

Alex stood and walked Cassidy to the door. "I love you, Cassidy," she declared plainly.

Cassidy smiled at Alex. "I know. I'm sure you will never know how much I love you," Cassidy said. She kissed Alex on the cheek. Cassidy looked over at her father one last time. "I hope you make the right choice."

Chapter Sixteen

It only took seconds after Cassidy had left the room for Eleana to erupt. "You knew?" Eleana questioned her father.

Callier steadied himself. "We had an alliance, Eleana. You don't understand. We swore, all five of us to protect you above anything else. Whatever I have done was for that cause alone. There was a great deal at risk..."

"At risk? What the hell is it with you? All of you? You had a great deal at risk? What about Claire? What about Cassidy? What about me? You had a great deal at risk?"

"Eleana," Krause placed a hand on her arm gently.

Eleana tugged away from him violently. "No, Jonathan. I want an answer. An actual answer for once."

"What is it that you expect me to say? That I am sorry? I am. I'm sorry for many things," Callier said honestly.

Eleana scoffed at his words. "Sorry is a pitiful word. Were you sorry then?"

"I was sorry for Claire, Eleana. We all were. If I had any knowledge that you might have been exposed..."

"I don't even care about that right now. What about Cassidy? Were you sorry for her too?" Eleana asked.

"I didn't know about Jim," Callier reminded his daughter.

"Didn't know he was actually alive—yes, I know. You thought he was dead, right? Killed to preserve your....What did you call it? Alliance?"

"Eleana," Krause called softly. "Nothing he can say…"

"Nothing he can say can change the past. I know that."

"None of us wanted this," Callier said. "This…"

"You created this, Papa. You, The Admiral, Mr. McCollum, Jonathan's father—all of you. You created it. And now, what? You want to pretend that this was some crusade for the greater good? Whose good, Papa? Where is the good in all of this?"

"You don't understand, Eleana. We could not let the alliance fracture. If we lost control of the programs…If we had not tried to change the course. It would have destroyed lives. It…"

Eleana's disgusted chuckle sent a shiver up her father's spine. "You are pathetic. Your alliance? It is fractured, beyond repair. This Collaborative of yours—who do you think destroyed lives?" she asked with the shake of her head. "Did you not hear Cassidy? You shattered children—your own children."

"We tried to protect you."

"You failed," Eleana said flatly. "Je ne vous connais pas. (I don't know you)."

"No matter what you feel. I'm your father, Eleana, and I love you."

Eleana closed her eyes and spoke softly. " Non, Edmond. Vous êtes un étranger. (No, Edmond. You are a stranger)." Eleana looked back to her father one last time and shook her head sadly. Without another word, she calmly left the room.

***

Cassidy had just put Mackenzie in her highchair when she heard a car pull into the driveway. "This cannot be good." She walked the short few paces to the study and opened the door. "Alex? Someone just pulled in the driveway."

Alex exchanged a glance with Krause. "I'll go," he said.

"Where's Kenz?" Alex asked.

"In the kitchen."

"Take her and go upstairs," Alex said.

Alex had no idea who could have known they were all here. She had no message from Jane. That caused immediate concern for Alex. Had it been Brady or Fallon, she would have expected a call. She looked at McCollum. Without a word, Alex walked to a safe underneath her father's old desk. In less than a minute, she was standing in front of James McCollum. She had stripped the man of his weapon when they had arrived.

"Take it," Alex handed him his pistol. "Go with Cassidy." She followed him out the door and called after Cassidy. "Tell Eleana to stay with Claire. Your father will protect you in case," Alex stopped when she realized the irony in her words. "Do not let anything happen to them," Alex told McCollum. He nodded and followed Cassidy up the stairs.

"Me?" Edmond asked.

"Go back in the study and call Jane. Tell her what just happened and that we seem to have company. See if you can find out where Brady and Fallon are. Lock the door behind you."

Edmond complied immediately. Alex took a few deep breaths, exhaling each forcefully. She made her way to Krause. "I'm not armed."

"I know. Let's hope you don't need to be," he said.

Krause waited with his hand on the door knob. He looked out the small hole in the door, waiting for a face to come into view. He steadied his breathing, feeling an uncharacteristic nervousness emanating from Alex. Normally, they were both controlled and unemotional in uncertain situations or dangerous ones. That was a necessary survival skill. What had just transpired would have been enough to unsettle nearly anyone. Alex's family was upstairs. That made this situation all the more tenuous.

"Just stay behind me, until we know," he told Alex.

Two quick knocks came. Krause could not see anyone. Another knock, this time louder. "I know your home," a voice carried through the door. "Come on, Alex."

Krause jumped back when an eye met his and the owner of the eye stepped back and deliberately into view. "Christ Almighty," he groaned as he opened the door, his gun at his side. "It's Hawk."

"Geez, Krause! Do you greet all of Alex's friends this way? Taking the older brother role to a whole new level," Hawkins teased.

"Hawk?" Alex stepped into the foyer. "What the hell are you doing here?"

"I figured with this crew you would be serving lunch soon," Hawkins quipped. Alex pulled her into the house forcefully. "What?" Hawkins asked. "Was I supposed to bring pizza or something?"

"You could have called," Alex said. She gave Jonathan the nod to give the all clear to everyone.

"I thought Tate would have let you know I was coming."

Alex shook her head. "I'm going to kill him," she groaned.

"You sure are jumpy," Hawk said.

"Can't imagine why," Alex replied.

"Why then?" Hawk grinned.

"How about my dead father-in-law is upstairs and two of my ex-lovers are in the house. How much more do you think Cass can take?"

"What can't I take?" Cassidy asked from behind Alex.

Alex looked upward, closed her eyes and took a deep breath. "Who did I piss off?" she mumbled. Alex turned and smiled at Cassidy. "Cass, this is Charlie Hawkins, my former…"

"Partner," Cassidy finished the sentence. "Yes, I remember. Nice to meet you, Agent Hawkins," Cassidy said with a smile.

"Hawk," Hawkins gave Cassidy her preferred name. "Everyone calls me Hawk. Nice to meet you too."

Cassidy felt her phone vibrate. She passed Mackenzie to Alex and took her leave to answer it.

"Hey, Helen," Alex heard Cassidy's voice grow more distant.

"So what are you doing here?" Alex asked Hawkins.

"Shit, Alex," Hawk chuckled. "That baby looks kind of like you."

"You think?" Alex beamed. "I think she looks like Cass."

"Is Nicky the…"

"What are you doing here, Hawk?"

"Got some information I think maybe we should talk about."

"Am I going to like this information?" Alex asked.

"Bah!" Mackenzie called out happily.

"Yeah, that's what I'm afraid of Kenz," Alex told her daughter. "Oh, hell, I don't see how this day can possibly get any worse now. Let's have it."

"Alex!" Cassidy called out as she hurriedly came back into view.

Alex turned and looked at her wife. Cassidy was pale and Alex could see the phone trembling in her hand. "Cass? What is it?"

Cassidy shook her head. "Dylan."

***

Alex took the phone from Cassidy's hand. "Mom?"

"Alexis…"

"Where's Dylan?"

"He's still on the mountain," Helen said.

"How badly is he hurt?"

"I don't know. It's not life-threatening. All the Ski Patrol told me was that he took a good spill. He injured his arm and they want to check him out. They worry about concussions," Helen said. "Rose is with him."

"Does she have her phone?"

"I think so, but Alexis the chances you will get her are slim. I just wanted you to know they are taking him to the emergency room at the local hospital."

"We'll be there as soon as we can," Alex said.

"Alexis, it is almost four hours from you. It's supposed to start snowing…."

"We'll be there," Alex said. "Call Cass as soon as you know anything."

"I will. You need to calm down. He'll be okay. We can handle it," Helen said.

"I know you can. We'll be there as soon as we can," Alex said again. She looked at Cassidy. "He'll be okay."

"I know, I just hate that we are so far away," Cassidy said.

"Me too."

Hawkins cleared her throat. "Alex? What about the…"

Alex's jaw tightened. "Go in the kitchen. I'll be there in a second," she told Hawkins. "Cass, go pack us what we need. Sounds like we might be stuck there until Wednesday. Plus, who knows how Speed will be feeling."

"Alex, can you do this now? I can….."

"Nothing is more important than you and our kids," Alex said. "Nothing."

"I'll get Kenzie ready."

"Hey, Cass?"

"Yeah?"

"Maybe I am crazy, but if we're going to the cabin…Maybe…"

Cassidy nodded. "What about Edmond?"

Alex smirked. "We'll stick him in back. I think Eleana could use the space."

"I'll tell my father."

Alex watched Cassidy climb the stairs. "She'll tell me what?" McCollum asked hesitantly.

Alex spun around and smiled at him. "You lived in Siberia, right?"

"Yes?"

"Good. You're still familiar with snow," Alex said as she headed toward the kitchen.

"Snow?"

***

"Not that I am not happy to see you," Alex began, "but, I need to leave soon. So, what is it that you needed to tell me?"

"Tate picked up some chatter at Carecom from the night everything went down," Hawk said.

"Why am I not surprised the NSA is listening to my company's business?"

Hawk shrugged. "You know how it is. He didn't get much."

"What did he get?" Krause asked.

"Something about a distraction."

"Okay?" Alex sought an explanation. "And?"

"I know….I'm getting there. At first, that was all he had. There are some other words: keep, place, Admiral, and, well, it sounded like FBI, but that one was hard to discern. And, Alex? It was two voices. One might have been your security guy. Who is doing your background checks?" Hawk added.

"Why? Need a job?" Alex asked.

"Alex?" Krause shook his head. "Marcus saw two people that night. We already assumed one was your security man, and that there is a reason he has disappeared. But, think about it. The only words McCollum got from him were compromise and see."

Alex sighed. "I know. You're thinking what I am thinking?"

"Hello! What are you thinking?" Hawk asked.

"The break into Carecom was a distraction from something else. I'm sure there were some incentives, but they wanted us on another trail," Alex asserted.

"Think they are looking to compromise MyoGen for some reason? Maybe Ivanov knows something we don't," Krause said. "You heard McCollum. What if that program got so big that Ivanov somehow maneuvered ASA into the middle of it?" Krause asked.

"Shit," Alex rubbed her forehead. "Think that is why my father cut off the funnel to ASA? He suspected it?"

"Maybe," Krause said.

Alex looked at Edmond as he entered the room. "What did Jane say?"

Edmond shook his head. "She doesn't know where Brady and Fallon are."

"What do you mean?" Alex asked.

"I mean, she doesn't know, Alexis. They are off the grid—completely. She had them working some files from Rand and ASA…."

"Maybe they picked up on the same thing," Krause guessed.

"Why wouldn't they call in?" Hawk asked. "That's not like Brady."

"Yeah, well, Brady spent a year under, Hawk. He might not operate the way you remember," Alex said.

"You're not thinking he is working with The Admiral?" Krause asked.

"Not really, no, but I do want to talk to my father-in-law and get his take on that," Alex said.

"You trust McCollum to tell you the truth?" Krause was shocked.

"About that? Yeah, I do," Alex said. She had little reason to trust James McCollum, but his actions did not lead her to believe he would compromise them now, certainly not if he loved Cassidy. And, that was about the only thing Alex was sure about where McCollum was concerned—he loved Cassidy.

"Perhaps, they headed to MyoGen," Edmond suggested. "If they thought that you might be…"

Krause agreed. "Makes sense, Alex," he said. "When do you…."

"I can't go," Alex said. "Cass and I are on our way to Maine."

"You're leaving?" Edmond asked.

"Yep. You and your old friend are too," Alex told him. "It'll give you a chance to catch up with Mom," she said with a smirk. "And, you're going to help with something." She glanced back to Krause. "Dylan got hurt."

"Is he…."

"Okay, I think. Badly enough that they are taking him to the hospital. Cass and I need to go."

"It's okay. Eleana and I will see if we can't catch up with Fallon and Brady at MyoGen," Krause offered.

"What about me?" Hawk asked.

Alex's lips curled into a mischievous grin. "Oh, I have the perfect assignment for you."

***

"You can't be serious," McCollum looked at Cassidy in complete disbelief.

"I'm completely serious," she said as she closed a suitcase.

"Cassie, I don't think that is a good idea. I never intended to tell your mother…"

"I'm sure. If I heard you correctly earlier, you never intended a lot of things," she replied. "What did you intend?" she asked her father. "Wait, let me guess? You thought you could come in here, turn all of our lives upside down and then just leave again? Am I right?"

"It would be for the best."

"For whom? For you?" Cassidy challenged.

"For you, for Rose…For all of you."

Cassidy nodded. "Is that what you think? That you can just come into people's lives and open old wounds—that you can profess that you love someone and then just walk away?"

"I've hurt you enough."

"So? Your answer would be to hurt me more?"

McCollum was confused. "I don't think…"

"No, you don't think. At least, not like I do. I told you—it's your decision. If you want to be a part of my life, it can't be what it was. You don't know me anymore. I'm not sure I ever knew you at all. It doesn't change the fact that I love my father," Cassidy sensed her father was about to speak. "I'm not finished. You can make whatever decision you wish. You should know, I am done with the lies and done with all the secrets."

"Did you hear what I told you earlier?" he asked.

"Every word. What did you think? That would scare me into submission? I'm not your asset, Dad. No matter what you decide, I will tell Mom the truth. And, I will tell my children when they are old enough, and I do mean all of it," Cassidy said. "For now, I will tell them only what they need to know, but I will not protect your lie. I have one of my own that has torn me apart for too long already."

"You did what you had to do," McCollum said.

"No, I did what I chose to do, just like you. I have to live with that for the rest of my life. I don't have to live with protecting yours, and I don't intend to."

"Cassie."

Cassidy picked up Mackenzie. She stepped closer to her father. "Everything you have missed," she said to him. "For what? It's your choice, Dad. But, I don't care about the answers or the issues in the world right now. I care about my family. So, if you aren't going to come with us—don't be here when we get back."

"My staying could endanger you all the…"

"Your leaving will do that too," Cassidy said. "For what it's worth," she said as she took her leave. "I hope you stay."

***

"Claire?"

Claire rolled over and looked at Eleana. "You've been crying," she observed. Eleana looked at her friend helplessly. "Come here," Claire told Eleana.

Eleana walked slowly to the bed and fell into Claire's arms. "Are you going to send me away again?"

Claire sighed and pulled Eleana closer. "Why are you crying?"

"Why did they do it?" Eleana asked.

"I don't know," Claire said. "I don't know why any of us do what we do at times," she confessed.

"Some of us weren't given much choice," Eleana said softly.

Claire hadn't needed to hear the conversation downstairs to imagine what had happened. She kissed Eleana on the forehead. "Whatever he told you, now you get to choose what to do with it," Claire said.

"What about you?" Eleana said. "I…"

"I will be okay," Claire promised.

"I'm sorry."

"For what?" Claire asked.

"For not knowing, for leaving you, for…"

"Stop," Claire said. "Stop." She pushed Eleana away slightly so that she could look into her eyes. "You can't save me, Eleana. Wasn't it you that told me that?"

"I didn't know that…"

"That doesn't matter."

"Yes, it does," Eleana said.

"Maybe. It doesn't change things. You can't change who I have been."

"I don't want to change you, Claire. I love you. I just want to..."

"Help me? I know. Maybe one day you will be able to. Now is not that time."

"Why do you keep pushing me away?" Eleana asked painfully.

"Because I need to change me, Eleana. I don't know if I can. The one good thing I have done in my life is love you. It's the one thing I would never change. And, I need to start there. Someone helped me realize that," Claire said.

"Cassidy," Eleana guessed. "Cassidy told you to..."

"No, you know her better than me," Claire reminded Eleana. "She just said some things that made sense to me."

Eleana sniffled. "She does that."

"She reminds me of my mother," Claire spoke so softly that Eleana barely heard her.

Eleana smiled as she recalled Claire's mother. She had been a gentle woman. Eleana's mother was far more rigid and disciplined with her than Claire's mother had been. For years, looking back, Eleana wondered how Marjorie Brackett survived living with The Admiral. The thought made Eleana sick—she hadn't. Eleana took a minute to think about Claire's words. She felt the sincerity in them, and she could see the likeness as well.

"I guess she's kind of like everyone's mother sometimes," Eleana said. "I always have thought of it more as an older sister, but it's true. It's kind of spooky, actually. She just knows things. I wonder if that happens when you become a mom," Eleana mused.

Claire smiled at Eleana's curious expression. "One day you can tell me if it does," Claire said.

"What?"

Claire kissed Eleana gently on the lips. "I love you, El. You need to let me go."

"I don't know how."

"I know, that's why I am doing it for you. See? Being the bitch can come in handy sometimes," Claire tried to lighten the mood.

"You're not a bitch."

"You see something no one else does."

"That's not true, Claire. And, it doesn't matter anyway. You need to see it for yourself," Eleana said.

"I know," Claire replied.

"You really want me to go?"

"No," Claire confessed. "But, you need to."

Eleana nodded. She leaned in and captured Claire's' lips in a tender kiss. "Not goodbye," she whispered. "Just…"

"I'll see you," Claire said. She watched Eleana as Eleana opened the door and then closed her eyes.

Cassidy bumped into Eleana in the hallway. "Eleana?" Eleana shook her head. Cassidy smiled knowingly. "It's because she loves you," Cassidy offered.

"I know, but that doesn't make it hurt any less."

"It never does," Cassidy agreed. She kissed Eleana on the cheek. "Jonathan is looking for you." Eleana nodded. "Let him in," she said. Eleana nodded silently again and walked down the stairs.

Cassidy looked at Mackenzie. "This family is a mess," she said.

"Bah…Moo. Moo."

Cassidy giggled and stepped into Claire's room. "You okay?"

"Nope," Claire replied honestly. Cassidy chuckled. "I told you," Claire said. "I don't tend to lie. Just, people don't usually like what I have to say."

"Alex and I have to leave."

Claire surprised herself with her question. "Everything okay?"

"Nope," Cassidy answered. This time, Claire chuckled. "I don't like to lie either. Too messy," Cassidy said.

Cassidy smiled at the lingering question in Claire's eyes. She knew that everyone in the house, except Eleana, doubted Claire would ever change at all. Cassidy didn't care much what anyone thought at the moment. She had no idea how much Claire would change or whether the changes would ultimately be for the good. But, she had no doubt that Claire had already begun.

"Dylan wiped out skiing. We need to get to Maine."

"Is he okay?" Claire asked genuinely.

"I'm sure he'll survive. If it puts him out of commission for any time, he will not be happy."

"Cassidy?"

"Yeah?"

"Is there like some weird thing that happens when you have kids? Like a radar thing or something?" Claire asked.

Cassidy laughed. "I don't think so, why?"

"No reason."

Cassidy scratched her brow and pursed her lips. "Take it easy on those pills. Jen will be here tomorrow."

"I'm not stoned!" Claire defended herself. "Why does everyone think that?"

"Just behave yourself," Cassidy warned as she began to leave.

"Hey, Cassidy," Claire stopped her. "I hope Dylan is okay."

Cassidy nodded. "I'll see you."

"Yeah," Claire whispered as Cassidy closed the bedroom door. "See you."

***

"Anyone who can tame Alex deserves my respect," Hawk poked Cassidy as they approached Claire's room.

"It's nice to have a face to accompany the name," Cassidy said sincerely.

"Oh no, I don't think I want to know what she told you," Hawk said.

"All good," Cassidy promised. "Well, most of it anyway," she winked.

"She thinks so highly of me she's letting me babysit," Hawk complained.

Cassidy laughed. "You might find the company more interesting than you'd imagine," she said.

"I've no doubt Brackett is interesting. I never wanted children," Hawk chided. "Don't have the patience."

Cassidy nodded. "She might surprise you."

"Do I detect a note of admiration in your voice?" Hawk asked curiously.

"You detect a note of empathy," Cassidy corrected Alex's former partner.

"You do realize who that is in there?"

"I do. I just wonder if any of you really do," Cassidy offered. As if on cue, Kenzie started babbling loudly in the distance. "Sorry," she said. "Duty calls."

Hawk watched Cassidy head toward the sound of Mackenzie's voice. She looked the bedroom door in front of her and groaned. "Duty? Ugh. Thanks a lot, Alex. What did I do to deserve this? I didn't think it was that bad."

***

Alex wished that they had Cassidy's SUV as she loaded two bags into her mother's trunk.

"Maybe it's a good thing he's not coming. Besides the fact that Edmond is ready to kill someone, this car is small," Alex tried to make light of the fact that James McCollum had seemingly decided to stay behind.

Cassidy's defeated smile made Alex want to pummel the older man all over again. There was a part of her that was relieved. She had no idea how they would handle the news with Rose, and at the cabin, they would have to tell Dylan something. But, that all seemed inevitable no matter what. And, Alex had thought that the cabin would be safer both emotionally and physically for the fallout. She leaned in to kiss Cassidy on the forehead and caught sight of McCollum carrying a small bag.

Alex whispered in Cassidy's ear. "Don't look now." Cassidy turned around slowly. Alex extracted Mackenzie from Cassidy's arms. "I'll get Kenz strapped in."

McCollum took a step forward. "Hi," Cassidy said.

"I'm still not convinced this is a good idea," he said.

"Me neither," Cassidy said flatly. McCollum looked at her in amusement. "I told you, I am done with lies," Cassidy said.

"Cassie, what about Dylan? How are you…"

"Well, I guess we tell him the truth," she said. "The parts we can. You had to go away somewhere. There was an accident. It was so far away that no one found you until Uncle Pip did, and he brought you home. Until then, we all thought you were dead."

"Sounds crazy to hear it."

"It is crazy," Cassidy said. "Doesn't make it not true. Come on," she told him.

"Your mother…."

"That's between the two of you. Alex will call Helen on our way."

"You think that will help?" Buffer the shock I mean?"

"Nope," Cassidy replied flatly as she climbed into the back seat with Mackenzie. McCollum froze, not sure what to do.

"You do remember how to get into a car?" Cassidy asked.

"I...."

"Sit next to your granddaughter," she instructed him.

Alex turned around from the front seat. "Is it me, or does this feel more like National Lampoon's than the X-Files?"

"This is a bad idea," McCollum whispered to himself outside the door.

"I heard that," Cassidy said. "Get in the car, Dad."

McCollum took his seat and looked at Cassidy in amazement. "How did..."

Alex laughed in the front seat. "You want to keep your secrets safe in this family, don't speak," she advised him. "Cass has bat hearing.

"Drive the car, Alfred," Cassidy said.

"Yes, Mrs. Wayne."

"Bah!" Kenzie screamed out. "Moooooo!"

"See? The cow!" Alex declared as she pulled out of the driveway.

Cassidy closed her eyes. National Lampoons—accurate.

Chapter Seventeen

Eleana had been silent during their flight and still had not spoken. Krause had been trying to sort through the facts. Somehow, his thoughts kept turning to the woman beside him. Cassidy had pulled him aside before she left.

"You need to tell her the truth."

"Who?" Krause asked Cassidy.

"Eleana. Tell her, Pip. She needs you right now. Her whole life just got ripped out from under her. Claire, who she might have been, all of it."

"So did you," he replied.

"Yes, but I have what I need," Cassidy said. "It doesn't stop the anger and the hurt, but it does help. You need her too."

"Cassie…"

"Pip, she is not me. You never lost me, because you never really had me," Cassidy said truthfully. "There's only ever been one person for me. I just hadn't met her yet."

"I know."

"You have Eleana. Don't lose her," Cassidy said.

"I don't know where to begin."

"Yes, you do," Cassidy said. She kissed him on the cheek.

"Tell Dylan I said hi, okay?"

"I will. Tell Eleana," Cassidy said again.

"What do you think?" Eleana asked Krause softly from the passenger seat of the rental car.

"About getting into MyoGen?" Krause asked.

"About any of it," Eleana said.

"I think, I love you," Krause said, surprising Eleana.

"What did you say?"

"I said that I love you," he repeated.

Eleana laughed. "You have interesting timing," she commented.

"I'm kind of new at this," he said.

"Breaking into buildings?" she quipped.

"Relationships."

"Is that what we have?" Eleana asked hesitantly.

"I hope it can be," Krause said honestly.

"You think we're going to die, don't you?" she asked him.

"What?"

"You do. You think that we're walking into a hornet nest."

Krause chuckled. "Distinct possibility," he said. "I do."

"Think we're going to die?" she asked.

"No," he laughed. "Love you."

"Gets easier to say, huh?" she teased him.

"I guess it does."

"You could have picked a time when we were alone."

"We are alone," he reminded her.

"Not in a car, at night, on our way to possibly be killed by hornets," she said.

"Did you take one of Claire's pills?" he asked.

"I was about to ask you the same thing," Eleana replied. "And, I love you too."

"Well, good—we can die in love," he joked.

"Not funny."

***

"What did you do to Toles?" Claire asked Hawk.

"Excuse me?"

"To pull babysitting duty," Claire said. "Pass the chips."

Hawk stuck a potato chip in her mouth and handed Claire the bag she was holding. "I could ask you the same thing. You're like her captive. Oh, how the mighty have fallen," Hawk said. "Sparrow falls from the sky."

"Clever—Hawk."

"I thought so."

"I'm sure. So?" Claire munched a chip. "We're stuck here. What do you want to do?" Claire asked. Hawk grinned. "Not that I wouldn't, but, at least, let me shower first."

"Clever," Hawk returned.

"That's what my daddy always said."

Hawk nodded. "No offense, Brackett, but your father is the biggest asshole I have ever met."

"Made a good impression, huh?"

"Almost as good as that idiot Kargen," Hawk said. "Pass that bag."

Claire took a handful of chips and threw the bag gently to Hawk. "Kargen was a Tool."

"I agree."

"So? You were Toles', what? Girlfriend?" Brackett asked.

"Could ask you the same thing."

Claire choked on a chip. "Great sex a handful of times does not make a relationship," Brackett said. "You?"

"Short lived. Alex doesn't do relationships."

"Does now," Claire said.

"What's up with that?" Hawk asked curiously.

"She could do a lot worse," Claire commented as she reached for the soda next to the bed.

"Alex is a good catch."

"I didn't mean Cassidy," Claire chuckled. "You ask me, Cassidy got the short end of the stick in the deal."

"Got a crush on Mrs. Toles?" Hawk poked.

"Nope. Just telling it like I see it."

"So? If we are really stuck here, what do you want to do?"

"Shower."

"Okay? You need help?" Hawk asked.

"Are you offering?" Claire flirted.

"Beats watching you munch chips in that bed."

"You know, if I felt better, I might take that as a come on," Claire said.

"If you felt better, it would be one."

Claire laughed. "You sure you can handle this?"

Hawk smirked. "I think I should be asking you that question."

"Smooth," Claire said.

"Most of the time," Hawk replied as she helped Claire up. "Why didn't Alex get you some crutches or something?"

"You know how it is," Claire said. "Anything to keep me in bed."

Hawk laughed. "You're not what I expected."

"Yeah, I get that a lot lately," Claire replied.

Hawk opened the bathroom door and looked at Claire. Claire reached for the shower and winced. "Oh yeah, you can do this yourself," Hawk said.

"I can do it," Claire said.

"You get hurt any worse and Alex will kill me. No way. For whatever reason she wants you safe."

"She wants me watched."

"Probably true. She made me swear that I would take care of you," Hawk said. "She didn't even offer to pay me. Don't they have kids? Since when is babysitting free?" Hawk complained.

"She actually said that?" Claire asked.

"Yeah, she did. So, help me help you. Make it easier for both of us."

"Trust me, Hawk, when you get my clothes off, it is going to be anything other than easier for both of us," Claire smirked.

"I'm going to kill Alex," Hawk groaned.

***

"What the hell is this place?" Brady asked Fallon.

"You tell me, I'm just a beat cop, remember?"

"Fallon, you are hardly a beat cop and everyone knows it," Brady replied. "And, anyway, I think that's a more noble profession."

"I'd have to agree," Fallon said.

"Thinking of going back to your roots?" Brady asked as he led Fallon deeper into one of Rand Industries' labs.

"Maybe," Fallon said. "No offense? This shit is not what I signed up for."

"Yeah."

Fallon moved toward a long table that sat at the left side of the room while Brady investigated the beds and machines that were placed at its center. "Hey?" Fallon called over.

"What is it?"

"Not sure. Take a look," Fallon said. Brady moved beside Fallon and looked at a computer screen. He stroked his chin and groaned. "Think somebody knew we were coming? Wanted us to see this?"

"No," Brady said. "I think somebody else was here."

"Why would they leave this open to the world? If they wanted to dump it—why not wait until it finished?" Fallon asked as he typed on the keypad of the computer to try and save the files running and deleting.

"Only one reason," Brady answered.

"Yeah? What's that?"

"They didn't expect anyone would ever see it."

***

Alex pulled into the hospital lot and parked the car. "Not here," she said to McCollum.

Cassidy moved to unbuckle Mackenzie. McCollum noticed her hand shaking. He understood immediately that he was the cause. Helen had called during their drive to let Cassidy know that Dylan did not have a concussion. He did have a broken wrist and a sprained ankle. She had told Cassidy that they were waiting for some more x-rays to determine if anything needed to be done before setting his wrist and casting it. Cassidy was relieved about Dylan, but her uneasiness was increasing steadily about seeing her mother. She wanted to put the task on her father. The more she thought about it, the more Cassidy understood how cruel that would be to do to Rose. Somehow, Cassidy needed to find a way to prepare her mother for the unfathomable.

McCollum moved to unbuckle Mackenzie and took Cassidy's hand.

"Cassie, you don't have to do this. I will tell her."

Cassidy shook her head. "I need to prepare her," she said. "You can't know what it was like for me to see you standing there. And, I owe that to her. Mom is...Mom was the most important person in my life for nearly all of it. If I don't tell her, I would feel like I was lying to her. I can't bear that."

"I understand," he told Cassidy.

Cassidy took a deep breath. "Will you be all right here?" she asked with concern.

"I have spent time in much darker accommodations," he told Cassidy. Cassidy offered him a somber smile and nodded as she exited the car. Alex peered into the backseat. "I'll be here," McCollum promised. "Take Edmond. It might help."

Alex remained still for a moment. "Whatever happens, you should know one thing," she said.

"You'll kill me if I hurt her again?"

"Probably, but that's not what I was going to say," Alex told him. "It means a lot to her that you came," she said. "I can't say I understand, but she really does love you." Alex was positive the older man was beginning to tear up. "Don't let her down."

"I don't know if I can promise that."

"Don't bag on her," Alex said. "Take the blows and stick it out." Alex closed the door to the car and took Cassidy's hand. "Ready?"

"What did you say to him?" Cassidy wondered.

"I just told him the truth."

***

"I can't get any signal," Brady said. "You?"

"No."

"Shit. Is it still downloading?"

"Yeah," Fallon answered. "But, if I did this right, it should be downloading to Alex in real time on her secure server at Carecom."

"Definitely not your everyday cop," Brady said. "Let it run."

"Just let me check one thing," Fallon said. "I want to make sure she sees it."

"Make it fast, Fallon. There's a reason it wasn't completely wiped."

"I know," Fallon said. "That's why I have to get it to Alex—no matter what."

***

"Mom!" Dylan yelled when he saw Cassidy open the door to the examination room he was in.

"I'll let you two talk," Rose said. She kissed Cassidy on the cheek. "I'm sorry, Cassie."

"Not your fault, Mom," Cassidy assured her with a smile.

"I'll see you in a bit, Dylan," Rose promised.

"Okay, Grandma. Can we still get pizza?"

Rose laughed. "I'll see what we can arrange," she said as she left the room.

"I bagged, Mom," Dylan said sadly.

Cassidy smiled at him. "I heard. How's the arm?" Cassidy moved swiftly to his side. She kissed him on the forehead and ran her fingers through his hair.

"You're not mad?" he asked.

"Mad? Dylan, why on earth would you think I would be mad at you?"

"Mom, Black Bear is like a bunny slope," Dylan said.

Cassidy bit back a laugh. "It happens," she said.

"Not to you," Dylan proclaimed.

"Oh, yes, to me too," Cassidy admitted. "I just have been lucky that I haven't broken anything."

"It hurts," he confessed.

"I'll bet it does," Cassidy replied just as Alex peeked in.

"Hey? Up for some more company?" Alex asked.

"Alex!"

"Hey, Speed. How are you feeling?" Alex asked him.

"My ankle hurts worse than my wrist," he said.

"I'm sorry, Speed."

"It's okay. It was my fault," Dylan said.

"Your fault? That you fell?" Alex was puzzled.

"Yeah. I got ahead of Grandma."

"Dylan," Cassidy said firmly. "You know that you need to stay with an adult."

"I know, Mom. Just, I was doing so good! You should have seen it...I don't know what happened," he said sadly.

Cassidy smiled. "It happens, Dylan. It will happen again," she said. Cassidy caught Alex's stare as Alex's eyes flew open. Cassidy chuckled. Something about skiing made Alex's overprotective nature kick into high gear. "Hopefully, next time you will land a little softer. Learning to fall is part of the deal, Dylan."

"I know. I tried to do what you taught me," he said. "It just happened so fast."

"Usually does," Cassidy observed. "You know, your grandfather broke his nose once skiing Black Bear."

"No way!"

"He did. He was skiing backward, teaching me. He hit some ice, I think. He went over backward like a cartoon. It was actually kind of funny," Cassidy recalled, "until he sat up and I saw the blood pouring down his face."

"Gross," Dylan said.

"Pretty much," Cassidy agreed. "I was scared to ski the next day. He made me go anyway, right back to Black Bear."

"I won't be able to ski anymore this year."

"I know," Cassidy sighed.

"Am I going to miss soccer?" Dylan asked fearfully.

"I don't know, sweetie," Cassidy said honestly.

"Hey? Where's Kenzie?"

Alex answered. "She's with Grandma and YaYa."

Cassidy looked at Dylan proudly. "I'm proud of you."

"You are? I bagged!"

Cassidy chuckled. Dylan could be a perfectionist at times, and he was quite competitive. It reminded her of Alex. "Yeah, I am. YaYa told me you made Grandma laugh."

"Grandma was upset," Dylan said. "I think she was scared."

"I'm sure she was," Cassidy agreed. "Would it be okay if Alex stayed with you for a bit while I go see Grandma?"

"Am I in trouble?" he asked nervously.

"No," Cassidy answered. "You learned a lesson, I hope."

"Yeah, don't lean so far right."

"Dylan…."

Dylan smiled mischievously. "Don't get too far ahead of you or Grandma."

Cassidy grinned. Dylan had grown up so much in the last year that it scared her at times. He was quickly becoming a young man. "You can tell Alex about the trails," she said. "She doesn't know much about all of that."

"Okay," he agreed happily.

Cassidy kissed Alex on the cheek. "I'll be back."

"I'll be here," Alex promised. She whispered in Cassidy's ear. "Mom knows," Alex said. "She'll be nearby. Lean on her if you need to."

Cassidy nodded. "I'll see you in a bit. Come get me if the doctor comes in?" Cassidy asked.

"You know it," Alex said. She sat down on the edge of Dylan's bed. "So…Tell me what this double diamond thing is."

***

Hawk studied Claire Brackett as she slept. Claire had fallen asleep on the couch in Alex's mother's living room after Hawk had helped her downstairs. Claire needed a change of scenery, and so did Hawk. Eventually, they had opted to flip on the television and Claire had drifted off during a marathon of Get Smart reruns. One moment, Claire had been laughing. The next, Hawk heard soft snoring coming from the couch.

Helping Claire shower had proved both humorous and a bit disconcerting. Hawk could not deny that Claire Brackett was a beautiful woman. And, Claire was an incurable flirt. It took more restraint than Hawk had expected not to seduce Claire. She had not taken a lover in longer than she preferred to think about, and she had little doubt that Claire could have quelled the dull ache that had taken up residence in various parts of her body. But, Claire had met the situation with humor, another surprise for Charlie Hawkins.

Claire Brackett did not fit the profile of the agent Hawk had always heard about. She seemed to Hawk to be amazingly unguarded. At first, Hawk had assumed that it had to do with the medication that both Alex and Cassidy had warned her about. But, Claire had not taken anything since before Hawk had arrived. Claire had grown quiet a few times, but most of their time had been spent in conversation that flowed more naturally as the hours passed.

The first couple of hours had been strained between them, both attempting to gauge the other's motives and personality. Hawk had seen glimpses of the agent referred to as Sparrow a few times in those hours. She had caught Claire watching her with a discerning eye. It didn't offend her any more than she expected her examination of The Sparrow bothered Claire. It was in both their nature to be cautious, and for good reason.

Hawk still wasn't sure how or when it happened, but at some point, their conversation had turned. She had raided Helen's kitchen and the two would be rivals called a truce that included polishing off a tray full of junk food and a two-liter bottle of Diet Coke. Hawk smiled remembering Claire's puzzlement regarding their snacks.

"Can you explain to me why anyone who stocks this much junk food has diet soda in their house?" Claire asked seriously. Hawk shrugged. "It makes no sense," Claire griped. She picked up a package of cupcakes. "180 calories! For one fucking cupcake, Hawk! One! Diet soda? Why? It's useless like non-alcoholic beer. Who the hell wants non-alcoholic beer?"

Hawk chuckled at the memory. "Who are you, Claire?"

***

"Mom?"

"Cassie, I'm sorry about Dylan. He's so fast. He just…"

Cassidy smiled sympathetically. "He knows better than to go off. It's not your fault."

"That may be, but I still feel awful," Rose said. "He tried to be brave," she told Cassidy. "He didn't even cry, but I could tell he was afraid when the ski patrol came. That wrist…"

"He's okay, Mom," Cassidy reminded her mother. "He'll have a story to tell."

"He reminds me of your father sometimes," Rose said a bit wistfully. "So competitive at times. You were never like that, always wanted to include everyone, not surpass them. Must have skipped through you to Dylan."

Cassidy could feel her hands shaking. Her stomach was turning violently. She moved to sit beside her mother. "Mom…"

"What's wrong, Cassie? You look a little flushed? Are you sick?"

"No, I'm not sick."

"Oh, my God! Are you pregnant again?" Rose asked excitedly. Cassidy let out a nervous chuckle. "You are! I don't believe it….You're going to need that farm…."

"Mom," Cassidy chuckled again. "I'm not pregnant." Rose looked at Cassidy doubtfully. "I swear, I'm not pregnant."

"Cassie, you…"

"I'm not, Mom, although we are talking about it. Not for a while," Cassidy said.

"Then what is it?" Rose grew concerned.

Cassidy strained to offer her mother a smile. "I've never told you about Alex's….Well, what she does at Carecom."

Rose smiled. "You mean she's not the president of the company?"

"No, she is. She just…"

"Is that what this is about?" Rose asked. "I have some ideas, Cassie. A few more now than I did a week ago."

"What do you mean?"

"Helen told me a few things."

Cassidy nodded. "What did she say?"

"Only that Alex did not completely leave her former job at the NSA. She did say that Alex's father and Edmond were involved in the government and that Carecom supports some government programs."

"The CIA," Cassidy said bluntly. "It's a corporation that supports the CIA."

Rose's stunned expression made Cassidy's breath catch in her throat. She had attempted to rehearse in her mind what she would say to the woman before her. Perhaps, it would have been better to just allow Rose to see the truth as Cassidy had. Time to prepare might not be for the best. For Cassidy, she could not consider the option of deceiving her mother. On some level, she felt guilty for not running to the woman beside her immediately. There had been moments in the last two days when Cassidy had desperately wanted to do that. Cassidy had closed the bedroom door, shut her eyes, and fought the urge more than once to run to the safety of her mother's arms just as she had when she was a child.

Rose had been Cassidy's refuge for most of her life. She still was in many ways, but Alex had come to fill that role in a way that no one ever had or would again. And, Cassidy now filled that same role her mother had for Dylan and Mackenzie. That was life. It turned in cycles—birth, life, death. For all its upheavals and surprises, the cycle of life remained the constant that gave each person a sense of permanence and purpose. Where, Cassidy wondered, did the reappearance of someone you had mourned long ago fit into that equation?

"Cassie?" Rose took Cassidy's hand. Cassidy's tear filled eyes lifted to meet her mother. "What is it? You can tell me anything," Rose reminded her daughter.

Cassidy's smile did nothing to conceal the torment and regret that painted her irises. She closed her eyes and forced herself to breathe. Slowly, Cassidy opened her eyes and met the familiar, loving, compassionate gaze her mother held. "I could explain a million things to you," Cassidy said. "And, not one of them would matter when you see the truth for yourself. I know that."

"Cassie, what's wrong?"

"What Helen told you is true. Alex's father, Edmond….Jane's father—they all worked in intelligence," Cassidy said. Rose listened. Cassidy sucked in a nervous breath. "The thing is, Mom, it wasn't just their fathers."

"Cassie?"

Cassidy looked down and nodded as if to convince herself that she could continue. She looked back up at her mother. "Dad worked with them too."

Rose smiled. "I know."

"You knew?"

"No, I didn't know. Your father was tight-lipped about a lot of things, Cassie. He never talked about work much. He preferred to concentrate on you and spending time as a family when he was home. That's one of the reasons I loved him so much, I think. I never asked and I never cared—not until the drinking started."

"Mom…"

Rose sighed heavily. "I took out one of your father's old albums the other night to show Helen," she said. "There was a picture of your friend Edmond and your dad. That's how Helen ended up telling me about Alex and…Well, a few other things," she explained.

Cassidy nodded her understanding. "Alex….Mom—Alex and Pip," Cassidy faltered.

"Cassie, just tell me."

"I don't know how," Cassidy whispered. "They have been working together for a while. Alex….They found some things….Pip, he went to go look….They…Well, they thought that Alex's father might still be alive. Just…"

"What? How could he be…."

"Mom, please….He isn't," Cassidy said. "Pip did find someone. It wasn't Nicolaus." Cassidy watched fear color her mother's expression. She wondered if somehow Rose anticipated her next words. "Mom, Dad…Dad is alive." Rose appeared to go catatonic. "Mom?"

"That's impossible."

The hollowness in Rose's voice and the haunted look in her eyes made Cassidy shiver. "Mom, I'm sorry. It's…."

"They made a mistake."

Cassidy fought to suppress her emotions. "No, they didn't."

"You can't know that," Rose argued. She pulled her hand from Cassidy's and looked away.

Cassidy's sadness finally eclipsed her control. "I do know. I've seen him," she said. Rose's eyes met Cassidy's again. Cassidy wasn't sure what she saw there now—fear, doubt, anger? She took a deep breath and reached for her mother's hand. "It's him. I promise it is. Mom, he's here."

"I..."

"Edmond is taking him to the cabin in our car now."

"Why?" Rose whispered.

"He needs to tell you that," Cassidy said.

Rose remained silent for long moments. Cassidy sat beside her, holding Rose's hand. She half expected to see Rose's temper flair. Her mother's reaction surprised her. Rose was lost in a sea of emotion and confusion. It broke Cassidy's heart watching the woman who had raised her. It startled Cassidy when her mother finally spoke.

"I'm so sorry, Cassie."

"Sorry? Mom, you have nothing to be sorry for."

Rose's tears spilled over her cheeks as she finally allowed herself to look at her daughter again. Cassidy reached over and wiped her mother's tears. "I can't believe he would do that to you," Rose said.

Cassidy smiled solemnly. "I'm all right," she promised.

"You were everything to him—to both of us," Rose told Cassidy. "I...I don't...How can he..."

"A friend of mine told me recently not to try to understand. She was right," Cassidy said. "I will never be able to understand him," she told her mother. "But, it is him. If you don't want to see him, I will have Edmond take him back to Helen's."

"No," Rose said bluntly. Cassidy noted the quiver of anger in her mother's voice. She hated it, but she preferred it to the despondent cadence minutes before. "No. I need to."

"I understand," Cassidy said. "Edmond will come back for you and Helen. Do you want me to be with you when..."

"No."

"Mom..."

"No, Cassie. No. He came here with you?" Rose asked. Cassidy nodded. "You've talked to him?"

"At length," Cassidy admitted.

"And, you believe him? Whatever he has told you?"

"Not completely. About the important things—yes."

Rose shook her head. "This cannot be real."

"I know."

"You're sure?"

Cassidy smiled regretfully. "There are a lot of things I am not sure about," she confessed. "I'm so sorry, Mom," Cassidy said. Against her will and under her mother's gaze, she began to cry. "Please don't blame me. I'm sorry."

Rose pulled Cassidy to her. "Blame you?"

"I didn't tell you when he…"

Rose rocked Cassidy in her arms. Internally, she doubted that any of what Cassidy said could be true. It seemed far too much like a bad plot in a soap opera. She felt Cassidy quivering in her arms, shaking as she had when her father had died. "Shhh, Cassie…It's all right, Cassie. It's all right. I promise."

"It's not, Mom. It's not all right—not any of it."

Rose let her tears fall unrestrained and mingle with her daughter's. She had comforted her daughter through the greatest loss of both their lives. Now, she held her again as if someone had torn open an old wound that could never completely heal. "It is, Cassie. It is. It will be. I promise."

Cassidy let her mother hold her. She had no desire to let go. She had intended to comfort the woman holding her. In a heartbeat, Cassidy had found herself reduced to the longings of a child who was unable to understand the reality of loss in life. As it had always been, her mother's arms immediately surrounded her. Somehow, Cassidy understood that this is what they both needed. There were no reasons and no explanations that could heal pain. Time and love were the only remedies. That started here.

Alex stepped into the room, ready to tell Cassidy that Dylan was headed for his cast shortly. She stopped and held her breath at the scene before her. Could anything be worth this? Alex felt a tear cascade over her cheek. She made no attempt to suppress it nor to wipe it away. Nothing was worth this pain. Nothing. She silently slipped from the room unseen.

Alex looked up at the ceiling as her tears began to gather pace and intensity. She found herself speaking silently to the most unlikely person. "Dad? Why? Why? What could be worth all this?"

"Alexis?" a soft voice called to her.

Alex opened her eyes. Helen wiped Alex's tears as Alex fell into her mother's arms. "Why?" Alex choked on the word.

Helen closed her eyes and held her daughter. "I don't know," she confessed. "I wish I did," she told Alex. "I love you, Alexis."

"Mom?"

"I know, sweetheart. He loved you too. Maybe someday you will believe that," Helen said. She kissed Alex's head as Alex let the floodgate of emotion spill over. "It's all right, Alexis. Let it go. Let it go. It will be okay. I promise."

Chapter Eighteen

"**N**o!" Claire sat up like a bullet shot from a gun.

Hawk flew out of her chair and to Claire's side. "Claire?" she called. Hawk put her hand on Claire's back and could feel Claire's rapid, shallow breathing. "Claire? What is it?"

"You need to get Alex."

"What? Why? Claire..."

"Hawk, please. Please. I think I remembered something. Why didn't I see it?" she chastised herself. "You need to get Alex on the phone, please."

"Why?"

"Please, Hawk. She doesn't know. None of them do."

"Claire, slow down. Slow down. What did you remember?"

"Fisher, O'Brien...Cassidy wasn't his objective," Claire said.

"What? What are you talking about?" Hawk tried to get Claire focused.

"My father, Hawk. You don't understand. They didn't want McCollum. That wasn't O'Brien's objective. Not Fisher's. Not the same goal as my father's."

"Claire, I can't call Alex with this. I don't know what you are talking about."

Claire's answer stopped Hawk's heart. "Dylan."

***

333

"What the hell is Daniels doing here?" Eleana wondered aloud.

"Same thing that we are."

"What are the chances we are going to find anything now?" Eleana asked. "Think about it, Jonathan. Don't you think they will have destroyed or, at least, moved things by now?"

"I do. That's why Jane pressed Alex for the merger, I think."

"They were never going to let her…"

"Not easily, no. But, it did get us some access and it did spook Rand. That has put more things in the open then a lot of people intended."

"You think this was all about forcing their hand?" Eleana asked him.

"Yeah, I do. Jane wants to know who killed John, who made that call. It's an obsession. But, I think she suspects something she's not telling any of us. And, I think it's connected to this."

"About John?" Eleana asked.

"Maybe."

"You know, don't you? Who had him assassinated, I mean."

Krause sighed. "If I believe Claire, her father did."

"She told you that?"

"She was out of it," he commented.

"You don't believe her?"

"I think she believes it," Krause said. "And, it wouldn't surprise me," he admitted. "But, he wasn't alone. There's no way possible in that."

"How do you know?"

"They called me to arrange it."

"What?"

"It's a long story," he said. "We had it set up. Should have looked like the perfect failed attempt. It was a test."

"A test?"

"Yep. As much as they wanted him out, and I still am not sure why they were so hell bent on that," he said. "They also tested my loyalty. The ultimate test—love versus duty. What do you subscribe to?" He chuckled caustically as his sights narrowed on a figure in the distance approaching Daniels.

"I don't get it."

"Eleana," Krause turned to her briefly. "There's nothing to get. It's a game."

"It's not a game, Jonathan."

"Yes, it is. That's all it's ever been. McCollum and your father are right."

"How can you say that?" she asked him in disgust.

"Because, it's true. It's all about perception. These people all feel entitled to do what they do. It doesn't matter what I think or you think to them. They don't care about that. You think people who would program their children to do their bidding give a shit about what happens to those children? That's why they are called assets."

"It's cold."

"It is," he agreed. "People invest a lot of energy in these assets," he observed. "That's really the game. Like chess," he chuckled as he waved Eleana to follow him a few steps toward a large delivery van.

"People's lives are not a board game."

"Um, you said people. I said assets. Who's the pawn, the rook, the knight?" he asked her rhetorically. "Assets are pieces to move. If you don't see yourself as human, but as an asset," he said. "If life to you is just about that duty, which is really a game…Then what matters at all?"

"That's depressing," she said.

"It's all some people have, Eleana."

"You sound like you are defending them."

"No, I'm just acknowledging the reality. You think your father and Cassidy's father are the devil."

"I think they are selfish," she declared. Krause made no reply, focusing on finding a way to get closer to Ambassador Daniels and the man approaching him. "You don't?" she asked him.

"I think they are misguided assets," he said.

"You're kinder than you think," she mumbled.

He took a deep breath and looked at her. "No, I'm not. I've just seen more than you have," he told her.

"You think what they did was right?"

"I think they did what they thought was right," he corrected her. "And, I don't believe they did it for themselves. That makes them different than him," Krause nodded toward Daniels. "You're not a pawn," he looked at Eleana. "At least, not to your father, neither was Cassidy or Alex. Your fathers wanted you left off the board," he said, turning back to Daniels.

"Your father didn't want that for you either," she said honestly.

"My father was a hard, demanding man, who made it clear what was expected of me early on."

"I didn't mean the one who raised you."

Krause nodded. "I know. That is the father I knew," he said. Krause saw an opening to get within hearing distance of Daniels. He took a moment to address Eleana again before moving them closer. "Eleana, people are what they know. You are who you are because of what you have seen, what you have been taught, what you have been shown. We all are. You think your father is hard, cold like mine was. Yet, you are soft and warm—caring and compassionate, like Cassidy in many ways," he smiled. "You learned that because you were shown that. That is what Cassidy's father meant by perception. You give and you love because at your core you believe people are giving and loving."

"Jonathan…"

"It's not difficult for you to love, to say I love you. Not like it is for me. It's taken me a long time to learn and it is still foreign to me at times."

"But, you did learn."

"I'm still learning," he said. "Perception does not shift overnight. Some people's never will," he told her.

"Then why bother trying to change it at all?" she asked him.

"Because once in a while someone does change," he said. "Once in a while, you are able to change it for one person. That's really the best you can hope for." He looked ahead again. "We need to get to that storage shed. Stay close to me. I want to hear this conversation."

"Jonathan?" she tugged on his jacket. "We're not our fathers," she said.

"We are, more than you think."

"I'm not…"

He leaned over and kissed her gently on the lips. "Who are you hoping to protect, Eleana?" he asked. She looked confused. "Why do you do it?"

"Because, someone has to. Someone has to try and leave this world better. To try and…"

"For who?"

"I don't know. The people I love…for…Dylan and…"

"Ah, for your children?" he guessed. "Not so different after all," he said.

"I would never."

"Different paths with the same purpose," he said. "Come on. Let's see what our friend the ambassador has to say."

***

Edmond pulled Helen's car in front of the cabin. Rose sat looking out the window of the car. Helen had respected her friend's need for silence.

She held Rose's hand in a gesture of comfort. "Do you believe it?" Rose asked Helen without turning toward her.

"That the man in there is your husband?" Helen asked. Rose nodded. "I do."

Finally, Rose moved to face her friend. "I don't know if I can do this."

"You can," Helen said.

"How can I?"

"Because, if nothing else, Cassidy needs you to," Helen replied honestly.

"I don't know what to feel."

"You don't need to know," Helen told Rose. "Just let yourself feel whatever it is."

"And, if I hate him?"

Helen smiled. "You have every reason to, frankly."

"Would you? If it had been Nicolaus that they found?" Rose asked.

"I would have been angry. I might have thought that I hated him, but," Helen sighed. "I still would have loved him."

Rose nodded. "I'm sorry, Helen. I wish it had been."

"I know. I do too, but not for my sake."

"Alex?"

"At least, Cassidy believes that man in there loves her. I'm not sure Alexis will ever believe that about Nicolaus. And, that is really his fault. He pushed her so far away for so long. If he only knew how much she wanted him to pull her closer. How much she needed that. They don't think. They do what they were taught...try to control a situation."

"Is that what this is? What he did? Jim...He was always affectionate with Cassidy. I can't believe he would put her through what he did only to come back and...It's beyond forgiveness," Rose said. Helen smiled. "Why are you smiling?"

"Cassidy told me she could forgive him for herself. She wasn't sure she could ever forgive him for hurting you."

Rose closed her eyes and shook her head. "I don't know where she gets that from. She…"

"I do. She gets it from you," Helen said. "Don't try to feel anything," she advised Rose. "Just feel it. He deserves whatever he gets, and that is your choice to give," Helen said. She opened her door. "Edmond and I will be in the bedroom. We have some things we need to discuss."

"Helen?" Rose stopped her friend.

"Would you? Forgive him?"

"I don't know," Helen answered honestly. "I just know I would still love him."

***

"I can't get her," Hawk said. "Wherever they are, she must not have a signal."

"What about Brady? Fallon? Fallon can go there. She'll listen to him."

"Claire," Hawk tried to calm Claire. Claire was so agitated, Hawk felt she had to comply. She still did not know what exactly had convinced Claire that Dylan was in danger. Hawk did know that Claire was adamant she talk to Alex. Alex was out of the loop at the moment. She was about to try and pump Claire for more information. The expression of utter desperation on Claire's face stopped her and she sighed. "I'll try," she promised.

Claire nodded her thanks.

***

"Fallon, come on! Let's go. Leave it. We need to go—now," Brady ordered. Fallon grabbed a piece of paper and started writing something down. "Christ, Fallon! We need to go."

Fallon grabbed the paper and nodded. "I can't believe we never saw it. We need to get to Alex. If Brackett or…"

"We don't even know if it means anything," Brady said.

"Yeah, neither does anyone else who might have seen it," Fallon said.

"She's kept them safe this long, Fallon. I pity the person who goes after one of her kids."

"I'd prefer not to test that theory."

"Well, then move it. The faster we get out of here, the sooner we find Alex," Brady reminded Fallon.

Fallon followed Brady swiftly toward the door and stopped suddenly. "Do you hear that?"

"What?" Brady asked. "Don't get spooked. Come on."

"Listen!" Fallon demanded. Brady fell silent and tried to tune into whatever Fallon was hearing. "What is that?" Fallon asked. He looked back at the lab.

Brady's eyes widened. He watched as the computer screen they had just been studying went suddenly black. "Run! Now!"

***

"You're sure?" Ambassador Paul Daniels asked the man standing before him.

"I am. The General was clear. They are vulnerable."

Daniels nodded. "Fine. I will get this to The Admiral. You're sure that the objective was not met?"

"No, I can only tell you what the records referenced. It's there."

"And the records?" Daniels asked.

"They were moved as you requested weeks ago. Those are the hard copies of Petrov's files."

Eleana whispered in Krause's ear. "What would Anton Petrov have to do with MyoGen? He's ASA's guru?"

Krause shook his head, intent on listening to the conversation a few feet away.

"And, O'Brien's?" Daniels inquired.

"Only what you have here. Unless Petrov kept logs somewhere else."

"Understood," Daniels said. "The General is expecting your report."

"Yes, sir."

"Don't call me sir," Daniels demanded. "Your flight leaves in an hour to Boston. Don't miss it."

Krause felt the tension in his forehead like a vice grip. He watched as Daniels retrieved a phone from his pocket.

"Jonathan, we need whatever that officer gave him," Eleana whispered.

"I know. Not yet," Krause replied. He wanted to keep listening. Krause had no idea if what Paul Daniels held in his hand would be of any use at all. The conversations the ambassador was engaging in might turn out to be the best information Krause would get. He would bide his time.

Eleana felt her hip vibrate. She pulled out her phone. "What the hell?" she lowered her voice so that even Krause could barely hear her. "Claire?" she asked. Krause looked back at her. "Are you okay? What?"

Eleana tapped Krause and pointed back to the van they had been behind moments earlier. He nodded his understanding and mouthed the words "be careful" to her. Eleana smiled reassuringly. Krause watched her move quickly to their previous location and pulled his focus back to Daniels. "What the hell are you up to, Paul?"

***

Helen glanced back and smiled as a show of support to Rose before she disappeared from sight. Rose held her breath and waited. It seemed to her is if hours had passed, but she was certain it had only been seconds before he appeared. She watched him walk into the room and stop a few feet in front of her.

"Rose," James McCollum spoke her name as if he were worshiping it.

Rose's expression was unreadable as she closed the distance between them. She stopped less than an arm's length away and looked directly into his eyes. Without warning, her hand flew to his face, smacking him so intensely that his jaw moved.

"You son-of-a-bitch," she said venomously.

McCollum did not reply. He turned back to fully face her and was stunned when he felt her fingertips tenderly brush across the red splotch on his cheek. She seemed to be studying the outline of his face as her hand traced it. It was as if she were trying to convince herself that he was real, that he was truly the man that she had once loved. It was James McCollum's turn to hold his breath and wait.

"Do you know how much I missed you?" she whispered. "All those years. Every year. Every time Cassie did something. When Dylan came and then Mackenzie. When I watched her standing there with Alex, so in love. You were supposed to be there," she said without giving him the courtesy of looking into his eyes.

"I'm sorry," he said.

"Why are you here now?" she asked him.

"There are a lot of reasons," he said, surprised that her question had not been directed to why he had left.

"Tell me," she directed him. "I deserve that much."

"The truth?" he asked.

"Even if I don't believe it," she replied.

McCollum swallowed hard. "I've thought about that a lot today. I told myself it was for Cassie, for Dylan. That it was to keep them safe, to protect them," he told her.

Rose finally looked into his eyes. His hand cupped her cheek and she closed her eyes. Twenty-five years had not changed the familiarity of his touch. Standing before him, anger rolling through her veins like thunder, confusion clouding her thoughts, the only clarity at all was in his touch. Once she had fallen in love with James McCollum, she had accepted that she would never love again—not like she had with the man before her. He had made her laugh. He had allowed her to cry. He had challenged her ideas and inspired her to think for herself. He listened to her as if she were the most interesting person he had ever known. And, he had given her the greatest gift of her life—Cassidy.

"Maybe it was," he said. "To keep them safe. She's an amazing woman now. A woman," he shook his head slightly. "With all your fire and compassion," he said.

"And your eyes," Rose whispered emotionally.

"I missed you," he admitted. "All these years, hearing stories, seeing photos, watching your lives from a distance. Maybe it was more for me than it was for any of you," he confessed.

"I don't…"

"You don't have to say anything," he said. "I don't expect you to forgive me, and I don't expect you to…"

"Love you?" she guessed. McCollum looked at her, his heart plummeting and then beating wildly. "I don't know you," Rose said honestly. "I don't know if I ever did. My Jim would never have left me. He would never have devastated his daughter knowingly. He would have protected her from that pain."

"I…."

"I can't promise you anything," she said honestly. "Only that I have always loved the man I married. It didn't change when he drank himself into a stupor and pushed me away. It didn't end when I mourned an empty casket," she said. "And, it never faded in all these years. There was only one person for me in this life. I married him and I mourned him long ago."

McCollum nodded. "If I could…"

"Don't say it. I could scream. Most of me wants to, but I won't. I can't. That's not what Cassie needs from me."

"She would understand," he said.

Rose smiled earnestly. "Yes, she would. She forgets I am her mother sometimes, now that she is one. It's not her job to protect me. It's mine to keep her safe, any way I can, from anything I can."

"She's lucky to have you."

Rose shook her head. "You see? That is where you and my Jim differ. He would have understood," she said. "It's always been me who was lucky to have her." Rose smiled sadly at the man before her and went in search of Helen.

McCollum stood frozen in place. "You're right," he whispered. "He always loved you too."

***

"I don't know, Claire. Tate doesn't know where Brady and Fallon are" Hawk said. "Can't you just tell me?"

"Give me your phone."

"Why?" Hawk asked.

"Hawk, please?" Claire asked urgently. Charlie handed Claire her cell phone and sighed. "Eleana? It's me. No…I'm okay. We can't get Alex. No one knows where Fallon is. Just listen. I had a dream, but it wasn't a dream. It was a memory. You know? Like, all of a sudden I can remember all these things. Conversations, places….Things about people. Alex has to know…"

***

"Claire? Wait. Slow down. Slow down." Eleana said. "Why do you need Alex?"

"El, remember I told you I kept O'Brien close for a reason?"

"Claire, I don't…"

"Just listen. I remembered something. I don't know how I never saw it before. It's like all the pieces were jumbled for so long, you know? Like, I just kept going because nothing made sense anyway. Now it's….It's like I can see it. Like a fog lifting or something."

Eleana tried to steady her nerves. Claire was rambling and Eleana needed her to focus. "Claire, did you take…"

"I'm not stoned, El!"

"Okay, I'm sorry. Slow down and talk to me. What is it you didn't see?"

"It wasn't Cassidy they wanted."

"What?"

"O'Brien, my father…They didn't put Fisher on Cassidy to find her father, El. At least, I don't think so anymore. It makes sense."

"Claire, what are you talking about?"

"O'Brien. I heard him talking to Dmitri once. I was half asleep, just tuned it out. He could be such an asshole."

"Claire! Focus!"

"Sorry, I feel like….Anyway, Kargen was dressing him down, you know. He told O'Brien that he failed in his objective. O'Brien said something about it not being his fault. It was Cassidy's call and it made sense with the directive The Admiral gave him."

"What directive?"

"Congress, I think. The election—all that shit. My father works to place lots of people in office. Anyway, Dmitri said that no directive superseded the objective. O'Brien said there were plenty of assets. They didn't need him anyway. But then O'Brien said he was useful in unexpected ways."

"I don't understand."

"Dylan, El. He was talking about Dylan."

"Claire…"

"I'm telling you. Then I remembered what he said once. He said he wasn't the pawn I thought he was. He had what my father really wanted and he had hidden it someplace my father would never think to look."

"You think he meant Dylan?"

"Yeah, I do. I didn't put it together then. But, if Cassidy was out of the way, and if anyone knew about John…"

"John Merrow? What about him?"

"That he's Dylan's dad."

"What are you talking about?" Eleana asked.

"You didn't know? I figured Krause would have told you."

"How do you know that?" Eleana challenged Claire.

"Oh, something he said once. I figured it out. Plus, Dylan looks like him. He's way too cute to be O'Brien's. Surprised no one sees it."

"Who did you tell?" Eleana asked.

"No one," Claire said. "Not my business. Besides, I liked John."

"Jesus, Claire. It's a stretch. I'm not sure that Alex is…"

"Listen, I'm telling you it makes sense. My father? Even if I'm wrong about O'Brien, my father will see it the way I do."

"Even if you are right, why would they all of a sudden move on it?"

Claire groaned "El! All of a sudden? Not all of a sudden. Now? Think about who is back. The mastermind himself, my father's ghost?"

"Your father doesn't know McCollum is back," Eleana reminded her.

"Grow up, El. I love you but open your eyes. My father knows. I guarantee you he knows. He probably knew before you and me that McCollum was on his way back."

"Okay. You think he wants McCollum."

"Bonus round. If he thinks Dylan knows something, who better to uncover it?" Claire posed her question.

"Shit. Okay, I'll call you back."

"Eleana! Did you hear me?"

"I heard you! Just sit tight. I promise I will call you back."

***

"Well, he seems sure," Daniels said.

"I will confirm it," Admiral Brackett said.

"You really think the boy knows something?" Daniels asked doubtfully.

"It's possible. That was, after all, O'Brien's objective."

"Yes, but that objective failed according to what I have."

Admiral Brackett laughed. "Viktor wanted Lynx, Paul. You know that as well as I do. He would have done anything to flush him out. And, he is hell bent on objectives. Meet them at any cost. He did not appreciate the deviation. Dylan should have been with your boys in school, Paul. That was not a negotiable item for Viktor. A great deal was invested in O'Brien, and not just money. You think Viktor Ivanov wanted to hear O'Brien's excuse that Cassidy made that decision?" Brackett laughed. "He told Viktor that her decision to keep the boy in public schooling was best for his congressional career. Congress was not his objective. It was my directive. Viktor does not like to lose, and never to me," Brackett gloated.

"Perhaps, but his role was beneficial for Ivanov as well. So, why take risks over a missed objective? Pride?"

"Partly, yes. In Viktor's mind the boy is his—his right."

"And, you? What's your interest? To take from Viktor? To what end?" Daniels asked.

"O'Brien was not known for his caution. He was known for his boastfulness and his bumbling," Brackett said.

"I agree, but Christopher O'Brien was not a fool either, Bill. He played the game more expertly than most give him credit for. You know that as well as I do. No one suspected he was a seed. No one."

"Not no one," Brackett replied firmly.

"John Merrow's thin suspicions are hardly cause for action now. He's been dead a while."

"Death is a funny thing sometimes."

"You think Merrow is alive?"

"No," Brackett scoffed with a chuckle. "He's as dead as it gets. But, he took precautions."

"You don't think he knew about Lynx?"

"Of course, he knew. Or rather, my old friend told him. But, I suspect that only came after he told Nicolaus the truth."

"The truth?" Daniels wondered.

"That Dylan O'Brien was his son."

"What are you talking about? Did O'Brien know that Dylan was Merrow's kid?" Daniels asked.

"No."

"But, Merrow told you?" Daniels asked skeptically.

"Of course not. I have other sources."

"The General," Daniels guessed.

"Of course. She tells him everything. How do you think I knew to look for Lynx?"

"And, the boy?"

"Oh, Paul, come now. We both know that people hear things they do not remember. Whether or not the boy was exposed to SEED is not the point. That certainly could have advantages, and that is why we wanted O'Brien to gain control. Alexis threw a wrench in that plan," he muttered. Brackett chuckled. "Nicolaus was always throwing up roadblocks. Fool.

Seems it runs in the family. If O'Brien had what he claimed, if he had actually managed to secure that information, that list—it is possible the boy knows something."

"That's a stretch," Daniels observed. "It's a big risk for a long shot."

"Not really," Brackett told him. "They are vulnerable. Lynx is there—in the open. Alexis will be reluctant to carry with the boy there. She's softened. Worst case scenario, we secure Lynx and the boy. Best case scenario? We discover something we didn't expect to find. Either way, we can eliminate the obstacles."

"You want to kill Alex?" Daniels asked.

"Do you see another option?"

Daniels sighed. "What about Cassidy? What about…"

"War has its casualties, Paul."

"And, Claire? If what he says is true, she could compromise you."

"Ancient history. No one trusts Claire. I don't even trust Claire. She's no threat to us. Never has been a threat to anyone but herself."

"Elliot might disagree with your assessment," Daniels responded sharply.

"Elliot might have been your friend," Brackett said. "He was an obstacle that needed to be removed. He knew too much."

"I doubt Edmond would agree."

"Edmond is weak," Brackett said. "Too afraid to do what is necessary and look where that has gotten us? The family is everything, Paul. If you cannot control your children, how can you keep control in the broader world? When they choose to leave that path…"

Daniels was disgusted. He had never cared for Admiral Brackett, but he had done his duty as assigned. The Admiral was his handler. Paul Daniels signed his life over to the agency early on. It had never been a question. It remained the only thing he believed he could depend on. But, to compromise a child? He had stomached the murder of more than one friend, counted it as part of the acceptable risks in the world he belonged to. He did not mourn. Men like Elliott Mercier and Russ Matthews had sworn the same oath he had. They understood the risks and the expectations that accompanied that oath. Merrow, Krause, Toles, O'Brien, Kargen, The Admiral's daughter—all well-versed in the realities that could befall them at any time. You did not enter this life with the fear of death.

He understood what Admiral William Brackett was saying. Daniels had been given this path, groomed and prepared for it in some way at every turn in his life. He was a seed, just as his friends Russ Matthews and Elliot Mercier had been, the same as Claire Brackett. His sons now followed a familiar path. They would be educated at one of the finest private institutions in the country. They would travel the world and learn about culture and language. Inevitably, they would be accepted to one of the most prestigious universities to study an appointed field, or perhaps they would accept an appointment to West Point or The Naval Academy. That would be determined later. That was William Brackett's definition of family. Daniels had always believed it was a sound theory. Who better to trust than a parent? Who better to groom than a child? Now, he found himself asking what the limits of the theory were.

The ambassador had no issue with his sons following a prescribed path. For all its risk, it provided a good life. Daniels had comforts most desired. He had a stunning, intelligent wife who supported him without reservation regardless of his transgressions. Daniels traveled in the company of presidents, kings, and spies. His world was the world that popular films and books were made of, and he loved it. He never questioned that it would not be the same for his sons. He was beginning to see a flaw in his theory. His children were hardly grown men. He had never seen their education, their programming as a compromise. Rather, he saw it as edification and preparation. Daniels loved his children. That was an undeniable reality. If someone sought to take him from his sons solely to manipulate his children for their own gain? If, in this game he played, his children became expendable pawns? What if The Admiral began to question what Daniels' boys might have heard? It was all an excuse. William Brackett had a long-held vendetta against The Broker and Lynx. He blamed them for the fracture in The Collaborative. This was not about duty nor was it devised as a plan for the security of any objective other than Admiral William Brackett's ego. Daniels made a silent decision. One he understood would likely end more than his career.

"I understand," Daniels said. He had sensed a presence not far away for some time, and he knew after his brief call earlier with The General, who that presence belonged to. His objective had just changed. For the first time in Paul Daniels life, he would follow a directive of his own making. He would give the man listening what he needed—a chance. "You'll be sending me to Toles then?"

"Don't be ridiculous. That's not your role. I have it in hand. I'm looking forward to catching up with my old friend."

"Bill, do you think it is wise for you to confront Lynx personally? Situations are unpredictable. You've been out of the field a long time..."

"I won't be alone, and I can handle myself," Brackett chuckled.

"And if you succeed? What? Dylan would be placed with one of..."

"Leave that to me."

"Fine. What do you want from me?"

"The first wave begins this week. You need to be in London. Mitchell is on the trail. That plane..."

"Understood. I will handle Ian."

"Good. Be careful, Paul. Mitchell is not an easy mark," Brackett warned. "He is not family. Only thinks he is."

Daniels hung up the phone and pursed his lips. He took a deep breath, expecting the heavy barrel of the gun he now felt placed to his back. "Hello, Jonathan," he said.

Chapter Nineteen

Dylan had fallen asleep against his mother in the backseat of the car. Alex opened Cassidy's door and smiled. Dylan looked small to her at the moment, cuddled beside his mother. He had changed and grown so much in a short time that Alex often found herself longing for the boy she had first met. It was selfish, and Alex knew it. She was immensely proud of her son. She wished so many times that she had seen his first steps, heard him babble for the first time. Often, the time she spent with Mackenzie prompted a sense of longing in Alex.

Alex remembered the first time Dylan had crawled into her bed and snuggled against her. It was a memory that she replayed often. She had known that she was in love with Cassidy. She knew that Cassidy loved her. That night, the way Dylan sought comfort between them, the feel of Cassidy's hand resting on them both—Alex understood at that moment that she had a family.

Cassidy looked up and tried to determine what she saw flickering in Alex's eyes. "You okay?" she asked.

"He looks so small," Alex said.

Cassidy looked down at Dylan and kissed his head. "Looks can be deceiving," she joked.

Alex laughed. That was the truth. "I'll get him," Alex said.

Cassidy stepped out of the car, gently letting Dylan fall against the seat. "Should you really do that with your back?" Cassidy asked in concern. Dylan was hardly the six-year-old little boy she used to carry up the stairs.

He had grown like a weed, begun to fill out into the beginnings of a handsome young man. She often missed the feel of his legs wrapped around her waist, and his head resting on her shoulder. She loved watching him as he changed and explored, but Cassidy missed his closeness at times.

"I can carry our son," Alex assured Cassidy.

Cassidy grinned and patted Alex's shoulder. "I didn't mean to insult your strength," she teased.

Alex groaned and reached into the car to extract Dylan. He mumbled and then let out a small moan that Alex immediately recognized as pain. Her heart went out to him. "It's okay, Speed. I've got you."

Cassidy watched as Alex stood to her full height. Dylan's legs wrapped around her. His left hand looped around Alex's neck and he let his head fall on her shoulder. "Alex?" he mumbled in confusion.

"It's okay, Speed."

"Where's Mom?"

"I'm right here, sweetie."

"I don't feel so good, Mom."

"I know," Cassidy said. She smiled when Alex rocked him slightly. "Come on, Alex will get you to bed."

"Can you stay with me?"

"Mom will stay with you, Speed."

"No, both of you," he asked groggily.

"Yes, Dylan," Cassidy said. She understood that the pain medicine, the pain from his injuries, and exhaustion had lowered all of Dylan's defenses. She had felt a similar need earlier when she fell into her mother's arms. And, there was a small part of Cassidy that wished she would walk into the cabin, find her parents in the big bedroom, and crawl in between them. No matter how adult anyone felt, Cassidy was certain everyone craved that at times—the security of their parents' arms—to feel safe.

Cassidy opened the door to the cabin for Alex and was surprised to see her parents sitting with Helen and Edmond in what appeared to be a civil conversation. She had spoken to both her mother and Helen from the hospital. Cassidy wasn't sure what she anticipated would be happening when they arrived home. Whatever it was, this was not it. She was more stunned when the first person to speak was her father.

"How is he?" McCollum asked.

"Tired mostly, I think," Cassidy said.

Dylan grabbed on tighter to Alex's neck. "Alex?" he mumbled sleepily. Alex grinned. Dylan, if she was not mistaken, was a bit high on his pain medication. "I bagged," he said sadly and yawned. "I'm tired, Alex. Will you lay down with me?" he asked.

Alex kissed Dylan's head. "Yeah, Speed. I'm tired too. Come on, let's get you to bed."

"Where's Mom?"

"I'll be right in," Cassidy promised.

Alex leaned in and kissed her cheek. "Are you going to be okay if…"

"Go on," Cassidy said. "I promise, I will be right there." She kissed Dylan's head and stroked Alex's cheek. Alex smiled at Cassidy and nodded to the room before continuing on.

"What's going on?" Cassidy asked when she saw cards on the table.

"Safer than conversation," Helen said.

"And, better with wine," Rose added.

"Are you two drunk?" Cassidy asked.

"On my way," Rose lifted her wine glass.

Cassidy noted the slight chuckle that escaped her father's lips. She seriously considered the fact that all four of the people at the small table had lost their minds. "Uh-huh." She shook her head. "I'm going to bed. This is too bizarre for me to deal with."

Helen rose from her seat and followed Cassidy down the short passage that led to the largest bedroom in the cabin. "Cassidy?"

Cassidy sighed. "I don't know what I expected."

"No one knows how to handle this, Cassidy," Helen said frankly. "Don't think your mother walked in and went back twenty-five years," she said. "He's here. He's your father, and she would do anything for you."

"I know. I thought she would be furious."

"She is," Helen said with a smile. "Actually, I thought seriously about locking up all the kitchen knives." Cassidy chuckled. "Wine and cards seemed a better alternative. She's not ready for his reasons," Helen explained.

"I wasn't either."

"No," Helen agreed. "I'm sure that's true. But, that is not her father. It's her husband. You don't know what that is like, Cassidy. It's awful losing your parents, no matter how old you are, believe me. Losing the person you love....Losing the person who…"

Cassidy reached out and touched Helen's arm gently. "I know," she said. "Believe it or not, I've tried to imagine what that would be like. If it were Alex and me…"

"Alexis would never leave you, Cassidy, not like that. One day, one of you will understand what I am talking about. I wish to God I could prevent that for both of you. Believe me, no matter how many years you have, it will never be enough."

Cassidy nodded. "I know." She leaned in and kissed Helen's cheek. "Watch out for my father," she warned as she opened the bedroom door.

"What do you mean?"

Cassidy turned and shrugged. "He doesn't like to lose. Cheats sometimes," she said. "He doesn't think I ever noticed. He used to stack the deck when we played Go Fish to make sure he started with pairs."

Helen rolled her eyes. "Rose and I will keep Kenzie with us."

"Thanks."

"Get some sleep," Helen said.

Cassidy walked into the bedroom and closed the door. She was content to stand and watch Alex holding Dylan.

"Aren't you tired?" Alex asked. Cassidy climbed onto the bed, leaned over Dylan and kissed Alex tenderly. "Mm. What was that for?"

"How's your back?" Cassidy asked knowingly.

"Hurts like a bitch," Alex admitted.

"Not so little anymore, is he?" Cassidy commented.

"No, but he is to me."

"I know." Cassidy stroked Dylan's hair and put her head on the pillow.

"What are you thinking?" Alex asked.

"I was thinking about that night we were coming back from Nicky's restaurant."

"Which night was that?" Alex asked with a playful smirk.

Cassidy giggled. "Not one of those nights," she laughed. "Although, when we get back, I think that sounds like an excellent plan."

"Consider it done."

"I was thinking about that first night," Cassidy explained. She heard Alex's breath catch slightly and moved to caress Alex's arm in comfort. "I know what you are thinking."

"No, you don't."

"Yes, I do. You're thinking about Carl Fisher."

"If he was...."

"I was thinking about you and Dylan."

"Me and Dylan?" Alex was confused.

"Yeah. Do you remember? You probably don't....When we went to pick Dylan up, I forgot to get his..."

"Booster seat," Alex chuckled. "Yeah, I remember. He was a lot lighter then."

Cassidy smiled and looked at Alex. She moved to trace the curve of Alex's cheek with her fingertips. "I came down the stairs and you were rocking him. He was holding onto you tightly. You put him in the car and whispered to him so gently."

"Surprised you, huh?" Alex said.

"Not really," Cassidy told Alex. "Just made me love you. I knew. Funny, I didn't know I knew then."

"Huh?" Alex was confused.

"I knew then, deep down that I wanted that with you."

"What was that?" Alex asked.

"A family. Crazy, right?"

"Not really," Alex replied.

"I realized it out there just now. More than I ever have, I think. I think about that moment sometimes. It was the first thing that popped into my mind when I found out Mackenzie was coming," Cassidy said. Alex was surprised. "It was," Cassidy told her. "I couldn't wait to see you do that again with our baby."

Alex took Cassidy's hand and kissed her palm. "I'm sorry that things are so messed up," she said.

"They aren't." Alex looked at Cassidy as if she had been dropped on her head. Cassidy fought to keep her laughter to a giggle. "Okay, they are."

"You scared me there for a minute," Alex winked. "I promise you, Cass…I will find a way to make it better. I won't let…."

"Stop," Cassidy said with a kiss. "Stop it. You do make it better, Alex. This? This makes it better. I told you a long time ago that I don't need you to be the sweeping hero. You're not Batman."

"I know, I'm Alfred," Alex tried to lighten the sudden tension she felt.

"You do have a way with dishwashers," Cassidy complied with Alex's need for levity. Alex chuckled. "The point is, I don't need you to save the world or even keep me safe from all of it, because you can't, neither do Dylan and Mackenzie."

"Cass, it's my job, and I don't mean as an agent. I have to protect you."

"You can't all of the time," Cassidy said bluntly. "I love you for trying so hard. This is what matters, right here. That night? That night that we came home and you found that picture taped to my door?" Alex shuddered visibly. Cassidy took Alex's hand. "I don't think about that part, Alex. Believe me, I was terrified. The most fear I felt was when you pulled your gun and disappeared around the back of that house in the dark—looking for God knows what. I wanted you back that instant. Not just in my sight…"

"Cassidy…"

"No, you need to hear this. I know you. All I need, all any of our children will ever need is you just to rock them when they are afraid."

"I'm not going anywhere," Alex promised.

"I know that too. I'm just telling you that this is what matters to me—these times. Just being with you, even when you make me want to scream."

"I like those times too," Alex cracked.

"You are incorrigible," Cassidy laughed. "You know what I meant."

Alex smiled. "Yeah, I do," she admitted. She felt Cassidy's arm drape over Dylan as Cassidy's head fell back on the pillow. "I love you, Cass."

"I love you too," Cassidy replied through a yawn.

"You think Speed is okay here? I mean, I don't want to hurt his…."

"I think we are all right where we are supposed to be," Cassidy replied.

Alex let out a contented breath. She closed her eyes and smiled. "Yeah, you're right, as usual."

***

"Well, Ambassador? I would ask how you've been, but I really don't care."

"You can put the gun down, Jonathan."

"I don't think so," Krause said as he stripped Daniels of the weapon he was carrying. "So? Why don't you tell me what I just heard? Who is headed to Alex?" Krause demanded with an eerie calm.

Eleana had been making her way to Krause when he moved on Daniels. She reached them both in a sprint. "Jonathan…."

"The Ambassador was just about to explain why he was talking about my sister and my nephew to Claire's father," Krause explained. Eleana immediately understood that Claire's fears were being realized. "He wants McCollum that badly?" Krause asked.

"Jonathan," Eleana tried to get Krause's attention.

"When are they moving?" Krause asked Daniels.

"Now, I would guess," Daniels replied evenly.

"Jonathan, it's not just McCollum he's after," Eleana chimed urgently.

"I know. Dylan. I heard. Why?"

"Does it matter?" Daniels spit venomously.

Krause ignored him. "Eleana, call Alex and warn her that company is on its way, and they know who is with her."

"No one can reach her," Eleana said. "Probably the snow. Claire and Hawk…."

"Claire and Hawk what?" Krause demanded.

"Claire's remembering things all of a sudden…"

"Eleana…."

"Jonathan! Put your feelings about Claire aside for once!"

"You might want to listen to Agent Baros," Daniels advised.

"Shut the hell up!" Krause yelled. "Call Fallon. They are in New York going through files. He's close enough to get to Alex."

Eleana shook her head. "Hawk tried. Even called Tate, they are offline. Fallon and Brady, no one knows where they are."

"Fuck!"

"How do they know where Alex is?" Eleana asked.

"Only one way. Should have seen it long ago. Everywhere we were led, all the obstacles…Like someone was one step ahead of us from the beginning. Because they were," Krause said as he pushed the gun into the flesh of Paul Daniel's back. Daniels remained still and silent.

"Jonathan?" Eleana implored him.

"There is only one person who knows where we all are at any given time. Only one person who knew who we were looking for all along. There is only one person she trusts completely and she tells him everything," Krause explained. "General Waters. Am I right, Ambassador?"

"Oh, my God," Eleana shook her head in disbelief. "Matt? Matt would never betray Jane."

"You'd be surprised what people will do," Daniels said. "Put the gun down, Jonathan. You can have the file. It will explain many things. Just put down the gun and let me make a call."

"Why would I do that?"

"Because, I am the man who can help you right now."

Krause had less than a second to make his decision. He looked at Eleana. "Do you trust her?"

"Who?" Eleana asked.

"Claire. Do you trust whatever she told you?" he asked. Eleana was stunned by the question. "Eleana!"

Eleana snapped to attention. "Yes. Yes, I trust her."

"Call her now. Tell her that her father is on his way to Alex. They are our best chance now."

Eleana nodded and put a few paces between them. Krause heard her voice growing quiet in the distance. "Claire?"

"You are going to send The Sparrow to save Toles?" Daniels laughed. "Brave—or stupid."

"Shut up," Krause said. "Give me the file."

"And then what? You kill me?" Daniels asked.

Krause chuckled. "That's too kind." Daniels took a deep breath. Krause moved to subdue the ambassador fully. "We have a lot to talk about."

"What makes you think I will say a word?" Daniels spat.

"You will. And, if you don't? I know someone who can help you."

"If you reach them in time," Daniels replied.

"For your sake, I hope we do. Because, Paul?" Krause whispered. "If anything happens to my family? I promise you, you will pray for death."

***

"Claire, what are you doing?" Hawk grabbed hold of Claire's arm.

"I'm going with you."

"You can barely walk!"

"He's my father, Hawk. You know what? He has fucked with one too many people I care about," Claire declared as she struggled to fasten her bra. Claire grabbed her shirt. She moved to extend her arm into the sleeve and yelped in response. Hawk took a deep breath and walked to Claire. She grabbed the shirt from Claire's hand.

"What are you doing?" Claire asked heatedly.

"Helping you get dressed. We need to move. We'll be here until morning if I let you do this yourself."

Claire watched as Hawk methodically buttoned the blue shirt. Hawk's eyes followed her hands while Claire's eyes followed Hawk. When their eyes met, Claire froze. Hawk smiled, leaned in and placed a chaste kiss on Claire's lips.

"I don't know who you are," Hawk said.

"That makes two of us," Claire agreed.

Hawk smiled and extended her hand. "Come on, Gimpy—let's go save the savior."

Claire chuckled. "I won't be gimpy forever," she commented as Charlie helped her down the stairs.

"I'm not sure if that is a threat or a promise," Hawk replied.

"Depends on which you prefer," Claire deadpanned.

Hawk laughed. She helped Claire put on a jacket just inside the doorway. "You'll need that," she said. Claire looked at Hawk in questioning. "I don't need a gimpy agent with pneumonia," Hawk explained.

"Hawk," Claire grabbed Hawk's arm. Hawk was stunned at the terror she saw in Claire's eyes. "He will do it. He will kill Alex. He'll kill them all if he thinks that he can…"

"Maybe you can help with that."

Claire shook her head. "He'll kill me too, or worse."

"Worse?" Hawk asked.

"Yeah. Make me forget."

"Claire, I'm not going to let that happen," Hawk said with conviction.

"She's…."

"What?"

"Cassidy, I might not be to her….But, Hawk? She's the only friend I ever had besides El. At least until…"

"Let's go," Hawk said. "I don't let my friends die," she told Claire.

"Alex," Claire muttered as Hawk opened the door to her Jeep for Claire.

"Her too."

***

Cassidy woke up feeling more rested than she had in days. She could feel the chill in the air from the snow that had fallen most of the night. She wondered if the trails would be open on the mountain this morning. Oddly, she felt the desire to ski. At times, it had helped her to clear her thoughts. At times, it had helped her connect with her father. She needed both. She smiled at the sight of a sleeping Alex with Dylan sprawled across her. Typically, Alex rose before the sun. It was ironic. Cassidy was sure that the events of the last few days had taken the greatest toll on Alex. Alex struggled with feeling helpless. She had a need to make things better for the people she cared about. That was easy to accomplish with the physical realities of life. Alex could carry Dylan when he was hurt or sick. She could protect them from physical danger. Cassidy had witnessed that when Carl Fisher had captured her. Emotions existed in a different universe.

Alex could not take away Cassidy's confusion or pain. She tried in every way she knew how to, but at the end of the day all Alex could do was hold Cassidy and tell her that she loved her. That was enough for Cassidy. For Alex? Alex needed to do more. Cassidy wished that somehow she could make her wife understand that even if Alex solved all the riddles in the world, and managed to forge world peace, there would still be pain to confront. Alex knew that, of course, she just could never seem to accept that loving Cassidy was enough. Cassidy didn't need all the answers, the solution to her life was lying beside her, and if she guessed correctly, cuddled with her grandmothers down the hall.

Cassidy pulled herself from the bed quietly. She retrieved some warm, clean clothes and made her way to the shower, hoping that perhaps she could get a few runs in before the day started for everyone else in the cabin.

***

"Help is on the way to Alex," Jane told Krause. "They should be there before the day begins, before Bill arrives."

"Claire called Eleana a few minutes ago. They're on the mountain now. They just need to get to the cabin."

"Jonathan, do you think Claire is a safe bet?"

"I think Eleana trusts her on this. I trust Eleana. I hate to admit it," he said. "Claire is…Well, she's not changed as much as she is different." He heard a soft sigh escape Jane's lips on the other line.

"I think I can imagine," Jane replied. "Being betrayed by the one person you trust more than anyone will make you see things differently."

"Jane," Krause called softly over the phone. He imagined that she had spent the last few hours trying to convince herself that there had been a mistake. General Matthew Waters was considered by most to be reputable, forthright, and ethical. Krause would never have dreamed that General Waters would use his sister. He could not comprehend what would have made Matt align himself with William Brackett. Then again, much of what Jonathan Krause had confronted in the last few years continued to astound him. It never became normal.

Jane put her face in her hands. "I can't believe it."

"I'm sorry," Krause said sincerely. "I have Daniels. I have some interesting information too. Not complete, but it's more than we had. Do you want me to make my way to Matt?" he asked cautiously.

"No."

"Jane, I know that you love him. I know….But, Jane…"

"I will handle it, Jonathan," she said.

"How?"

Jane sighed. "I will handle it."

Krause wasn't sure he wanted to know what that meant. "And me?"

"Secure the ambassador as usual."

"If I do, if I go through the usual channels, Matt will know within minutes."

"I know."

"Jesus, you're going to let him hang himself," Krause said.

"He's already done that," Jane said sadly.

Krause understood. "It doesn't mean he had a hand in John's assassination."

"Of course, it does," Jane said flatly. "We both know that, but thank you for denying it for my sake," she said honestly.

"Janie," Krause called gently to her over the line. "I…"

"You have someone else to worry about," Jane observed. "Secure the ambassador. Take Eleana home."

"Fallon and Brady?"

"They obviously did not like pushing paper," she said. "Perhaps you will collide."

"You think they are on their way here to MyoGen?" he asked.

"Stands to reason."

The theory made perfect sense to Krause. Neither Fallon nor Brady would have taken kindly to reviewing transcripts and reports amid all the insanity that had unfolded. "If I see them, I will…"

"Send them home," Jane said. "This ends today."

"It never ends," Krause observed honestly.

"No, it doesn't," she admitted. "But, it can end for a day."

"If you need me…"

"You have your directive," she said.

Jane set her phone on the table and took a deep breath. The one person she had always trusted completely had betrayed her at every turn. She had told her brother everything since childhood. Jane wondered if John Merrow had suspected anything about Matthew Waters. If he had, he had spared his wife that suspicion. If he hadn't, Jane was certain it was for the same reasons she had not. They didn't want to see what was right in front of them. It was too painful to believe that someone you loved could be so cold.

She shook her head in disbelief. Was it really necessary to suspect the worst in people to protect them? Ironic and sad if that were the truth.

"I'm sorry, Matt. There is just no other way."

***

Dylan woke and went in search of his mother. He hobbled into the large living space and startled at the sight of a tall man walking through the door with a bundle of wood.

James McCollum smiled over the load he carried and placed it by the fireplace. "Good morning, Dylan," he said.

Dylan was unsure and took a step back, only to bump into something solid. "It's okay, Speed," Alex's voice assured him. She paused. Why hadn't she and Cassidy talked about this? Where was Cassidy, she wondered? "This is Mr...."

McCollum stepped forward. "You can call me Jim," he said with a smile, extending his hand to Dylan. Dylan accepted his gesture and nodded.

"Jim is…Well, he's…."

"He's someone very important to your mom," Rose broke through the uncertainty and tension. "I'm sure she will tell you about it when she gets back."

"Where is Cass?" Alex asked.

"She left over an hour ago for the trails, hoping Bear Claw would be open early now that the snow stopped," Rose explained.

Alex looked out the window. "How's she getting there?"

McCollum laughed earnestly. "She'll manage."

Alex looked over at a sullen Dylan. "What's wrong, Speed?"

"If I didn't bag yesterday, I'd be with her."

"On Bear Claw? Isn't that that double diamond thing?" Alex asked.

Dylan giggled. "Yeah. We'd do Black Bear or Allagash. Then she'd let me watch her," he explained.

Alex was puzzled. Rose smiled at her. "There are monitors in the small lodge that sits halfway up the trail. You can watch the different trails from there. Bear Claw has the most cameras," she said. "Why don't you take Alex there?" Rose suggested to her grandson.

"Is that such a good idea?" Alex asked. "Speed, your ankle is still swollen."

Dylan shrugged. "I can make it."

Alex was skeptical. She expected Cassidy might have her head on a platter for even letting Dylan try, but the determination in his voice convinced her to let him. Plus, she needed to put some distance between herself, Dylan and James McCollum. Dylan would inevitably have questions. Alex was a bit surprised Cassidy had left at all, much less without telling her.

Dylan saw Alex's apprehension. "I've hurt my ankle before on the mountain. Mom helped me, but I still had to ski to the bottom," he told Alex. Alex sighed. Cassidy was full of surprises. She guessed that she would still be discovering things about her wife in thirty years.

"Take the snowmobile," Rose said.

"Dylan, go get dressed. Do you need help?" Alex asked him.

"No," he said as he limped from view.

"I'm not sure this is such a great idea," Alex admitted. "Why didn't she tell us she was leaving?"

"Alex," Rose began. "Dylan will be all right. For Cassie, that mountain is a place to escape. She grew up here, so has Dylan in many ways. I know you don't understand."

"No, I do," Alex replied. Rose grinned.

"Ever seen Cassie ski?" McCollum asked. Alex shook her head. He nodded. "There won't be many people on that run this morning. It's late in the season, and with the snow…Well, you should get some glimpses of her. Not as exciting as watching her in the terrain park, but…"

"Terrain park?"

Dylan reappeared with a sweatshirt in his hand. Alex smirked and helped him pull it over his head. "They have jumps and stuff," he mumbled through the fabric.

"Like ski jumps?" Alex asked nervously. McCollum and Rose both chuckled at the wonder and fear in Alex's voice.

"Not like what you are picturing," Rose assured her.

"It's cool, Alex. Mom is really good."

Alex nodded. "I just never realized she was so into it. I mean, I've heard you talk…"

"You thought I was just bragging like some of those soccer moms I have seen at Dylan's games?" Rose guessed.

Rose had told Cassidy numerous times that some of the women on the sidelines made her crazy. It had never been in Rose's nature to embellish Cassidy's talent. Cassidy was the same way with Dylan. Dylan was quite the young athlete and he thrived on his summer soccer games. Cassidy cheered for the entire team, and Rose had heard her council Dylan more than once on the need to be a team player. He was not as big as some of his teammates, but he was fast and coordinated. Rose had never allowed Cassidy to get cocky, and Cassidy was determined to instill the same message in Dylan.

"Well, I am bragging. I'm just not exaggerating. Go see for yourself," Rose said. "Besides, with all these kids you seem to want, she might not have much time for this," Rose added. Alex's eyes grew wider and Rose laughed. "Oh please, Alex. I swear if you could have had her pregnant the day Mackenzie came home, you would have."

"What were you saying about exaggerating again?" Alex asked her mother-in-law.

"She's not exaggerating," Helen defended her best friend with a yawn as she entered the room carrying Mackenzie. "You know, Alexis, you could take the pressure off Cassidy and have the next one yourself."

"Who says there's going to be a next one?" Alex replied.

"Oh, please," Helen and Rose chimed in unison.

Alex grumbled. "Speed, why don't you eat something while I get ready and then we'll go."

"Can we eat there instead?" he asked.

Alex grinned. Anything that might get her out of the lion's den faster sounded like a good idea. Helen and Rose reveled in teasing Alex. She truly did not want Cassidy's father and Edmond to see the way the two older women could make her blush.

"Sounds good, Speed. Are you sure you are up to it? What about your wrist?"

Dylan wanted to go to the slopes. "It's okay," he said. Alex looked at him skeptically. He shrugged. "It hurts," he admitted. "I'll be okay, Alex. Please?"

"Only if you promise me that you will tell me if you need to come back. If I think it's too much, we will turn around. I'm not sure this is the best idea, Dylan. And, only if you understand we are not going all day, just to see Mom and then we are coming back here. Understood?"

"I promise, Alex."

Alex smiled. Dylan was determined. "Give me a few minutes to shower and we'll go." Alex sidled up to her mother. "How high is half way up the trail?" she whispered.

Helen shrugged. "It's halfway, Alexis."

Alex groaned and headed for the shower. "What the hell kind of answer was that?"

***

"Claire? Are you okay?" Hawk asked as the Jeep approached the cabin. "Hey, listen, we made it here in time."

"You don't know my father," Claire said.

"It's only a little after 7:00. We beat them."

"Or, they are waiting," Claire suggested.

"If they are, we'll handle it."

Claire looked out the car window. She felt an unfamiliar sensation rising through her veins—fear. What kind of person kills the person they supposedly love? What kind of person deliberately harms his child? Claire Brackett had done many things in her young life that she was aware would make people shiver. She wondered how much of it had been by her choice. Surprisingly, that answer seemed to hold little concern for Claire. Whether or not she would have done it without her father's interventions did not change the facts. She had taken life. She had used people for any number of reasons. Then again, she did not deal with people often. She dealt with assets. Claire had thought she understood that distinction.

Claire closed her eyes when she felt the Jeep come to a halt. There had only been a handful of people who had ever shown Claire Brackett genuine kindness. In her life, people used kindness as a tool to acquire what they wished—information, connections, physical gratification—it was seldom a gesture without expectation. Perhaps, Claire mused, she did not deserve it—kindness. She had lost everyone who had ever cared for her at all. Her mother had always been gentle with her. John Merrow had tried on more than one occasion to reign her in and convince her that there was far more in life than the games she played. Eleana had loved her beyond what was reasonable. Eleana held Claire, challenged Claire, and confronted Claire when no one else would dare. She had lost all of them in some way. Cassidy had reached out to Claire against the caution and concern of everyone around them. Claire still could not comprehend why. What had any of them seen to even try?

"No more of this," Claire whispered.

"Claire?"

Claire turned to face Hawk. "No more taking parents from their children. No more."

Hawk hopped out of the Jeep and went to open Claire's door.

"What are you doing here?" McCollum began to make his way cautiously toward the vehicle. He had gone outside to split some wood for the fireplace. It gave him a reason to step away, and James McCollum was grateful for the air in his lungs, even if it was cold. Hawk opened Claire's door and Claire emerged gingerly.

"Claire?" McCollum's surprise lit his features.

"Where's Alex?" Hawk asked.

"She took Dylan down to the lodge," he answered. "What are you doing here? You're not supposed to be up," he looked at Claire.

"Cassidy here?" Claire asked.

"No, they went to watch her ski. Claire, what's going on?" he asked.

"My father is on his way here. He knows you are here. He won't be alone," Claire said. "We tried to call but Alex's phone..."

"None of us have had any reception since early yesterday evening. Betting the storm took out the tower."

"How do I get to the lodge?" Claire asked.

"It's about a mile down the mountain. There's a shuttle that comes by on the main road. Alex took Dylan on the snowmobile. Or, you can drive down to the base. Take the first Bear Claw lift. It leads to The Den. That's where they are," he said calmly.

"Claire," Hawk turned to her. "You cannot make that trip. You can barely walk. I'll go, you stay here."

Claire balked at the suggestion. "Are you armed?" Claire asked McCollum. He shook his head no. "Too exposed, Hawk. Too exposed. It's safer if I go. Give me the keys to the Jeep."

"Claire!"

"Damnit, Hawk! We don't have time for this!"

"Alex's Glock is in Helen's car," McCollum told them.

"Get it," Claire said. "I'll bring it to her."

"Claire, don't you think Alex might be more receptive to me," Hawk argued.

"Hawk, if my father comes here, they are all unarmed. Trust me, I would prefer to stay. I'm not fast enough if…"

Hawk sighed apprehensively as McCollum returned with Alex's gun. "Claire, be careful. Your father wants me," he told her.

"Not just you," Claire said. "He wants Dylan."

"What?" McCollum went pale.

"Hawk will fill you in."

"Claire, wait," McCollum said.

"No time."

"Claire! Mackenzie is in the cabin. You need to take her to Alex. Cassidy can take the kids in the Jeep," he explained before flying into the cabin.

"Is he fucking insane?" Claire asked. "I can't watch a baby!"

"He's right, Claire."

"Fuck!"

McCollum burst through the door to the cabin and headed directly for Rose. "I need you to listen to me." She looked up at him. His pupils had narrowed to pin points. "Get Mackenzie and Helen and meet me outside. You need to get to the lodge now. Rose, please, I know you have no reason to trust me, but I am asking you to."

"What's going on?" Edmond asked.

"Bill. On his way with company," McCollum explained.

"How do you…."

"Claire is outside."

"Claire?" Edmond asked.

"Edmond! Nous savons tous les deux qu'il ne sera pas hésiter! (We both know he will not hesitate)!" McCollum urged.

"Go," Edmond looked at Helen. "Please, Helen…Take Rose and Mackenzie and go."

"Not to rush our goodbyes," Hawk poked her head in the door. "But, we've got company on the way."

Edmond helped Helen with her coat while Rose bundled Mackenzie hurriedly, fumbling in nervousness. McCollum took over Rose's task handily and passed her their granddaughter. He led her through the door to Claire. "Stay with Claire. She'll keep you safe until you get to Alex." He nodded to Claire. Helen and Rose climbed into the back of the Jeep with Mackenzie and he leaned in the door. "It might never matter to you again," he told Rose. "But, I love you."

"This is not what I signed up for," Claire grumbled.

"Is there another road?" Hawk asked. "Another way to the cabin."

McCollum nodded. "Safest the way you came, but," he looked back at Claire, who had pulled herself into the driver's seat. "Go down to where the fork was, turn left and go up the mountain for about a quarter mile."

"Up? Why up?" Claire asked.

"Go up until you see the next fork. There are some condos up there. Take a right and go down. Just in case" he said. Claire smiled, understanding his directive. If anyone were close, they would not pass Hawk's Jeep coming from the cabin. A few extra minutes was worth the diversion. "Claire?" he said. He looked back at Rose. "Don't worry about us. You get them out of here, Cassie too. No matter what."

Claire nodded and turned the Jeep over. She looked at the occupants of the back seat and shook her head in utter disbelief. "This is not what I signed up for."

*＊＊

Admiral William Brackett climbed into a black Hummer. He took a deep breath and readied himself to come face to face with his old friend James McCollum. McCollum was not a person to be underestimated. When he had served in the field, he had often been tasked with the most dangerous and often gruesome missions. McCollum was an engineer by trade. He was also a master marksman, proficient in martial arts, physically intimidating when needed, and highly intuitive. Brackett closed his eyes. A call from General Matthew Waters had left him with a greater measure of confidence in this chosen course of action.

Waters had spoken with his sister. He informed The Admiral that she had called him regarding his contacts at Rand. She was sending Krause and Baros back to ascertain what Gray had not been able to show Alex before Carecom had been compromised. Agent Fallon and Agent Brady were pushing paper, Waters had said. The Admiral's daughter was convalescing under the watchful eye of Agent Hawkins. Jane's greatest concern was for Dylan, who had apparently met with a small accident. Brackett could not have devised a more perfect scenario if he had coordinated it all himself. The only question marks left to be answered were Joshua Tate and Marcus Anderson. Neither presented any significant worry for Brackett.

"How far out?" he asked the two men in the front of the car.

"Twenty minutes."

"Good."

"You want to surprise them?" the driver asked.

"Oh, they'll be surprised," Brackett gloated. "All of them."

Chapter Twenty

"**F**uck! Fallon! Fallon!" Brady moved the agent on top of him and shook him lightly. "Fallon? Damnit. Shit, Fallon."

Brady reached into his pocket and pulled out his cell phone. "Fuck!"

He threw the smashed piece of metal and plastic aside. The smoke surrounding him was thick and clogging his lungs. He coughed and spit. His leg throbbed and his head was spinning. Brady checked Fallon for a pulse and closed his eyes. "Goddammit, Brian," he whispered. He reached into Fallon's coat pocket and fished for Fallon's cell phone. "We can't be here," he muttered to Fallon. Brady pulled himself upright and began to drag Fallon behind him.

Fallon stirred slightly. "Go," he managed to whisper.

"Brian…" A rumbling above them directed Brady's sight upward.

"Get out," Fallon directed him.

"Not without you."

"Without me. Get to Alex."

"Brian," Brady argued. The rumbling steadily shifted to a constant creaking.

"Now, Brady," Fallon opened his eyes. He knew that Brady could not see the hole in his back. Fallon could feel it. Something had pierced him deeply in the explosion. There was no way he was walking or crawling anywhere. Fallon suspected that if he could make it out of this nightmare of wire, steel, and dust he would likely never walk or crawl anywhere again. Alex needed the files he had sent. That was the most important thing.

"Fallon, I will get you out of here."

"No, you won't," Fallon said bluntly. He grabbed Brady's jacket. "Tell Alex—take care of Kate. Take care of those kids, all of them."

"Brian…"

"You know I'm right. Let this beat cop get some rest," Fallon managed the hint of a smile. He had resigned himself to his fate. He had hoped that it would never come to this, but Brian Fallon had no illusions about life as a cop nor as an agent. He had accepted the risks long ago.

"You're no beat cop," Brady told him as bits of plaster fell on them.

Fallon coughed up some blood through a chuckle. "Always a beat cop," he said as he closed his eyes. "Get out of here."

Brady looked down at Fallon for a moment. "Fuck me," he muttered. "I'm sorry," he said. Brady pulled himself into a kneeling position and began feeling his way through the rubble. Fallon was right and Brady hated it. The least he could do for the man behind him was to honor his request.

***

"I don't understand it," Krause said.

"What?"

"Brady I get. I mean, he's been off the radar for over a year. But, Fallon? I can believe he'd move on a suspicion, but to not check in—at all?"

"You think they were compromised?" Eleana asked. "Maybe we just missed them. If they drove, they would have been hours behind us," she reminded Krause.

"Maybe," he muttered. Krause was tense. "I don't like it."

Eleana pulled him to face her. "Alex will be all right," she told him, sensing his worry.

"I don't like any of it."

"Neither do I," she told him. "You can't do anything about it right now," she said. "You have to trust that Claire and Hawk will get there. They will. Jane will come through on her end. She loves them too, Jonathan." Eleana noted the deep sadness in Jonathan Krause's eyes and moved to kiss his lips gently. "Jane will be okay," she said. "We'll get through this. We always do."

"That's the thing, Eleana. Not everyone always does," he said.

Eleana kissed him again. "No, they don't," she admitted somberly. Her thoughts traveled to her friend Russ Matthews. She would not be in Jonathan Krause's arms had Matthew's not moved quickly to save her when the American Embassy had been attacked in Moscow. She thought about Claire's mother. "Jonathan?"

"Yeah?" he asked as his hand caressed her back.

"I don't want to think about any of it right now," she told him honestly. He looked at her compassionately. She traced a small scar over his eyebrow with her fingers. "Just love me right now."

Krause smiled. He leaned in and kissed her tenderly. "I don't deserve you," he told her.

"Yes, you do. And, I deserve this."

"What's that?" he asked.

"To have someone love only me."

Krause smiled. "That, I can do," he promised.

***

Alex let Dylan lean on her for support as they made their way toward the ski lift. She watched the chair lift climb the mountain and swallowed hard. Dylan pulled on Alex's hand to guide her toward the platform. "Isn't there another way up there?" she asked.

Dylan looked at Alex curiously. "No."

"So, you just sit in this until you are halfway up the hill?"

Dylan studied Alex. "Yeah. Come on, it's fun."

"Can't we just take the snowmobile up there?"

"No," Dylan said. "This lift will drop us just above The Den. We just walk down the path."

"See? Your ankle still hurts," Alex observed. "Can't we see her down here?" Alex had only skied twice in her life, neither had been an enjoyable or successful endeavor for her, something she had no intention of sharing with her son or her wife.

Dylan giggled. He was starting to understand that his hero was a bit afraid. "Alex? Are you scared?"

"What? No!"

"It's okay, I was scared at first too. This one is easy."

"Uh-huh. Speed, how are you going to hop off of the lift with that ankle?" Alex asked.

"Boots help," he said. Dylan's ankle was sore, but he was excited to be with Alex, and he was looking forward to seeing his mother on the slopes. "It's not far, Alex. I promise, I can do it."

Alex took a deep breath and nodded. There were only a few people ahead of them in line. She was startled by a voice behind her. "Couldn't keep him away, huh?" Alex turned to find Cassidy lifting her ski goggles.

"Mom!"

"Hey. What are you two doing here?" Cassidy asked.

"Grandma said we should come watch you."

"Oh, I see," Cassidy replied. "Well, in that case, care to share a ride?"

"I thought this went half way?" Alex asked.

Cassidy smirked. She had guessed that what prevented Alex from skiing was the lift. Helen had made a few comments to that effect. "It does. There's another lift on the opposite side of The Den that takes you to the top," she explained. Alex nodded. Cassidy smiled. They were next. "Be brave," she whispered in Alex's ear. Alex looked at Cassidy like a deer caught in the headlights.

Dylan sat beside his mother happily. Cassidy leaned into Alex's ear as they began their ascent. "No worries, love, I will protect you." Alex grimaced and Cassidy chuckled.

Dylan poked his mother. Cassidy leaned in so he could whisper in her ear. "I think Alex is afraid of heights," he said. Cassidy winked at him.

Cassidy noted Alex's white knuckles on the bar and took pity on her. "You didn't have to come," she said.

"I wanted to see you," Alex replied. Cassidy took Alex's hand and held it. "Cass?"

"Hum?"

"How high is half way?"

***

Hawk reached inside her jacket. "I trust you know how to use that," she said to McCollum, handing him a Glock.

"I do. Suppose you fill us in on why Bill Brackett is interested in my grandson."

"I would, but I don't really get it. Something about his father using him. I don't get it. I just know Krause thinks Admiral Brackett is on the way. Claire was determined to get here first."

Edmond looked across the room at McCollum. "SEED? Is it possible that Dylan was part of SEED?"

"Anything is possible," McCollum admitted.

"If O'Brien used Dylan," Edmond began.

"If I hadn't already killed the son-of-a-bitch," McCollum groaned.

"Not too worried about surprising us," Hawk commented from the window in the common room. She could hear a vehicle approaching.

"Well, we'll see who will be surprised," McCollum commented. He gestured to Edmond to take a seat. The two sat across from one another, each with a cup of coffee on the table, a deck of cards spread between them. "Agent Hawkins," McCollum addressed the young woman. "Go in the bedroom over there. There is a closet right inside. In it, there is a panel that opens. I built it to hold Cassie's gear. You'll fit."

"What? I am not leaving you out here. Alex will kill me, not to mention Claire…"

"Just do it, Agent," McCollum directed her. "You don't know what we are dealing with. You said it yourself. I need to know. He will tell me, trust me on that."

"You don't think he'll go after them?"

"Not if he doesn't guess we're a threat. Just do it. I can handle Bill Brackett—trust me."

***

Alex and Dylan sat at a high top table that faced several television monitors. Cassidy had promised that she would join them after her run. Alex watched the monitors carefully, waiting to catch a glimpse of Cassidy.

"Alex! Here comes Mom!"

Alex's eyes zeroed in on the light blue jacket and she felt her lips curl into a smile. Cassidy was graceful. Her descent was fast, but fluid. Alex envied the freedom she imagined Cassidy felt at that moment. The slopes were almost bare. Alex sat in awe. It didn't surprise her that Cassidy had athletic abilities in the least. She'd seen evidence of that many times. Cassidy could be competitive, but it was always with herself. Alex had never seen Cassidy become frustrated or irritated by losing a game of any kind, not like both she and Dylan could at times. But, Cassidy did push herself. Alex admired the tenacity in her wife as much as she did Cassidy's gentle nature.

"Told you!" Dylan said. "She's really good!"

Alex nodded. "Yeah, Speed, she sure is."

***

"You're Bill's daughter," Helen commented.

"Who is Bill?" Rose asked. "What is going on?"

"He's my father, yes. You know him?" Claire asked as she approached the parking lot of the resort.

"We've met," Helen replied.

"I'm sorry," Claire responded. She turned to face the women in the back seat. "How do I find Alex?"

Helen nodded. "I'll take you."

Claire tossed the keys to the Jeep to Rose. "I think you'll be fine here. You can keep it running. If you feel like anyone is…Well, just drive away. Just go. They're not looking for you or Mackenzie," Claire said.

"What about…" Rose's apprehension was growing.

Claire looked at Helen. "Just tell me where to go. Stay with them. It's safer. And, anyway…I think you might have a clue what I mean."

"Not as much as you might think," Helen said. "More than I would like," she admitted. "Walk across the lot. There is a sign for Bear Claw. You can't miss it. Take the first lift to the lodge. It's only about 100 yards down the hill when you get off. You'll see it. That's where Alexis is."

"Okay. Just sit tight until I get back, unless you can't."

"What about Edmond and Jim?" Rose asked fearfully.

Claire smiled at the older woman. "If anyone can beat my father at his own game, it's Cassidy's father. Sit tight," she told them.

***

Cassidy lifted her goggles and squinted to focus on a familiar figure in the distance approaching the platform for the chair lift. "Claire?" She put her poles in the ground and pushed off forcefully.

Claire was determined to ignore the searing pain in her shoulder and her ankle. She had not taken any medication in over twenty-four hours.

Mentally, she slapped herself for not listening to Hawk and taking something before the car ride. With the weather, the four-hour trip had become nearly seven. Hawk had argued that Claire could sleep while she drove and that Claire needed something. The effects of the medication would be slim by the time they reached Alex. Claire would not even discuss it. She felt as if a fog were lifting from her mind and she had no intention of clouding it again in any way. As she struggled toward the platform ahead, she realized pain had its own unique way of clouding thought.

"Claire?" Cassidy came up behind the agent. Claire spun more quickly than she had intended and momentarily lost her balance. Cassidy grabbed her arm and steadied her. "What the hell are you doing here?" Cassidy demanded.

"I need to find Alex," Claire replied.

Cassidy immediately recognized the desperation in Claire's eyes. She wasn't sure if it had been brought on by fear or physical pain. "Why? Where is Agent Hawkins?" Cassidy asked.

"Cassidy, please. I know….I don't want to…She's with your father at the cabin."

"Why?"

"Cassidy…."

"Dammit, Claire! What is going on?" Cassidy demanded.

"My father," Claire said. "He knows your father is back. He knows he's here. Please, Cassidy."

Cassidy's heart dropped and she began to panic. "Mom and Mackenzie…"

"They're safe," Claire told her. "I brought them down. Alex's mom is with them. I promise—they are safe," Claire assured Cassidy. "Cassidy, you and Alex….You might not be. Please?"

Cassidy guided Claire toward the lift. "You are going to tell me what is going on while we are on this lift."

Claire looked at Cassidy hesitantly. "Cassidy…"

"Claire, I mean it. This is my family. I have a right to know."

"Maybe," Claire said. "It's not true, though," Claire mumbled as they reached the platform and waited for their turn.

"What's not true?" Cassidy asked.

"That the truth sets you free. Sometimes it just takes you prisoner," Claire said.

***

"Time to pay the piper, Edmond."

Edmond nodded his agreement. "Why didn't you tell me?" he asked.

McCollum smiled at his old friend. "You never lost that ability, Edmond."

"What are you talking about?"

"You always believed in Bill. Always thought somehow the five of us would remain true to our word," McCollum said.

"I was a fool."

"No, you were a friend," McCollum disagreed.

"And? Where did that get me? Where did it get Claire or Eleana? And, this? If I had known…"

"It would have changed nothing," McCollum said flatly. "Bill trusted you with more than he did Nicolaus. The Major took you into his confidence, gave you Ivanov to liaise with. It gave us clues. It bought us time."

"Little good that did for John and Elliot," Edmond reminded his friend.

"Elliott followed his own tune. He may have been your son, but he did not follow in your footsteps. He chose the game over any sense of purpose. That is not your fault. As for John…John knew where he was heading. He knew it for a long time, Edmond. That is why he went to Nicolaus. He needed to protect his children. And, that is why Nicolaus passed his work to Jane when the time came. There is a different meaning of family for some of us."

McCollum closed his eyes. He heard the vehicle outside and looked back at Edmond. "We cannot go back, my friend. It's time to move forward now. We owe them that."

***

Krause rolled over when he heard a rattling by the bedside. "Fallon? Where the hell have you been?" he asked heatedly.

"Krause," Brady's voice was raspy.

"Brady?"

"Krause....Fallon...Fuck. There was an explosion at Rand."

Krause shot up in the bed, waking Eleana. "Brady, where is Fallon?"

"I'm sorry, Jonathan." Krause sat shell-shocked. "He...He saved my ass, Jonathan."

Krause closed his eyes to quell the roiling of his stomach. Alex had never wanted Fallon in this game. Fallon had insisted. Krause had agreed with Fallon. Now, he berated himself for that decision. Alex's worst fears seemed to all be coming true. Everything they had sought to protect was hanging in the balance.

"Why were you at Rand?" Krause fell back on the only thing he could—the job.

"Doesn't matter. Listen, we found something. Thought we had time. Makes sense they would blow it to hell."

"What did you find?" Krause asked. Eleana sat beside him watching him thoughtfully.

"You might call it a map."

"What kind of a map?" Krause asked.

"Something called SEED. Handlers, assets, objectives," Brady said. "Krause?"

"Yeah?"

"O'Brien was on that list."

"I know," Krause said.

"It's worse. So was Dylan."

Krause nodded silently. "I know that too."

"How? Brady asked.

"Ran into an old friend at MyoGen. He had some interesting files. Incomplete but enlightening."

"Maybe what we sent will fill in the gaps," Brady said.

"Sent?"

"Fallon redirected the dump to Alex's secure server."

Krause smiled. Fallon had proved himself over and over again. "Are you injured?"

"Yeah, was about to call Jane for an extraction."

"No. She's otherwise engaged. Can you get somewhere secure?"

Brady coughed. "Yeah, I think so."

"Do you need..."

"Nothing life threatening. I think my ankle is broken, some smoke inhalation, a few deep cuts. It can hold."

"Fine. We'll be there in a few hours. Call me when you have a location."

"Krause?"

"Yeah?"

"I'm sorry....About Fallon."

"Yeah, me too."

"Jonathan?" Eleana asked when he placed the phone back beside him and closed his eyes.

"Was that Brian?" Krause shook his head. "Jonathan?" she implored him gently.

"We need to pick up Brady."

"Where is Brian?" she asked with growing concern. Krause stroked Eleana's cheek. "No..."

"I'm sorry, Eleana."

Eleana fell into Jonathan Krause's arms. "When will this end?" she asked.

"I don't know," he confessed. "I don't know."

***

Cassidy walked into the lodge and leaned her skis against the wall. "Come on," she said to Claire.

"Cassidy, I am really sorry."

Cassidy turned to Claire and nodded. "Let's go."

Alex started to walk toward Cassidy, excited to see her wife when she caught sight of the person walking a pace behind. "Dylan, stay here."

Cassidy noted the stiffness in Alex's gait. "Alex..."

"What the hell are you doing here?" Alex demanded of Claire.

"Alex," Cassidy took hold of Alex's arm. "Just listen to her, please. I'm going to get Dylan," she said.

"I'm waiting," Alex said.

"My father is on his way here."

"Here as in where we are?"

"Here as in where you are staying."

"Jesus Christ...Mackenzie...."

"She's okay," Claire said calmly.

"How do you...."

"She's in Hawk's Jeep with your mother and Cassidy's."

"Where's Hawk?" Alex asked.

"At the cabin. Alex, it's not just Cassidy's father he wants."

"What are you talking about?"

"He thinks O'Brien might have...He thinks Dylan might know something."

"I need to get to the cabin. My gun is in the car."

"No, it's not," Claire said with a slight grin.

"What?" Alex asked. Claire pulled Alex aside and handed her the Glock. "How did you?"

"McCollum gave it to me."

"How did he?"

"I don't know," Claire said.

"Claire, only Hawk is armed."

"I doubt that is true now," Claire said.

Cassidy smiled at Dylan. Inside she was shaking like a leaf, but she did not want him to see that. "Hi," she greeted her son.

"Mom? Why is Ms. Brackett here?"

"You remember her?"

"Yeah, she took me with Uncle Brian once."

"Yes, she did. She's here to see Alex."

"Is Alex leaving?" Dylan asked.

"I think so. You and I are going to go meet Grandma and YaYa and have some breakfast. We'll catch up with Alex later."

"But, Mom...I can't ski down."

"It's okay. I'll ride down with you."

"Mom?"

"Yes?"

"Who is Jim?"

Cassidy smiled. "Well, why don't we save that for the ride?" she suggested. Dylan nodded. "I'll be right back," she promised her son. Cassidy ran her fingers through Dylan's short hair and made her way back to Alex and Claire.

"Cass…"

"Don't," Cassidy told Alex. There was no anger, only fear in her voice. "You can get to the cabin from here. There's a trail behind the lodge. It actually isn't that far, just on the other side of Allagash. You'll see the signs for the summit lift. The snow is pretty deep, but you will see my tracks. Just follow it. It leads you to the woods behind the cabin."

"Claire, go with Cassidy," Alex said.

"No way!"

"Claire! You can barely walk. You will only slow me down," Alex argued calmly.

Cassidy sighed. "There's a ski patrol station when you reach Allagash. That's only about an eighth of a mile. If you can get there…"

Alex nodded her understanding. Claire started back for the door. "Where are you going?" Alex asked.

"Getting a head start so I don't slow you down."

"Alex," Cassidy implored her wife.

"Cassidy, take Dylan and get the kids out of here. Get some distance between you and this place. Do you hear me? I will call you when it's safe."

"Alex, my father…"

"Don't underestimate him," Alex told her.

"Dylan. Why?"

Alex pulled Cassidy to her. "It doesn't matter right now. Just go."

"Alex," Cassidy began to cry.

"Trust me," Alex said.

"I do."

"Then trust that I will call you," Alex said. She kissed Cassidy tenderly. "Take Dylan and go, Cass. Please."

Cassidy nodded. "I'll be waiting."

Alex smiled at Dylan and waved. "I'll see you soon," she promised.

***

McCollum looked up as the front door to the cabin began to open. Brash as ever, he thought. He looked back down at the table and spoke. "You are back early," he said without looking at the person in the doorway.

"And, you have been gone forever."

McCollum looked up at Admiral William Brackett at the same moment Edmond turned to face their old friend. "Bill?" Edmond asked as if he were surprised.

"Hello, Edmond. Sorry to drop in so unexpectedly. Where's the family?" he asked. McCollum remained stoic and silent. "No matter. I'm sure they'll be back from wherever they headed off to soon. It gives us a little time to catch up."

A tall, muscular man stood just behind The Admiral. "You want me to find them?"

"No. I imagine they are off enjoying the mountain. They have to come back sooner or later. Surprised you didn't join them," Brackett addressed McCollum.

"I'm not exactly the guest of honor here."

Brackett laughed. He took a seat at the table. "Oh, but you are," he said. "Keep an eye out," he told the man in the door. Brackett turned back to McCollum and Edmond Callier. "So? Let's catch up."

***

"Shit," Claire yelped as they moved down the trail.

Alex sighed heavily. She pulled Claire toward a tree. "Just stay here."

"No way, Toles. I'm not running away from him this time."

Alex nodded. "I know. Just wait here." Alex took off in as much of a sprint as she could manage.

"Toles!" Claire called. "You're not leaving my ass here!" Claire leaned her head against the tree and caught her breath. She had managed to keep pace with Alex, but she was quickly losing that ability. She took a deep breath and pushed down the pain before pressing forward.

***

"Mom? Is everything okay?"

"Everything is fine, Dylan."

"You look worried," he observed.

"Well, I am," she admitted. "Alex has been worried about work," she told him honestly. "She has to meet with some people back at the cabin," she explained. "Grandma and YaYa are waiting for us."

"Why is Ms. Brackett here?"

Cassidy smiled. "Her father and Edmond are friends."

"Oh," he replied. "Who is Jim, Mom?"

Cassidy took a deep breath. "Well, Dylan, that is a hard question for me to answer."

"Why?"

"Because I am not really sure myself."

"But, Grandma said that he was someone important to you."

"He is," Cassidy admitted. "I'm going to tell you something and I want you to listen. Okay?" she said. He nodded. Cassidy looked out over the mountain as the lift began its descent. "My father loved this. Looking out over the mountain."

"I do too," he said.

Cassidy looked back at Dylan and smiled. "I can't really explain it to you because I don't really understand it myself. I was only about your age when my father had his accident."

"I know."

"Mm. They never found my father. His car went into the river. They looked," she said. "It was a bad accident. We just all assumed he was dead. He never came back." Dylan looked at his mother curiously. "Jim....Dylan, Jim is my father. He is your grandfather."

Dylan considered her information. "He didn't die?"

"No."

"Why didn't he come back?" Dylan asked. "He made you so sad."

"He did. I don't really know, Dylan. He couldn't come back for a long time. He was far away."

"Did he forget where you were or something?" Dylan asked.

"He forgot a lot of things," Cassidy replied honestly.

"Did he forget who he was?" Dylan tried to understand.

Cassidy sighed. She smiled sadly at her son. "Yes, I think he did," she replied, realizing that it was an honest answer. "In a way, he did—yes." Cassidy felt a tear slip over her cheek.

Dylan took his mother's hand. "Don't cry, Mom. He remembered."

Cassidy nodded and chuckled in spite of her falling tears. "I guess maybe he did, Dylan. Maybe he did."

***

"Matt."

"Janie!" General Matthew Waters rose from his seat happily. "What a surprise!"

Jane nodded. "I'm not the only one it seems with some surprises."

"Are you all right?" he asked his sister. "Janie? What is it? What's wrong?"

"Why, Matt?"

"Why? Why, what?"

"Why did you do it?" she asked.

"What did I do?" he asked.

Jane shook her head sorrowfully. "John trusted you. I trusted you."

"Janie, what is this about?"

Jane took a deep breath. "Dylan is safe, Matt."

"What are you talking about?"

Jane threw a file onto his desk. She nodded to it. "Christopher O'Brien: Handler: Viktor Ivanov. Objective: Cassidy McCollum—Program SEED."

"What is this?" he asked looking at the file.

"Keep reading," she instructed him. "Matthew Waters: Project Lynx. Handler: William Brackett. Objective: Continuation Project Lynx. Program Integration—Program SEED."

Matt nodded. "So?"

Jane smiled at him ruefully. "Why? Why would you align yourself with The Admiral? You fought our father over that for years."

"It's not that simple," he said. "It was given to me, Jane. I did what was expected."

"Given to you? You had a choice to make. We all do."

"No, I didn't. I never had a choice. What do you know about it?" he shouted angrily. "You made the choice, Janie. After everything, you made the choice!"

"What the hell are you talking about?"

"You know who implemented Lynx?"

"Of course, I know. Jim at our father's direction."

"Yeah, and do you know who was slated for that program? You think that SEED is the first of its kind? Come on, Janie."

"What are you saying?"

"I'm saying Dad made a deal. You were left aside," he told her.

Jane closed her eyes. "If he agreed that you would be placed. Matt…"

"Everything I did was for you."

Jane looked at him and shook her head again. "No, Matt. It wasn't. That was our father's choice, not yours. You're right, I did make my choices. Some, I am not very proud of at all. I would never have compromised my children like he did. I cannot believe that you would allow that. My God, you sanctioned it. You…"

"It's all about family, Jane."

"Whose family?" she asked. "You mean the family our father used to talk about? That's not family, Matthew, that is just business."

"We are given our family, Jane. Family demands loyalty. If someone betrays that…"

"You're wrong. Family is not given, Matt. It is created by our choices."

"It's all in motion already."

"What is that?" Jane asked.

"The Admiral and Viktor's plan. It's unfolding as we speak. The seeds are everywhere."

"Yes, I know. But, seeds are not much good if no one waters them," she said. She turned to leave.

"You're leaving? Just walking away?"

Jane turned back. "What do you expect me to do, General? Shoot you in your office?"

"It's true, isn't it? The Broker? He was Sphinx," Matt said. "You knew where to look because he passed it to you."

Jane smiled. "You listened to Dad's bedtime stories too much," she said. "It sparked your imagination about too many things." She started to leave again.

"Jane…"

"Have a nice day, General."

"I'm still your brother."

"My brother was a man who understood family. My brother would never have murdered his sister's husband, betrayed her confidence about the son he loved and never got to know. He would never have put her through that pain. You, Matt, are General Waters. My brother said goodbye a long time ago."

Jane turned on her heels and left him in his office. She closed his door and fell back into it, the air stolen from her lungs. "I am so sorry, John. So sorry."

***

Claire had her hands on her knees trying to catch her breath when she heard a motor approaching.

"Get on," Alex instructed her.

"You came back."

"Don't make a big deal out of it. Coming or not?" Alex asked.

Claire climbed on back. "Can't say I ever expected to put my arms around you again," Claire cracked.

Alex chuckled. "Well, we have at least one thing in common," she said as she sped off.

***

"So, what have you been doing in the cellars of Siberia all these years?" Brackett asked McCollum.

"Undoing your madness."

"See, that's your problem, Jim. You never had any vision," Brackett said. "You and Nicolaus and this idea that there are limits. There are no limits unless we create them."

396

"Bill!" Edmond interrupted him. "My God, look what you did to your daughter."

"I didn't make Claire who she is. She did that."

McCollum chuckled in disgust. "No, you just made her forget who she was. You think that is different somehow?"

***

Alex pointed ahead to Claire. She cut the motor on the snowmobile. "Three o'clock, I see him," Claire said.

"I'll take care of him," Alex offered. "You get to the back of the cabin."

"No," Claire said. "I recognize him. You head for the cabin. I'll take care of him."

"Are you...What the hell?" Alex stopped short. Her sight fell ahead to where Marcus Anderson was creeping up behind the subject of their discussion. "Anderson?"

"Good morning, ladies," a voice greeted Alex and Claire. They both turned to find Tate leaning an unconscious man against a nearby tree.

"Tate?" Alex asked in disbelief.

"Nice to see you too, Alex."

"How did you?" she looked back toward Agent Anderson as he approached.

"Jane," he explained. "Krause had a run in with Daniels."

"We need to get in there," Claire said.

"They are just talking," Tate said.

"How long have you been here?" Alex wondered.

"Just long enough," Tate replied.

"Where is Hawk?" Claire asked in concern.

"I'm not sure. I didn't hear her in there."

"Alex," Claire urged Alex.

"Hawk can handle herself, Claire. Anyone else?" Alex asked the men.

"Just the Admiral. Jane's plan apparently worked. He's cockier than usual."

"What plan?" Claire asked.

"Later," Tate said.

"I want to get closer," Alex said. She looked at Anderson. "Marcus, Cassidy is with the kids. I think she was headed to the restaurant just before the resort."

"I've got it covered," Marcus assured her.

"Come on," Alex beckoned Claire. Claire tipped her head in surprise. "I want to hear what they are talking about, don't you?"

Alex and Claire moved toward the cabin. Alex managed to peer in the front window. Tate was right. Brackett had his back to the door. He was nothing if not confident. McCollum caught her eye and nodded almost imperceptibly. Alex understood the subtle message. Cassidy's father felt he had control—stay put.

"This new world order of yours," Edmond said. "This is worth Claire? Eleana? Jesus, Bill. We agreed. The five of us. We promised."

"Always the idealist, Edmond. What did you think? Lynx was Donald's project. You thought he would end that?"

"Donald Waters was as arrogant as he was foolish," McCollum replied.

Tate looked at Alex. "Jane's father?" he whispered. Alex nodded.

"No, you lost your faith in the family long before the rest of us," Brackett accused McCollum.

"What the hell are you talking about? We are back to this? Rose has nothing to do with this," McCollum spat.

"Everything to do with it. You went outside the family and look. You began to see a different pathway. Tainted Nicolaus with it. And, Edmond?

He has too much of his mother in him. Always ideals with you three," Brackett told him.

"You are not seriously suggesting that Jim's marriage is to blame?" Edmond uncharacteristically raised his voice.

"Family, Edmond. Family. We were brothers once," Brackett said. "The ultimate bond. The same duty."

"Duty?" McCollum laughed. "You're a fool, Bill. You and Donald and this twisted idea you have of family. Isn't Claire your family? What about Marjorie? Jesus, you fucking murdered your wife in front of her daughter!"

"She was in a position to compromise us with Ivanov. She would have too."

"Why?" Edmond asked. "The truth."

"She found out about the school. About Claire's training. About Claire's...."

"Programming?" McCollum guessed.

"If you will. She worked inside, you know that. She had more information than I did most of the time. To tell you the truth, I wondered if she might be Sphinx," Brackett admitted.

"So, you killed her," Edmond surmised.

"I did what had to be done."

"And, O'Brien?" McCollum asked.

Brackett shrugged. "Ivanov's pawn originally. Part of Petrov's project. A seed."

"And?" McCollum urged. "Tell me, Bill. It's just us. What was his objective?"

"Simple really, marry Lynx's daughter and start a family," Brackett said.

"Why?" McCollum asked.

"You walked away. Made no contribution, James. But, you had information. No one is ever that cautious. Your family holds answers they do not even know they possess," he said. "Cassidy would have surpassed them all had she not interfered."

"Cassie is not your asset. That was not Rose's decision. It was mine to keep Cassidy from those schools."

"Perhaps. It runs in the family, apparently. Your daughter saw to it that the boy stayed out of the program."

"What is he talking about?" Alex whispered to Claire. Claire shrugged.

McCollum laughed. "She demanded he go to public school," he guessed. "Kept him from the program without even knowing it."

"Mm," Brackett said. "But, O'Brien…He got ambitious. His bumbling hid his brilliance. He traced those wires into his campaign. Right through ASA and back to MyoGen."

"That's why my father cut off the funds to ASA," Alex whispered to Tate. "They were funding SEED somehow at MyoGen."

"Found some data, so he claimed," Brackett said.

"And, you think Dylan knows what it is?" McCollum asked.

"I think he knows where it is."

"Long shot."

"Worst case scenario I recover one of Ivanov's assets and alleviate some annoyances in the process," Brackett said. McCollum struggled to suppress his anger. "Not that we didn't try before. John screwed that up."

"You never expected Alexis and Cassidy," McCollum chuckled.

"No. Fisher should have accomplished the task. It would have cleared O'Brien," Brackett said.

"To take custody of Dylan," McCollum surmised. "He's just a boy."

"He's family," Brackett said. "If O'Brien did expose the boy at all, knowing his objective could be a major asset. O'Brien squarely in play would have been a benefit now that it is starting. The boy? That would have pacified Viktor and given O'Brien more leeway."

"To take your directives and feed you information," McCollum guessed. Bracket shrugged. "And now, you think I am going to help you? Help you program Dylan? You're insane."

"You will if you want your grandchildren to be safe. Consider that my way of honoring our friendship."

Alex burst through the door gun blazing. "You son-of-a-fucking-bitch!"

Admiral Brackett turned in surprise. "Alexis."

Alex's hand was shaking in anger. "You are not going to touch my children."

"So much like your father," Brackett laughed. "You think I am the only person you have to worry about? Grow up, Alexis."

Claire stepped around Alex coolly.

"Claire," Brackett greeted his daughter. "You look surprisingly well." Claire kept moving forward. He turned his chair to face her. Claire stared at her father. "You have something to say?" he asked her dryly.

"No," she answered as she drew her gun.

McCollum moved quickly. He swiped Claire's legs out from under her and knocked her backward. Brackett began to laugh. "I know what I need to know," McCollum said. He pulled his gun. One loud blast and Admiral William Brackett was slumped over in his chair.

McCollum stepped back and moved to Alex. She was still standing, pointing her gun at Brackett, her hand shaking with anger. McCollum lowered her arm and took the weapon. "No more, Alexis. We made this, not you, not Claire. You do not need blood on your hands. That belongs on mine and his. No more."

Claire pulled herself up and moved hesitantly toward her father. She stood over him, staring blankly. She wanted to feel something. She wanted to feel anything. She looked across the room at Alex. They stared at each other for a moment. Claire realized what she felt—relief.

Hawk burst into the room with her gun in hand. "What the hell?"

Claire turned and looked at Hawk. Hawk saw Claire wavering and walked deliberately to her. Claire looked into Hawk's compassionate eyes and immediately fell to the ground. She cried. She cried for her mother. She cried for what she had become. She cried in relief, relief from fear that had permeated every moment of her life for sixteen years.

Hawk folded Claire into her arms and looked up at Alex. Alex smiled at her sadly. Alex turned to James McCollum. "Dylan?" she asked.

"I don't know, Alex," he said.

"Can you…"

James McCollum grasped Alex's arm. "No. He's a boy. Let him be that boy. Even if O'Brien had done anything, it would need a trigger and that trigger died with O'Brien."

"How can you be sure?"

"Alex, please trust me. If the time ever comes that you grow concerned, we will talk. I don't think it will. Let him be that boy. Nothing good will come of exploring a maybe. Trust me, please."

Alex nodded as Tate made his way to remove The Admiral. "I need to call Cass." McCollum nodded. "Jim?" she addressed him by name. He looked at her curiously. "Thank you."

Chapter Twenty-One

Alex thought that she should feel strange with the occupants of the cabin. Oddly, she felt a sense of comfort. Mackenzie had fallen asleep on her shoulder and Alex could not bring herself to let go of her daughter. Dylan was sitting with Jim McCollum. It was evident that Dylan was curious about the man. Alex smiled slightly at the gleam in McCollum's eye as he spoke to Dylan. There was still a great deal of tension among the adults. McCollum saw Alex from across the room. She watched as he smiled at Dylan and walked toward her.

"A moment?" McCollum requested. Alex nodded. She reluctantly passed Mackenzie to her mother. Helen offered her a reassuring smile and Alex followed Jim McCollum outside.

"What are you going to do?" she asked the older man.

"I don't know," McCollum confessed. "Stay here for now, I think. Cassie was right. Whatever might come to pass, it has to be new, at least where my family is concerned."

"You made a good start today," Alex observed.

McCollum's defeated sigh surprised Alex. "No. I murdered a man I once considered a friend."

"Claire would have, if you hadn't," Alex said.

"I know. I couldn't allow that. She's suffered enough."

"She's caused her share of suffering," Alex reminded him.

"We all have," he looked at Alex. "When we met, I thanked you for taking care of my family," he said. "The truth is, they are your family now, Alex."

Alex nodded. "I can't speak for Rose or Cassidy," she said. "I don't know what they will do, but I am not blind," she said. "It might not be what you want, but they both love you."

McCollum's halfhearted smile told her more than any words could have. He reached into the pocket of his jacket and pulled out an envelope.

"What's this?" Alex asked.

McCollum shrugged. "It's a letter, to me. I think, perhaps it is meant for you now," he said. "You read it," he told Alex as he started to walk back into the house. "You know, Alexis," he addressed her by her given name. "Your father was a complicated man at times. He was my best friend. And, I can tell you that no matter what you think, he was always very proud of you."

"I don't think…"

McCollum nodded. "It's funny what self-loathing will do," he told her as he entered the house. Alex opened the letter.

My Friend,

The time is approaching. You will forgive this method of communication. It is best for now. You wanted to know what it was like. I was not there. I hardly felt I should attend. I do know that Alexis is happy with Cassidy. Strange, isn't it? That they found each other in spite of all of our hope to keep them away from this madness. I wonder at times if there is a conspiracy greater than our own that somehow dictates where we fall.

You are the only person who has ever understood the burden I carry. I have passed that now, and it makes me sick to do so. But, she is the one person…The only person I believe will remain true to our work. I don't know that it will ever end, Jim. Too many people. The map is beyond what I can even draw. Like the ever-expanding universe, I wonder when it will collapse in on us.

I did see your grandson, several times. He is a handsome young man, bright too. I see a great deal of Rose in him, and your Cassidy, but he also reminds me of his father. I marvel at them. John, Jane, Alexis, Cassidy. They are so unlike us, wanting to change the world and believing they can. I wonder when we lost that. I wonder if we ever possessed that.

Jonathan has his path. I cannot intervene. I have tried. But, I am certain in time that they will discover the truth. And, there is truth. I have come to understand that now. When the veils of perception are pulled away, truth is always at the center, waiting to be discovered. Perhaps, we had forgotten that. I am sorry that my time has come. I cannot watch over them any longer from here. In truth, I failed in that endeavor miserably. For that, I could never expect forgiveness.

My solace now is in knowing that we did create something better without even trying. I see it in my daughter's face and I do not have the stomach to look in the mirror afterward.

I am forever grateful to you. She will be in touch. You will find protocols enclosed. I hope one day you will be able to have what I leave this world without. Be well, old friend.

Nicolaus

Alex folded the letter and placed it in her pocket.

"Alexis?" Helen walked out the door and to her daughter.

"Why didn't he ever tell me?"

"I don't know," Helen said honestly. "I wish I could give you the answers you are always looking for. Your father loved you. Why he couldn't tell you, I don't know. It tormented him and it broke your heart. Such a waste. He loved all of you. Someday Nicky will need to accept that as well."

"What about you?" Alex asked.

Helen smiled. "I loved him, and I always will. No matter what he did, I can't change that and I would never try to. I love you, Alexis—all of you. You and Nicky are a part of us, the best and worst we shared. Jonathan? He is a part of your father," she said with a smile. "How could I not love him? Just like you love Dylan."

Alex nodded. "It's cold out here. Let's go inside."

"Are you all right?" Helen asked.

"I will be," Alex said. "I just have some decisions to make."

"I know."

"How do I know which one is right?" Alex asked her mother.

"Follow your heart, Alexis. That is where they all lost their way," Helen said.

Alex walked back inside and removed her coat. Her eyes found Claire, who was sitting on the end of the sofa, silently staring off into space. Alex had been a bit surprised at the obvious affection she had witnessed between Claire and her former partner. But, Claire was not the same. And, Hawk was someone who Alex understood needed a partner who could challenge her. She chuckled. She had her reservations, but Alex was certain that Cassidy would demand they give Claire every reasonable chance, particularly after the day's events.

"I don't know what to say to her," Hawk admitted as she came up beside Alex.

Alex nodded. Her eyes were focused on Cassidy as Cassidy approached Claire. "Do you love her?" Alex asked.

"I just met her."

Alex chuckled. "Does that matter?"

"Maybe," Hawk replied. "How can you love someone that fast?"

"Hawk, do you think you could? Love her, I mean?"

"It's Claire Brackett," Hawk said with a sigh. "Maybe, I can't explain it."

"You don't have to explain it to me. Be her friend right now, Hawk. Maybe that is what she needs, at least for now," Alex said.

Cassidy sat down beside Claire. "Hey."

Claire looked at Cassidy. Cassidy's heart ached at the pleading expression in Claire's eyes. "I'm sorry," Claire said.

Cassidy nodded. "Claire, you very likely saved all of us today."

"And, you might never have been in that position if I hadn't been involved with…"

Cassidy glanced over at Alex. Alex understood the silent request. She started toward Cassidy, then stopped short to answer her phone.

"You can't change the past," Cassidy observed to Claire. "Sometimes you just have to do the best you can to make a difference today.—to become a little bit better right now."

"I don't even know who I am," Claire said. "How do I do better?"

"Seems to me you started that today," Cassidy told her. Cassidy put her hand on Claire's knee. "You have people to help you along the way."

"Do I?" Claire asked helplessly.

"Yes, you do," Cassidy promised. "But, really that is all up to you to decide."

Alex walked over to Cassidy. Cassidy looked up at her and felt her heart drop dramatically. She had seen that expression of turmoil before on Alex's face. "It's Brian," Alex said. Cassidy looked at her fearfully. "Pip called. He and Brady….They were at Rand. There was an explosion in one of the labs. He…"

Cassidy closed her eyes against a crushing pain in her chest. "Oh, God…Kate."

Alex hung her head, pinched the bridge of her nose, and sighed.

Claire looked at Alex. "He'd tell you that it was his choice," she said, knowing that Alex was blaming herself. Alex looked at Claire, her gaze open and confused. "Fallon," Claire said. "He wanted in," she told Alex. "He was a good agent. It's not your fault, Alex."

"Doesn't feel that way."

"I know it doesn't. It isn't. He'd be the first person to tell you that," Claire said.

"She's right," Hawk said. "I didn't know him well. But, Claire is right."

"That doesn't help Kate and the kids," Alex said.

"Then, I guess we will have to," Cassidy told Alex. Alex nodded. Cassidy looked back at Claire and smiled. "Thank you," she whispered. She stood and took Alex's hand, leading her from the room.

Cassidy closed the door to the bedroom and kissed Alex soundly. She reached up and brushed away Alex's tears. "I'm sorry, love."

"Me too," Alex said as her tears continued to fall.

"I love you, Alex," Cassidy promised. "I know this will sound horrible."

"What?"

"I loved Brian."

"I know you did," Alex said.

"But, right now I am so grateful that it wasn't you. That it wasn't my father, or God…"

Alex took Cassidy's face in her hands. "Not horrible, just honest."

"I don't want to lose you."

Alex nodded and kissed Cassidy. There was nothing to say now. She led Cassidy to the bed and pulled Cassidy into her arms. Alex closed her eyes. She listened to the voices in the other room. Somehow, they had managed to shelter most of their family from the day's madness. She wondered how they would continue to do that. Someone was delivering Kate Fallon the news every law enforcement spouse feared the most. Three more children left to mourn a parent. Alex was tired. There were still so many things to sort out. She guessed that Cassidy's father would stay at the cabin—at least for a while. She found herself wondering what Claire would do now. It was obvious something was developing between Claire and Charlie Hawkins. Alex hoped that it might be something to tame them both a bit. Alex heard Dylan's laughter lifting through the cabin and smiled. Cassidy often told Dylan when he fell short on the soccer field or a test at school, that all he could do was try and do a little better tomorrow. Maybe that's all there was to do.

"I love you, Cassidy."

"I love you."

***

"What is it?" Jane asked through the phone line.

"They've hit in London," the man answered.

Jane sighed. "What was the target?"

"Passenger plane."

"Are you certain it was Ivanov?" she asked.

Ian Mitchell took a deep breath. "It was The Admiral's call as near as I can tell. I'm sorry I could not get the exact target in time."

"Not your fault, Ian," Jane said.

"Jane? I did get the second target. Just not the date."

"Go on."

"FBI Los Angeles. Sometime soon. And, Jane? The word Cesium was used."

***

March 9th

Cassidy went in search of Alex. It had been an emotional day. Alex had maintained her composure until Brian Fallon's eldest son James had approached her and asked if she would help him become an FBI agent like his dad. Cassidy watched as Alex's face fell. Alex had nodded and told him that when he was older if that was still what he wanted, she would help him as much as she could. Cassidy could tell the conversation had upset Alex. Loss was never easy and they had both suffered a great deal of loss over the last few years.

Cassidy walked into the rec room in the basement of the Merrow townhouse just as Alex was finishing a call.

"No," Alex said. "Call Jonathan. I know. I've made my decision. I know you do. Thanks, Jane. Me too. Yeah...I'll tell her."

"How is my best friend?" Cassidy asked. "I feel like she's avoiding me these days."

"No, she's just dealing with some things," Alex explained. "She just told me to tell you that she wants to come up with Stephanie next weekend. If you are up for a visit."

"Mm. I am, but right now I am worried about you."

"I'm okay."

"Nice try, Alfred. Even my tacos didn't cheer you up."

Alex chuckled. "I love your tacos."

Cassidy raised an eyebrow at Alex. "Up for a game?" she nodded to the pool table.

Alex smirked. "Why? Need a lesson?"

"Who says I'm the one who needs the lesson?" Cassidy challenged her wife.

"Ha-ha. You can teach me how to get on a ski lift. I still get to be the billiards instructor."

"Are you questioning my form?" Cassidy flirted.

Alex closed the distance between them. "Never."

Cassidy closed her eyes as Alex's lips descended on hers. "On second thought," Cassidy said. "Let's go upstairs."

"Tired?"

"No," Cassidy said as she pulled away and started out of the room. "Coming?"

"Right behind you."

Cassidy led Alex into the master bedroom. She closed the door, faced Alex and slowly pulled her sweater over her head. Alex's breath caught and she licked her lips. "Jesus, you are beautiful, Cass."

"You're in love," Cassidy replied as she stepped closer.

Alex's hand fell down Cassidy's shoulders, over her arms, and then traveled upward across Cassidy's breasts to her throat. Cassidy closed her eyes. She took a deep breath and captured Alex's hand. Slowly, she opened her eyes again.

"What?" Alex asked, not certain what she saw flickering in Cassidy's gaze.

"Nothing," Cassidy said. "And everything." Alex smiled. Cassidy's lips found Alex's neck and sucked gently on her pulse point. Her hands moved to address the buttons on Alex's blouse. Cassidy's fingertips brushed across the swell of Alex's breasts and she sighed. She freed Alex of her shirt and bra. Alex followed her lead and removed Cassidy's bra swiftly.

Cassidy's touch meandered over Alex's flesh until it reached the button of her pants. Slowly, Cassidy trailed kisses over Alex's chest and stomach until she was kneeling before Alex. She lowered Alex's pants and kissed her way up Alex's legs, over her stomach until she was standing again, facing Alex.

Alex leaned in and claimed Cassidy's lips in an ardent kiss. Her hands addressed Cassidy's skirt and Cassidy stepped out of it. Cassidy pushed Alex back toward the bed and Alex smiled. Alex loved this part of Cassidy, the piece of her wife that could be aggressive and tender at the same time. She let Cassidy guide her backward onto the bed. She looked up at Cassidy as Cassidy moved to kiss her again.

"You," Cassidy said placing another kiss on Alex's lips. "Are my world, Alex."

Alex reached out and caressed Cassidy's face. "I do not deserve you," she said honestly.

"Yes, you do. We both deserve this, every moment of it, and I don't want to waste one," Cassidy told Alex. She kissed Alex deeply, her tongue brushing over Alex's softly, possessive in one moment and relenting the next. Cassidy's kiss fell lower, her breath caressing Alex's skin as she moved. She kissed each of Alex's breasts and forced herself upright to straddle Alex's hips, bringing their bodies together intimately.

Alex's head fell back momentarily. Cassidy grinned, seeing desire and arousal flush Alex's cheeks. Alex steadied her breathing and looked at Cassidy as Cassidy moved against her. Her hands found Cassidy's breasts and she watched in rapt fascination as Cassidy's eyes closed and Cassidy bit her lip in response. Cassidy's movements were sensual and unhurried. "Cass…"

"Alex, just feel me," Cassidy said. She opened her eyes and looked into Alex's as their dance continued. Cassidy desperately wanted to climb the cliff of desire with Alex and hold onto her as they fell together. She needed to feel alive, to know that Alex was alive and real. Death often served as a reminder to live. That is what Cassidy craved at the moment—to feel painfully alive. She gazed down at Alex, wishing that there were words to convey the swell of emotion rising within her. Desire existed between them often, but what made these moments intoxicating was the love that passed between them.

Alex's eyes had gone dark with need, and Cassidy could feel the urgency in them both rising. She took Alex's hands and held them to steady her as she increased the pace of her movements. Cassidy needed to be close to Alex, to feel a part of her. She dropped a hand to Alex's chest, feeling the rapid beat of Alex's heart. Tears welled in her eyes. Alex was here. She was alive. They were together. Amid the sensual and emotional haze of the moment, Cassidy found herself thanking God that it had not been Alex that was taken. Cassidy wanted Alex to understand how much she needed Alex, desired her, and loved her in every moment. At times, making love to Alex was the only way Cassidy felt she could adequately communicate that, and still Cassidy knew she would never be able to get close enough to the woman looking up at her.

"Cass," Alex traced Cassidy's cheek with her fingertips.

The reverence in Alex's voice as she spoke Cassidy's name was Cassidy's undoing. She felt herself start to fall with Alex without warning. Her hands fell on either side of Alex as Alex's hands dropped to Cassidy's hips, keeping her close as they both crested and fell again.

"Alex!"

Alex took Cassidy over the edge again until Cassidy fell into her arms, quivering lightly and repeating, "I love you," softly over and over.

"My God," Cassidy breathed. She pulled herself up to look at Alex. Alex brushed the hair out of Cassidy's eyes. "Do you remember the first time we made love here?" Cassidy asked Alex.

"Of course," Alex said. "It was the first time," she smiled.

"Mm…I didn't think that being with you could get better, that I could feel more, but I do. I swear every time I look at you, every time you touch me—I fall in love with you all over again."

Alex kissed Cassidy on the forehead. "Who's in love?" Alex teased her wife.

Cassidy chuckled. "I do love you," she said. She laid her head on Alex's chest and sighed in contentment.

Alex stroked Cassidy's back lovingly and took a deep breath. "I need to tell you something."

Cassidy felt a twinge of nervousness settle in the pit of her stomach. "Go ahead."

"I talked to Jonathan. I've asked him to take over my role at Carecom."

Cassidy pulled herself up and looked at Alex again in the faint light. "Alex?"

Alex sighed. "It's time."

"Alex…"

"I can't, Cass. Watching Kate and the kids today—it made me think of you and your mom. It made me think about Dylan and Mackenzie. I can't bear that. You standing there receiving that flag. I can't…."

"Alex, you know that there are never any guarantees about things like that."

"I know. I also know I don't need to make it more likely. Everyone that we know, my father, your father, Claire's father, Edmond…They all believe they are right, so much so that their children suffer. Dylan has already suffered because of it. They all have a reason for why they do what they do. Where has that gotten any of them? Where has it gotten us? I can't…I…"

Cassidy let out a heavy sigh and shook her head. "I would be lying if I told you that part of me doesn't long for that—for you to walk away. It'd be a lie, but Alex, this is part of who you are. You need to try and make a difference."

"There are a lot of ways that I can make a difference. You taught me that," Alex replied.

"You give me too much credit. And, my way may not be your way. You need to solve things, to…"

"Maybe," Alex conceded. "But, Cass, the thing is, you can't solve a puzzle when you become one of its pieces. You're in the middle, locked in place. You can't see the picture clearly. Sometimes, maybe the only answer to the puzzle is to distance yourself so that you can see it more clearly."

Cassidy stroked Alex's cheek. She leaned in and kissed Alex's lips tenderly. "Are you sure this is what you want?"

Alex nodded. "Positive."

Cassidy settled herself against Alex and let Alex pull her close. "I love you, Alex, no matter what. I need you to know that. No matter what you choose, I love you. That will never change."

Alex kissed Cassidy's head. "I do know. None of it matters without you, Cass—none of it. Nothing is more important than you and our kids—

nothing. I've said that I did it for you, for Dylan, for our family. Maybe it was. But, there are enough potholes in the road already without me placing landmines there. You say that I give you too much credit. I think you have that backward. I don't ever want to lose you, any of you."

"Never happen, love."

"Remember that you said that," Alex said with a chuckle. "When you get sick of me being around."

Cassidy kissed Alex's chest. "Just don't expect tacos every night."

Alex laughed. "How about every Tuesday?"

"We'll negotiate, coach."

"Vanilla cake for dessert?" Alex asked hopefully.

"Don't push it, Alfred."

Alex chuckled and closed her eyes. "Je t'aime, Cass."

"Et, je vous adore. (And, I adore you)."

Epilogue

One Year Later
July 30th

Cassidy walked into the living room just as Alex was hanging up the phone. The television was silently playing images of a bomb attack in Kenya that had occurred earlier in the day.

"I know. There isn't much you can do at this point. Just keep the lines open," Alex said. "I will. You be careful," Alex said as she disconnected the call. She looked at the images crossing the television screen and sighed deeply. With a shake of her head, Alex picked up the remote from the coffee table and clicked off the television.

"Pip?" Cassidy asked from behind Alex. Alex turned abruptly, her expression confirming Cassidy's suspicion. "Regretting your decision?" Cassidy asked. Alex just smiled. "You know, he would gladly give you back the reigns at Carecom," Cassidy said frankly.

Alex chuckled. "Tired of me already?" she asked Cassidy.

Cassidy laughed. "Nick is waiting for you outside."

"Are you sure you will be okay?" Alex asked.

Cassidy looked down at her belly and smiled. She patted it gently. "We'll be fine," she assured Alex.

"Cass, Nick can take the boys…"

"Alex," Cassidy said with a smile. "I am not due for another six weeks. Dylan and Cat have been looking forward to this for months."

417

"What about you?"

"I've been looking forward to it too," Cassidy poked. Alex nodded. Cassidy closed the distance between them. She had been teasing Alex relentlessly about Alex's overprotectiveness. They had both been surprised by the news that they were expecting twins. Cassidy had taken to teasing Alex that this was somehow Alex's master plan to fill the team bench as quickly as possible. "We are fine, all three of us," Cassidy told Alex assuredly. "If anyone starts trying to run for the end zone, I will call you—I promise."

Alex huffed slightly. "You went early last time. You heard the doctor."

"Alex, stop," Cassidy said. She laid a gentle hand on Alex's arm. "I'm not alone."

"Mmmm...I get it. This is so you and Barb can gossip with my mom about Nicky and me."

Cassidy shook her head in amusement. "Maybe," she conceded. "Admit it, you have been looking forward to this weekend almost as much as the kids."

Alex huffed again. It was true. She hadn't had much of a chance to spend time with her younger brother in over a year. She was stunned by Cassidy's Christmas present—a weekend of baseball in Boston. Cassidy had made all of the arrangements, tickets to three games, a hotel suite, and a tour of Fenway Park. Alex understood that the trip was meant not only for the kids, but it was also Cassidy's way of helping Alex and Nick reconnect. There was no way Cassidy was going to let Alex stay home. Alex suspected that had Cassidy been due the next day, the conversation would have been the same.

"Cass..."

Cassidy laughed and grabbed Alex's arm to lead her from the room. Alex followed her wife to the front door. Cassidy turned to face Alex and smiled broadly at the look of consternation on Alex's face. "Quit pouting, coach," Cassidy teased.

Alex put her hands on Cassidy's belly. "You two stay on the bench until I get back."

Cassidy rolled her eyes. "Go on. The first string is waiting," she said with a raise of her brow.

Alex leaned in and kissed Cassidy gently. "See you Sunday night."

"Yes, you will," Cassidy promised. She watched as Alex made her way to the car where Dylan and Cat were impatiently waiting with Nick and shook her head affectionately at the scene. "Now, get out of here, coach."

"Made her go, huh?" Helen asked as she came up beside Cassidy. Cassidy sighed. "Worried about her?" Helen guessed. Cassidy watched silently and waved goodbye to the foursome as they pulled out of the driveway. "Cassidy?"

"It's part of who she is," Cassidy said.

Helen nodded and closed the door. Alex had held true to her word. She had turned over control of Carecom to her older brother and resigned officially from the CIA. It had taken a while for Alex to decide what she wanted to do next. Cassidy was surprised when Alex announced that she had taken a position as an instructor at the State Police Academy. Alex seemed pleased with the decision. Two weeks later she bounced through the door with the news that she had gotten a second job coaching cross country and track at the local high school.

"She seems happy with her decisions," Helen observed.

"For now," Cassidy said.

"Mommy!" a tiny voice called out. Cassidy smiled as her daughter toddled toward her. Helen scooped up the toddler. "D.?" Mackenzie asked.

"Dylan is with Momma," Cassidy told her daughter.

Mackenzie frowned. "Baby?" she pointed to Cassidy's tummy.

"Yes, Kenzie."

"We pway?" Mackenzie asked.

Cassidy laughed. "Not yet, Kenz," she said just as she received another strong kick. "Soon," she said. "You can play with Jacob," Cassidy told her daughter.

Kenzie took that opportunity to wiggle from her YaYa's grasp. Helen set her down and watched as she sprinted as best she could away toward the family room where Barb and Jacob were. "Cob! Cob!" Mackenzie called as she hurried away.

"She never stops," Helen noted.

"Mmm. Just like her momma," Cassidy commented.

Helen chuckled. It was true. She and Cassidy had talked about it many times. Mackenzie reminded Helen of Alex often. Alex constantly made comments about how much Mackenzie resembled Cassidy. She did. The older Mackenzie got, the more apparent that was. She had Cassidy's features, although, given her already considerable height, Helen expected that one day Mackenzie might tower over Cassidy. Neither Alex nor Cassidy had ever discussed or divulged who their donor had been. Helen had her suspicions. Mackenzie was a blend of her parents in every conceivable way. She watched Mackenzie round the hallway corner and felt a smile tug gently at her lips. The toddler reminded her of Alex at the same age—curious about and into everything. Helen started laughing.

Earlier that morning, Cassidy had called for Helen's assistance after finding that Mackenzie had climbed into one of the kitchen cabinets and removed every single pot that Cassidy had stored there. Mackenzie had arranged them across the kitchen floor. When Cassidy asked what Mackenzie was doing, Mackenzie had grinned proudly and said, "Bekfast, Mommy."

That was Mackenzie. She didn't wait for anyone to show her how to do things, she inserted herself in the middle of everything and endeavored to learn how it worked. It didn't seem to matter if it was an adult conversation, her brother's models or Legos, or how the television worked. Mackenzie had a need to know. She emulated everything Dylan did. If Cassidy or Helen were cooking, Mackenzie needed a pot and a spoon to help. When Alex would stretch before leaving for a run, Mackenzie would mimic her every move.

Helen understood Cassidy's concerns. Alex had always been on the move in some way. She was insatiably curious and constantly looking for a new challenge. Helen also had come to understand her daughter quite well. She put an arm around Cassidy. "I think you underestimate the challenges that await her," Helen chuckled.

Cassidy smiled at the truth of the statement. Four children likely would present as many obstacles and upheavals as international conspiracies had. She laughed when she felt a strong kick in the ribs. "You agree, huh?" Cassidy said to her unborn children with a smile.

"Stop worrying," Helen told Cassidy. "It never does any good anyway. There's no way to stop the next minute from coming, and there's no way to guarantee what it will hold."

Cassidy laughed. She'd learned the truth of that simple statement the hard way. "I never thought she'd take the role of coach literally."

"She is full of surprises," Helen said.

"Mommy!" Mackenzie walked into the hallway covered in flour.

Cassidy covered her mouth and shook her head. "Where is Jacob?" she asked. As if on cue, Jacob appeared, his black hair resembling an older man's salt and pepper gray.

"Cookies!" Mackenzie screamed in delight.

Barb peeked around the corner "Oh my, God! What? They were watching Cookie Monster. I just ran to the bathroom."

Cassidy nodded. "What was that you were saying about the next moment?" she asked Helen.

Helen laughed and shrugged. "Like mother, like daughter—full of surprises," she said. "Come on, Kenzie. You and me have a date with the bathtub."

"Cookies, Ya...My cookies...."

Helen kept laughing. "We'll talk cookies while we take a tubby."

Cassidy watched as her mother-in-law and Barb steered the two toddlers up the stairs. She looked down at her belly and laughed. "God, help me. A bench full?" Cassidy kept chuckling as she left the room. She picked up her phone.

***

Alex hung up her phone and flopped onto the hotel bed.

"Everything okay?" Nick asked.

"Yeah."

"You seem worried about something," Nick observed. Alex smiled. "I'm sure Cassidy is fine, Alex."

"She is. The kitchen apparently could use some help."

"Come again?"

"Seems your son and my daughter decided to make cookies for Cookie Monster."

Nick cringed. "Uh-oh."

Alex laughed. "Eh, it's flour. It's white. It'll blend in with the cabinetry."

"That wasn't Cass just now, was it?" he asked. Alex sighed. "Jonathan?" he guessed.

"Just some questions," she said.

"Regretting leaving Carecom?" Nick asked.

"No," Alex said. "I just hope that I don't disappoint anyone."

"You mean Cassidy?" he asked. "Come on, Alex."

"No, I mean anyone. This is all new for me, Nicky. All of it."

"You'll be fine. Besides, you are the strongest person I know."

Alex laughed. "No, I'm not."

"Yeah, you are. You always…"

Alex stopped her younger brother's thought. "No, Nicky, you're wrong. I'm not the strongest person you know. I'm married to her."

***

Alex glanced over at the room's sleeping occupants. She opened the small envelope that Cassidy had packed in her bag. She slid the card out and smiled. The card depicted waves crashing against the shore at sunset.

Alex,

It's strange to me sometimes. I know there was a time in my life when you were not in it. It seems so far away to me now that I can barely recall it. Remember that first time you took me to the ocean? I sat across from you, looking into your eyes. I couldn't have known then that we would stand in that same place and you would commit your life to me. Somehow, I did. At least, I knew that you loved me. I knew that night, just looking at you, that I never wanted you to leave. Strange how life brings us together, isn't it?

Every time I see the ocean, I think of you. I miss you the moment you leave, whether it is for a few moments or for days at a time. I'm sitting here writing this. It takes me back to the first time you went away, the hollowness I felt in my heart. The joy I felt at the simple sound of your voice on my phone. And now, here I am watching our daughter line the kitchen floor with my pots and pans—our daughter. Our son is calling for you in the distance, and I can feel the new life we are creating moving inside me. I had to write this. I had to tell you that through all the changes, all the loss, and the sadness, all the questions that never seem to have answers—I have never been happier in my life. I have never loved you more, yet I know I will love you more when tomorrow comes. I wouldn't change one moment, not one. Because, if I sought to change even one thing that has come to pass, I might not have had the chance to love you. I might not be watching our children as they grow. I might not have you to miss, even for a moment.

I'm not the poet you always claim me to be. I'm not perfect, nor am I sure of many things. I am sure of you. I am sure that when the final sunset falls, it will be your arms greeting me, just as mine will always be waiting to hold you. Through all the joy and all the sorrow, you give me peace and purpose. You have given me the strength to face anything, knowing I am not alone. Thank you for loving me, Alex.

I will see you in a few days.

Je t'adore, my love. I can never hope to tell you what you mean to me.

À toi pour toujours,

Cassidy

Alex closed the card. She closed her eyes and pictured Cassidy the first time they had traveled to the beach. Cassidy was leaning back with her eyes closed and the wind blowing softly through her hair. Alex felt a tear slip over her cheek. When she took a minute to think about it, and she had thought a great deal about it, no one had suffered more, lost more, or had more to fear than Cassidy. No matter what came to pass, Cassidy had always remained steadfast—steadfast in her love for Alex. Also, steadfast in her compassionate heart. She'd questioned. She'd cried. Alex had never seen her wife truly falter, not even once.

Alex had once told Dylan that Cassidy was her hero. She opened her eyes and glanced at the sleeping boy beside her. He was so much like his mother. He was beginning to show a striking resemblance to John Merrow. But, Dylan's heart, Dylan's kindness, his need to give, that was Cassidy. Alex closed her eyes again. Cassidy was more than the love of Alex's life. She was Alex's harbor, Alex's anchor, Alex's guidepost, Alex's hero. Alex picked up her phone. She waited and listened for Cassidy's voice and the signature beep.

"Just closing my eyes, picturing the ocean. Thank you for the note. Your wrong, Cass. It's always been you who has given me strength, given us all strength. I learn from you every day. I still have a lot to learn, so I'm glad you are so patient. I'm watching Dylan sleep. I love you both so much, Cass. All of you...I promise I will be the best coach I can be. I might need your

424

help once in a while. Maybe we could take a ride to the ocean when I get back one day, if you are up to it, just the two of us. Before it becomes just the six of us," Alex said with a chuckle. "I'll see you Sunday."

Alex closed her eyes and let herself fall away. Miles apart, yet she felt Cassidy holding her. "Je vais passer l'éternité as t'aimer (I will spend eternity loving you). I promise. Je t'aime, Cass." *I promise.*

The End

The Alex and Cassidy Series

Intersection

Betrayal

Commitment

Conspiracy

Other Books by Nancy Ann Healy

Falling Through Shooting Stars

Made in the USA
Monee, IL
10 September 2022

13669212R00243